They come together or not...

Sugar
DADDIES

International Bestselling Author

J A D E   W E S T

Cover design by Letitia Hasser of RBA Designs
http://designs.romanticbookaffairs.com/
Edited by John Hudspith http://www.johnhudspith.co.uk
All enquiries to jadewestauthor@gmail.com

First published 2016

Warning.
This is a Jade West novel. You existing readers will know the drill by now. Read with caution.
For those of you who are new to my work, hello!
This book is dirty.
If you don't like them dirty, this probably isn't a book you'll enjoy.
If you do enjoy dirty, then make yourself comfortable. ☺
Thank you.

For Sue.

I couldn't have wished for a better friend.
This is for those long summer days out on the horses, for the laughs, the fun and the effortless communication. It's for those crazy made-up field names and the stupid ideas which never quite worked out as planned.
But mainly it's for the countless magical memories you've blessed me with. xx

Chapter ONE

CARL

The envelope icon continued flashing at the bottom of the screen, but I ignored it, along with the lingering glances in my direction. Rick was exceptionally talented in many areas, but subtlety wasn't one of them.

He was twitchy, and it wasn't from the copious amounts of coffee he'd been guzzling all evening, he was excited. Rick was *usually* excited, naturally wired with a high metabolism and the expressive kind of features you can read a mile off, but this was a special kind of excitement.

It was endearing. Although I'd never tell him so.

He pushed his chair away from his desk, spinning to face me, yet still I didn't react.

I enjoyed the game far too much.

Our home office is *intimate*. The tension stretched until he broke, with a mock groan.

"Well?! Have you looked?!"

"No," I said.

"Pissing hell, Carl, will you just *look*? Please?"

I angled my laptop screen down and stared at him, long and sternly, trying my best not to break a smile.

"I'm busy. Foster proposal. Tender deadline tomorrow."

"Piss off. There's *always* a deadline tomorrow. Five minutes, just check it out. I only need a yes. One little yes. She'll get a yes, I promise."

I sighed for effect. "Who is it this time? Another Penelope Pout? *I want a boob job, and an Audi TT and world peace*? No, wait... Another broke but talented artistic genius, seeking true love on *Sugar Daddy Match-up*? You like those..."

He coasted his chair across the floor, propped his elbows on my desk and jabbed a finger at my laptop. "Just *look*. She's nothing like the others."

"You always say that."

He smiled. "Yeah, but I don't always mean it."

I minimised my document and called up his email. *Sugar Daddy Match-up! You have mail!*

I hovered over the link, then folded my arms. "So, give me the elevator pitch. Why this one?"

He rolled his shoulders, tipped his head from side to side. "Elevator pitch, you got it." He held up a finger. "She's hot, like really hot. Not a Penelope Pout, no fake tan, no epic contouring, not even false lashes. She's just hot. Cute, too."

"Blonde? Brunette?"

"Blonde. Wavy. Natural. Blue eyes."

I nodded. "Go on."

"She's local. Much Arlock."

"Local?" I conceded a point to him in the name of convenience.

Much Arlock was only a thirty-minute drive from Cheltenham. Hardly anything. "Ok, I'm listening."

"She's a little bit quirky, in a good way. Not all-out boho, just... she has personality."

"I'd hope so, Rick. We want a companion, not a whore. Although a whore would be a whole lot cheaper."

"Like I said, she has personality. She seems nice. Funny."

I laughed. "You can tell that from her profile picture can you? Pulling the funky chicken is she?"

"Just fucking look, will you?" He pushed his glasses back on his nose, and smoothed down his beard, eyes twinkling.

Boho. Another one. Could I handle another trendy little free-spirit in the house? Probably. The thought didn't altogether turn me off.

I clicked the link, and Rick leaned over, angled my screen so he could share my view. I resigned myself to the inevitable apathy, another pretty face in the catalogue of pretty faces looking for a healthier bank account and a nice rich cock. Or two. Two on offer didn't seem to hinder our success any. Far from it.

The face that greeted me wasn't out of any catalogue. Her hair was a cascade of natural blonde, tumbling over slender shoulders to rest at the curve of her vest top. Her eyes were alive and kind, pastel blue and full of mischief, and her smile was bright and genuine. A sweet little nose, with a sprinkling of freckles over glowing skin. Nice tits. Narrow waist. Long legs in faded denim, crossed under her as she leaned back, her palms splayed on the grass beneath.

She was beautiful. Beautiful and different from the others, he was right. A seashell necklace and two gemstone bracelets were her only adornments.

7

Bohemian, yes. But just a little.

Rick gave me the overview, but it sounded distant.

"Her profile says she's twenty-two, not too young. Just about to finish up university. Worcester. Business degree. Still lives at home. Drives. Works two jobs. She's outdoorsy, all-out natural, likes pizza and KFC, though. All the unhealthy stuff. Probably even likes service station sandwiches. You'll get on well."

"We can't all pull a PJ party and work from home every day. Your de-humidified little veggie snacks hardly cut a day on the road." My voice came out dry as my tone got serious. "This one. Does she know? Is she... suitable?"

I didn't pull my eyes from the screen yet I knew he was rolling his.

"Don't start. She knows *some* of it."

"Some?"

"*Some*. From our profile."

"So tell her the rest."

He groaned at me. "Listen up, Mr *tell it like it is*, we need *time*. She needs to get to know us. We haven't even met her yet."

"Ok, so let's meet her, and then we'll tell her. Lay our cards flat on the table and see if hers match up."

He shook his head. "Six months, you promised."

"I promised *three*."

"You said *six*, after Nicole from Northampton ran screaming for the hills, you said *six*. You sat right there, just where you are now, and *you* promised *six*."

"Under duress. I've changed my mind."

He clapped his hands in front of my screen, forcing my attention. "*Six*, Carl. We're going with six months this time. I mean it."

His tone tickled me. "Who died and made you Lord of Sugar Daddy dating? We all know who wears the trousers around here, Richard." I smirked. "Don't pretend you don't like it that way."

"I'd like it a whole lot better if we managed to coax a three-way just a smidge beyond your boar-headed *negotiations*. This isn't some sales deal. It's about... people, Carl, *people*..."

"*It's all about the soul, man...*" I mocked. "*I* negotiate. That's what I do."

"Not this time." He shook his head. "Six months. Let me handle this one." His eyes were like a puppy dog's. "Please... just let me handle this one..."

I scrolled down through the email. "Where's the obligatory nude?"

"There isn't one."

I raised my eyebrows. "No tit shot? Not even underwear?"

He smiled. "Nope. Not a thing."

I was strangely impressed. "She does know we come as a pair, yes? She knows it's two at once or not at all?"

"She knows she will need to... accommodate..."

"Such a delicate way of putting it. She's happy with that, is she?"

"It's clear on our profile. She referred to it in her message. It's pretty explicit... not slutty, she's no tramp, but she's... clear in her intentions..."

A tickle of excitement ran through my balls.

"...her name's Katie, by the way."

Katie. It suited her.

"Katie Serena Smith... and she's keen..."

I scrolled past her picture, to the message below.

I've never done anything like this before. I'm sure

almost every other message says the same, but I really mean it. I really have never done anything like this before… but I want to.

I'd be lying if I said I wasn't on a sugar daddy website for the money, but I wasn't expecting to find anyone close enough, and I definitely wasn't expecting to find a profile like yours.

I've fantasised about taking two men at once since I was old enough to know it was possible. You ask in your profile if I've experienced sex like this before, and I haven't. I don't know how it would feel to have two men inside me, and I don't know that I'd find it easy, but I want to try.

You ask if I've ever opened up enough to take two men in my pussy, and no, I haven't, not even close, but I think about it every day since I read your profile.

It's taken me a while to pluck up the courage to message.

But I'm ready now.

I really want this.

You ask what I want out of the arrangement, and I'm not really sure how to quantify it.

I'm just a small town girl with big dreams, that's why I'm on this site. But it isn't just about the money. Not anymore.

Katie. X

Explicit but not slutty. No grandiose claims of riding two fat dicks all through the night. No graphic demonstration of her pussy-stretching capabilities, and we'd had plenty of those. No *take me, big boys, take my tight little cunt*, or, *you've never known a pussy as hungry for two as mine.* None of that.

I tried to get a measure of *Katie*. "If she can't quantify it, what does she want? Not college fees presumably, and she doesn't look the type for a cosmetic surgery wish list."

He shrugged. "A small town girl with big dreams... who knows. That's cute, though, right?"

"*Cute.* Yes."

Rick's grin showed his dimples. "She's seriously cute. I think I'm in love already."

"With a declaration like that, how could I possibly say no?"

"You wouldn't say no anyway. You haven't stopped staring at her."

Astute little asshole. I tapped my fingers on the desk. "Alright, message her back. It's a yes from me."

He punched the air. "I knew it." He wheeled himself back across the floor, tatty jeans trailing the carpet. "I fucking love you, Carl Brooks, you will *not* regret it."

"One last shot," I said. "Then we're out. Profile deleted. I'm done with this."

He gave me a salute. "Yeah, yeah, one last shot. This one's our girl, I can feel it in my bones."

I laughed. "In your boner, you mean." My cursor hovered over minimise, but I didn't click. I didn't want to click. *Maybe, just maybe.* "Message her, then, now. Set it up."

He reclined in his seat, hands behind his head. "Don't need to," he said with a smirk. "I messaged her before I sent you the email."

Katie

Hi, I'm Katie, pleased to meet you. Handshake? Hug? Air kiss? Maybe not. Hi, I'm Kate. So good to meet you, finally. Finally? Does that sound desperate?

I reversed the car at the bottom of the street. Again. Clunky gears made me over-swing and they ground like teeth on chalk. Nasty. I could just feel the curtains twitching. They'd be calling neighbourhood watch before long. I'd already circled the road three times in the past fifteen minutes, and still I was early.

Hi, Rick! Carl! I'm Katie. Katie Smith. So lovely to meet you! No. Too gushy.

I put the car in neutral and looked again at my surroundings. The road was suburbia central, and I was surprised the street itself wasn't paved with banknotes. I felt totally out of my comfort zone, a pathetic little duckling bobbing on the waves.

But I should have known it would be like this. It should be like this. It would be considerably more concerning to rock up on some deadbeat estate somewhere and find my sugar daddies weren't all they were cracked up to be. I'd checked this place out on Street View, many times, but Street View doesn't account for scale. These properties were big.

It seemed so easy in the safety of my own fantasies, but now it was a whole other ballgame, parked up in money town with a bellyful of butterflies and a serious case of fight or flight.

Fight or flight. More like fuck or flight.

The thought gave me jitters.

Maybe that's what they'd expect. Pleased to meet you, strip now, please and show us your pussy.

Rick said not, but he would, wouldn't he?

Still, that wouldn't be the worst that could happen. Murder on money row, sugar daddy slut gets butchered in Cheltenham suburbia.

Unlikely, I'd checked them out. Facebook profiles, electoral roll, the business connect website. They were everywhere, bold as brass, and all the lines matched up neatly. Plus, I'd left a practical dossier of information on them in my dressing table drawer. Even Much Arlock's sleepy police force could crack that crime in a heartbeat.

I stared over at their house, realising all over again that my car was going to look like a bag of shit on their driveway. My car would look like a bag of shit on anyone's driveway.

I took a breath. Here goes nothing.

I pulled my battered old Ford onto their property, and immediately wished I'd given it a jet wash. Mine was covered in mud and scratches and probably half a hay bale, and theirs were gleaming. Gleaming and new. A posh Range and some sporty silver BMW, pristine on their fancy pink-bricked driveway. At least I'd made the effort to spruce myself up. I turned off the engine and kicked off my pumps, replacing them with the killer heels I'd stashed in the passenger footwell. I checked my makeup in the rearview mirror, lipstick still behaving in a shade only one darker than nude, and a few token dabs of mascara. I'd pass. Hopefully. I shimmied my dress further down my thighs, conscious of flashing my slutty little knickers as I clambered into plain sight. Long legs are both a blessing and a curse, harbouring the ability to turn a perfectly respectable dress into a whore-gown with just one false wiggle. Finally I reached for my bag, checking my paperwork just one last time. Paperwork, yikes. This was some crazy shit, but my dreams weren't getting any smaller.

I could do this.

I needed to do this.

I took a breath and stepped out into the cool evening air, a welcome relief against burning skin. My dress was the most expensive I owned; a soft pink strapless number with a demure little diamante rose at the bust.

My strides defied my lack of confidence, my heels clacking against the ground as I approached their front door.

Rick and Carl, Carl and Rick.

I hoped it would be Rick who answered. Rick seemed nice, and kind, and cool. Rick was hot, and funny. I could fall for Rick. He had full-sleeve tattoos and his clothes were nerdy-chic. He had messy brown hair and dark eyes, and a full-on hipster beard. He was a designer, too. What's not to love?

Carl, on the other hand. I'd never spoken to Carl. Carl seemed... intense. Intimidating. Posh suits, and steely muscles, and chiselled features, and absolutely everything I wasn't. The corporate bogeyman under my country-girl bedspread. Maybe the photos made him look more that way than he really was.

I knocked on the door and my heart thumped like a crazy bitch, my breath raw in my throat as I saw a shadow move behind the glass.

The door swung open and I couldn't breathe, just plastered on the warmest, brightest smile I could muster and it stayed. It stayed because it was Rick who answered, and he was smiling, too. His smile was incredible, big and genuine, and it gave him dimples. He had tight black jeans on over brogues, and a purple tie over a short-sleeved checked shirt. Rick Warner, graphic designer extraordinaire, was absolutely goddamn fucking gorgeous, way more gorgeous than his gorgeous pics. One for the win.

"Katie! Hey!" He beckoned me in like a long-lost friend, and wrapped me in colourful arms that were hotter in the flesh than they were in any online photo, and he smelled of both the ocean and cherries simultaneously. His chest was hard under his shirt, and he was taller than I'd expected, as tall as me, even in heels.

He pushed the door closed behind us, and reached for my hand and it felt alright. I could do this.

Or so I thought.

Until there was him. Mr Stern. And he was massive. Massive and perfect. And really stern. His eyes looked like they hunted girls like me for breakfast.

"Carl, this is Katie. Katie, this is Carl."

Carl took a step forwards, and I instinctively took a little shimmy back, but his hand had already landed on mine, squeezed hard. "Introductions aren't entirely necessary, Rick," he said, and I wasn't sure how serious he was. "Pleased you could join us, Katie. I've heard a lot. All good."

"Same," I said. "I mean, bits, from Rick."

I've heard you're intense, and serious, and great in bed. I've heard you're not as scary as you first appear. I've heard you work all over the country, closing mega technology deals worth enough to make the eyes water. I've heard you're driven, and smart, and really nice when you get to know you.

I've heard I have to take you both at once. That's the condition. Your condition.

I've heard that's what gets you off.

But I couldn't fathom any of it, I could only burn under the way his eyes ate mine. Green, like bay leaves, flecked with silver. His hair was dark and slick, and his shirt was crisp and white, the collar so sharp it could cut. He was wearing tailored trousers, even on the weekend, and his watch was expensive and caught the light as I watched his hand shaking mine.

"So, Katie, what brings you here? Why us?"

Direct.

Rick jabbed him in the arm, elbowed him pretty hard. "I'm sure Katie would like a drink, Carl." He wrapped an arm around my shoulders, angling me past his confrontational other half, where my body skirted Carl's just a little too closely. My skin prickled and my legs felt like jelly, as though he was melting me.

I couldn't fuck him.

He'd destroy me. Turn me into a puddle of gooey nothing.

But I was giddy at the thought. Giddy with everything. And it all seemed so stupid, this whole thing was crazy stupid. A silly girl out of her depth, thinking she could cut it as some kind of high class escort to two bisexual guys, just because she took it up the ass a few times at college and enjoyed it.

A lot.

Ok, I enjoyed it a lot.

But still.

Fuck.

Rick led me on through the hallway into a huge, airy kitchen. The place was gorgeous, framed energy drink adverts lined the walls above glossy white ceramic tiles, and the tops were black marble.

"You did these?" I asked, pointing one out.

"Sure did." He smiled at me, and I'd have relaxed completely if I hadn't felt the heat of Carl behind me. "Wine? Spirits? Soft drink?" Rick raised his eyebrows. "Power-up lime, the drink of champions?"

I smiled back. "Water, please."

He took out a mineral water, one of those posh ones in glass bottles, dispensed some ice from their super cool fridge-freezer, and handed it over in a twisty glass. I sipped, and my throat was tight with nerves.

"A little apprehensive?" Rick asked, and his eyes were twinkling. "Hey, don't sweat it. I'm nervous, too." He looked behind me. "We all are."

I didn't believe that somehow.

"This is... surreal..." I managed. "It feels so different in real life." I checked myself. "Not bad different. Just different."

"We should go through to the lounge," a deep voice said. "It's more comfortable."

My heart pounded.

I followed him mutely, with a paper smile on my face all the way. I chose a seat in the far corner, a big white leather armchair that swallowed me up. Rick took one of the pouffes beside me, arranging himself casually with his legs kicked out towards mine. Carl took the chair opposite, and there was nothing casual whatsoever about him. He sat forward in his seat, with purpose, eyes on mine.

"Do you have any questions?"

Plenty. But I couldn't think of a single one besides the obvious. Are you going to fuck me now? Here? On your lounge rug while my heart pounds ten to the dozen? Are you going to insist I take two cocks right from the off, and judge me if I squeal? Are you going to be disappointed when I wimp out of anal and cry that it's been a while?

Am I going to be good enough?

I pictured my dreams, everything I'd ever wanted, and all the ways they'd seemed impossible before I'd stumbled across the Sugar Daddies article in Glitz magazine.

I needed to be good enough for this.

I took another sip of water and focused my mind.

Questions. He wanted questions.

"I have a few," I said.

And then the questions came.

Chapter
TWO

Katie

I started with the innocuous. "You guys have been together three years?"

Carl stared at me, and my heart wouldn't stop pounding. "I'm sure Rick filled you in."

So much for an ice breaker.

Rick took a breath, and smiled all the brighter. "Three years, yeah. Met through adult hook up, just for threesomes, and when things didn't work out for Carl and Melanie we just kept on going with other women until one day we kept on going without. Just us." He leaned back on the pouffe and I admired the swirls of colour on his forearms. "But we don't want *just us*. We're far too greedy and far too bi." He laughed a little, and behind the warmth of his smile I caught a hint of nerves.

Carl cleared his throat. "Our routine makes it challenging to find women compatible with our... requirements. Hence we were advertising."

Were advertising. The choice of tense didn't go unnoticed.

"Makes sense," I said. "So much is online these days. Dating made simple…"

Green eyes pierced me. "We haven't found it to be all that *simple* so far. I'm hoping that's about to change."

My skin was burning, and I hoped I wasn't pinking up. I brushed my hair back, feigned confidence. "I hope so, too." I took a sip of water and decided to go all in. "So, these… requirements? What are they?"

Rick leaned forward in a heartbeat, all ready to start talking, but Carl spoke first.

"We want a woman who will share our preferences in the bedroom, indulge us often, and keep us in pleasant company outside of it. We want a relationship without drama, without endless questioning about *where this is going*, or *what's going on*, or concerns over pointless mundane trivialities." He paused, his eyes on my bare knees. "We want a woman who can accommodate us both at once." Another pause, and those smouldering eyes felt like they were prising my legs open.

"Yes, of course," I said, as if he'd just asked for extra sugar in his tea.

"We want someone who can stay neutral to both of us, who isn't going to get notions of falling in love with just one man. We don't have time for that kind of emotional involvement. We want someone we both find attractive, who turns us both on. A lot." He smiled, and he had such perfect teeth. "It's safe to say you tick those boxes."

I didn't know what to say, so I said the obvious. "Thank you."

His eyes looked me up and down, and my confidence faltered. "What about you, Katie? What are your *requirements*?"

Shit. "I want…" I took another sip of water to ease my throat. "I want to experiment. I want a dynamic I can be comfortable in..."

"And two cocks?" Carl smirked. "You want to feel two dicks in your pussy at once, yes? As per your message. We enjoyed your message."

Rick shot him a glare. "She wants to get to know us, Carl. She's only just walked through the bloody door."

"She *is* getting to know us. I'm just stating the obvious, why not call a spade a spade?"

Rick scowled at him. "Why not just have a drink and relax?"

"Because that's not why we're here." Carl fixed me back in his gaze and I found myself licking my dry lips. "That *is* what you want, isn't it? Two men at once?"

I nodded, certain the blush was creeping up my cheeks. "It's... it's my fantasy..."

"And now that we're all here, in the same room, is it still your fantasy? How about it, Katie, do *we* measure up to *your* fantasy?"

Rick visibly squirmed, and his eyes were full of apology, but I didn't mind. I had metal. I had to have metal, or I wouldn't last five minutes of this crazy shit.

"Yes, it's still my fantasy. You're a very attractive couple."

Carl nodded, seemingly appeased, and I felt strangely satisfied by his approval. "Good." He got to his feet and stepped away, grabbing an envelope from a corner cabinet. He handed it over. "Our paperwork."

Shit really was getting real. I pulled my own envelope from my bag and offered it to him. His fingers touched mine as he took it and I swear I felt the spark. He gave me a nod as if he'd felt it too.

I pulled out their documentation, STI test results less than a month old. They were clean, both of them. Carl had already finished with my paperwork by the time I'd finished He offered it to Rick, but Rick waved it away. "We should have had a drink," he said. "Sorry."

I shrugged. "Better to get the formalities out of the way, right?"

He went to answer but Carl started up again. "You're on the pill?"

I nodded. "Yes. I'm very careful."

"And you're comfortable with this being an exclusive arrangement? No other partners on the side."

"Yes."

"How long are you willing to commit?"

I drank the rest of my water. "I'm unsure... I was thinking a few months. Maybe six?"

"Six months works. We can talk again after six. Renegotiate the arrangement. Iron out any issues."

There was an edge to his words that sent a shiver up my spine. A brooding heaviness, and it felt so ominous.

Rick piped up, his tone light. "Of course we'll talk," he said. "Often. Nothing is set in stone, we're people, right?" He laughed. "This thing isn't going to be signed in blood. We can be flexible; make sure everyone's happy."

Carl pulled out a mobile phone. "So, what are you hoping for in terms of the financials, Katie? Do you have a figure in mind?"

I suddenly felt dirty, and fought back the nerves. *Money. I hate talking about money.* "I'm really not sure... do you?"

"We paid our last companion two grand a month, but she only did one weekend out of every two. She had children."

Their last companion. Nothing like making a girl feel special. I brushed it aside. "That's... generous. Very generous."

"Not that generous. You should hold out for three."

I forced a smile. "Maybe I will."

Rick reached out, put a hand on my arm. "We're more than happy to give you three."

Three grand a month. My legs were shaking. I could do a lot with three grand a month... If I kept my waitressing job, just weeknights... I could have saved enough in six months, enough for everything, or at least a shot.

My voice came out raspy. "What would you expect for three grand a month?"

The air felt heavy until Carl answered. "Three weekends out of four, ideally. A sunny disposition at all times. And sex. Lots of sex."

"I can do that." I wished I was as sure as I sounded, but three grand would make me sure.

"Fine." Carl tapped at his phone. "What's your email address?"

"Katie S loves horses at gmail dot com."

He raised his eyebrows but didn't comment. "Sent."

My phone buzzed in my handbag and I pulled it out. Email. *You received a payment from Carl Brooks. Click to accept.* I clicked and there was £1000 waiting for me, just like that. My heart stuttered. I had to work weeks for that kind of cash in my regular jobs. I tried to keep a poker face. "Great. Thank you."

"That's just for this weekend," he said. "If you want to stay, that is."

Rick's hand was on my wrist again. "You don't *have* to stay, Katie. Really. Don't feel obligated. And if you do, there is a spare room, plenty of spare rooms... we've got more spare rooms than you can shake a stick at."

"I'll stay," I said, even though my nerves were skyrocketing. I had an overnight bag in the car, just in case. I looked straight at Carl, begging my heart to still. "Do you want to... shall I, um... now?" I reached around for the zip on my dress, cheeks burning.

The look he shot me was full of shock, and even a little indignation. "No," he said. "You don't seem cheap enough to spread your legs the moment the cash comes out, and we're certainly not cheap enough to take it that way."

I felt strangely taken aback. "I just thought... sorry..."

His eyes were so hard. "You're not a prostitute, Katie. I don't expect you to drop your knickers the minute you walk through the door."

I shrivelled under his glare, turning into a gawky little girl. "I thought that maybe... sorry, I misunderstood."

Rick groaned, loud enough to get our attention. "Drinks, please..." he said. "For fuck's sake, let's get a fucking beer. Jesus Christ."

He didn't even wait for affirmation, just took himself through to the kitchen.

I was pleased to follow him.

The atmosphere changed in the kitchen. The air felt lighter, and the evening sun lit up the room through the huge townhouse windows. Rick pulled out a beer and offered me one, but Carl was already at the wine rack, pulling out a bottle of red and holding it up for my approval.

"A good year," he said, and uncorked. He poured, and I caught a heady whiff of fruit.

I took my glass and swirled the wine around, took a sniff. "Nice."

A thousand pounds richer. I couldn't quite believe it. Real money. In my account. I smiled, and I meant it, and then I drank down a large enough glug of my wine that Carl smirked at me.

Rick hitched himself onto the marble counter, tapping his brogues against the cabinet underneath. "We got off to a weird start," he said. "We're really not that bad, I promise. We're pretty laidback."

I didn't quite believe him, but I smiled anyway. "You have a wonderful place."

"That's down to Rick," Carl said. "He's the designer."

Rick looked out of the window rather than soak up the praise. "You want anything here, just help yourself. Feel at home. We want you to be comfortable here, don't we, Carl?"

Carl sighed, eyes heavy as they met mine. "Yes, yes." He tipped his head towards Rick. "He's a free spirit, *man*. Rick is all about ambience, and communication, and..." He reached behind him and jabbed at some weird grill like contraption. "...shrivelled up tofu crackers. He's quite the hippy."

"Dehydrated," Rick groaned. "They're dehydrated."

"Whereas I'm a little more, direct. I like to be *direct*."

No shit. I knocked back some more wine. "What else do you do? For fun?"

"Work," Carl said. "We work a lot. Work hard. Work smart. Other than that we watch movies, hit the occasional club, hit the occasional tennis court, too. We have a gym in the basement, and a sauna and Jacuzzi. It makes working out a little easier. How about you?"

Wine made me brave enough to show myself. "I ride," I said. "Horses. Well, one horse. Samson." I fought back the urge to whip out the gallery app on my phone and bore them with ten thousand pictures. Now really wasn't the time.

They both nodded, a look passing between them.

"Makes sense," Carl said. "The horsey type, yes. Very good."

"You ride?" I asked.

"Oh yes, we ride." His eyes prickled me. "Just not horses." He wouldn't stop staring, and his gaze was hot. I took a step back, propping myself against the kitchen island. "So, tell me about Katie Serena Smith. Fresh out of university, a business degree under your belt. What next?"

I shrugged. "I'm planning on bailing out of the conventional. That's why I'm here."

I had both of their attention.

Rick held his beer up. "Conventional is overrated. We don't conform much in this household."

"What are you bailing out of?" Carl asked.

I held up my glass. "The boring. The mundane. The status quo. I studied business because I felt I *should* get a conventional degree. Now I want to live for me." I took a breath. "I want my own yard. Just a small affair, maybe six horses. That would do nicely." It felt weird to share my ambitions so quickly, and part of me twitched inside, twitching at the potential disapproval.

Carl tapped his fingers against his wine glass, weighing me up. "An eventing yard? Dressage, perhaps?"

I shook my head. "Neither. Just a little riding school. A couple of horses for a couple of kids, it's been my dream since I was a little girl."

He didn't look impressed, and I didn't expect him to. Rick was more forthcoming. He smiled and nodded, and uttered noises of approval.

"I only have the one horse," I continued. "But I want that to change, soon. It's why I'm here."

"Money to set up a stable?" Rick asked, not even a hint of condescension in his tone. "That's really cool."

I nodded. "It costs a fair bit, even for such a small scale."

26

Carl pointed a finger in my direction. "You could use your business degree for a few years, build up some real world corporate experience. You could walk into a decent sales or finance training role."

I stared at him. Mr Mega Corporate. Stared at the hard lines of him, the promise of steely muscle under his shirt. He worked out a lot, you could tell. He wasn't all hip and lean like Rick. He was solid. Like a bull. An angry bull. The wine was already hitting me, swishing warm in my stomach, and I tried to imagine him fucking me, his face in mine while he pounded me, the grunts of him as his flesh slapped mine. I wasn't sure whether the thought thrilled or petrified me. Maybe a bit of both.

Definitely a bit of both.

And he'd paid for it in advance. Paid for *me*.

I focused back on the conversation. "I could probably toe the corporate line, yes."

Carl raised an eyebrow. "But you're not going to?"

"No. I'm not going to." I kept my eyes steady. Determined. He wasn't the only one who had steel.

I breathed in relief as he looked away. "I do admire those who know what they want out of life."

Rick laughed. "Carl doesn't tolerate indecision easily." I filed that away for future reference. He dug in his pocket, pulled out some rolling tobacco. "Going to head out for a smoke," he said. His eyes sparkled, full of meaning. "Do you?"

I placed my wine on the counter. "I'll come for some fresh air."

Carl didn't move, not even a muscle, and I was glad. He held up his mobile as we made our way outside. "I'll just check my emails."

27

The garden was impressive, like the rest of the pad. A big wooden table with chairs, and two of those chiminea burners. There was a covered area for smoking, the whole place edged with a classy rock garden. It was as swish as the interior. Impressive and imposing. Rick rolled his cigarette as his eyes weighed me up.

"He's difficult, but he's really cool when you get to know him."

I raised my eyebrows. "No, he's fine."

Rick smirked, placing his roll up between his lips. "He's difficult. He knows it, too. He can't help himself."

"Really, he's fine." I smiled, and hoped I appeared genuine. In reality the guy intimidated the shit out of me, enough to set my nerves alight. A healthy thousand in my bank account made it a lot easier to stay put, but the thought of fucking the guy was enough to bring me out in a cold sweat. Rick on the other hand, Rick I'd do for fun.

His smile was so easy. "I'm glad you came."

"Thanks, me too."

"Some don't," he admitted. "For some it's all talk. I hoped you'd show."

"I'm serious about this," I said. "The idea suits me."

"How so?"

I let myself relax in his presence, catching the scent of him on the breeze. "I don't get much chance for dating. University, two jobs, horse to look after."

"But university's over."

"Just frees me up for more stable time."

"Priorities, I get it." He leaned against the wall. "You're nicer than I hoped. Your smile is cuter."

"Thanks." I leaned beside him. "You're nicer than I hoped. Taller."

"Seriously, don't mind Carl," he said. "He's really something when you get to know him."

"I'm sold," I laughed. "Don't worry, I can handle it."

"I really hope so." He reached for my hand, pulled me into him, until I could smell beer and smoke, and him. "You don't need to rush, by the way. Neither of us expect anything, not tonight."

But I did want something. I wanted him. The mess of his hair was perfect, the lean lines of him pleasing to the eye. His tattoos were hot, patterns and hearts and stars over tight muscle. He wet his lips, and I caught sight of chrome. A tongue bar. I wondered how it would feel against my clit, and the thought shocked me. The extent of my attraction to Rick shocked me.

"You said you had piercings, you didn't say which."

He poked his tongue out, showing it in its full glory. "Tongue, nipples." He paused. "Cock."

Excitement fizzed. "You have your cock pierced?"

He grinned. "You could say that."

I forced my mind back to Carl. No favouritism, as per the rules. "And Carl, does he?"

He shook his head. "No, he's a blank canvas, not even a hint of a piercing. How about you?"

"Only my ears."

I couldn't stop thinking about Rick's cock. About the piercings, and the tats, and the glint of chrome in his mouth.

He stubbed his cigarette in the ashtray. "Better go back in."

I nodded, but took his wrist as he made to pass. "How many times have you done this?"

"Women?" He stared at me. "Five from Sugar Daddy. A few before it."

Wow! "None of them worked out?"

"Some." He looked through the window, checking for Carl. "One we really liked. It's a long story." He moved his hand, took my fingers in his. "None of them worked out, no." He smiled and moved closer, and my breath stopped as his mouth paused just an inch from mine. "I'm pleased they didn't, though, to be honest."

"You are?"

His body touched to mine, fingers trailing up my back, and it was scorching. Chemistry. Fucking chemistry.

"I'm really pleased they didn't," he said. "Because not one of them made me feel half as excited as you have since you walked through our door."

I willed him to kiss me, just to feel the warmth of his mouth on mine, just to *see*. Just to *feel*. Just to squash the nerves, and the tension and the excitement. But he didn't.

"Carl will be waiting," he said.

CARL

I could see them through the window. Enough of them to know Rick had the hots for Little Miss Horsey.

It made me smirk to myself. Rick, with his heart on his sleeve. Literally as well as figuratively. His tattoos were full of them. Hearts and stars and weird patterns.

I wondered if he'd kissed her yet.

The flush on their faces as they came back inside made me consider it, but no. We have boundaries, and Rick sticks to them.

Trust.

It means everything.

I refilled Katie's glass, and she chugged another load back as though it wasn't vintage. I liked that about her already. She lacked any kind of pretence. She was spirited, and free. Classy, without being stuck up.

A body to fucking die for.

And a sparkle in her eyes that made it clear she wanted this.

Correction. A sparkle in her eyes that made it clear she wanted *Rick*. They always wanted Rick. Rick is fun, and sexy, and puts people at ease. Me not so much.

I could live with that. I didn't give a shit about that. But I did give a shit about time. Six months was too long to wait, six months was wasted time, a stupid dance that could lead to a fat pile of frustration.

Six months was unacceptable.

I needed to know she could deliver, and I needed to know a fuck of a lot quicker than six bastard months.

Rick wiggled his eyebrows at me, and Katie was attached to him, her hand in his. They'd be fucking already if I wasn't here, and I knew it.

"Have you eaten?" I asked, and she nodded.

"I grabbed something before I came over."

"Do you need to call anyone, let them know you're still in one piece?"

She shook her head. "I'm all good. Mum's at work. I'm a big girl, she doesn't worry about me."

"She's your mother. Mothers worry." I raised an eyebrow.

"I've never given her cause to worry," she said. "This is way above my usual level of crazy."

"You're quite safe," I said. "A risk that paid off."

"Yeah." She smiled, but her eyes were on Rick. "It did."

Drink always makes conversation so much easier. I kept my head, holding back on the wine while Rick knocked back the beers, and Katie loosened up on a couple of glasses of red. I let them talk, and I watched. I always watch.

Rick told her about graphic design, and made her laugh about some of his clients. Only Rick can make work funny like that. He asked her about her uni course, and her friends, and her horse.

She showed him a thousand pictures, but only showed me one.

She asked him a thousand questions, but only asked me a couple.

She touched his arm a hundred times, but kept her body an ocean away from mine.

Yet her eyes kept finding me, and kept staring, and there were nerves there, intoxicating nerves that tempted me to say fuck it, and grab hold of her tight little body and pound the fuck out of her over the kitchen island. I did nothing, just watched.

I checked my watch when they went out for another cigarette, and the time was getting on. Midnight called, and the stakes were getting higher. To fuck or not to fuck.

Her choice, and I couldn't call it.

She was under his arm when they came back in this time, his fingers trailing the soft skin of her forearm. She was resting against him easily, her smile bright and body relaxed. It made me feel surprisingly irritated, an outcast in my own kitchen, even though I knew the idea was ludicrous.

Rick's eyes told me the idea was ludicrous.

He grabbed another beer from the fridge and this time he came to my side, pressed his body against mine, his hands on my waist. Katie watched, and her pupils were big, the wine making her openly curious.

She was picturing us fucking, I could tell. I could practically see us behind her eyeballs. No doubt I'd be on top, Rick squirming under me while I pounded his hot little asshole.

She'd have that much right.

On cue she crossed her legs, and I watched the press of her thighs as she clenched.

She'd be wet. Wet and tight. Nervous and needy.

We should take her. Fuck her until she squealed like a wanton little bitch and earned her thousand.

Rick's breath was in my ear. "Bedtime soon?"

I nodded. "Definitely soon." I stared at Katie, loving the way she blushed with wine and self-consciousness. "Will you be wanting the spare room?"

She twiddled her hair in her fingers, and it wasn't meant to be provocative, I'm certain of it, just absent-minded, but I felt it right the way through my cock. "I think so," she said. "If that's alright? I mean, I'll stay with you, just, the first night is…"

"It's cool," Rick said. "We get it. Spare room is fine."

I didn't say a word, and there was no point.

We'd put her in the spare room, and she'd wriggle her way under the covers and pretend that's where she wanted to be, and maybe it would be.

But not for long.

She was too curious, and too excited, and her body wanted Rick too fucking much to stay put.

I'd put money on it. Much more than a measly fucking grand.

Time to check out my predictions. I squeezed Rick's neck, my fingers massaging his throat. "Let's call it a night."

Katie drank her wine back, placed the glass on the side. "I'll get my bag," she said.

I watched Rick walk her out, saw the huddle of them by her car. A big fucking thing for such a dainty looking girl.

"I'll show Katie up," he said as they stepped back inside, but I shrugged.

"No need, I'm coming up, too. We'll all go up."

I led the way, purposefully opening the guest room right next to ours. I pointed out the en suite, the tumbler and mineral water on the dressing table, and then I left her there, backing Rick out of the door with me.

Her eyes followed us until I closed the door.

And Rick was pissed at me. His breath was in my ear, all hissy and angry.

"You could have at least let me kiss her."

"Chill the fuck out, loverboy," I said, pacing through to our own room.

"Jesus, Carl. I could have warmed her up to the idea."

"She's fucking wet for it," I said, my voice low. "She's like a bitch on heat over the idea of your cock in her tight little snatch. You'd have to be blind not to see that."

"Both of us," he said. "She wants both of us."

I laughed. "Like fuck she does." My eyes met his. "But she will."

He pulled the bedroom door shut, but I shook my head and threw it wide. And then I unbuttoned my shirt while he watched, and his eyes were hooded, the swell of his cock plain as day in his fucking jeans.

"Now get naked and get on that fucking bed," I said. "And I'll prove my theory about Little Miss Tight Snatch next door."

Chapter THREE

Katie

I breathed a sigh of relief once my bedroom door was closed. Just me. Alone and in one piece. Albeit one slightly inebriated piece. Carl may be curt, and blunt, and really fucking intimidating, but he could sure pick a decent wine. I chalked up a point on his virtual scoreboard.

So far it went a little like this...

Rick. Score: 879. Hair, smile, tats, tongue bar, artistic, funny, nice chest, good hugs. Cool shoes. Dimples. Nerdy-chic. I opened my overnight bag and pulled out my satin slip. *Tongue bar.* That was worth at least a hundred points on its own.

Carl. Score: 001. Good wine picker.

Scrap that.

Carl. Score: 002. Good wine picker. Scary hot.

Is scary hot even a thing? I pictured Carl's looming muscular frame, his hard jaw. Chiselled from steel and softened to perfection with goat's milk and the tears of young virgins. That's how I imagined him. Yes, scary hot was a thing.

Rick, hot. Carl, *scary* hot.

Katie. Score: 1000.

I checked my mobile banking app again just to be sure, and the balance made me smile. Three grand a fucking month. *Nice work, Katie, well played.*

It seemed all so easy now there was a closed door between us.

I cast aside my heels, dress and push-up bra — and hell, what a relief. On closer inspection of my bedtime attire, I decided to stick with my slut-knickers — a scrap of lace that was more frill than substance — as much as anything because I didn't feel my regular bedtime panties were deserving of the opulence of this place. The room was more like a posh hotel gig than someone's spare. Another point for Rick, his interior decor skills were faultless. This room was cream and black, stark and striking, with a huge white bed and black scatter cushions. Shabby chic furniture, but the uber-expensive kind. I mean, I even had a bottle of mineral water on the dresser for Christ's sake. Who even does that?

I poured some out and glugged it back, then slipped my skimpy satin slip over my head. I'd never wear this crap at home, but it felt right here. I caught sight of myself in the mirror and it barely skimmed my arse, plunging down into a truly indecent v at my cleavage, too. I teased the knots from my hair, then struck a pose. Escort Katie looked confident as she stared back at me. Baby-doll satin and wine, a winning combination.

My confidence shrivelled faster than a piece of Rick's dehydrated tofu when I heard footsteps on the landing outside. In a panic I flicked off the light and dived into bed, burrowing under the sheets as though they had the power to render me invisible. I listened until my ears were ringing, but there was no more movement. The faint orange glow disappeared from beneath the door as the landing light went out.

I caught my breath, tossing back the bedcovers enough to feel the cool of the air.

It seemed I really had escaped a night of double-fucking. The thought was both a relief and a disappointment, but mostly a relief. There was a niggle, though, under the surface. The niggle that it would be so much harder next time around after having baulked and opted for the spare at the first opportunity. Maybe I should have fucked them, broken the ice and earned my money. I'd shaved and everything, and show me a single girl who wants to go to all the bother of shaving her bits for a non-event. Not this one.

I shuffled down into the mattress, and it was comfortable. Much better than my one at home.

Fuck, how I wished I was fucking Rick. Just Rick. His hot tatted body over mine.

But Carl.

Shit.

There was fear lurking under the bravado and I wished I couldn't feel it. Bravado was good, bravado kept you safe and happy and smiling, confident in the face of a world that wants to judge you and tear you down at every opportunity. Everyone loves the smiling, confident, happy-go-lucky girl, and mainly that was me. *Mainly*. But here I felt out of my depth, galloping into the unknown for the sake of a small-time dream nobody in the world except me took seriously.

I rolled onto my side, my knees to my chest, snuggling down into the pillows and heading for sleep.

Until the noises came.

Just one at first, and it was him, Rick. My heart did a little flutter.

His groan was loud and guttural, and slightly pained, followed by another that was even more pained. Sex noises are always so unmistakeable. They churned in my stomach, and made me feel guilty, and awkward, and... *horny*. My breath was shallow as I listened for more. Low, deep grunts in a staccato rhythm, and I couldn't stop my mind chasing them, wondering what was happening through the wall, even though the pulse between my thighs already knew. Oh God, I knew.

And oh my fucking God, how I wanted to see.

There was still enough wine in my system to urge me on, and my thighs fell open, fingers slipping inside my lacy thong. I wondered if Rick was pinned, held tight to the bed as Carl's steely body took him. I wondered how much it was hurting, if it really was as rough as it sounded, but soon his groans turned from pained to desperate, and altogether more frantic. I strained my ears for more, hoping for the sound of flesh slapping flesh. Hoping for the sound of Carl, too. Maybe he was whispering, maybe his mouth was on Rick's ear, telling him how good it felt, how tight he was. Maybe he was talking about me.

Maybe he was talking about what he was going to make me do for my three grand a month.

Maybe next time it would be *me* grunting in pain as Carl slammed me into the bed.

The idea set me on fire, and I could hardly think, hardly breathe, lost to everything but the dirty need to take two men. *Those* two men. I'd wanted Rick on sight, probably more than I'd ever wanted anyone in my life. The genuine confidence in his swagger, his ease in his own skin, the way he flicked his tongue piercing when he knew I was staring at his mouth. But here, safe in the room next door, I wanted Carl, too. I wanted him in a way that scared me, right from the depths of my seedy fantasies. I wanted to be nervous of him, I wanted him to intimidate me, and use me and make me take it all. I wanted to cry out like Rick had as he forced his way inside me.

My clit was on fire under my fingers, my pussy so needy as I slipped two inside, but the noises quietened too soon and left me bereft. I held my breath and listened hard to catch the faintest sound, but there was only a series of quiet groans. The promise of a louder volume was enough to get me out of bed, tiptoeing to the wall. I pressed my ear to the brickwork, and they were still going at it. I could hear the noises from their bed, the thump of wood against brick as a headboard hit against the wall. And Carl, I heard Carl, but his voice was too low to make out any words. It was a no brainer. I drained the last of the water from my glass and placed it against the wall, my ear gently to it.

"Yes, holy fuck yes!" Rick's voice.

"Tell me!"

"All of it. Deep. I want it fucking deep."

A grunt.

A moan.

"It?"

"You. I want you, Carl. Right inside. Stretch me and fuck me deep!"

Another grunt. Louder this time.

A muffled groan. I imagined Rick's face pressed into the pillows.

More words from Carl but I couldn't make them out.

A grunt. A moan. I shifted the glass.

Nothing.

If only I could get a little closer.

So quietly I sloped to the doorway, teasing down the handle and praying it didn't creak. The door didn't betray me, swinging open with ease and allowing me to stick my head out onto the landing. There was a path of light from their bedroom door, and the temptation was too much. If I could just inch my way along, just enough, maybe I'd be able to see, just a glimpse. Tiny steps took me closer, edging along the wall with shallow breaths. I hit the jackpot as I reached their doorway, the definite sound of flesh slamming flesh, and Carl had a filthy mouth, grunting a string of expletives about Rick's tight asshole and how fucking close he was, and it was as hot as I'd imagined. I held my position, and slid my fingers back between my legs, brushing my clit as Carl promised to spurt his load into Rick's hungry ass. I had to see, just a glimpse, just for a moment.

I held my breath as I peered out, just in time to see Carl's muscular ass as he slammed his way towards climax. I couldn't get much of a view, not from there, but I couldn't stop, daring to step out just a little further. There was a bathroom just the other side of the landing, I could see the basin, I could be heading there, one last late night pee before bed. Innocent. It could be innocent.

Carl's orgasm paralysed me. It fixed me to the spot and stopped me dead. It was raw, and violent. Muscles taut and brutal as they took what he needed. Rick whimpered and it was the most beautifully erotic sound. He wanted it, a stream of *yes, yes, yes* as Carl finished up, two deep thrusts, and his thighs were quivering, tight with exertion.

Mine were quivering, too.

I forgot myself. Gawping openly as Carl rolled from Rick's back, and my eyes must have flown wide as Carl turned over, breath still ragged as he scooted to the side of the bed and dropped his feet to the floor. I tried to step into the shadows of the bathroom, but I was too late and Carl's eyes burned me alive, hammering into me as though I was the next hot piece of meat for the pounding.

I reached the bathroom doorway as Rick rolled over, too. His eyes sought me out and they were hooded and hazy, his hair dishevelled. He smiled, but I couldn't smile back, I was nothing but nerves.

"Bathroom," I stammered. "Needed to go. I'm so sorry."

I flinched as Carl got to his feet, his thick cock still hard and veined, and so big my pussy clenched, but he didn't head in my direction. His smile was dirty and victorious, and I felt like a bunny in a snare. "Strange," he said. "Since you have an en suite."

Busted.

I wished the ground would swallow me up.

Carl disappeared out of view, and I heard him pissing. The sound was strangely horny. I stared at Rick and he stared back at me, and he was still smiling. "It's alright," he said. "You can watch, it's cool. We don't mind."

But I felt like such a sneaky little bitch.

I was trying to think of words, but my palms were sweaty and my fingers were twitchy. I held them together, contemplating my next move. Into the bathroom or back to bed?

A flush of a toilet and the sound of running water, and then there was Carl again, and scary hot didn't even come close. His chest was a wall of muscle, his abs taut and defined. His thighs were thick and solid, and the V of his hips was deep and perfectly sculpted. And his cock, oh my God, his beautiful cock. Even at half-mast it was still a monster. He stared me out and worked it slowly with his hand, barely even making an effort, and yet it was swelling before my eyes, bigger and bigger, and I couldn't stop staring.

I'd never take both of them. Never. I struggled to comprehend taking just him.

"Are you joining us?" he said, his voice hypnotically low.

I didn't have a voice at all, trapped in the headlights.

He smiled and it was a dirty smile. "Rick needs to come. He'd appreciate your help."

I tore my eyes from Carl, and Rick was still smiling, his posture relaxed.

"So, how about it, pony girl?" Carl asked. "Are you joining us, or not?"

And suddenly I was aware that he was staring at my tits, or more precisely my nipples that were poking through thin satin. He licked his lips, and my poor heart. It jumped and hammered, and my mouth was dry and my pussy was soaking wet. Rick rolled onto his back and took hold of his dick, and there was a glint of metal in the lamplight.

"Well?" Carl prompted. "What's it to be? I'll do the honours if you won't."

Fuck or flight.

I glanced back along the landing, to the shadows of the guest bedroom.

Fuck or flight. Fuck or flight. Fuck or flight.

Another glint of metal caught my eye as Rick moved, and his cock was big, too. My mind whizzed at the thought of two big cocks pushing into me, stretching me. And *deep.* Carl demanding I take them all the way.

Carl pulled back the bedcovers and stepped aside, waiting.

Fuck or flight.

I took a breath.

And then I stepped inside.

CARL

Victorious.

I couldn't resist flashing Rick a look that told him so, but he wasn't looking at me, he was looking right at her. I can't say I blamed him. The girl was born to be fucked. An entirely indecent nightdress offered her no modesty. It barely covered her nipples, pulled tight over the creamy swell of her tits. They were bigger than they'd appeared in her dress, spilling over the fabric and resting heavily against her ribs. Her nipples were hard little nubs and they betrayed her, as did the dark little bunch of her knickers, wet enough that the fabric was pressed to her slit. Her legs were long, and riding sure suited her. Her thighs were toned and strong, her arse shapely before it nipped into her waist.

She was carrying a little flesh around her hips, and it was delightful. The girl's body was delightful. And my cock was hard again.

She'd noticed, too, eying me warily, despite her blatant hunger for a piece of Rick.

She'd intended to fuck. There's no way she'd have opted for the fantasy nightdress otherwise. That suited me, too. I have no time for games or the useless pretence of being coy.

In silence we took each other's measure, and she showed her grit.

The girl made her way over slowly, delicately, eyes wide and lips parted. I watched the rise and fall of her breasts as she breathed, sensing the thump of her heartbeat as she battled her nerves.

The wine would have certainly helped.

She approached to within reach and I patted the bed, indicating she should take up position beside Rick. The bed was more than ample for three, we'd been sure of that when we'd purchased it. It was decadent and comfortable, with exceptionally decent springs. She tested it out, her tight little rump perched on the edge.

Her eyes met mine, and she gasped as I stepped closer, pulling her legs up and away from me and shimmying over to Rick.

It's always such an error of judgement on their part. They invariably think that Rick is the *nice* one. The *safe* one. And while Rick is both of those things, he's also a dirty, kinky little freak who's easily as brutal as me in the right conditions. Stretching is his thing, stretching and body fluids, and boundary-pushing filth.

It's one of the reasons I love him.

I do love them dirty.

Rick met my eyes and I knew the drill immediately. He was ready to fuck, and he was ready to fuck hard.

Katie was jumpy, she flinched as I climbed up beside her, squirming away before I'd even touched her. I probably wouldn't touch her, either, not this evening.

I let my eyes wander over her, unapologetically blatant. I loved the way her breath caught, the flash of nerves across her face.

"Take your nightdress off," I said, and she did. Pulled it up and over her head without hesitation. She was blessed, perfect tits. Tawny nipples, pebbled and ripe. She wriggled out of her knickers without being asked. Good girl. Her thighs clamped shut as I stared at her pussy. She was shaven perfectly smooth, her mound clammy and swollen. She'd been fucking playing alright. She started as Rick draped an arm over her, but she was all smiles for him. He took her shoulder and pulled her closer, and she moved for him, sinking back against the pillows, her thigh pressed to his.

His eyes met mine and I gave him a smirk, knowing what was coming long before she did.

He'd be a surprise to her.

He was exactly that. Her eyes widened as he uncoiled like a snake, pressing his mouth to hers and pushing his tongue inside. She gave the cutest little moan, and wrapped her arms around his neck, letting him claim her mouth like a man consumed. He took her swollen tit in his hand, and squeezed her, pinched her nipple until she squirmed, his breath deep as he sucked her tongue between his lips. She parted her thighs as his hand moved lower, letting out a squeak as hungry fingers slipped inside her slit, seeking out the ripe little bud of her clit. He spread her for my pleasure, and there she was, a pink little rosebud, glistening like the sweetest jewel. My mouth watered.

He pressed a thumb to her, circling her with the ball against her hood, and she was wet and squirmy, a horny little bitch who'd had this coming and knew it. Her fingers gripped at his shoulders, her heels grinding against the covers, moaning as he slipped two fingers inside her and pumped deep. She was tight, but she was horny, spreading wider to let him in. He changed his angle, coaxing with his fingers until her breath hitched. Rick's some kind of fucking g-spot dowser. He never fucking fails.

"You're so tight," he groaned, and she liked that. She smiled, and there was a playfulness in her eyes, partially hidden behind the nerves.

We'd have fun with this one. So much fun.

Rick kissed his way down her throat, tickling her with his tongue bar. He sucked her tight little nipple into his mouth, and nipped her, and she liked that, too. She tipped her head back and closed her eyes, whimpering as he moved down enough to blow on her clit. His tongue found the spot, a silver dart seeking her out. I loved the way his tongue lapped, quick little jerks, bringing her up. The girl was a squirmer, hands gripping the sheets as she bucked against his face. I breathed in the musky scent of her, her wet little noises nothing short of a delight. Her eyes were closed tight, head tipped back, lost to everything but the sensation.

Until I called her name.

She looked at me with a start, and there was a gasp, a flutter of fear, but I didn't move, just met her gaze and held it. Demanded it.

I watched her as she crested and then came with a shuddering moan, and she didn't look away from me, not even when Rick slipped a third finger inside her and ploughed her hard, his wrist a fucking piston, jamming in just the right spot. She moaned and squirmed, and gave us another delight. The girl was a gusher, soaking Rick's fingers as she climaxed, and her whole body jerked and trembled, waves of endorphins rippling through tight flesh.

She positioned herself without words, instinctive fingers coaxing Rick between her legs. She must have felt the steel of his Prince Albert, because her eyes widened afresh, straining for a look before he sunk balls deep. Too late.

"Fuck," she hissed. "Oh God."

He took her knees and pressed them to her chest, and he fucked her. Fucking hell, he fucked her, and her face was a picture. The realisation nothing short of a wonder as the man took her hard and deep, the hard ridge of his belly slapping her thighs. She turned her head towards me and bit her knuckle, her hair rippling on the pillow as he rammed his way home. He pressed his mouth to her ear and breathed, clammy hair pressed to hers.

My hand worked my cock, heady with sounds and smells and

horny fucking visuals, hyperaware of the slam of Rick's cock inside that sweet little cunt and the way his balls were tightening.

He looked at me, and I looked at him, and I nodded. He smiled.

He pulled Katie's knuckles from her mouth, and guided her dainty little fingers to my cock. She met my eyes for just a second before they tightened around me, and I gripped her hand in mine, working her up and down my shaft in time with Rick's thrusts.

She was a good girl. She gripped tight and let me use her, grinding my dick against her palm until my balls were aching.

Rick reached the edge, and Katie moaned like a bitch on heat as he changed angle. She curled her toes, and arched her back and bit her lip, but she didn't stop working my dick.

"Fuck," Rick groaned, and it sent me over the edge, spurting thick into Katie's sweet little palm.

Rick's hand slapped the wall, bracing himself, and he came inside her tight little snatch with a hiss of expletives that turned the air blue.

Dirty-mouthed little cunt.

And then he collapsed on her, catching his breath while she caught hers.

Long seconds passed before he laughed. An easy sound that chased every scrap of tension from the room.

I sank down into my spot, an arm under my head as my cock twitched and settled, smiling as Katie held her cum splattered fingers up to the light.

Rick's eyes sparkled as he guided her fingers to his mouth.

And then he licked them clean.

Chapter
FOUR

Katie

A couple of hours sleep is never kind, but neither was my body clock. I opened my eyes as the first hint of light cut through the drapes, and my mouth felt like I'd been sucking on a baboon's ass.

Carl. Score: 001 and a half. Good wine, scary hot. Minus half a point for gakky wine-dry mouth in the morning.

I risked a glance over my shoulder, relieved to find it was Rick's breath on my naked skin. The room was baking like a sauna, and I was burning up, even without covers, hyper-aware of the heat as his legs tangled with mine. I risked a shimmy towards the edge of the bed, but he stretched in his sleep, and his arms captured me, pulled me tight against his chest. Shit.

I could feel his cock against my ass, and he wasn't soft. Maybe that wasn't such a bad thing. Maybe another good fuck would seal the deal well and truly.

But Carl. God Almighty, Carl... I wasn't sure my freshly-fucked pussy was ready for that.

SUGAR DADDIES

I lay statue-still and listened, and there was Carl's breath, steady and deep. He sounded close, surely just the other side of Rick, and the thought spiked my heartrate. Yeah, I definitely wasn't ready for that. My fingers tingled at the memory of his solid monster dick, the rush of adrenaline as he pumped himself off in my hand.

I held my breath and eased myself from Rick's grip, inching away so bloody slowly that it felt ridiculous. My concentration was at its peak, a tentative foot on the carpet as I made to stealth-exit, but no. Rick's fingers found my arm and squeezed and he was after me, voice sleepy and thick.

"Pumpkin carriage awaiting, Cinderella?"

I lay back beside him, keeping my voice low so as not to wake the beast beyond. "Pumpkin leaves before midnight. I well and truly missed that ride."

I felt his smile against my shoulder. "You definitely got a ride..."

I couldn't stop myself smiling. "Yes. Yes I did."

He propped himself up on his elbow, and I felt his eyes on me in the darkness. "How about round two?" His fingers grazed my arm, tickled my ribs, then crept down my belly, but I shifted away.

"I have to go," I whispered.

"Bailing on me in the darkness?"

I ghosted a laugh. "It's morning, and I'm not bailing."

"Who the hell calls this morning?"

"Samson," I said. "He definitely calls this morning."

"Ah." He rolled onto his back. "Samson would have to get used to a Sunday morning lie in if he was mine."

"He's so worth the early start."

"I'll take your word for it."

I dropped both feet to the floor. "Can I leave?"

I loved the low husk of his laugh. "So long as you promise to come back."

I got to my feet. "I'll be back."

A couple of blinks into the shadows and I could make out the tumble of sheets, the hard lines of Carl's body at Rick's side. I watched Rick shift position, press himself to Carl's chest. "Don't be a stranger," he whispered.

I took that as my dismissal, grateful he didn't insist on a goodbye kiss from my baboon-ass lips. I felt the pathetic little scrap of my nightdress under my toes and scooped it up, but my knickers were nowhere to be found. I patted my way around with naked feet, hoping to strike lucky, but no. I'd have to leave them.

A memento.

I pictured them jacking off together, thick cocks shaft to shaft with only the flimsy piece of lace between them. The thought was surprisingly horny.

Much more horny than the boyfriend at college who'd steal my dirty panties and stash them under his bed. I found fifteen pairs under there once. Fifteen jizz-encrusted fucking pairs.

Asshole.

I crept to the bedroom door, and it was open. The light was brighter on the landing, and it was easy to return to my room. *My* room, for all the ten minutes I'd spent in there. I flicked on the lamp and tossed last night's clothes into my case, taking only a minute to bunch my messy hair into a bun and brush my teeth in the en suite. I pulled out my daywear from the bottom of the case. The height of fashion — a tired pair of jodhpurs, an oversized t-shirt, and my *I love my horsey* socks. All great except my boots were in the bastard car.

I looked in mortification at the glitzy stilettos I'd swaggered in

50

on. Bollocks.

Jodhpurs and pink fucking stilettos. What a total idiot.

I smoothed down the bed and rinsed out my glass in the sink, then made my way down the stairs, keeping to the edge to avoid any creaks. I eased down the front door handle with baited breath, but nobody followed me. Almost to safety, almost...

Until a fake-cheery voice called out a *good morning* from the driveway next door. Oh crap. *That* kind of neighbourhood. I turned to face the greeter, and it was a woman, middle-aged, with a parlour-pretty spaniel ambling around her feet. She was wearing one of those posh fleece jackets, and a spotty neck scarf. Definitely from money. I could have died when she looked me up and down, eyes lingering an age on my horsey socks in stupid heels. Mortification doesn't even come close. She held up a hand. "Cindy," she said. "Are you a... relative?"

"Friend," I said, and my cheeks were burning. Guilty. I don't even know why I felt guilty, but I did, like I had *slut* tattooed on my forehead for the whole world to see.

"Friend, yes..."

And she knew it. She fucking knew it. *Gah.* I fumbled with the central locking until my car let me in. "Katie. Pleased to meet you," I lied.

"Yes... you too. I'll be seeing you?"

I nodded, and smiled, and did this crappy little half shrug before throwing myself into the driver's seat. I kept the smile on my face while I tossed aside my heels, so desperate to get out of there that I started the car up in nothing but my stupid socks. I cringed afresh when my car rumbled and spluttered and choked loud enough to wake the whole fucking neighbourhood, and pulled away quickly, waving at Cindy like she hadn't just caught my walk of shame down some bi couple's driveway at six a.m.

I pulled out of money town and breathed more easily.

I did it. I really fucking did it.

And it was good.

I was good!

Score!

It's so easy to feel like some kind of sex goddess in the aftermath. That bloom of confidence when you're at safe distance and assure yourself you've got this shit nailed. *No big deal. See you around, stud.*

But it was a big deal. Big money, big dicks.

Just... *big*. The whole thing was big.

Crazy fucking big.

I had a glow between my legs and a smile on my face, and a nice big thousand in my bank account and life felt pretty damn sweet. It felt sweeter still when I pulled away from Cheltenham, back towards home turf. I headed straight for Woolhope and the yard, turning off the motorway and making my way back through the countryside. Roads turned to lanes and the sun rose over the horizon, bathing the world in the beautiful light of a fresh day, and the thrum of excitement fizzed its way through me. It never gets old. Never.

I pulled into the yard, crawling the car up past Jack's house and into my familiar spot at the side of the feed barn. Jack was already out, shifting woodchip from one bin to another.

My stomach did a little lurch at the sight of him. He wasn't old, mid-fifties at most, but he looked defeated. A haggard old man in the frame of someone in his prime.

He looked as though he was made from the land. A proper farmer type, with a kindly face and weathered hands... and just lately with eyes that roved a little too much.

Lonely. He was just lonely. He didn't mean it.

He raised an eyebrow as I stepped from the car in just my socks.

"Don't ask," I said.

"Wasn't going to." He smiled. "Long night?"

"You said you weren't going to ask."

"Didn't ask about the socks, just your night." His eyes twinkled, and he lit up a cigarette.

"Had a date," I said. "It went... well."

"So where is he?" he said. "Not well enough that he's coming to meet your boy?"

"Nah," I grinned. "Nobody's meeting Samson until it's serious. He doesn't need a string of stepdaddies at his stable door." I fished my boots from the back of the car, and Jack closed the distance.

His expression was heavy, and it made my heart drop. "Bank's been on at me again."

I tried to smile. "I just need a few more months."

He sighed. "Dunno if I've got months." He looked me right in the eye. "No way you could, um, ask your dad?"

I rued the day I'd ever blabbed and blurted about my stupid pissing father.

The thought turned my stomach. "I'll get the money," I said. "Just not from him. I'd rather eat my own shit."

He pulled a face. "I know, lass. Sorry I asked. You know what it's like, times must."

"I know."

And I did know. I knew how tough times were around here for Jack. His wife had run off last year, taking the yard's head foreman along with her, and Jack was left to pick up the pieces, running a woodland maintenance business virtually single-handed through the tough winter months while prices rose all around him and profit margins got squeezed. There were just a couple of stables on his land, and a run-down excuse for a dressage ring, but I'd been here years now, and I loved it. It was *our* place, Samson's and mine, we belonged here. I just wanted to make it official.

Jack was willing to rent me the land, but he needed the cash and he needed it upfront. Otherwise he was going to have to sell. Sell and turf me off.

The thought was horrible.

We were right by the woods here, acres and acres of perfect riding. I'd been dreaming of running a stable here since I first set eyes on the place, and it had been cemented in concrete the second Samson had arrived on the horse lorry, and I'd led him into his stall. It felt right here.

"I could give you a bit now, if you need it…"

He shook his head. "I shouldn't, Kate, just when you can, you know? I don't want to have to sell."

I pulled out my mobile. "Five hundred do for now?"

He looked so sad. So awkward. "Fuel bill's in. Gonna set me back six-fifty."

Ouch.

I ignored the seedy twist of pain as I transferred seven hundred. So long, bank balance. It was a nice few hours.

"Done," I said. "And a little extra. For any little extras Samson might need."

He never did, and Jack would never use the extra money for Samson, but we danced the little dance anyway.

He smiled. "Better get old donkey ears out. He's been giving me some shit this morning."

Jack said that every morning, and every morning it was just something to say. I smiled anyway.

I rounded the corner to the stable block and my heart did its little jump it does every single time I set eyes on my beautiful boy. He already knew I was coming, ears pricked up and eyes fixed in my direction. On sight of me he gave a little whinny and tossed his head, and I smiled. His eyes were big and brown, and so kind, and his ears were long — a little like a donkey's, as Jack would say — and his nose was velvet soft.

"Hey," I said, and he butted me, tickling my cheek with his forelock. I scratched his ears and rubbed the white flash of his blaze, and my big baby looked so bloody big today, shuffling around his stall all eager to come out and play. I grabbed a head collar from the hook and slipped it on, sliding the bolt on the stable door and leading him out. His step was bright and bouncy, eyes excited as I hitched him to the post and headed for the tack stall.

He whickered as I set his saddle down on the railing, snuffling my pockets for mints as I brushed him down.

Samson was a big brute of an Irish Draught cross. An ex-hunter, certainly owned by someone who was more about the excitement than the skill. I'd picked him up from auction, my heart in my throat as I'd bid against some dealer from the Forest of Dean. Fuck knows what would have happened to Samson if I'd have been outbid, but I'd known he was for me from the moment our eyes met across the sale yard. I hadn't even had a chance to ride him, let alone to get him vetted before I bid, but it didn't matter. I took a chance, and it had paid big, even though he was way too inexperienced for his age, jumping way too big and way too awkwardly, and shying at everything on earth when we rode out alone. I'd persisted, through it all. All the teething problems, all the schooling, all the knocks and bumps and falls. We'd learned together, him and me, and it was the best feeling.

He was almost black, his coat the very darkest bay, and his mane was thick and full, his tail long. He breathed against my shoulder as I teased the pugs from his forelock, holding still as I planted a kiss on his nose.

"Let's go."

I saddled him up in a flash, and grabbed my helmet, swinging myself up onto his back before I'd even fastened my chin strap. He strode out with his head high, ears pricked as we made our way out past the other horsey faces in the stalls and further out past Jack. He waved as we cleared the barn, and I squeezed Samson to a trot as we headed up the drive and onto the lane.

The saddle felt harder than usual against tender flesh, every pace a reminder of the fact I'd been fucked the night before. I'd really been fucked the night before. Potentially harder than I'd ever been fucked, and definitely deeper. Rick fucked like a porn star. The thought made me grin. One in the pussy, one in the hand. Maybe I could be a little porno minx myself.

The nerves came flooding back, the memory of the adrenaline and the endorphins and the fear, and it put me back in my place.

Hardly a porno minx, but I'd done alright. I think.

They'd both come. That's alright, right? Even if Carl had pretty much jerked himself in my hand, that still counted.

I sighed to myself. That counted.

Next time I'd do it better. Next time I'd strip like a professional, spread my legs wide enough for two and tell them to come take what they paid for. A shudder ran through me. Or maybe not.

SUGAR DADDIES

Samson picked up pace, and we rode out across the common, a gentle canter as we rounded the corner to the parking area. I gave him a pat and encouraged him on, and he did me proud, head down and pace even as I slowed him to a trot at the entrance to Haugh Wood. I tried to concentrate on my posture, on the finesse in my leg work, but the motion was too intense. My pussy still felt freshly fucked, tender in my seat, and all I could think of was them.

Naked bodies, and primal sounds, and the smell of sex in the air.

Rick's grunts, so pained... so... desperate. The memory made me hot in the saddle, cheeks burning up in the freshness of the morning, and my thighs clenched involuntarily. I bounced higher and landed forward in the saddle, pressed myself to the pommel, hard enough that the hard leather knob pressed against my clit and sent sparks flying. *Fuck.*

I looked around, but the track was deserted. Just us. Me and Samson. I coaxed him forward, and his trot was bouncy. I stopped rising to the beat, pressing myself to the ridge of the leather as Samson picked up his feet. *Fuck.* I slipped my feet from the stirrups, and spread my thighs, holding myself forward in the saddle, and moving, grinding.

Rick's grunts. The slam of flesh against flesh. Carl's tense ass, the thrust of his hips. The swell of his cock in my fingers. And Rick. Metal against my clit. The squelch of his fingers as he twisted them inside. And the wetness... oh fuck, the wetness...

A flutter between my thighs, Samson's trot so steady. I coaxed him on, faster, and I was rubbing, rubbing myself in the seat.

Fuck.

Rick's eyes as he pressed my thighs to my chest, the way he'd fucked me, hard. The way he'd thrust all the way inside, the way he'd

57

closed my fingers around Carl's big hard fucking cock.

Fuck.

I held myself to the pommel. Breath ragged. *Thump, thump, thump.*

Two cocks at once. *Their condition.* Carl's strong hands lifting me up, his fat cock pushing inside my asshole and making me grunt and cry out like Rick. The thrust of his hips, and I'd be squealing, stretching, taking him. And then more, so much more. Rick's fingers at my clit, rubbing me, forcing their way inside, stretching me open, and I'd be squirming...

Oh fuck.

And I'd take them. I'd take them both. Two fat cocks, two bodies grunting and thrusting and slamming into mine. Carl would tell me what to do... Rick would tell me how good it felt... and I'd be lost... stretched raw by two big fucking dicks.

Oh fucking fuck.

I pulled Samson to a halt and slipped my hand down my jodhpurs, standing in the stirrups and bracing myself as my fingers found my pulsing clit and rubbed their way to orgasm.

The wood was alive with the rousing chirp of songbirds. Samson rustled his nose in the undergrowth, and there was the squeak of leather as I rocked in my seat, nothing but a ragged bag of nerves, desperate for orgasm. I came with just a hiss of breath, my groans choked in my throat, and the euphoria swept through me, calming my thumping heart.

I smiled, and laughed at the absurdity, convincing myself it was safe. Until I heard voices, the familiar *ching* of a bicycle bell.

Bollocks. I kicked Samson onto the straight before I'd even fastened my jodhpurs and he went charging, cantering free as I gave him loose rein.

I laughed. Flushing bright. Embarrassed and excited and endorphin crazy.

This was us.

This was me.

The wind in my face. The familiar triple-beat of his hooves on soil, and I lost myself. I lost myself in the ride.

We were alive. We were free. We were everything.

I was grinning as he slowed to a trot, giving him a pat as he gave a big snort and dropped to a walk. That's my boy.

We completed the circuit, a good long hack that saw the cyclists out in force by the time we headed back to Jack's. Samson had worked up a healthy sweat, his head bobbing nicely and ears pricked forward, and I was still aching, a nice low throb between my legs. My clit was still tender, tummy tickling at the thought of being taken by two cocks.

I dropped to the ground back at the yard, legs like jelly as I hitched Samson back up to the rail. I loosened his saddle and took it down, and took off his bridle, hosing him down with a flash of cool water in the morning sun as he munched on his breakfast.

I was about to turn him out into the field when my mobile started up in my pocket.

Unusual.

People rarely call me in the mornings.

I pulled it out, and the screen flashed a name I really didn't want to see:

Sperm Donor.

Fucking hell.

The dread engulfed me. The same dread I'd been feeling at the sound of his name since I was ten years old and couldn't choose to ignore the shit out of him. The murky soup of feelings I couldn't explain, didn't want to explain.

Didn't want to begin to make sense of.

Ain't nobody got time for *issues* like that.

What the fuck could the sperm donor possibly want at nine a.m. on a Sunday morning?

My finger hovered over answer, until I decided I couldn't give a shit what he could possibly want at nine a.m. on a Sunday morning.

I let him go to voicemail.

Fuck him.

Chapter
FIVE

CARL

"So much for that, then. At least you got a fuck out of it." I shot Rick a scowl. "Better than a fucking hand job. I told you this shit was a waste of time."

Rick's smile didn't ease up any. "She's coming back."

"Sure she is. This year, next year, sometime never." I went through to the bathroom and brushed my teeth, letting out the first stream of morning piss with my cock still at half-mast. Rick always gets the fucking pussy first.

He appeared in the doorway, and I saw his eyes twinkling in the mirror. "She's still keen. She said so."

"You saw her leave, then? Didn't think to tell her she could stay around and earn the rest of her cash?"

"She went to sort out her horse. Early morning stable stuff."

I rolled my eyes. "Great."

"You can hardly say anything, you're the biggest fucking morning person I know."

"I *have* to be a morning person."

He smirked. "You like her, too. I know you like her. It's alright, you know. You can let your asshole crown slip just a little."

"We don't know her," I said, and I meant it. We didn't know her. Didn't know shit about her. Not besides the fact that she's a pretty girl who likes horses. And Rick's cock.

He stroked himself in the doorway and it was obvious why everyone likes Rick's cock so much. "Should have insisted on at least a blowjob before she ran off."

"Your turn next," he said. "Keep it fair."

"I don't think she's interested in my turn."

"Bullshit." He laughed. "You're always like this."

"*It's* always like this. You getting carried away, loving everyone the minute they step through the door, bedding them and giving them the fucking spiel and then giving *me* the big surprise act when things go tits up a few months later."

"Not this time, this time it's different. She's different."

I could feel myself scowling, held myself back. "Let's tell her what the deal is, then. If she's so different."

"Don't start." He stopped stroking himself and shot me a look.

"I'm being serious, Rick."

"So am I. Don't fucking start," he said. He pushed me from the toilet bowl once I'd finished my piss and sat himself down. I finished brushing my teeth, smiling at the hisses and splutters his ass was making.

"Nice."

"You tore me a fucking new one last night."

"And it worked. Little Miss Horsey came running, did she not?"

"Yeah, it worked."

I ruffled his hair. "You fucking loved it."

"Didn't say I didn't." He smiled at me, and there were those fucking puppy dog eyes again. "I really like her."

"Here we go..."

"I do."

I rinsed my mouth. "You always really like them."

"Not like this. She's funny, and she's nice. She's really kind, you can tell, she's got a nice energy. She feels..."

"Tight?" I smirked. "Nice tight snatch, has she?"

"That isn't what this is about."

"But she has?"

He grinned. "Yeah, she has."

"I should hope so. We're paying her enough."

I leaned against the sink as he wiped his sorry ass. "You don't even mean it. You just say it for something to moan about."

He had me there. "Let's just see if she turns up again before you go professing your undying devotion, shall we?"

I walked away to dress, pulling on a t-shirt while he watched.

"*You* have my undying devotion, Carl."

"I should hope so." I grabbed some jeans from my wardrobe.

"You know you do," he said. "I love you."

Fucking Rick and his blurts of affection. "Thanks."

He flushed the toilet. "And that's it, is it?" He washed his hands. "*Thanks*?"

"Thanks. Very much?" I buttoned up my jeans.

He propped himself in the doorway, and his body was incredible in the morning light. His cock was thick and perfectly proportioned, the glint of silver in the end demanding my eye. "And...?"

"And what?"

"Are you going to say it?"

I feigned ignorance. "Say what?"

"You know what. You never fucking say it."

I sat on the edge of the bed, admiring the view. "Surely Little Miss Horsey hasn't got you running insecure? I barely even touched her."

"This isn't about her," he said. "It's about us."

I pulled a face. "Jesus Christ."

"I'm being serious, Carl. Can't you just fucking say it?"

"I love your tight little asshole, Richard. I love it very much."

"Fine." His eyes darkened, and his shoulders turned rigid, his movements jerky as he pulled his clothes from his chest of drawers.

I laughed. "Sensitive this morning."

"Just... whatever, Carl."

He pulled on some boxers and I rolled my eyes at his back. "Seriously. You know I don't need to spell this shit out. We're not five, Rick. What do you want? Little love hearts and flowery kisses?"

"Whatever."

"Christ, Rick, what's this even about?"

He folded his arms and faced me, and his gaze was firm. "Why can't you say it?"

"I can," I scoffed. "I'm just not so... gushy."

"You can't," he said. "It makes you uncomfortable, doesn't it?"

I didn't answer.

"Is it because I'm a guy? I thought you were over all that?"

My words came out harsh. "I *am* over all that. I've *long* been over all that. Fucking hell, Rick, that lasted a fucking week, at best."

"What, then?"

I scowled at him. "Like I said, I'm just not so extravagant with my words. What difference does it make? I'm here. You know exactly how things are."

"Maybe I want to hear it. You always want it straight up from everyone else. Why can't you say it?"

"That isn't even vaguely the same thing." I got to my feet. "That's a ridiculous parallel." A dark strip of lace peeped from under the covers. I pulled it out. Katie's knickers. Without thought, I held them to my nose. Breathed her in. *Nice.*

"I just want to know. It's good to hear sometimes." He sighed. "Unless you don't."

I ran the gusset between my fingers. "Unless I don't what?"

"Feel like that."

"Like what?" The lace was fine, and the scent of her was glorious.

Rick slapped the chest of drawers, uncharacteristically irritable. "Just forget it."

"And you're going to be all hissy now, are you?"

He shrugged and he was walking away. Rick never walks away.

It made me lose my shit.

I grabbed him by the elbow and his eyes were wide as I pulled him back. He slammed into the wall with a thud and I pinned him, my shoulder pressed to his as I pulled down his boxers. And I said it. Even though the words made me icky to my stomach, exposed and uncomfortable and highly fucking awkward, I said it.

"I love you."

His cock was hard against my thigh. "Say it again."

I took his cock in my hand, wrapped the lace of Katie's frilly knickers around him. He groaned as I worked his shaft. "Don't fucking want much, do you?" I squeezed until he groaned. "I love you, Rick. Since you fucking insist on hearing it. I love you, I love you, I fucking love you. Hearts and roses and soppy fucking kisses. Is that what you want, Rick? You want to hear me make a fucking sap of myself? Is that what makes you fucking hard, pretty boy?"

"Fuck, Carl. *Fuck.*"

His fingers were at my jeans, and I was relieved. My balls were tight and hot, the scent of sweet pussy lingering on my tongue. His hand wrapped around me, and he jerked me hard. Fast. Ramping up the pace until I grunted in his ear.

He pulled me to him, pressed his cock against mine, and I groaned as the ridges of his piercings pressed into my shaft.

"Fuck..."

He groaned for me, then threaded Katie's little knickers between our thrusting fucking meat. "Gonna fuck her. Both of us. I know you want it..."

I thought of the pink little bud of her. Her shaven slit. "Of course I fucking want it..."

"Gonna fucking stretch that cunt, Carl. You want it as much as me. Gonna be so fucking tight in there, Carl. So fucking tight."

"Fuck, Rick..." The rhythm was relentless, hips and dick and fingers.

He licked my lips and I sucked his tongue. Then pinched, the barbell hard against my teeth. He groaned and it was wet. I didn't let him go, and he wriggled and squirmed.

I pressed harder against him, bucking harder.

His hands gripped my ass, held me to him, and there were no fingers, just cocks, cocks and grinding fucking flesh.

I let his tongue go free and he pressed his head to the wall, closed his eyes. "Gonna open her up for you, Carl. Gonna make her nice and wide. I know what you need."

"Fuck..." I hissed.

"Gonna make her take it, make her beg... open her up until you're all the way inside, Carl. Oh, fuck, she's gonna be so fucking tight. Such a tight little fucking snatch."

"I want to... I want..."

"I know," he breathed. "Gonna fill her up, Carl. Fill her right fucking up."

And I was coming, spurting and hissing and shooting my load all over his fucking belly. All over mine.

"Yes..." he hissed, and he was coming too. I felt the jerk of him, the frantic judder of his dick against mine.

I caught my breath against his shoulder, and he laughed.

"Wasn't so fucking hard, was it?" he said. "Three little words." He took a deep breath. "Say it again."

"Now you're pushing your fucking luck," I said.

Katie

I stepped through the door at midday and Mum shot up from the dining room table. She hovered while I kicked off my boots in the hallway.

"What?" I said.

"You know what."

Urgh. I rolled my eyes.

"Don't tell me he called you. What a prize fucking prick."

"Watch your mouth," she said, and I shot her the finger.

I smiled and so did she.

"I'm not talking to him," I said. "He can piss off."

"He said he's been calling for a week."

"*No*," I said. "His *office* has been calling for a week. Him, no. *He*

67

called once. Earlier. I was busy."

"Semantics. He's been calling for a week."

"I don't give a shit what he's got to say. I'm not interested in any little non-family get-togethers. I'm not interested in Verity's new fucking show pony. I'm not interested in how wonderful his wonderful life is." I tossed my phone from my pocket to illustrate my point. "I really don't care. I want none of it."

"He's your dad…"

"He's my *sperm donor*. Nothing more."

She pulled a face. "That's horrible, Katie."

"*He's* horrible."

"He's still your father." She grabbed my phone, held it out to me. "Call him."

I shook my head. "No fucking chance."

"You should call him. He wants to speak with you about something."

"I couldn't care less what he wants."

"You will," she said. "Call him."

I took the phone but made no move to dial. "Why will I?"

Mum ran her hands through her hair, and it curled at the ends in the exact same way mine does. We could have been sisters. People often said so. "Ask him!"

"You tell me," I insisted. "What does he want?"

She sighed. "He has an opportunity for you."

"Then I'm really not interested in calling," I laughed. "I don't need his *opportunity*."

"This is different," she said. "You need to consider this one."

"I don't need to consider anything from him." The promise of three grand a month held me in warm arms. "I can sort my own shit out."

She leaned against the table and took a breath. "Harrison Gables."

The name stole my breath. I gawped for long seconds. "What about Harrison Gables?"

Harrison Gables was the best horse whisperer in the whole universe. He's the best of the best. The guy works miracles. He works with the wild horses on the cowboy plains in the US, and he's known worldwide. I'd give anything to meet him, but he rarely indulges an audience.

My heart fell before she'd even finished the words. "Verity is going..."

I should have known. Of course Verity would be going. Princess Verity could do anything, have anything, go anywhere. Of course Princess Verity would want to go and meet Harrison Gables, not least because *I* wanted to go and meet Harrison Gables. I couldn't hide the resentment from my voice. "Why tell me that? That's so fucking unfair."

She shook her head. "No! That's the thing! He wants to send *you*."

My belly fluttered and twisted. "Me?! Why?"

"Maybe because you're his *daughter*?"

I tried not to shoot her nasty eyes. All this time and she still defended him. She'd never stopped defending him. It was sad really.

I forced myself to breathe, telling myself this was some stupid game, some stupid trick, even though my heart was daring to hope, daring to dream.

"What does he want? He must want something?" I couldn't stop the pout. "Verity need a kidney donor or something? Maybe they want to harvest my *sub-standard* DNA to save *precious*. He'll need to come up with more than Harrison Gables in exchange for my organs."

Mum rolled her eyes. "Ask him," she said, and gestured to my phone. "Who knows? It could be something *good*. Have you considered that?"

No. I hadn't considered that. There was little point. It was never good. I stood mute, just staring. *Harrison fucking Gables.*

"Alright," I relented. "I'll call him."

Mum looked relieved. She chivvied me along with frantic hands, and then she said the ominous words.

Ominous words that never boded well.

"Think before you give an answer," she said. "I mean it, Katie, you need to *think* about things. Don't go bladdering in there making rash decisions."

I dialled the number before she could make me promise anything.

CARL

"Call her," I said. Rick was staring at his phone, pretending to be tapping away on some thing or another, but I knew. His brows were too serious.

"No."

"Call her. See if she's coming back this afternoon."

"No!" he said. "Just give her some time, will you?"

I smirked. "Don't pretend you aren't shitting it. You want to know if she's coming back. So, call her."

"You're wasted, you know that? You should start up an agony aunt column. *Ask Doctor Carl*. It would be an instant hit."

"Mock all you like, my advice is sound. People just don't want to hear the truth." I turned my nose up at his little veggie crackers and grabbed some bread from the bread bin. "You don't really think she's coming back, do you?"

"I do actually," he said. "I know she'll be back. I'm just not sure when."

"Next weekend. If she wants to get paid."

He rolled his eyes at me. "And that's what I'm supposed to say, is it? *Hey, Katie! You'd better be back here Saturday. It'll be two dicks next time. We'll have lube.*"

"What's wrong with that?"

He sighed, and nibbled at his veggie delight. "It's just so... base."

"And?"

"And... just... non-seductive."

"We're supposed to pay her *and* seduce her now, are we?" I stuck the bread in the toaster. "Surely she should be seducing us, no?"

"Doesn't mean we can't make an effort."

"We made an effort."

"You uncorked a bottle of red. Big deal."

I groaned. "So, what do you suggest? Candlelight and truffles?" I smirked. "Then dick?"

"This place is intimidating."

I laughed. "Is it hell. It's just a fucking house, Rick, not a bastard castle."

"That's not what I mean," he said. "She's walking onto our turf. It's intimidating."

"And this is where we *live*."

He sighed. "Let's go away. Take her with us. Just for the weekend."

"Out?"

"Brighton. Manchester. Anywhere."

"And then what?" I watched the steam from the toaster. Rick and his soft fucking ideas.

"And then we drink, and relax, and have fun." His eyes sparkled. "And then she takes two cocks."

"She isn't going to take two first go, Rick, even I know that."

He shook his head. "She'll take two, trust me. It's all in the technique."

"We'll tear her apart."

"Trust me."

The toaster popped. "I'll be happy to trust you," I smirked. "Just as long as you can pissing well get her there."

He smiled. "So, we'll go? Brighton?"

"Wherever you want," I said. "No expense spared..."

He punched the air.

"...on one condition."

"What condition?"

I took a seat at the table. Focused on him deadpan.

"You've got to promise me we'll both be buried to the balls in that tight little snatch before the night is out. Otherwise it's no fucking deal."

He held out a hand. "You've got yourself a deal, partner."

Katie

"Katie!"

Urgh. His fucking voice. Such a snobby, self-righteous fucking prick.

"You called?"

He sighed, made a right fucking mountain out of it. "You could have returned my calls sooner. It's unfortunate I had to call your mother."

"She said."

"Did she explain? It's a great opportunity, Katie, I'm very serious."

I didn't have time for this crap. "What do I need to do to meet Harrison Gables? My kidneys aren't for sale, and neither's my pissing soul." *Just my pussy. Ouch.*

He sighed again, full of them. He's always bloody sighing. "Won't you just come to the office, as I requested your mother? We can talk there. Properly."

"I've no interest in talking properly," I snapped. "Just tell me now."

"Katie..."

"No," I said. "Tell me now."

He really did groan then. An exasperated groan that pissed me the hell off, but I kept my mouth shut while he said his piece.

"One month's apprenticeship with Harrison Gables at his ranch," he said. "One whole month, just you and Verity, his absolute attention."

I could have cried. The idea was inconceivable.

Inconceivable and no doubt rammed full of conditions.

And impossible to achieve any other way.

He had me and he knew it. He really knew it.

"And I have to see you?"

"Tomorrow," he said. "At my office. Stroud."

"I can't do tomorrow," I lied. "Thursday? Friday?"

73

He groaned and I heard paper flicking. "It will have to be the following Monday, then," he said. "One p.m. Don't be late."

"And what will this meeting be about?" I asked. "What do you want?"

"A week on Monday," he said again. "Be there."

And then he was gone.

Asshole.

SIX

CARL

I'd do anything on earth for David Faverley, but his petulant, spoiled excuse of a daughter was trying my patience, and I'd been in the same room as her for a mere twenty-nine fucking minutes.

Our intern programme at Favcom Technology was renowned as the best in the industry. I'd like to say it was my baby, but I'd be lying. David had been running the scheme for a lot longer than I'd been in the business, in fact, the scheme was responsible for the fact I was even in this business at all. I believe there are pivotal moments in life where fate crosses your path, takes your measure and decides to give you a shot. Maybe it's a chance opportunity, maybe it's that moment you hit the peak of your curve and the cards stack in your favour, or maybe it's that one person that sees right through you, ignores your past and your hang ups and the massive fucking chip on your shoulder and catches sight of something more.

David Faverley was that one person for me. The guy who looked beyond the shell of the arrogant little prick in his office and saw something in me worth investing in. So, here I was, almost twenty years later, at the head of his Techstorm sales subsidiary, shoulder to shoulder with him at every business meeting that meant anything, director across the board for every single one of his enterprises. Yet, I rarely broadcasted it. Scrap that, I never fucking broadcasted it.

Respect is never a given, it's always earned, and titles mean shit. I want the people in my teams to respect me because I've given them reason to. Trust me because I've proven myself trustworthy. Work hard for me because I work hard for them. And despite my reputation as a hard-headed steely sack of shit, I'm really not so bad, or so people tell me.

I have just three rules in business, and in life. Give your all, grab hold of opportunities, and show gratitude for all you've been given.

Verity Faverley defied all fucking three of them.

She didn't want to be here, that much was obvious; trussed up in her brand new designer fucking workwear, her stiletto-heeled shoe tapping aimlessly in the air as she stared at my presentation slides. Her expression was both pouty and glazed, and as she yawned for the third time in ten minutes it was just about time to pull her up on it.

"Am I keeping you awake, Miss Faverley? I'd strongly suggest an earlier bedtime if you're going to be on form for nine a.m. sharp."

Eighteen other faces in the room, and not one of them looked at her. She had that kind of aura, the one that says *my daddy's your boss, don't fuck with me*, but that really doesn't mean shit to me. Every other person in this room was here out of merit. Every other soul in this room wanted to be here, wanted the shot, wanted to grab hold of the opportunity and make something of themselves. Every other person, *I'd* chosen. But not this snotty little bitch.

She shot me a look of pure disdain. "Whatever, *Carl*."

I gritted my teeth. The problem with working so closely with David Faverley was that I'd inadvertently spent too long around his kids to maintain a healthy level of professional courtesy. Sebastian and Dominic, the elder two, had been similar. *Hey, Carl, yo, Carl, how's it going, Carl?* But they'd learned. A few days into the internship had knocked the familiarity clean out of them, and then it had returned stronger, more genuinely, and with mutual respect.

Somehow I doubted the road would be as smooth with Verity. She was here purely because *Daddy* was making her be here. By all accounts because of some crappy little US trip he'd used as leverage, and it seemed that this time she believed he'd hold out on his conditions. No internship, no fucking jolly at the end of the six months.

I pointed at the current slide.

"My requirements are simple. Everyone will do their best. I don't care where you've come from, I don't care what you know, or what you've done, or what a couple of cruddy pieces of paper claim you're worth. I judge on what I find, and I find effort and determination to be worth a thousand university degrees. Don't try and coast through this programme, because I'll know it, I've already seen it a thousand times over. You have a problem, you bring it up and we work through it, other than that, I expect your all when you're on my team, and for the next six months we're a team. Understood?"

Eighteen heads nodded, while Verity's looked at her Gucci watch.

"Miss Faverley, is that understood?"

She rolled her eyes. "Yeah, Carl, I get it."

But she didn't. She didn't fucking get it, because spoiled little bitches like Verity Faverley have never had to work for anything. She's the youngest. The pampered princess in the ivory tower. Her mother's little china doll.

A brat.

"We'll be starting from the ground up, no exceptions. Everyone is on equal footing here, following the same path as the hundreds before you. You'll start in the call centre, developing your customer service skills, your communication skills, your professionalism and your product knowledge. You'll be learning to sell without visual cues, without a smart suit, without a company car, or flashy business cards, or a title under your belt. And then, when you're ready, *if* you're ready, you'll get a shot at higher level account management, maybe a placement in one of the field sales divisions. Maybe you could even transfer to marketing. The world is your oyster, and we hope most of you, *most* of you, will stay." I smiled at the rag-tag collection of newbies before me. "Any questions?"

A few tentative hands went up, and I addressed their queries one by one. All the regular. *When will we have to make live calls? What products will we be working on? I don't know much about the technology yet, is that a problem?*

Verity had not a single one.

I gave them a smile and watched them settle, breathing out a sigh as they began to relax into day one of their new life. And then I threw them a curveball. I docked my phone on the speaker stand at the front, scrolled through songs until I found the *Rocky* theme. This moment would singe itself into their memory, the disbelief and the shock and the humour. Maybe sometimes the horror. This moment would begin the breakdown of their reservations, pushing them through their self-consciousness. Initiation by fire, and it had purpose here.

"Everyone sings. *Everyone*," I said. "I'd better hear you, or you'll be out on your ear on day one." I scanned the faces, registering the first flashes of horror. I don't know quite why it is that singing in public petrifies people so universally, but Christ it does. "Everyone will do their very best. Stand up, please."

Nineteen people got to their feet, some shifting awkwardly from foot to foot, some grinning, some already blushing. All of them ready to give it a go, except one.

"Music is an anchor, and sales is a performance based career. Find your songs, the ones that lift you up, make you feel like you can take on the world and everyone in it. Find them and use them, often. This is mine."

I pressed Play.

And then I led from the front, and that always surprises them most of all.

I can't sing, not really, but I love music and I love to move. I listen to music wherever I go. On long drives to meetings, through hard workouts on the rowing machine, preparing for an important negotiation, crunching the numbers at month end. I love music and I love to dance, and I put both of those into practice in front of a room of new recruits, and they smiled and laughed a little, and slowly their voices grew louder, their expressions more open as they joined in with the tune. A roomful of people bellowed out the Rocky theme, and some of them found their groove and even did a little fist pump, and that one guy at the back stepped up to the plate and became that one guy who always throws himself right in, and he jogged on the spot and punched the air in front of him, and I liked him. I really liked him. He'd be one to watch.

I stepped between the chairs, listening to every single person, making sure all of them were singing strong, and then finally I stepped over to Verity on the end of the front row. Her face was deadpan, not even a hint of a note. I chivvied her along, a hand on the shoulder, my voice in her ear, but she did nothing, just stared at me like I was some idiotic piece of shit. My expression turned, grew stern, my gestures becoming more urgent until she rolled her eyes at me.

I stopped singing.

"Come on," I said. "Give it a go."

"No way," she said. "It's stupid."

People around her quietened, their ears pricked.

"It's not stupid, Verity. Stupid is trying to form relationships on the phone with a stick up your ass and inflexibility of communication."

"It's *stupid*," she repeated. "I'm not going to make an absolute tit out of myself, not for *you*."

"You're already making an absolute tit out of yourself, Miss Faverley, I'm just asking you to *sing*."

Her eyes widened and turned sour. "Fuck you, Carl. I'm not singing. No way."

I tipped my head to the side. "Then get out."

She folded her arms. "Sorry?"

"I said, get out." I returned to the front and turned off the music. "You're dismissed, Verity, you can leave."

"But, I…"

"But nothing. You give your all, or you quit."

"That's ridiculous, just because I won't sing your stupid crappy song." Her cheeks turned pink and angry, but I didn't back down. "We'll see what Dad has to say about this," she hissed.

I gestured to the door. "Be my guest, he's in suite four-two-four."

She scanned the crowd, and everyone dropped their eyes. "You'll be sorry," she snapped, and then she was gone, a whirlwind of self-entitlement stomping her way down the corridor, heels clacking like pistol shots.

I smiled at the rest of the candidates. "Equal footing, as I said. No exceptions."

I took my phone from its dock, noting the message icon before I slipped it into my pocket. The room felt lighter somehow, barriers coming down. There was more eye contact, brighter smiles. Good.

All good.

"Right," I said, changing the slide. "Let's get started."

Katie

Tourist season turned Much Arlock into a hiker's haven. The cafe was rammed for the lunchtime special, people nipping in for a sandwich after a morning's walk along the Malvern Hills. I grabbed table four's orders from the hatch and flashed Benny a smile as he wiped his brow with a dishcloth.

My resignation letter was in my pocket, but there was a sadness to the idea of handing it in. I'd been working here since I was old enough to carry a tray without spilling it. Saturdays at first, just around school, then holidays, and now four afternoons a week. The money was crap, but the job was alright. And Benny was so bloody nice.

Slowly the lunchtime rush eased off, and I wiped down tables and waited. Eventually, Benny stuck his head around the door. "You wanted to speak?"

My stomach lurched, the letter burning me. "When you get a second."

He beckoned me over, and my legs felt stiff as I moved. I wanted to hand in my notice, and yet I didn't. I wanted the time, and not the safety net, not the safe little wage packet this place offered me. It would make it far too easy to bail on Carl and Rick, and I didn't want to bail, I wanted to chase the rainbow.

I handed over the envelope and Benny's eyes fixed on me. "You have a new job?"

I nodded. "Sorry, Benny."

"No need for sorry," he said. "You have a degree, all grown up. It's time."

His smile brought a lump to my throat. "I've really loved it here."

"And here's really loved you." He put a hand on my arm. "You must come, for toasted teacakes, often. My treat."

I nodded. "Thank you."

He slipped the letter in his apron pocket. "This job, with your father?"

Urgh. Another one I regretted telling. I really should get better at keeping secrets. Once it slipped out, they never fucking forgot about it.

"No," I said. "Nothing to do with that prick."

"Pity," he said. "Your father knows good business." I looked at his friendly eyes, heavy browed with grey. Benny was South African, accepted by the locals slowly over the years, until he was now a piece of the Much Arlock furniture. "Where are you leaving us for?"

I tried to recall the standard line I'd made up. "I'm helping out a designer. Cheltenham."

"I didn't know you were into the art." He smiled. "A designer... yes..."

"I'm not," I laughed. "It's the customer facing side. I'm his...

82

assistant..."

"Ah, yes." He grinned. "Good."

I felt like such a fraud. "Yes, it's good."

He pulled out the calendar. "You finish next week?"

"Please," I said, and then remembered the sperm donor phone call. Another fucking *urgh*. "And I'll need Monday off, if I can. My *father* wants to talk to me."

Benny scribbled on the rota. "Maybe your father has a good business offer."

I checked for customers but there was only the old deaf couple by the window. "Maybe my father can go fuck himself."

"Katie!" he blustered, but he was laughing. "You just hear him out, yes? For old Benny."

God. Another one.

"Yeah, yeah. I'll hear him out."

The bell above the door chimed as a party of regulars came by for coffee and cake, and our time was up.

"Thanks," I said. "I appreciate everything you've done for me. I really do."

He waved it away. "Good partnership," he said. "That's all."

My phone vibrated in my pocket as Benny turned back for the kitchen. I pulled it out as the table of regulars got seated.

One message. One email.

Which to answer first?

I clicked the message.

> Rick: I've got an idea. Fancy a hook up
> this week?

I felt it between my legs, the memory of his piercing against my clit. My cheeks were burning as another message pinged through.

> Rick: I mean a chat, not a fuck. Sorry,
> that sounded bad!
>
> Rick: Unless you want a fuck?

I smiled, and then there was another ping.

> Rick: Ignore me. I meant a chat. A hang
> out. Some chill time.

The table were engrossed in the menu, even though they had the same cakes every time. I sent off a message.

> Sure, I'd like that. When? I can do
> Wednesday. Maybe Friday.
>
> Rick: Wednesday? Lunch? Come here. I'll
> cook.
>
> And Carl?
>
> Rick: No Carl.

No Carl? I didn't know whether to feel relieved or worried.

> Ok, cool. See you then.

I took the coffee order before remembering the email. I clicked to open as I waited for the coffee to filter.

Favcom Tech. Confirmation of your interview.

What the fucking hell?

I scanned through the text. A fucking interview?! On Monday?!

So much for a fucking chat.

I fired off a text to Mum.

> I'm not taking a fucking job with him.

Mum replied in a heartbeat. Just hear him out. Please?

Such a simple reply. No. Fucking. Chance.

> It's not a job. It's an internship.

84

Great experience.

So, she knew exactly what he was after. I could have strangled her through the handset. No!

What about Harrison Gables????

I steamed the milk, and I was pissed off. So fucking pissed off. I typed a response.

Fuck Harrison Gables, and fuck the fucking sperm donor, too.

She'd replied by the time I delivered the tray to the table, and I could have guessed what it said a mile off.

I know you don't mean that. Please go, just to see. For me. Love you. x

Pissing hell. What was with the world? Please go, for me, for me, for me...

I took a breath.

I didn't need him or his poxy job, and I'd tell him so. I'd tell him what I thought of his stupid Harrison Gables blackmail, too.

And then I'd tell him to go fuck himself, and at least I'd be in person to give that sperm donating sack of crap the fucking finger.

CARL

I loosened my tie and ditched my jacket over the chair, guzzling down a couple of mouthfuls of beer before Rick even asked the question.

"So, Princess Faverley?" he quizzed. "Just as good as you were expecting?"

I nodded. "The brat wouldn't sing."

"Ouch."

"Quite. So, I sent her packing. She ran to Daddy, you know how it goes."

He sucked in breath. "And what happened?"

I smiled at the memory. "He sent her back five minutes later, with an apology."

Rick's eyebrows shot up. "An apology? No fucking shit!"

"A token apology."

"Did you accept it?" He grabbed himself a beer.

"After she sang the Rocky theme..." I couldn't help but smirk. "Solo..."

Rick shook his head. "Jesus, Carl. She's gonna hate your fucking guts."

"She can hate my guts, I couldn't give a toss, just as long as she learns to apply herself to the programme, or gets the fuck out of it."

He paused, and I made him wait, didn't say another word.

"Did you get my message?" he asked, finally.

I took a swig of beer. "Yeah, I got it."

Rick shrugged. "So? It's good, right?"

"That our little *sugar baby* wants to head over and *chill* on a Wednesday afternoon? She probably thinks you're paying."

He scowled. "Don't ruin it. It means she's still keen."

"It means she's after more cash."

"Or more cock." He leaned back against the kitchen island. "Can you be here?"

I stared at him. "When have I ever been here on a Wednesday afternoon?"

"Fine," he said. "So, what if she wants to fuck?"

I shrugged. "Is that what you want?"

86

He sipped his beer. "Maybe."

"Maybe?"

He tipped his head. "Maybe, yeah."

I propped myself on the worktop. "Solo?"

His cheeks pinked. "No..."

"Oh, come on, Rick. When have you ever invited one over in the week?" And he hadn't. The idea was absurd. Together or not at all, that normally stretched to everything.

He sighed. "She's just..."

"Just what?"

"Just... different."

I took a breath. "She must have a magic pussy if you're all hung up on it after one little fuck."

"It's not just that."

"Of course it's just that," I said. "What do you think you are? Fucking soulmates?" He looked shifty. Awkward. It bothered me. I fucking hate secrets. "What is it?" I said. "Spit it out."

He turned away, pretended to wipe something down from the sink. "Nothing."

"Don't give me that shit," I said. "You're up to something."

He groaned. "For fuck's sake, Carl, why do you always fucking do this?" He reached in his pocket and pulled out a piece of paper. He hovered as I reached for it. "Before you read this, know that I had to really dig, and this isn't recent, and it doesn't mean anything."

"Yeah, yeah," I said. "Just hand it over, what did you fucking find?"

"And I'm seeing her." He kept it above his head. "I'm seeing her Wednesday regardless, and I'm scoping it out, and I like her. I really like her."

"Just give me the paper, Rick." I took it from his hand, and he looked away as I unfolded it. A collection of Facebook statuses. Quizzes, and comments on other people's tags. My eyes soaked it all in. "So, it's done," I said, folding it back up. "Another pointless exercise."

He slammed his hand on the counter. "I knew you'd be like this."

I downed the rest of my beer, telling myself I wasn't bothered, that this was just another par for the course, but I felt strangely disappointed.

He shook his head. "Just let me scope it out."

"I don't have fucking time," I snapped. "Find someone else."

"Please, Carl, just give me a chance…"

I sighed, and there was disappointment. Definite disappointment. "I don't have time for this shit." I grabbed another beer and stepped away, but he didn't follow.

He stood with his arms folded, and his expression was resolute and steely and all fucking loved up. "I'm seeing her on Wednesday," he said. "And you can either be there or not, but I am."

"So, why tell me?"

"Because we're honest with each other. Because I want you to know," he said.

"And now I know." I shrugged. "Do whatever you want, but I'm out."

He took a couple of steps in my direction, and his voice had an edge of desperation. "Six months, you promised."

"And you rendered them unnecessary."

"But I *didn't*. Don't you see that?"

"I see exactly the opposite."

He scowled, shook his head. "What about the weekend? What

88

about stretching tight little cunt and taking her together? Hey? You telling me you don't want to do that now?"

I sighed. "Fucking hell, Rick. I don't know."

"Fine," he said. "I'll cancel her. I'll call it all off, right now." He pulled out his phone and began to text, but my hand landed on his wrist.

And I had nothing to say, no fucking reason, and he knew it.

His eyes were victorious.

"I'll see her Wednesday," he said. "I'll work it out."

And I didn't argue.

I didn't say another fucking word.

Chapter
SEVEN

Katie

Do I smell like horse? I pulled my t-shirt to my nose, took a whiff. Hmm, maybe a little. I pulled my emergency perfume from my handbag and spritzed the shit out of myself, then rubbed my fingers in my armpits to check for body odour. Safe enough. I'd just have to hope I didn't have any stray bits of hay dangling from my underwear. It's been known to happen.

One of the perils of heading straight to a lunch date after a morning at the stables.

I vacated my vantage point at the end of the street, then rumbled onto Rick's driveway. The Range Rover was missing. Made sense that Rick's was the sporty little BMW, it suited him. I switched off the engine and my heart was pounding, which was standard, but there was more than nerves today. I'd woken early, even for me, and I was excited. Ridiculously excited. So, this was *crushing*? I'd never really had a crush before. I'd liked plenty of guys, but it was always just a like. Occasionally a strong like. Sometimes even a considered *yes, I'd like his dick in my ass, possibly many times*, but never something that had me waking up before dawn with a big goofy smile on my face.

Rick. His point score was going up every time I pictured his face, every time he sent a text, every time I rubbed myself off to the thought of his hot pierced cock. And now I was at his door, with the promise of no Carl, just us.

That shouldn't feel as good as it did, and definitely shouldn't feel as good as the thought of three grand a month landing in my bank account. *Keep your fucking head, Katie, keep your fucking head.*

Rick opened the door before I'd even locked my car, and today he was barefoot, low slung jeans hugging his hips. He was wearing a simple t-shirt, but it was bright yellow, emblazoned with *life is art* in a funky font. He looked awesome, and his smile told me he was pleased to see me, too.

Yep, this was definitely crushing.

I was shorter in flat pumps, short enough that his lips pressed to my forehead as he pulled me into a hug, his arms wrapping perfectly around my shoulders. I leaned into him, my tits pressing to his chest, hands snaking around his waist to land on the top of his ass, and there was that ocean smell again, only the ocean never smelt as good as it did on Rick's beautiful inked skin.

"Hey, pretty lady." His smile was boyish and animated and delicious. "Pleased you could stop by."

He took my hand and led me inside, and the place felt so alive today. A radio blasted out soul music as the afternoon sun spilled through the kitchen windows, and there was a hint of a breeze from the open patio doors. He turned the music down and grabbed me a water from the fridge, then clinked my glass with his own.

"Cheers."

I smiled. "Cheers."

"Lunch is on." He pulled the oven door down enough to peer inside, and the smell hit me. Chicken. Barbeque.

I raised an eyebrow. "Aren't you, um…"

"Veggie?" He smiled. "Yeah, I am. But you're not. I'm not one of those *thou shalt not* types. Eat what you want." He pulled out a salad bowl from the fridge, and he'd even made that artistic. Chunky colours in flamboyant shapes. Cucumber stars, and tomatoes in neat little triangles.

"You shouldn't have…" I started, but he waved it aside.

"Used to it. Carl's virtually an anti-veggie. He has a side of beef with his beef, that guy."

Carl. I felt like an intruder upon hearing his name, hitting on his boyfriend while he was out of sight. I fucking hate cheating. The thought gave me shivers, feeling way more seedy than selling my ass for three grand a month. *Go fucking figure.*

"Where is Carl?"

"Work," he said. "He's sorry he couldn't make it."

I only wished I was, too.

He gestured behind me, to the laptop on the kitchen counter, the stool placed in front. "Beauty of working from home. My time's my own. Mostly."

"That's what I want," I said. "My own timetable."

"Best feeling in the world." His eyes looked me up and down. "Or one of them." His gaze burned me, his low laugh making me blush. He pulled out some bowls, and sauces, and a couple of serving spoons, laid them out on the kitchen island and pulled me up a stool. "Thought we could eat here."

I took a seat. "Works for me."

I was glad I'd opted for casual. It felt so much nicer to wear my own skin. My jeans were my best pair, and my t-shirt was one of my newer ones, and I'd even worn a couple of bracelets to jazz it up a little, but I was definitely me today. It felt good to be me in front of Rick Warner, and his smile told me I was doing just fine. I liked that. I liked *him*.

"How's your big hairy boy?" he said.

I gawped at him. Just gawped. Not once had anyone I'd been fucking ever asked after Samson before, not without prompting.

"Samson," he clarified, like it was needed. "How is he?"

"He's good." I grinned. "He's great. We're in training for the summer eventing circuit. I think we'll do well this year." I crossed my fingers, held them up. "I *hope* we'll do well this year."

He mirrored my gesture. "I'll keep mine crossed, too. And my toes." He pulled on some oven gloves and took out the chicken. "Maybe we could come and watch. Me and Carl, I mean."

"Watch me and Samson?"

He shrugged. "Yeah. Maybe we'll see you pick up some rosettes. That would be cool. We could be your cheerleaders. Don't be fooled by Carl's stoic exterior, he's got some moves." He pulled a couple of *Saturday Night Fever* gestures, wiggling on the spot with his oven-gloved hands on his hips, and it tickled me.

I couldn't help but laugh. "You seriously want to come and see me and Samson on the eventing course?"

He fixed me in an easy stare. "Sure I do. Why, is that some dating no-no or something?"

I held up my hands. "No, I just... I thought..."

His stare didn't waver. "You thought this was all about sex?"

"No!" I protested.

He laughed. "You totally did. And it's not. I mean sex is sex, and it's fucking great, and I can't fucking wait to get you under me again, don't get me wrong. But that's not it. Not all of it."

My mouth felt dry as he ditched the oven gloves and forked chicken wings onto my plate. "So... what is *it*?" I said. "What else is there?"

He handed me the serving spoon, and watched as I piled some salad alongside my chicken. "That depends."

"On what?"

"On you."

"On *me*?"

He nodded. "Yeah, on what you want."

I drizzled some olive oil over my greens. "Last time I checked you were the ones who were paying. Surely it's about what *you* want, no?"

He shook his head. "That's not quite how it works." He forked himself some cucumber stars. "See, we want... *things*... we want... *someone*..."

The piece of tomato in my mouth felt big all of a sudden. I struggled to chew, and struggled harder to swallow. "*Someone*? Like... more than a..."

"More than a fuck once a week on a Saturday, yeah." He sipped his water, but his eyes didn't leave mine. "Much more than that."

I felt my colour draining. *Much more than that*. What could be much more than that? A live-in whore? A sex slave? A maid? *A girlfriend?*

He waved his hands. Held them up. "Sorry, I shouldn't have said anything. Too much, too soon."

"No," I said. "It's just... I don't..." I took a breath. "I'm not really sure how this stuff works. I just read a couple of reader's letters in

Glitz, and it all sounded so easy and cool and glamorous. And hot. It sounded hot."

"There aren't any rules," he said. "It's just people. People want different things. I guess we need to find a zone where we all gel."

"Yeah," I said. "I guess so."

I had no idea what kind of zone a guy like Carl would gel in. The idea turned my legs to jelly.

"Me, personally," he said. "I want fun. Companionship. Someone who'll make us laugh. Someone who fits. Someone who's kind. Someone who takes cock like a trooper and still wants more the next morning."

My cheeks burned. "And then what?"

He shrugged. "And then she stays. Maybe. If that's what she wants."

"Stays?"

He looked me straight in the face. "Decides she doesn't want to leave and our cool little duo becomes an even cooler trio." He shook his head, slapped himself on the temple. "Shit. This really isn't for now. I only fucked you once already, I'm kinda hoping for more before I scare the shit out of you."

"I'm not scared," I said, but it was at least partially a lie. "I just... I don't know..."

"You can't know," he said. "You only just met us." He sighed. "I just wanted you to know this isn't just some flash in the pan idea. It's not about throwing money at a bit of pussy."

"Noted." I smiled.

He laughed, a belly laugh. "You're so fucking scared now."

I laughed back. "No!"

"Yes," he grinned. "You are. Forget I said anything."

"Really," I lied. "I'm not."

He licked his lips, and his tongue bar glinted, the atmosphere tightening in a heartbeat. "We'll fuck you first. A lot. Then you can think about it."

My stomach tickled, and I wanted him. I knew I wanted *him*. I shouldn't think it, and I certainly shouldn't say, but the words were already in my throat. "If it was just... if *this* was just... regular... it would be..."

"Easy?"

"Easier..." I admitted. "I mean, if it were just... if this were... us..."

His expression turned serious. "Carl and I come as a pair," he said. "Always."

I shook my head. Mortified. "Shit, I'm sorry. I didn't mean. I was just... thinking aloud... I shouldn't..."

"It's alright. I get it. One on one is simple. Classic boy meets girl. Girl fancies boy. Boy wants girl. They fuck. They swoon. They fall into a groove." He smirked. "I get it, that could be us. I feel that."

"I shouldn't have..." I repeated. "It just slipped out." I wanted to kick myself. Hard. "I'm sure I'll like Carl."

"You'll get to know him," he said. "And when you do, you'll love him. I promise."

"I'll love him, will I?" I laughed to lighten the tension. "You seem pretty confident."

"I *am* confident. Carl's hot, and smart, and funny — even if he doesn't always seem that way. He's determined and he always gives his everything. He's loyal, too."

"When did you know it was love?"

He smiled. "When he gave me his ass for the first time, and I was way more interested in him than his girlfriend's hot pussy. It doesn't

96

happen all that often, the ass thing. He's not much of a taker."

I smirked. "So, the girlfriend got booted?"

He shook his head. "The girlfriend was a scheming bitch. She fucked off."

"No loss, then."

"Not for me," he said. "More so for Carl."

"So, you're looking for a third for your happily ever after? Carl, Rick, and Miss Unknown."

"Something like that. Like I said, it isn't a concern for now."

I couldn't help feeling a little unnerved inside, the prospect of more taking grip of my lungs. I picked up a chicken wing, forced myself to smile as I ate it.

"You *did* say you didn't want the status quo." He held up his glass. "Here's to finding out, hey?"

I touched my glass to his. "Sure thing. I'll drink to that."

He took a swig, then clapped his hands together. "Enough of this heavy bollocks," he said. "Let's shut up and eat our bloody lunch before my blabbermouth runs away with me."

Sounded good to me.

Rick moved the music to the living room after lunch, one of those seamless setups that pipes your tunes from room to room. He took the sofa, and so did I, and so naturally my knee rested against his. He'd made me laugh, so much. Made me smile, so hard. So many stories, of travels, and graphic design, and love, and sex, and life. Mainly I had stories about Samson, but he was interested. Genuinely, too. I could see it in his eyes.

I could spend a lot of time around Rick Warner. A fuck of a lot of time.

An early lunch was turning into a late one, but he hadn't made any attempt to return to his project, and I wasn't pushing it. I could have happily stayed there, slumped on his sofa while we talked the afternoon away, substituted mineral water for cold beer and laughed my way through until dawn.

"So, yeah," he grinned. "She, um, didn't last long. Told me I was a freaky piece of crap and took off out of there."

"In her underwear?!"

"In just her fucking knickers." He laughed. "Seriously, it was a pathetic excuse for a thong." He gestured to his crotch. "Barely covered her fucking slit, I tell you."

The thought made me giggle. "She drove home like that?!"

"Yep. Through rush hour traffic."

"And that was the very first time you tried watersports?"

His eyes glinted. "What makes you so sure I tried it again?"

He had me. My cheeks burned. "I dunno. You just seem that kind of guy…"

"Ha!" He held his hands up. "You got me. Seriously, though, don't get too nervous. I won't throw up any filthy surprises, I promise."

"I trust you," I said. "I'm brave like that." I smiled at him and he smiled back, and there was something in it. Something unspoken, and heavy, and probably the result of too many sex stories.

I shifted in my seat, trying to ease the need between my legs, but all it did was hitch my knee further up Rick's thigh.

He licked his lips, and I watched his mouth as mine opened. *Shit.* And then he leaned forwards, his hand on my leg, hot through the denim, his breath warm on my open lips. Fuck, I wanted him. Not for the money, not to seal the deal, or get him on side, or take away my nerves for the big double-fucking that was heading my way.

Just *because*.

His lips brushed mine, and his eyes were dark, his lashes so close they tickled my skin.

"Kiss me," I whispered. "Please..."

He paused, hovering so close. "This is a grey area..."

Carl.

The thought was a spray of cold water, and I blinked, shifted, put my hand on his chest and moved away. "Shit, sorry. I didn't mean..."

He took hold of my thigh, strong hands pulling me back, hitching my leg over his to spread me wide. Even in denim, I felt exposed. "A grey area," he said. "Not a no-go area."

"But Carl..."

"Carl knows you're here. He knows I want this."

My breath was nothing but a hiss. "But you said... together, or not at all..."

"We usually mean it..."

Usually? I gasped as his tongue touched my cheek, moved down to my neck. He kissed my throat, and I squirmed, sinking down, letting my thighs fall open. "Fuck..."

"No sex..." he whispered. "We can't... but just a kiss... one little kiss can't be wrong..."

I moaned as his mouth pressed to mine, and my lips were already open, welcoming his tongue. His piercing felt so good, so nice as it circled my tongue. He pressed me into my seat, my head tipped back and at his mercy, and I could feel his hard-on as he moved, the swell against my thigh as he sucked my mouth, sucking my tongue deep into his. I had nothing but breath and need, and it turned me from rational Katie to some other Katie I didn't recognise. A Katie who wanted this guy so bad I twisted my fingers in the tangle of his hair and gripped him tight. A Katie who rubbed her thigh against the swell in his crotch and fought back the urge to dig her way inside his clothes.

Just a kiss.

But it wasn't just a kiss. It was a writhing, heavy, free-for-all, our mouths clamped together as we made out like two horny teenagers, only Rick was no teenager. His kiss was skilled, and dirty and deep, so horny it made my clit spark, my pussy throbbing against the seam of my jeans. He read my body, pressed his hand to my crotch, rubbing me hard through the stiff fabric.

"I want you," I breathed into his mouth. "Fuck, I want you."

His fingers teased me, his rhythm steady between my legs. "What I'd fucking give to see how wet you are..." I groaned as he pressed hard. "I bet you're fucking sopping. Your sweet little pussy so fucking wet for me."

I held his wrist, encouraged his movements. "Please... Oh fuck, yes, please..."

"I wish..." he rasped. "How I fucking wish. I'm so fucking hard... What I'd give to explode inside your hot little slit... what I'd fucking give..."

"Dirty boy," I groaned. "I love your dirty mouth."

"Tell me," he said. "Tell me what you want..."

My senses were reeling, my body jerking against his hand. "I want you to fuck me," I said. "I want your gorgeous fucking cock in me..."

"Nice," he smiled against my cheek. "More..."

My voice was just a whisper. "I want to feel you inside... I want you to fuck me, hard... I want you to take my ass, and make me fucking squeal…"

"You want to be stretched, little girl? Is that what you fucking want?"

Oh fuck, my clit was clanging like a church bell. "Yes… oh, fuck, please… I want you to stretch me…"

"Gonna open you up so fucking wide," he growled. "Gonna take your fucking cunt with two fat cocks, stretch you nice and fucking big… two big fucking dicks in your sweet little pussy… gonna feel so fucking dirty… gonna feel so fucking tight…"

"Yes…"

"Wanna see all the way inside you… all the way into your pink fucking hole…"

"Yes…"

"Gonna make you wet… make you stretch… make you fucking gape for me…"

The heel of his palm, so hard against my clit. "Fuck…" I ran my fingers down his chest, over his abs, until I found the swell in his pants. I squeezed him through his jeans. "Fuck me…"

"I fucking shouldn't…" he groaned. "Fuck…" But he was grinding against my hand, moving over me.

"Just a quick one. Hard and fast. Please…"

"I can't…" he said. "I can't…"

I cried out as he pinned me, his cock against my pussy, just two layers of denim keeping us apart. He fumbled with his zipper, and his breath was fast, so fast in my face. I stared at him, eyes wide, thighs spread and ready for more, but he paused before his dick was out, the haze clearing.

"Shit," he said. "Carl. I just… can't…"

I tried to find the resolve to push him away. "Grey area?"

He shook his head. "It's not so fucking grey, not really." He pressed his forehead to mine. "Shit."

I sucked in breath. "It's ok," I said. "We won't..."

"But I want to," he said. "I want to so fucking much." He gripped the leather of the sofa at the side of my head. "Why couldn't he have just taken fucking lunchtime off?"

"He must have known..." I whispered. "He must have known we'd be... wanting..."

He shook his head, and his eyes were clear and focused. "That isn't why you're here," he said, and there was a tone to it. A tone that made my heart sink.

I moved from underneath him, and he shifted to accommodate, pulling up his zipper and leaving his cock well alone.

"Why am I here? Why did you call me here knowing Carl was out?" The questions came out with a ragged desperation, and I hated it. I hated the thought of surprises.

And I hated the thought of this being over.

"I didn't want to say..." he said. "Not yet. It's too early, way too early, but Carl... Carl needs..." He sighed, then rubbed his face, his breath deep.

I sat upright, closed my thighs. "Carl needs...?"

"Carl wants to know whether..." He sighed. "Carl has... requirements..."

"Two cocks at once, right?" I said.

He shook his head. "That's not it." He brushed a wisp of hair from my cheek. "I didn't want to talk about it, not so soon. But it's important. Carl is... insistent... he wants to know... *needs* to know..."

"Needs to know what?"

He looked so awkward, so uncharacteristically unsure. He stared at me, and I willed him, willed him just to spit it out.

"It's important, like I said." He looked at the ceiling. "It's a sensitive situation... something you need to know about..."

"Tell me," I said. "Just tell me..."

Rick's eyes were dark and horny, his breath still fast as he prepared to answer my question. "Carl needs..."

But another voice told me. It boomed from the hallway. "Lunch," it said. "Carl needs his fucking lunch."

I stared open-mouthed at the doorway, and Rick did, too. And my cheeks were burning, just like Rick's were.

"Carl," he said. "I didn't think you'd be coming. You never come."

I untangled myself entirely from Rick, smoothed down my t-shirt, praying he wasn't angry, praying I wasn't about to be turfed out with my dreams in tatters.

I expected questions, and jealousy, and maybe a bit of outrage, but there was nothing of the sort. Just a sly smirk on Carl's face.

"I hope you didn't eat it all up without me," he said. "I'm fucking ravenous."

CARL

You've got to love walking in on people unexpectedly. The guilt was written all over their faces, dishevelled yet fully clothed, Rick all ready to spill the big condition. Maybe I should have let him, hung back in the hallway and listened to the drama unfold, watched our sweet little pony girl make her excuses and bail on us, just like those before her.

I should have let it happen, and then we could have moved on to plan B. Only plan B sucked donkey balls, and as much as I argued the point when Rick told me so, I thought it, too.

Maybe cute little Katie Serena would surprise me. Her baby blues looked me up and down, her smile nervous and apprehensive as she watched me walk through to the kitchen. Barbeque chicken. Rick really did have it bad.

I was pulling apart a chicken thigh when they joined me, and Rick shot me a look. A *what the fuck* look.

They stood close, shoulder to shoulder, the tension between them smoking and spluttering while I ate my lunch.

"Good day?" Rick asked.

I shrugged. "Busy."

I fixed my eyes on Katie, and she looked away with a blush. "I thought I should be here to finalise the plans."

Rick raised an eyebrow. "The plans?"

"The weekend. Brighton. I guess you haven't finished asking Katie if she'll join us."

Katie looked from Rick to me and back again. "Brighton?"

Rick's eyes were full of questions, his shrug almost unperceivable. "Ice breaker," he said. "Night out. Cocktails, tunes, dancing."

"Sex," I said.

She didn't flinch. "Sounds great."

Good girl.

I forked up a token piece of tomato. "We'll leave Saturday morning, nine sharp. Return Sunday evening."

She nodded. "Sure." She turned to Rick. "I'd better go, got a shift this evening."

"I'll see you out."

Of course he would. I smirked. "Bye, Katie, I'll be seeing you." I let the words hang heavy, wishing I was close enough to feel her heartbeat as it thumped in her chest.

"Bye, Carl." Her smile was warm and sweet, despite her apprehension, and there was a pang of familiarity in my stomach. I couldn't place it, and it made no sense, and yet this girl, this sweet little package of blonde and freckles and tight ass, was already under my skin.

And she was already well, well under Rick's. He led her out by her hand, and there was a tenderness there. He had it bad alright. Sap.

I cleared the rest of the chicken, and was already in the hallway with my keys in my hand when Rick came back inside.

"What was that?" he said. "I was all fucking set."

I stared past him, listening to Katie's rust bucket of a car chug from the drive. "A few weeks," I said. "We'll give her a chance."

"A few weeks? What good will a few fucking weeks do, Carl?"

And I didn't know. I really didn't know.

He took hold of my hand, lifted it to his mouth, and sucked in my sticky fingers, scraping the barbecue sauce off with his teeth. My nostrils flared, a flourish of tingles through my balls.

His eyes never left mine as he sucked on my thumb, sucked hard until it was clean.

He stepped back, "I'm sure I heard your cock twitch," he said, passing me a tea towel. "I'm already hard."

"I'd noticed," I said, wiping my hands and discarding the towel.

"I want to fuck you," he said and grimaced at my raised eyebrow.

I pulled him to me, pressed my lips to his. He tasted of her, and that my made cock twitch even more. Then he was hugging me, tight. I hugged him back.

"I've got to go," I said. "I'm presenting at three."

He blew out a sigh. "Yeah, whatever."

"You could have fucked her."

"I wanted to."

"But you didn't."

"No."

He pulled away. "Why are you here? I thought you couldn't make it?"

"Saturday," I said. "We'll really get her measure on Saturday."

He didn't reply, not until I was in the doorway, the Range bleeping as I pressed unlock.

"You like her, don't you? Fucking hell, Carl, you really like her. That's why you're here."

I gave him a wink before I pulled the door shut.

Chapter
EIGHT

Katie

Not nervous, not nervous, not nervous. Definitely not nervous. No way.

I'd packed too many clothes for a night away, virtually the entire passable collection from my wardrobe, but what was a girl to do? A night out in Brighton could mean anything. Posh dinner? Ballroom dancing? A basement rave? Partying on the beach?

Should have packed those glittery pumps. They'd pass for beach party attire. Crap.

Rick smiled across at me, and I wished I could see his eyes through his shades. "Not too long now." He turned the music up a notch, but Carl tapped the back of his seat.

"I'm expecting a call," he said, gruffly, and Rick turned it back down. He shook his head at me, and I laughed. My neck prickled as Carl leaned forward, his chiselled face appearing so close, right between our seats. "Some of us have to work," he said, and then his phone started up.

He'd been in the back seat the whole journey, his laptop on his lap and his phone beeping and whizzing. I didn't mind. I liked it up front with Rick. I liked it a lot.

Maybe I even liked the guy in the back seat a little, too.

I relaxed into the leather of the seat, the sun hitting my skin through the window as the world outside passed me by. I could do this. Carl, I mean. Maybe not do him do him. The thought of fucking him still brought me out in a cold sweat, but this, being with him. This I was getting used to.

His humour was dry, and he was uptight, and snarky, and a mega workaholic, but he was alright.

I was surviving Carl Brooks.

I was loving Rick Warner.

And I had three lovely fucking grand in my bank account.

Three!

Three lovely grand in my bank account, two fat dicks in my pussy later, and an industrial bottle of lube in my suitcase. Lube and paracetamol. And sanitary pads, for the internal bleeding I couldn't imagine avoiding as Carl's monster dick tore into me. Not really, I didn't have room in my case for non-essential toiletries. I smiled at the surrealism of my predicament, and Rick smiled back, put a hand on my knee. I put mine on top and squeezed, and I knew then I'd be alright.

I'd never been to Brighton. It was taller than I was expecting, a string of big hotels on the front, and the sea to my right. I pressed my face to the window and my heart jumped as we passed the bustle of the pier. I should have definitely brought my glittery pumps. Rick pulled into the underground parking of a grand looking hotel just a short way beyond, prime position, and Carl groaned as his mobile signal cut out.

"Fuck," he said.

We parked up, and got out, and Carl was already wandering away, his phone in his hand as he stared at the screen and angled it for signal. Rick touched a hand to my elbow and winked at me, and then he leapt after Carl, sneaking behind him to whip the phone from his fingers. He pranced away as Carl rushed after him, and I laughed as they played a stand-off, Rick poised on one side of the Range Rover as Carl came after him.

"Prick," Carl said. "I need that."

"Nah," Rick laughed. "Not this weekend."

"Yes, this fucking weekend!"

"No way!" Rick made a dash for it, and I laughed as Carl charged after him, and then there was a shake down and in a beat Rick had shoved the phone down the front of his jeans, and he was smirking, hip thrusting as Carl tried to get a grip on his belt.

"You think that's going to fucking stop me? I'll have your pants round your fucking ankles, I don't give a shit."

A family of four approached from the stairwell and stood mute by their Mercedes, and I laughed, oh hell how I laughed, hard enough to double over as Rick got close enough to the exit that Carl's phone started ringing in his pants. He gyrated his crotch, jumping about, his face a picture as the handset chimed and buzzed against his dick.

"That's important!" Carl growled, and I had to cover my face with my arm, laughing so hard I couldn't breathe. Rick handed it back with a grin once the call had rung out, and Carl jabbed his arm. "You're such a fucking idiot, Richard. Such a fucking dick."

But even Carl was smiling. He dropped the smile as he saw me laughing.

"Glad my professional humiliation is amusing you, Katie," he said. But he was playing, I saw it in his eyes. He looked from me to Rick and back again and then he groaned and pressed the off button. "Fine. I'm done for the weekend."

Rick threw an arm around his neck and pulled him close, landing a big wet kiss on his cheek, and it made my tummy lurch. "I fucking love you, Carl."

"Pleased to hear it," Carl said, and wiped his cheek down with a grimace, but that was playing, too.

I think Carl Brooks played more than I'd have ever expected, hiding behind a gruff exterior, all steely and corporate and stern.

I gave him another point. Carl. Score: 003. Good wine, scary hot, really a little bit funny when you get to know him.

Rick grabbed my hand and Carl grabbed my case along with his own, and we made our way up to reception where nobody seemed to raise an eyebrow that the three of us were checking into one double. But of course they wouldn't, our double was a whole fucking suite. Two huge rooms of grandeur on the top floor with a balcony overlooking the front, and it was awesome. It had been a long time since I'd been to the seaside, never mind among such opulence, and the excitement boiled over. Rick leapt on the bed and did a bounce, and I joined him, up and down on our asses while Carl checked out the view.

And then Rick pinned me, his inked arms holding me to the bed while he flicked his tongue up my throat, and I let out a pleasurable moan.

"Get a fucking room, kids," Carl said, and the husk in his tone gave me shivers. I watched him unpack his case, a couple of dark shirts and a black pair of jeans, a pair of shorts I really couldn't imagine him wearing, and some boxers, folded up neatly. He looked at Rick and then he unpacked some more, and my thighs felt like jelly strings as he lined up a load of sex toys on the dressing table. Dildos and plugs and a big bottle of lube. I tried to play it cool, relaxing at Rick's side as though I wasn't absolutely shitting myself. Carl loosened his cuffs, rolled his sleeves up as though he was about to get stuck into manual labour, and I nearly did shit myself.

He must have seen my expression, as he smirked.

"Later," he said.

Rick turned my face to his, and he was smiling. "Chill," he said. "You'll enjoy it. I promise."

My throat felt too dry to even risk replying, and I couldn't think of the words to say if I'd wanted to.

"We're wasting the day in here," Carl said. "Let's go. Sunshine calling."

I kicked off my pumps and swapped them for sandals, and headed to the bathroom to swap my jeans for cut-off shorts, tossing my hair for a bit of extra volume before I was ready to don my pink shades and head outside. The day was warm and bright, and it chased my reservations away. We took a table on the beachfront for lunch, and we drank fruity cocktails while Rick talked about the string of old family holidays he'd been on as a child.

One of four kids, he said, loads of fun. Well-to-do parents with loads of money and an easy demeanour. It was easy to see why he was so confident.

"I was the cool one." He grinned. "Bit of a joker."

I could believe that.

He finished up his stories and looked between us both, waiting for one of us to pick up the baton and share our own tales. When Carl looked away I figured it was my turn.

"Mum took me away when she could," I said. "Those crappy little budget caravan breaks in the school holidays, where the food is nothing but value burgers and the pool is a higher percentage of child piss than it is water. It was on the edge of Bognor Regis, a total shithole. Loved it, all the same."

I couldn't imagine either of those two knowing what I meant, but Carl surprised me.

"I went once, same park. Only holiday I ever had, just for a couple of days. Best time of my childhood."

"Only holiday?" I asked.

He nodded. "They didn't really have the budget to take us kids away, not from the hostel."

"The hostel?" The question was out of my mouth before I thought, and Rick put his hand on mine, squeezed.

"Ice cream," he said. "I think it's time for ice cream on the beach."

I could take a hint. "Sure," I said. "Sounds a great idea."

We walked slowly, and I threaded my fingers with Rick's as he threaded his with Carl's, and it felt nice here, absorbed by the crowd of other unusual parties, colourful people in colourful clothes, gay and straight and everything in between.

"You mentioned your mother," Carl said. "What about your father?"

"I don't have a dad," I replied in a beat. "My dad is nothing but a blank space on my birth certificate."

"Sorry," he said.

"Don't be," I said. "I'm not."

He looked at me over Rick's shoulder, and his eyes were so green in the sunlight. "I don't have a dad, either," he said. "Not one that matters. People should learn to keep it in their fucking pants if they're not man enough to step up to the plate."

We agreed on something, that was for sure.

"And now I feel like the odd one out," Rick laughed.

"You are the odd one out," Carl smirked. "Always."

"Whatever." Rick grinned, wrapped his arms around our waists and pulled us in tight, so tight that the scent of Carl knocked into me when he did, and he was dark and deep and smelled like leather on skin. "I'm the glue that holds this shit together."

"Not tonight," Carl said, and his tone dried my throat once again. "Tonight it will be Katie holding us together." He smiled and it kicked up my heartrate. "Quite literally."

Literally. I pictured the lube on the dressing table, the rope-like veins in Carl's huge meaty dick, and wondered if I'd actually be able to take just him, never mind both of them. Oh fucking fuck.

Carl ordered his ice cream first. "Strawberry and chocolate," he said. "Always a winning combination." He took his cone and I could have combusted when he licked it, his eyes fierce on mine.

He was challenging me, challenging me to break and run. But no. No fucking chance.

I leaned into the counter and tried to look cool. "Double scoop strawberry," I said. "Got to love a double serving." I took a lick. "Yummy." I winked at Carl and he actually smiled.

"Clever," Rick said, "then I guess I'll have the banana split, with chocolate sauce... and plenty of nuts," he added.

Carl laughed, slapped him on the back, and his grin when he looked at me was a grin I'd never seen before. I'd held up to the pressure, I could see it in Carl's eyes. Just a flash of admiration, or acceptance. I don't really know what it was, but it thrilled me.

Sun and cocktails and ice cream and a quick change of clothes, and we were out again, grooving to the beat at Club Wave, a dance bar on the beach, with loud tunes and disco lights, and dry ice and drag queens. I was covered in black sequins, a backless dress that barely covered my ass and sparkled under the lights, twirling in heels with a pink glitter nail polish on my toes. And there was Rick, in a tight white tee, his hipster jeans showing off the v of his hips as he danced at my side with glow-bands around his wrists. Rick had moves. He pumped the air and he twirled, whooping as the bass picked up. Rick was hot, and alive, and free.

He pressed to my side, a hand on my waist, claiming me as his lips tickled my bare shoulder, and I wanted it. I wanted to be his.

The track changed, and it was one I knew, one I liked. I jumped on the spot, cocktail confident and ready to party, then slung my arms around Rick's neck as he picked me up, spun me in his arms, only to drop me at Carl's feet. The heat of Carl's body sent shivers up my back. I tossed him a look over my shoulder, and he stepped closer, so close, the wall of his chest pressing against my bare skin.

He snaked his hand around my waist as Rick pressed into the front of me, and I moved with them, sandwiched between two firm bodies, Rick's thigh between mine as he took hold of my hips and rocked to the beat. I stretched up my arms, and tipped my head back, and Rick's lips landed on my collarbone, tickled me. Here we go. But I was ready, confident in my sparkly clothes, confident with the glow of alcohol in my belly. My outstretched arms reached back for Carl, my fingers finding the back of his neck and tangling in his hair. His hair was smooth, and soft, his skin warm.

His hand on my waist moved upwards, slowly, his fingers

splayed against my ribs, and I sucked in breath as his fingertips reached the swell of my breast. Rick's tongue bar felt so nice against the tenderness of my throat, and I smiled, angling my head back on Carl's shoulder as he squeezed at my tit.

Yes.

His crotch pressed to the small of my back, and he felt even bigger there, a solid pole of hot fucking dick. The feel of him made me squirm, and I turned my face towards his, grinding my ass back at him.

Kiss me.

I was nervous, under the alcohol. Nervous enough that my tummy was a fluttery mess. The nerves lessened as Rick's thigh pressed hard to my pussy, his hips rocking enough to feel just right.

I looked at Carl, his face so chiselled under the disco lighting, so at odds with the glitter and sparkle of this place.

Kiss me.

My eyes fluttered, then closed, my lips parted as Rick sucked at my neck, and then there was a ghost of stubble, Carl's cheek against mine before he landed his lips at the corner of my mouth. I felt his fingers in my hair and he angled me further, eyes dark as he hovered, his lips just a whisper from mine.

Kiss me, just fucking kiss me.

And he did kiss me. His lips were hard, yet soft, demanding, yet teasing. His tongue was strong, pushing between my lips to hunt mine down, and we danced there, in my mouth, and we hit the same beat.

Hot breath, and hot hands, and Rick's tense fucking thigh against my clit, and I squirmed, and writhed, my hands busy between two hot guys, two firm bodies, two soft heads of hair. My mouth busy between two hot mouths, two needy tongues, two men growing more insistent with every ragged breath. I coaxed Carl tighter to my back, circling my hips to tease his cock, and he thrust and ground and hitched me up against him, the length of him pressing into the crack of my ass as Rick pressed himself against my pussy.

Sandwiched. Pinned hard between two dicks. Two hard cocks straining to be inside me, and I wanted it. I wanted them.

My fingers became braver, ghosting Carl's cheek as my body accustomed itself to the bulk of him. He still intimidated me, his steel still giving me shivers in the deep, dark depths of me, but I was coming to know him. And I was coming to like what I knew.

I focused back on our surroundings, on the hustle of bodies dancing all around us, and nobody was giving us a second glance, too caught up in their own groove. Men kissing men, men kissing women, women kissing women, a whole roomful of people feeling the beat and the heat and the promise of sex in the air. Rick's beard tickled my shoulder, and I smiled.

Yes. Yes, I could do this.

I wanted to do this.

I tipped Rick's face up and pressed my lips to his and I was smiling, and then I coaxed Carl forward, my hand around his neck, pulling him forward as I guided Rick back. Their lips met over my shoulder, and I liked it, I really liked it. Carl's mouth opened first, and I watched so closely, loving the way his tongue pressed to Rick's. I moved my pussy against Rick's thigh and I watched them make out, guiding Rick's hand to my tits to squeeze at me, pull at me, make me fucking tingle.

And then they looked at me, both of them, looked at me with their lips still glistening from their kiss, and their eyes were hungry and hooded, their gaze pointed.

I closed my eyes as two hot mouths came for mine, unsure of which tongue was whose as they tangled with mine. It was wet and messy and totally uncontrolled, disorienting me enough that I didn't know whose hand was on my tits, or which guy was pinching my nipple until I wriggled.

I wasn't sure whose fingers slipped between my legs and found my clit. Whose fingers slipped their way inside my thong and found me wet and desperate. Whose fingers slipped inside me and thrust to the beat of the music until I was panting against their open mouths and hissing out curses. "Fuck yes, fuck yes, fuck yes."

"Dirty girl," Carl rasped. "I love a girl with a filthy mouth."

I wrapped my arms around their shoulders, and I smiled my way through the butterflies in my belly.

"This dirty girl is ready for bed," I said. I looked at them, both of them, their eyes glinting hot under the party lights, and I knew what I wanted. "This dirty little girl is... ready."

As ready as I'd ever be.

Chapter
NINE

Katie

Ready. Yes. Ready.

And yet I felt so nervous. More than nervous. Scared.

Scared and excited. A strange combination. I guessed like a parachute jump, or swimming with sharks. Or taking that big fucking fence on a horse that was playing up. I always took the fence. I could take this, too. These *two*.

Carl slipped the key card in the door and held it open, and I stepped past him with a deep breath. The urge for crappy small talk bubbled up in me as the door clicked shut behind the guys, but there was nothing to say. *Nice evening. Phew, what a club. Who fancies a cuppa? Lovely cup of tea, always good before my pussy gets torn open, I find.* I'd be stalling, and for what? Two pairs of eyes were hungry, scoping me out in the quiet of the room, and it made me tingle from my tits to my toes.

They stood, shoulder to shoulder, waiting for my move, and they were gorgeous. Both of them were gorgeous.

I kicked my heels aside and my feet were grateful. My dress was easy to take down, it slipped smoothly from my shoulders, baring my breasts, and Rick smiled as I wriggled it down over my hips. Carl didn't smile, but he nodded, just a little. Just enough. My dress dropped to the floor and I stepped out from the fabric, making sure to keep my shoulders back and tits proud, portraying a confidence that wasn't entirely genuine.

"Nice," Rick said. "She's a picture, isn't she, Carl?"

And Carl surprised me. Took my breath away.

"Beautiful," he said. And he meant it. I could see it in his eyes.

He thought I was beautiful. Not just hot, or cute, or pretty. *Beautiful.* My tummy fluttered as I hooked my fingers inside my thong and slid it down, and I was wet already, the lace damp against my thighs.

Naked, and excited, and scared, and completely unsure of what to do next, so I made for the obvious choice, climbing up onto the bed and kneeling at the top, thighs spread wide enough that the air felt cool against my wet pussy.

It was the right move. Carl and Rick came closer, then gave each other a look. A smile. Rick pulled his t-shirt over his head and tossed it to the side, and Carl unbuttoned his shirt, slowly. I was spoiled, unsure where to look, flicking my eyes between the two as they dropped their jeans in unison. Rick's tattoos were divine, his abs tight and lean, and his cock, his cock was awesome. I was falling for Rick, and it was crazy, I got that feeling as I looked at him, that aching lurch of want. And there was Carl. Huge and ripped and so perfectly defined.

The guy was more than just a guy. He was imposing, and intimidating, and hot. Crazily, scarily hot. I dared to look at his cock, and my throat felt dry, but I smiled.

He'd fit. They'd fit. Surely. Definitely. Hopefully. I mean, you can push a whole fucking baby out of that hole, right?

Right?

But that hole felt like it had closed up tight, battened down the hatches and called a time out. My muscles were stiff, and tense, thrumming with nerves, and still my clit buzzed, wanting. I guess it didn't get the same memo as the rest of me.

I brushed my hair from my shoulders, gave a little shimmy, aiming for porn star but most likely falling well short, and then I beckoned them forward, invited them up.

And they came. Both of them. Climbing onto the bed and heading straight for me, two crazy hot guys with fire in their eyes, stalking me on all fours. I fought the urge to giggle, adrenaline making me giddy, but as they rose to their knees in front of me I didn't want to giggle at all. My tentative fingers reached out, coming to rest on two solid chests, and I stared at the path I made, brushing over two sets of abs. I'd landed lucky with these two. Really lucky.

Their cocks were both impressive side by side. Rick's Prince Albert was thick, a heavy ring that glinted in the lamplight. I took hold of his shaft, enjoying my first real look at him, and there were more. Two barbell piercings through the bottom of his shaft by his balls, and fuck they looked good. Carl's cock was darker, thicker, the veins so much more pronounced. My fingers looked so tiny as I took him in hand, gripping tight around his shaft, straining to enclose him, and falling well short.

I worked my hands in sync, up and down slowly, teasing two dicks like it was the most regular thing in the world, and I couldn't tear my eyes away. I didn't want to tear my eyes away. Rick groaned, and Carl rested a hand on my shoulder, and it encouraged me, gave me the confidence to work them harder, solid strokes, all the way up and down, and my fingers urged them to move, guided them closer until they shifted, hip to hip, shuffling until they were close enough that I could press their dicks against each other, shaft to shaft, and they grunted, and moved their hips, cocks rubbing, thrusting, and I held them, gripped them, stared so hard at the girth of those two swollen heads that my tummy tensed.

They were so fucking big.

Oh fuck.

Rick's fingers brushed my cheek. "That's good," he said. "That's so fucking good."

Carl's grip tightened on my shoulder, hips thrusting, and I could feel his eyes on me, burning me. Gently he pushed me backwards, and my heart pounded. "Lie down," he said. "On your back."

I tried to swallow but my throat was dry, and I couldn't take my eyes from those dicks, trying to imagine the both of them pushing inside. My clit thumped, but my nerves were wired. I looked up at them, looked between them, trying my best to smile confidently and pretend this was no big deal. But it was a big deal.

I pulled my hands away and they were jittery. I tried to hide them, but Carl took my wrist, held my hand up in his and watched as it trembled.

"You're shaking."

I closed my eyes and pictured us on the beach front, happy and laughing and having fun. I knew these guys, not completely, but enough. Enough to like them, enough to be honest.

"I'm so nervous," I said, and my voice was raspy.

I was expecting Rick to be the one to calm me, but Carl was first.

He raised my fingers to his lips and he kissed them. My tummy churned and it was a good churn. His eyes were fierce, but they were genuine.

"Relax," he said. "No pressure, no rushing. I promise you'll be just fine."

"More than fine," Rick added, and he was smiling. A dirty smile that brought out his dimples and set me on fire. "Trust me, we'll make this feel real fucking good."

I met their eyes, back and forth, and there was warmth there. It calmed me, enough that the shakes eased off. I took a breath.

"Do you want to do this, Katie?" Carl asked. "Forget the money, and the fact that we're naked with a dressing table full of dildos. Do you really want this?"

My answer was clear, even through the nerves.

"Yes," I said. "I want this. It's just last minute jitters." I smiled, took a breath. "I really want this. I promise."

I wanted this regardless of the money, *them* regardless of the money, and the thought was so crazy that I wasn't quite sure what to do with it. I lay back, pulling a pillow under my head and resting with my knees bent up, propped together.

"Good girl," Carl said. "Relax."

Hands on my knees, easing them apart, and I let them fall, let them spread.

"That's so fucking nice," Rick said. "Such a gorgeous fucking pussy." He joined me at my side, trailed his fingers up my stomach. It felt so good when his lips pressed to mine. I wrapped my arms around his neck and kissed him deep, and the bed dipped under Carl's weight as he lay to the other side of me. His fingers found my breast, circled then squeezed, tugging at my nipple enough to make me moan. He

122

scissored my leg with his, spread me wider, and I could feel his cock, a heavy thump as it landed on my hip.

Rick broke the kiss and angled my face to Carl, and I closed my eyes and waited, my lips parted and wanting. It made me moan when Carl pushed his tongue inside my mouth, made me squirm when he pushed in deeper, as though his was on a mission to possess mine.

"Fuck yeah," Rick whispered. "That's hot. That's so fucking hot." I felt him move, and then his breath on my breast. Carl's tongue was in my mouth and Rick's licked at my nipple and I made a little rasp.

Carl squeezed and Rick sucked and I liked it. My breath came out ragged, and they felt it, I know they did. Rick took hold of my thigh, spread me wider still, and his cock was against my skin.

I moaned into Carl's mouth. He squeezed my nipple hard, then he tugged, and his hand clamped my breast, squeezed and kneaded and made it feel so fucking good. My hips rose from the bed, desire drowning out the nerves.

Carl's lips broke from mine but he didn't pull away.

"That's better," he said. "That's a good girl, nice and relaxed."

If only he could feel the butterflies in my tummy. If only he knew how my body was tingling, my heart in my throat as my pussy clenched and loosened, my clit swollen and begging.

I could hear Rick's mouth, suckling, his lips slurping and smacking around my nipple. He nipped me and it made me start, but I was already asking for more.

"Yes," I whispered. "Oh God, yes." I held his head to my breast, gripped his hair as his beard tickled my skin.

I squirmed between two hot bodies, my legs hooked over theirs, pussy completely exposed, and I didn't care. I was way past caring.

"Suck my tits," I said. "Please suck my tits. Please..."

Carl's mouth took me aback. Carl's mouth was open wide when he clamped it to my tit. Carl's mouth sent me fucking crazy alongside Rick's.

Two men sucking my nipples, two men slurping and groaning while I held them tight to me.

Two men made it feel so amazing. Made *me* feel so amazing.

And then they slipped their fingers between my thighs.

I reached for their cocks and found them easily. Hard and throbbing and so fucking big.

A thumb at my clit and I didn't know whose it was. I didn't care.

Fingers slipped inside me, two at first, then three, only to pull away and be replaced by different fingers, different men, both inside me. They fingered me until I was wet enough that I could hear myself, and then they pulled their fingers apart, hooked inside me and latched tight. I felt myself opening, exposed. I didn't care. I fucking loved it.

Still they sucked, still I squirmed. Still I wanted.

Two men's fingers linked inside me, pressed together as they pumped in and out of me. Two men stretching again, pulling my pussy lips wide, loosening me as I bucked against them.

The thumb on my clit sped up, pressed harder, and I was losing it, feet scrabbling on the bedcovers.

Rick pulled away from my breast, pressed his mouth to my ear. "Come for us," he whispered.

A sudden hard pressure inside my pussy as they changed angle, and still those fingers were stretching me. The most beautiful ache. I felt like I was going to explode.

And then Rick was gone, shuffling down the bed until I felt his breath between my legs. His fingers moved faster, and so did Carl's, and it was rough, and so fucking wet. He licked at me, and his tongue found my clit. Metal and soft tongue, his rhythm just perfect.

"Oh God," I hissed. "Oh… oh…"

Carl moved from my nipple to my mouth, and he sucked my bottom lip as I groaned. He dipped his tongue inside my open mouth and licked at mine.

"You're perfect," he said, then his teeth pulled at my lip and my back arched in response. Oh how I wanted those beautiful cocks.

More fingers inside and I took them, held my breath at the pressure until it felt surreal, felt like my pussy was a gaping Jack-in-the-box, ready to explode.

I gripped Carl's dick and he grunted, and I wasn't scared anymore. All I could think about was having him inside me. Having both of them inside me.

"Oh… fuck… *fu… fu… fuckkkkk…*" Noises tumbled from my mouth as Rick's tongue lapped at my clit and brought me over the edge. I jerked and bucked my hips, and they ploughed me hard, fingers knuckle deep, a hot squelching mess as the orgasm ripped through me and lifted me shuddering from the bed.

Rick didn't stop licking me until I was done, and I could hear my breath in little gasps. I raised my head to look at him, and he was moving towards Carl, his lips puffy and wet from me. He kissed Carl's open mouth, and Carl groaned, his cock twitching in my hand, and then Carl licked at him, sucked at him, taking all the wetness of me from Rick's lips.

"Taste her," I heard Rick say. "Taste that perfect pussy."

Carl didn't need more prompting. He moved in a flash and his tongue squirmed where Rick's had been, strong hands pushing under my ass and lifting me from the bed. Strong hands holding my pussy to his face. It was sensitive, so fucking sensitive I squeezed my thighs shut, clamping Carl in position.

"Fuck me," I whispered and it was all for him. "Please, Carl. Fuck me hard."

He lifted my knees to my chest and held them there, positioning himself between my legs as Rick looked on.

"Fuck her," Rick groaned. "Fuck that sweet little pussy, Carl. Really fuck her." His cock was in his hand and he was jerking. "Pound that pussy, Carl, open her up."

Oh fuck, I wanted him to. I really wanted him to.

The head of him was so fucking thick. I felt it, heavy against my slit, working back and forth. Carl put his weight on me, pinning my knees to my chest, and he pushed, pushed his way inside. Oh shit. Oh fucking shit he was big.

I held my breath, and then I squeaked, He slammed home, all the way in until I felt him thump deep, and I felt so full, so fucking full.

"Shit," I said. "Oh my fucking God."

"Fuck her," Rick said, and his voice was ragged. "Fuck her hard. I wanna see you fuck her."

Carl poised all the way in, and my muscles clamped around him, over and over as I adjusted to the size of his dick. He leaned forward and propped his elbows at either side of my face, and his eyes were on mine.

"Look at me," he growled. "I want you to look at me as I fuck you."

I nodded and met his eyes as he pulled out and slammed back home. Tender and achy and fucking divine.

He slammed again and he grunted. I loved the way he sounded.

His hips picked up speed and force, bobbing me around on the bed underneath him as he fucked me hard and deep. I didn't take my eyes from him, my mouth open as I gasped and groaned and took it all.

"Fuck me," I hissed. "Yes! Yes!"

"You're tight," he said. "Really fucking tight. It feels fucking beautiful."

I hardly noticed Rick approach, nudging Carl's elbow aside enough to kneel at my head. His cock landed across my lips, and I moaned as I opened up enough to let him in.

"Good girl," he said as I sucked on the end of his cock.

One big dick in my pussy and another in my mouth, two pairs of eyes staring at me, two cocks hard for me. They were getting close, their thrusts more dramatic, the bed squeaking and creaking under the pressure.

"Gonna come," Rick growled. "Eat me up, baby, eat me fucking up."

I sucked him in, scraped his dick with my teeth and he hissed.

"Fuck," Carl grunted. "Now, fucking now."

He tipped me up, pressing my thighs flat against my tits, and my ass rose from the bed, Carl deep enough as he came that I whimpered around Rick's dick.

Rick's cum was thick and there was a lot of it. It filled the inside of my cheek and flowed to the back of my throat. I sucked him dry, took it all, and he stroked my face with clammy hands, telling me what a perfect girl I was. How lucky they'd found me.

Carl was still inside me, still unloading. I loved the thought of it, knowing that big thick dick was spilling his seed so deep.

I felt good, like I'd done well. I was proud, and it bloomed through me.

I wanted to make them prouder still.

Rick pulled from my mouth and Carl kissed me, digging deep for Rick's taste. He grunted his pleasure when he found it, and I felt him smile as Rick joined us, opening up the kiss to a three-way. I felt their breathing calm, and mine, too. I smiled as they pulled away, and I was happy, so happy.

"That was amazing," I gushed. "That was really fucking amazing."

Rick's eyes twinkled, and he looked proud, too. Triumphant.

"I'm so glad we found you," he said. "You're incredible."

Carl kissed my forehead. "Wasn't so bad, was it?"

I shook my head. "No. That wasn't so bad."

He pulled himself out slowly, and I felt raw without him. The two guys tracked down the bed and stared between my legs; hands touching me. I felt so exposed as they admired me, pulling my pussy this way and that and making positive affirmations.

"Nice," Rick said. "She's nice and ready."

"What do I look like?" I asked. "Am I... open?"

"Your pussy is divine," Carl said. He dipped his fingers in so I could feel it, and I felt so tender. Relaxed and loose, and wide. I tried not to think of the gape, of the view they were getting, but I really shouldn't have worried. They wanted more, angling me this way and that, teasing me wider.

"We can see inside you," Carl said. "It's fucking beautiful."

He reached for the bottle of lube from the dressing table and squeezed a load into his hand. It was cold against my clit. "We'll keep going," he said. "Don't want you closing up."

The thought brought a fresh rush of tingles.

Rick leaned over me, took a dildo from the row. It looked thick. Really thick.

I groaned as he tapped it against my pussy, and then he pushed it inside. "That's it," he said. "You're a fucking star, Katie. A real fucking star."

I put my arms behind my head and closed my eyes, concentrating on nothing but the sensation. It built slowly, one toy fucking me slow and deep, only to be replaced by another. More and more lube, more and more fingers on my clit. I hitched my breath as two toys ground their way into me, gave a little whimper, but it was a good pain, a good ache.

"Shit," I said. "That's intense."

"Two cocks," Rick said, and he was smirking. "Just not ours. Not yet."

Not yet.

It was tight, really tight.

"Push," Carl said. "Push against us, that's a good girl."

I pushed against the pressure and it ached and then it pained, just enough to make me squeal. I lifted my hips from the bed and circled and thrust, and they were pushing those toys right back at me. They fucked me, and I was sopping, pussy slippery with my wetness and an industrial quantity of lube.

I could feel how loose I was, loose but full, stretched and raw and horny as fuck.

"Push," Carl said again. "Take it. Take it all."

And I wanted it all, wanted it enough to make me grit my teeth and thrust back at them. "Fuck me," I hissed. "Both of you, I want both of you."

"You've got a beautiful pink gaping pussy," Rick said. "But we've still a way to go."

But I wanted it now, I wanted them now.

I propped myself up on my elbows, and the sight of those two gorgeous guys between my legs, eyes simmering and hungry and hot for me, was more than I could take. The fantasy boiled over, and Rick knew it. His eyes sparkled with knowing and he pressed his fingers to my clit.

"What a naughty little minx," he said. "You are really something special, Katie."

"I can take it," I said. "I want it. I fucking want it."

Carl's eyes were so green under the stark hotel room lighting. He was taking my measure and I knew it, staring me out as Rick strummed my clit, those two fat toys still wedged in my pussy.

"I want it," I repeated. "Fuck, I really want it."

Carl pulled the toys out with a slurpy plop and I let out a breath.

"You want it?" he asked. "I'm not sure you're ready."

I groaned as he pushed his fingers inside, and this time he didn't stop. He kept going until his hand was almost all the way in, and it burned a nice burn, ached a nice ache. Rick kept strumming, and my thighs were tense, straining.

Carl twisted his hand and it felt incredible, fucked up and messed up and so fucking surreal, but it was incredible.

"Do it," I said. "Please."

Rick looked at Carl, but Carl was looking at me.

"Please," I repeated. "I want you. Both of you. I want you now."

Another twist of his hand and I felt him sink deeper. He opened and closed his fingers inside me, just a little, and I felt all of it, every tiny movement.

"Ok, Katie," he said. "Come for Rick, come for him with my hand buried in your delightful little slit, and then we'll take you."

I sank back into the covers, loving the way the sensation built, and even though I was about to be fucked by two men, two *big* men, I wasn't nervous. The nerves were all gone.

I felt safe.

I felt wanted.

I felt like the most desirable woman on earth, lying there with my legs spread and my pussy filled to the hilt with cum and lube and the majority of Carl's big strong fist.

My breath was even but deep, eyes closed as I focused on the need to come. Rick was so good, so skilled. He knew the right spot, knew the right speed, knew exactly what it would take to send my tender clit over the edge again.

And I went over the edge again.

I went hard.

"Fuck," I hissed. "Oh fuck, oh fuck, oh fucking fuck."

And Carl pushed. He pushed until I felt a bit of a plop, and my pussy sucked him in, took his whole fist inside me.

"Yes," he said. "Good girl, Katie. Good girl."

I was borderline delirious, jerking and bucking and desperate to take them.

They didn't waste time. I was still coming down when Carl pulled his hand from my pussy. He took Rick's arm and nodded to the bed and Rick lay at my side. He reached for me and pulled me onto him as though I weighed nothing, and his cock was already waiting. I groaned as it slipped inside me, but there was no resistance this time. I was slurpy and wet and I slid up and down him like a watering mouth.

"Fuck, Katie," he rasped underneath me. "I love the way you feel.

I fucking love the way you feel."

He wrapped an arm around my waist and he held me to him, guided my head to rest on his shoulder as Carl appeared between my legs. He slapped the head of his dick against my clit. *Thump, thump, thump.*

"You've a beautiful cunt," he said. "A beautiful pussy for a beautiful girl. You're beautiful through and through, Katie. One day I'll show you how beautiful you look when you're spread wide open."

"Stretch me," I said, and my voice was low and thick. "Please stretch me big enough for two. I want two."

"This might hurt a little," he said. "Breathe."

It hurt a little. Quite a little. Hurt enough that I grimaced as Carl pressed his monster cock to Rick's and pushed his way into the same hole. My pussy didn't take him easy, not even after everything I'd taken already.

"Ow," I hissed.

Carl paused, stared at me, and his eyes were beautiful. "I can stop," he said. "We can take more time."

I shook my head. "No," I said. "I want you in me. Now!"

"Ok," he said. "Take it... take me..."

He pushed, and it hurt. He leveraged his weight on mine, and on Rick underneath me, and I was pinned. Pinned tight between two hot bodies, two grunting men. He pushed until he sank inside, and fuck how I stretched. I could feel them, two big dicks pressed tight, moving together as Rick began to thrust under me.

I could hear their balls slapping, feel the pressure of two cocks grinding.

It felt insane, insanely good.

"We're in," Carl said. "Both of us. Good girl, good fucking girl."

I grinned, delirious. "Yes... oh yes..."

He kissed me and I kissed him back, and I was no longer scared of Carl Brooks.

I was crazy for Carl Brooks' body. His cock. His brusqueness and his dry charm and his bossy manner.

I was crazy for Carl Brooks.

And I adored Rick. I adored the press of his lips to my cheek. I adored the way he held me tight as they fucked me, wrapped his arms around me and gripped me and kissed me and made me feel so special.

It was painful, and brutal, and the noises were disgustingly wet and squelchy, but it was beautiful.

It was oddly romantic. It was passionate. It was everything I'd ever dreamed.

Carl broke the kiss and pressed his forehead to Rick's and they smiled at each other. They kissed so tenderly that it took my breath, and I wrapped my arms around Carl's neck and pulled him close.

"Fill her up," Rick whispered, and there was a desperation in it. "Do it. Fill that pussy right up. All the fucking way, Carl."

Carl's breath quickened, and they lost their coordination, a free for all of thrusting dick inside me, and I bounced between them, taking it all with a grin on my face that wouldn't leave.

"Fill her, Carl. Do it. I'm coming, I'm coming, too."

They came hard. Deep.

They came so hard I flushed with pride.

Carl's eyes darkened as he caught his breath, and there was a steel about him. A hardness to his tone that cut through the haze.

They pulled out slowly and I yelped. Empty. I felt empty. And sore.

133

I felt the wetness dripping out of me.

"We're going to fill that horny little cunt full of cum," Carl whispered. "Going to unload all the way inside you, until you're full. All the time. All the fucking time. That's what I want, Katie. That's what I fucking want."

Words like that should never feel horny.

But they did.

They were the horniest fucking words I'd ever heard.

Chapter
TEN

CARL

This girl. This sparkling, lively, sweet, baby blue-eyed girl was something. She really was something.

Forgetting the fact that she was with us for money, forgetting the fact that she was practically half my age, a virtual stranger, and blatantly far more into Rick than she was into me, forgetting all of this, and then some, I could fall for a girl like Katie.

I couldn't sleep. Not even in the post-sex, post-alcohol bliss with two gorgeous naked bodies in the bed alongside me. I stared at the ceiling and wondered where this was going, where any of this was going.

And it worried me to think the answer was nowhere. Just like always.

A big fat fucking excuse for nowhere.

Rick always scowled and rolled his pretty eyes and told me to *chill. Chill, Carl, give it a fucking minute, man. Chill, Carl, not now, just not now. Chill, Carl, just see how things go. See how things go.*

See how things fucking go, Carl.

But I was tired of seeing how things fucking go. That's not who I am. I don't just coast. Not anymore.

I'm not a victim of fate. I'm not a victim of letting life pass me by without taking hold of it by the scruff and dragging it wherever the hell I want it to go.

Katie Serena Smith. Cute, small town girl with big dreams. Could I drag her wherever the hell I wanted to go?

She stirred beside me, stretching out her legs under the covers. She was hot, squirming, her arms reaching out of the warmth in pursuit of cooler air. I'd opened the drapes before I slipped in bed, happy to admire the dawn over the sea if sleep didn't find me, and it was coming. The first signs of morning light, blooming over the orange hue of the street lighting down below, and it illuminated the perfect little creature at my side beautifully. She squirmed again, and rolled in my direction, and her arm landed over mine. A flutter of her eyes and they opened, and she started, just a little.

I turned to face her and she put a dainty little hand under her cheek, stared at me.

Rick was out for the count behind her, star-fishing as usual with one leg out of the covers.

"Hey," she whispered.

"Hot?"

She nodded. "Three in a bed, quite some heat."

I smiled. "Yes. Quite."

I slipped out of bed and pulled on some boxers, then went to the balcony doors to let some cool air in, but Katie slipped out after me. Her wince as she got to her feet didn't escape me. As much of a travesty as it was to cover her nakedness, I handed her the shirt I'd discarded, and she pulled it on, buttoned it up just enough to hide her modesty, and then she went outside.

I slid the door closed behind us.

"Wow," she said. "This is amazing."

"Yes. It is." She was looking at the sea, but I was looking at her. The messy cascade of blonde down her back, her eyes in the morning light. "How are you feeling? Are you... sore?"

She smiled. "I feel like someone shoved a boot up my pussy and kicked my ovaries. Repeatedly. Clodhoppers, with steel toecaps."

"Sorry about that."

"I'm pretty sure I've got internal bleeding." But she was laughing. "If I slip into unconsciousness, please call me an ambulance. It will likely be my womb falling out of the gaping hole you guys left me with."

"Maybe we should give you danger money. For the risk." But I was laughing, too.

"I just hope my bits go back together again." She grinned and her eyes were sparkling. "I'm too young for a saggy pussy."

"Pelvic floor," I said. "You'll be fine, I promise."

"It was worth it. Probably."

"Only probably?"

She shrugged. "Depends how long it keeps me from riding. There's no way I'll be mounting up for the next few days."

"Sorry," I said. "Should have thought."

"I was joking. It's all good." She leaned over the railings to check out the street below, and my shirt hitched up her thighs, draping beautifully over the rounded curve of her ass. Another day. Definitely.

"Yes," I said. "It's all good, Katie."

She turned to me and her eyes met mine, and there were nerves there. Nerves and questions.

"Was I ok?" she said. "I mean," she brushed her hair from her face, "did I meet your… *criteria*?"

Direct. I liked that.

"Yes. You were ok." I stretched out my arms, enjoying the morning breeze, and her eyes roved my chest. Landed on the swell in my boxers. "You were more than ok. You were incredible."

It made her blush. "Thanks."

"You want to continue? With our arrangement?"

She nodded. "Yeah, I want to continue." She smirked. "Definitely. Really definitely." Her eyes twinkled.

"Rick's quite something," I remarked.

"Yeah, he is." Her smile was so easy. So honest. "He says the same about you."

"He flatters me."

"I'm not so sure." She laughed. "I don't think you're all that bad."

"Not all that bad?" I tipped my head. "Is that supposed to be praise?"

"Yeah." Her laugh was intoxicating. Light and unguarded and fresh. "That's praise."

I watched the waves break on the pebbles, the litter pickers on the front, the straggle of people making their way places down below. Quiet. The calm before the storm of a sunny tourist Sunday. An illusion of stillness amongst the chaos that Brighton offers.

And that's how I felt. Like this was an illusion. A moment of quiet connection with a storm on the horizon.

My heart picked up its beat, and there was the urge in me. The urge to lay it all out on the table. Negotiate. Hammer out the details.

If there would even be any details. We never usually made it that far.

Chill, Carl, just give it a fucking minute, man.

"What do you want out of life, Katie?"

She raised her eyebrows. "That's quite a question for stupid o'clock in the morning." She paused. Took deep breaths of sea air. "Everyone always wants to know where you're going. *What do you want to be when you grow up? What do you want to study at university? What car are you going to drive? What's your life plan? What salary band do you want to be in when you hit thirty? When are you going to get a mortgage?*"

"I wasn't looking for your twenty-year plan." I smirked. "Just a rough idea."

She stared at me and her eyes were piercing, weighing me up. "You'll think it's stupid."

"Your stable idea? Why would I?"

"You just would."

"Why don't you try me?"

She shrugged. "I used to think there was something wrong with me, that I had some kind of defect because I wasn't as ambitious as my friends in high school. The career planners would tut and shrug at me and say I was worth *so much more*. I didn't want a degree from Cambridge telling me how clever I was, or some megabucks career path that would land me with a Mercedes and a three-bed semi in suburbia by the time I was twenty-five."

"So, what *did* you want?"

"I wanted the things in my heart," she said. "Still do. Horses. Freedom. Life. Riding was everything to me when I was growing up. Still is."

"A stable will complete you?" I was trying not to sound

patronising. I didn't want to patronise her.

She shook her head. "Not the stable. The joy."

"The joy?"

She nodded. "It was the best part of my week when I was growing up, that one little hour of riding on a Saturday morning. Mum works in care, and has done since I was born. Crappy money, long hours. We did alright, but she couldn't really afford the luxuries. An hour on a Saturday was all I got, and I was grateful. I loved it." She shifted position and a grimace flashed across her face. "Yowch, ovaries. Anyway, I want to offer that same joy. Set myself up in a little yard, a couple of horses, offering decent lessons. Affordable lessons. Maybe a couple of loan arrangements for kids in exchange for them helping out about the yard." She shot me a look of fire. "I'm not stupid, I mean, this will make money. Enough to live. I'm not some hopeless dreamer. It needs to make money to be sustainable. But just, enough." She checked out my eyes and smiled. "Told you you'd think it was stupid."

And I did. Partially. I thought it was a waste of a sharp, vibrant gifted girl who clearly had some brains in her skull. I thought she could be aiming for higher, bigger. A huge stable filled to the brim with horses — eventers, and racers, and show ponies, and a whole riding programme dedicated to the disadvantaged, if that's what she wanted.

"Why so soon? Why not live a little first? Tread the corporate boards to get a bit of experience behind you. Travel. Make some sound investments to see you through any dips in the road? You said your mother works long hours for crappy money, is that what you want? What about life? What about all the experiences out there to be lived?"

"I *am* living," she said. "The yard is where I feel alive." She sighed. "It's owned by a guy called Jack. A nice guy. The best guy. He'll rent me the stables and the land, but he's up against it. His wife left him, and his maintenance business is failing and the bank is after the clothes from his back." She met my eyes. "It's my shot. My dream. I just need a bit of cash to put it together. That's why I'm here, with you. Partly."

"Only partly?"

"Only partly, yeah. The other part is for me. Just because... you know." There was a blush on her cheeks again. "A girl has needs."

"Sacrifice a few years to pursue a career and maybe you could *buy* Jack's land. Have a stable of your own, not one you rent from someone else. A couple of years away from the dream to set yourself up for life, for the long haul."

She laughed. "I'm a graduate, big whoopy. Just some regular business graduate from Worcester. Who's going to give me a few hundred grand for a couple of years' work? I'll come out with a scrappy bit of savings and a few years of wasted time. I'd rather have the time. The bottom rung of a ladder you want to climb is better than a couple of rungs on one you don't, don't you think?"

And it was on my tongue. It was on my fucking tongue.

Right there. Right fucking there.

I leaned into her, and I took her elbow, and she stared up and me and her eyes were wide and her lips were parted, nervous. As though I was going to kiss her, as though I was going to press my lips to hers and tear that shirt from her body and take her poor, battered pussy right here on this balcony.

But I wasn't. I wasn't going to do anything of the fucking kind.

"Katie..." I said, and then I stopped.

141

Not to *give it a fucking minute*, *man*, but because the balcony door slid open and out stepped Rick, stark bollock naked aside from his glasses, with his hair a tangled mess all on one side.

Only Rick looks so hot when he's that fucking dishevelled.

Katie smiled, and he smiled back, and I stepped away. Recoiled like I'd been bitten, but they didn't notice.

"Morning, campers," he said, and kissed Katie's pretty mouth. He slung an arm over her shoulders and pulled her a few paces in my direction so he could do the same to me. "Let's go get an early breakfast, I'm fucking famished."

I drove the way home, and Rick took the back seat this time. Katie was in more pain than I'd anticipated, and I felt a little guilty for it. She'd pulled herself up into the passenger seat with a grimace on her face but claimed she was dandy, just a little bruised. That would be true enough, but I still felt guilty all the same.

Conversation flowed like a dream on the way back up country, stupid stories, and old jokes and politics and the occasional silly YouTube video, but it was mainly flowing in their direction. Rick leaning forward in his seat to stare at Katie's phone screen, or tickling her neck through the gap in her headrest. They were in deep, into each other like some corny old romance flick. If old romance flicks covered the bonding experience of double penetration, that is.

I think they call it instalove.

I was amused. Not quite jealous.

Encouraged, but not enough to let the prospects turn me into a stupid optimist.

I was happy.

We were happy.

So happy that I pulled the car off the motorway at the wrong junction and headed for Woolhope. They didn't notice at first, too engrossed in a game of 'what would you rather?'

Would you rather eat a donkey's penis or take a cracked rib?

Would you rather fuck Angelina Jolie or Brad Pitt?

Would you rather have no sex for the rest of your life or ten hours sex every day for the rest of your life?

Would you rather die now, or never at all, not for the rest of time?

"Would you rather find another stupid game, or walk the rest of the way home?" I said, but I was joking.

"Spoil-fucking-sport! Out he comes, Mr Grumpy!" Rick laughed.

"Quick-fire round, your turn," Katie said, and her attention was all on me. "Would you rather... work the rest of your life or retire right now?"

"Work the rest of my life."

"Would you rather... have bogeys for saliva, or piss for saliva?"

I raised an eyebrow. "What the fuck kind of question is that?"

"Answer!" Rick said. "You HAVE to answer!"

I shrugged. "Piss? Jesus, I'll go with piss."

"Would you rather live in a zoo or an aquarium?"

"Zoo."

"Would you rather have twenty kids until you die or never see a kid again?"

"Twenty." I looked at her. "I'd rather have twenty kids than no kids."

She rested back in her seat. "Rather you than me. Kids would totally wreck the cool-as-fuck house you guys have got going on. I think you'd rethink if it happened."

"No," I said. "I wouldn't."

Rick leaned forward, stuck his chin on my shoulder. "Um, where the fuck are we?"

And Katie noticed. She sprang to life, staring out of the windows. "Woolhope," she said. "We're heading for Woolhope." She turned to me. "Why are we heading for Woolhope?"

Rick chimed in. "Yeah, Carl, why are we heading for Woolhope? You got a sudden urge to mount a horse?"

I shot him a look in the rearview mirror. "Katie's feeling a little worse for wear, I figure it's the least we can do." I glanced in her direction. "You want to see your horse, I presume? Muck him out or whatever you horsey folk need to do of a weekend."

She nodded. "Yeah, but I was... I was going to do it later... get Jack to help."

"And now there's no need, is there? We can help."

Rick seemed happy enough to go along with it. He patted her shoulder and she tipped her head, pinned his fingers against her cheek. "We can help. Good call, Carl."

"It's up here," she said. She pointed to a pub on the right. "Turn off here, over the common, then swing up to the left, you'll see it." I followed her directions and she became visibly animated, restless in her seat despite the boot-kicked cervix. "Here," she said. "It's up here."

I turned down a long bumpy driveway. *Weston's Maintenance Services.* It looked like an agricultural yard, a little worse for wear. Some rusty old machinery out the front of a farmhouse, a few chickens dashing about the place. She pointed to a space in front of an old rickety barn, and I parked up. She was out of the car before I'd even turned the engine off, and her expression was a wonder.

144

Rick jumped out after her and she took his hand, started pointing things out. She made him poke his head in the barn as I locked the Range, and then pointed down a concrete path, her eyes locked on me.

"He's down here," she said. "Do you want to meet him?"

I felt like I was meeting the parents. That's how serious she was.

I nodded. "Lead the way."

She ambled along in spite of the soreness and Rick flashed me the biggest smile over his shoulder. His smile said *I love you*. It also said *win*. Seems he wanted to meet the horse as much as she wanted to introduce him.

We trudged past a stable block and I can't say I was all that impressed. Rough around the edges was putting it kindly. It was the kind of dirty you get from age, mud and lack of funds, not from lack of care. The roof looked as though it was a bodge job, and some of the doors looked about to fall off. Then there was mud, a lot of mud, and there'd been rain here, enough that I feared for my shoes. She trooped on regardless of care for her pumps, and led us through a wood-chipped dressage ring that was missing a couple of sections of fencing, until she stopped, at a gate, and there were open fields beyond.

I scanned the pasture and there were a couple of horse-shaped dots in the distance. I was trying to guess which one was hers when she surprised me.

Sweet little Katie put her hands around her mouth and she bellowed.

"Samsonnnnnnnnnnn."

It was quite a volume.

She stepped up onto the bottom bar of the gate and did it again, and I was about to suggest we just walk on down the field and catch the beast as I presumed most horse owners needed to do when there was a rumble of hooves, thumping up the grass at some pace. I stepped away from the gate on instinct, and so did Rick, and the horse came into view, charging up the bank at reckless speed. Katie leaned over regardless, holding out her arms and calling his name, and I nearly grabbed her, nearly pulled her back and out of harm's way before the hairy brute ploughed into her, but he didn't. He pulled to an instant halt, and he was all snorts, and nudging. His big furry head was over the fence, butting her in a way that I can only assume was affectionate, and she was giggling, happy.

"This is Samson," she said, like an introduction was necessary. "This is my big baby boy."

He was a big fucking boy. A huge black beast with a white stripe down his face. She kissed his nose, and reached up to scratch his ears, and Rick scratched his ears, too.

"Come see him, Carl," she said. "He's friendly."

But the beast didn't like me. Not all that much. I stepped forward and I was tense, and wary of him, and he was wary of me. He eyeballed me, then flinched, taking a step back and snorting like a fucking dragon.

"Steady," she said to him. "Hey, boy, steady."

"He doesn't like me," I said.

"He will," she laughed. "He's just nervous of you. You must be... tense."

"Tense?"

"They pick up on body language," she said. "Energy, emotion, fear, anger. Whatever. They pick up on everything."

"You're too fucking stiff," Rick laughed. "You're not at the office

146

now, you know. You need to loosen up, chillax. Let it all hang out."

I beckoned to the horse, tried to keep my tone light, but he'd have none of it. He didn't care for me at all.

I felt strangely disappointed.

"Never mind," Katie said. "He'll get used to you." She realised what she'd said and her eyes widened. "If you come back, I mean."

"We'll be back," Rick said. "Won't we, Carl?"

Two sets of eyes on me, looking to me, looking for answers to a question I couldn't answer. Not really.

"Sure," I said. I started walking back the way we came. "Now let's get shovelling this fucking horseshit before I change my mind."

Chapter
ELEVEN

Katie

I should've gone home. I mean *technically* I'm only theirs for the weekend, and Sunday night was in the realms of overtime, surplus to the requirements of our arrangement. But I stayed.

I stayed because I wanted to, because they offered, because I liked them.

Both of them.

I stayed because I wanted to fall asleep between two hot bodies again. I stayed because, despite the fact I could still feel the ache of the pounding I'd taken the night before, I wanted them again.

I wanted them so much I was a sticky hot mess.

I sent a text to Mum, letting her know I was out for another night, and one to Jack, asking him to mind Samson until I showed up after my stupid meeting with the sperm donor, and then I settled down for the evening, kicking back between Carl and Rick on the sofa, listening to Rick's soul compilation and drinking posh tea. And then they'd stripped naked, and I had, too, and we'd jumped into their massive white bed with me snug in the middle, and their arms had held me tight.

But they hadn't fucked me.

And even though my battered cervix was relieved, I can't say I wasn't a little disappointed.

It appeared Carl and Rick were gentlemen. Gentlemen who'd been super keen to point out I wasn't *on duty*. That I could take it easy. That they weren't expecting anything.

So they'd kissed me and held me, without even a hint of anything more.

I'd have taken both. I'd have even tried to take it like a trooper and open my legs for another cervix bashing. But how can you say that? I mean, *should* I have said that? What's the etiquette on that kind of shit?

They were paying *me*. And part of me wished they weren't, that this was just me and them, just because.

But that was crazy fucking thinking. Crazy. And thoughts like those weren't going to get me my little riding yard or bail Jack out of trouble.

Thoughts like those could get stuffed.

I'm an early riser, but Carl beat me on Monday morning. He was already up when I opened my eyes to find myself sprawled happily on his empty side of the bed. The bathroom was still steamy when I took a pee and brushed my teeth, and I found him downstairs, listening to the early morning news on the radio while he spooned up muesli. I sat myself down at the island and gave him a smile.

Carl was scary hot again this morning. Intimidating. He wore a jet-black suit with angles that were killer. He was clean-shaven and bright-eyed and his jaw looked made of steel.

"Breakfast?" he said, and nudged the muesli box in my direction. "We have toast, eggs, bacon. Rick probably has one of those breakfast nut bars or some other trendy squirrel food in the cupboard." He pointed behind me. "Bowls and plates are in the top. Cutlery in the drawer underneath. You'll soon learn your way around."

"Busy day?" I asked, and it sounded so lame.

"Always." He stared at me for a long time and I couldn't read him. His business face was on, and it was impenetrable. Cold. Matter of fact. Then it softened into a smile. "New recruits," he said. "Always a pain in the ass, invariably worth it in the end. And meetings. I have meetings. Always so many fucking meetings."

I wanted to ask what he did. Where he went. What made a guy like Carl Brooks tick the way Carl Brooks clearly ticked about business. But I couldn't. I didn't know quite where to start with the chit-chat.

I'd checked him out on Business Connect — sales director for some swanky agency — but Business Connect just gives you the words, it doesn't give you the picture. Not really.

He finished up his muesli, swilled the bowl in the sink, and then he was gathering up his things, with just enough crossover to catch Rick as he ambled his way across the kitchen and propped himself on a stool alongside me. Rick didn't look like a morning person, not at all. He was still yawning, stretching in his seat. His hair was ruffled and his eyes were sleepy.

Rick was gorgeous when he was sleepy.

Carl leaned over to kiss Rick's hair, and then he kissed mine. He smelled fresh, and hot, and his lips were firm. He squeezed my shoulder and his fingers were forceful, and I wanted him. I really

150

wanted him.

"Play nice, kids," he said, and then he was gone, a briefcase in his hand and his phone already pressed to his ear.

"He's a hot sonofabitch," Rick laughed. "And thus begins another sixty hour working week, minimum. The guy doesn't stop. Ever. I swear he works in his sleep, too."

"What about you?" I said.

"Twenty-five max. It's all about the creativity." He grabbed an apple from the fruit bowl. "So, pretty girl, what's your plan for the day? Do I get to keep you?"

I wished. I liked the thought of being kept by Rick.

But urgh, no, *sperm donor*.

"I have to head out for one o'clock. Stupid piece of shit thing I can't get out of."

"Work?"

It didn't occur to me to lie. I shook my head. "Just, some shitty thing. A meeting."

He raised an eyebrow and didn't look away, waiting for more, and I thought about spilling the truth, but every time I did people never let me hear the end of it.

David Faverley's daughter?! You're David Faverley's daughter? The David Faverley? Of Favcom? Wow!

I heard he's worth a billion. Is he really worth a billion?

Like I gave two shits what he was worth.

Everyone within a fifteen county radius knew David Faverley, and sometimes I was dumb enough to let it slip that I shared some of his shitty DNA. But not today.

Today I was just a girl who'd give David Faverley the finger and tell him where to stick his shitty little blackmail endeavour.

Asshole.

Rick changed the radio station and grabbed his laptop and started it up in front of me. Emails pinged in, and I caught sight of some of them, product briefs and blind testing feedback, and pictures of his adverts on billboards. Rick was amazing, and from the emails I saw it seemed that everyone else thought so, too.

In that one tiny moment I wished I was someone with a career, someone who could impress Rick and Carl the way they impressed me. But that wasn't who I am.

Rick didn't seem to care anyway.

He looked at his watch. "Seven thirty a.m. So, I've got you for a few hours?"

I nodded.

He closed his laptop and his eyes were hooded and gorgeous. "I think it's about time I gave you a proper tour of the house."

And now I was late, the woman on my navigation software blurting about a load of crap that didn't make any sense to me. I'd been around the block twice, looped the entire Favcom complex, and still I couldn't find where the crap I was supposed to park. Bollocks.

I was about to text him and say he could stuff his stupid meeting when I spotted a sign for visitor parking. Gleaming four-wheel drives, and little convertibles, and pushbikes, with a garish company *cycle for life* poster on the side of the bike rack.

Mine was the only heap of crap car there.

I was wearing my worst jeans on purpose, the ones with holes in the knees. I was wearing my most faded shitty t-shirt, too, once bright pink with '*bite me, baby*' on the front. And I had my scuffed pumps on.

I hadn't been here for years, not since I was small enough that it scared the shit out of me. Reception was now chrome and marble, and the reception desk was a huge aquarium with brightly coloured tropical fish swimming about. Talk about overkill. The receptionist was wearing grey, with one of those stupid ruffly neck ties. She smiled across the counter, but she was all gritted and condescending, I could see it in her eyes.

"David Faverley," I said, and she raised an eyebrow.

"David Faverley?"

"Yes," I said. "I have a meeting with him." She flashed me a look designed to draw blood, but I didn't flinch, just smiled.

"And who should I say is here for him?"

"Katie," I said. "Katie Smith."

She pursed her lips and eyeballed me before she picked up the handset. "I have a *Katie Smith* here for Mr Faverley. Claims she has an appointment."

Claims. Cheeky cow.

And then her eyes turned wide and she was pale, unsettled. She put down the handset and it looked like she'd seen a ghost. Her tone was light and her smile was bright and far too big for her face.

"Your father will send someone down for you soon," she said. "Please take a seat."

I took a seat, and helped myself to a coffee from the swanky machine. I flicked through a load of boring industry magazines that practically sent me back to sleep, and was flicking through the stuck-up, jargon-speak job adverts in the back of one when someone cleared their throat in front of me.

Another little minion, another little grey suit, but this one's neck scarf was polka dot, trying to be trendy. In fairness, it nearly pulled it off, too.

Minion lady held out a hand, and I shook it.

"Caroline," she said. "I'm on the intern team. I'll take you to your interview."

My interview, what a joke. I checked the clock on the way through reception, wondering what time I'd make it back for Samson, my poor abandoned Samson. Wondering if I'd manage a ride, just a little trot around the school, maybe a slow walk up the lanes. I wondered if Jack had picked his hooves out, and given him his farrier supplement and mixed up his dinner just the way he likes it.

I wondered about Samson all the way upstairs, via the glass-fronted lift, along the corridor with a million thick oak doors leading off, right up until our destination, where Caroline rapped on a door that said *meeting room seven* in boring etched letters.

She opened the door and gestured me in, and it seemed Caroline on the intern team wasn't staying for my stupid *interview*.

There was only one figure in the room, and my stomach churned, fell over itself. I wanted to be cool, wanted to be off-handed and calm and not give a shit, but I was ten years old again, and completely not good enough, stressing out because my pumps had odd-coloured laces and he'd think I was an untidy, mismatched, good for nothing girl.

The sperm donor had aged in the six months since I'd seen him. His hair was considerably more grey and he seemed smaller somehow. He stood from his seat and beckoned to a chair opposite him, and for a moment I thought he was going to try and do something ridiculous like hug me, but he didn't.

He couldn't hide his disappointment as he realised what I was wearing. His eyes showed his disapproval, and it made me angry, it made me so fucking angry.

I sat in his stupid chair and folded my arms and then I let him have it.

"You can stick your stupid poxy interview," I said. "I'm not taking a stupid job. Not here, not ever."

"Please, Katie," he said. "Please just hear me out." He pretended to care, pretended to smile. "How have you been? It's been months…"

"Good," I snapped. "I'm really dandy, thanks very much."

"I was hoping you could have made it to your Aunt Georgina's birthday party."

"I was busy," I said. "Had shit to do. I'm sure *Aunt Georgina* coped just fine without me."

He rustled some papers but didn't stop looking at me. "Aunt Georgina wanted you there, she wanted all of her nieces and nephews there."

"I'm sure she managed just fine with Verity to keep her company."

He sighed. "That isn't the point."

I leaned forward. "So, what is the point? Why am I here? Why are you blackmailing me with Harrison Gables, knowing full well it's likely my only shot? That's a power-crazed douche move, you know? Even for you."

"If you say so."

"I say so."

"Please," he said. "I was hoping we could have a productive discussion. About your future."

"What about my future?" I sneered. "What business is it of yours?"

He sighed again and slid across a glossy brochure. *Favcom Internship programme, investing in your future.*

"I don't need your *investment*," I said. "I'm doing just fine on my own."

"Six months," he said. "That's all I'm asking. You'll be paid well, and treated fairly, and will come out of it with a lot more experience than you went in with."

"I don't need experience."

"Everyone needs experience, Katie. You can't spend the rest of your life looking after Samson."

I hated the way he said his name. He had no right to speak his name.

"So, you planned to blackmail me with Harrison Gables?"

"I planned on incentivising you with Harrison Gables."

"In-centi-what? Is that even a word?"

"Motivate," he said, "Think of it as a reward, in the spirit it is intended."

"A reward for what?"

"For completing the programme." He pressed his hands together. "Your brothers took this course and passed with flying colours. Sebastian is a senior technician in R&D now, and Dominic is a level four accountant in the finance team."

"Whoopty doo, you must be so proud."

"I am," he said. "Of all of you."

"Save it," I snapped. "I don't need your approval."

"You have it anyway. I'm your father. I want to see you do well."

"Yes, well maybe I don't want you to see me do anything! Maybe I just want you to clear off and forget I existed. Should be easy enough for you, *Dad*."

He waved me quiet, just like always, and I felt the tears prick. Stupid fucking tears. I should never have come here.

I stood to leave but he stood, too, and his hands were out, his expression sad and horrible.

"Please," he said. "Let's start again. Just give me five minutes."

I shrugged and I hated it. I hated to want the incentive he was offering. I hated this place, and its horrible stuffy corporate everything, and my stupid horrible stuffy corporate father. "Five minutes."

"Your mother thinks you should take this opportunity. It would make me very happy if you did. Your sister enrolled, just last week, and you could slot right in, I'm sure you'd pick it up."

"It's already started?"

He nodded. "I should have told you sooner, but your mother advised against it, she said it would give you longer to talk yourself out of it."

"As if I was likely to ever talk myself into it."

I pictured Verity, flouncing around in her posh little pinafore. Bitch. I bet she was loving it, I bet she was doing so well, so bloody well, so much better than anyone else.

"There's no small print, no extra conditions. You complete the internship programme and I will send both you and Verity for a month on the ranch with Harrison Gables. It's that simple."

If only it was that simple.

But it *was* simple. He'd picked too well, too fucking well. And even though I was proud and stubborn and full of bitterness, I was still that little girl watching Harrison Gables on YouTube and marvelling, and dreaming, and imagining a day when I could be like him.

"What do I have to do?" I said, and my voice was quiet. "What does this internship programme thing actually mean?"

"Sales training," he said. "The best of the best. Some field experience. Some product experience. A little stint in marketing. You can specialise for the final section. It can mean whatever you want it to mean." His eyes met mine and they held firm. "Please," he said. "Katie, I know things haven't been smooth for you, and I know you don't think the best of me, but please, just think about it."

I'd done sales around college, insurance telemarketing to earn money for Samson's livery. I'd been alright. More than alright. My bonuses had bought him a new saddle, a fine job from a proper saddler.

"And there's no underhanded tactics, no moving goalposts? Just six months of a stupid programme and I'm on that plane?"

He nodded. "That's exactly how it is. Unless you want to stay."

Never. Not in a million years.

"Salary?" I said. "What's the salary?"

"Twenty grand to start. Bonuses on top."

Twenty grand could see me right, with my other little earner on the side. Twenty grand was nearly three times my rate at the restaurant.

"Working hours?"

"Nine to five, Monday through Friday. It's all regular stuff, Katie."

The thought of being away from Samson pained me. It fucking hurt. And I knew then he had me. I was already considering it, already feeling it.

Asshole. Fucking asshole.

"And who is going to give me this *best of the best* training? Let me guess..." I sneered. "You?"

He laughed aloud. "Christ, no. Do you really think I'm that arrogant?"

I didn't answer.

"Please, Katie, give me some credit. It's a long time since I founded this business, and a long time since I was at the coalface of business development. Sales has changed, marketing has changed. The programme is cutting edge, led by the best of the best. The best of them all, I promise."

"Great," I mocked. "I can't wait to meet this *best of the best*. It's going to be so much fun."

"So, your answer is yes?"

I stared at him. "I don't know you've left me with much choice."

"There's always a choice," he said, and blue eyes met mine. Blue eyes like mine.

Harrison Gables, I'm doing this for Harrison Gables. And Samson. And Jack, too.

"When do I have to start your poxy programme?" I sighed. "When do I have to sign up?"

"I'll introduce you right now," he said, and my stomach lurched. Torn jeans suddenly seemed such a stupid idea. I wanted to bail, say I'd come back tomorrow, at least wear something that looked like less of a teenage middle finger to an arrogant sack of shit father, but I didn't have time. He was already on the phone, instructing someone in.

"Please," he said. "My daughter, yes. She's ready to meet the team, I thought you could... Thanks, right." My stupid father smiled like the cat who'd got the cream, grinning away until there was a rap at the door. He stood, smoothed down his tie, and I wished I was in any other clothes than these. I folded my arms across the stupid slogan on my chest, and looked at the table top. "Katie," he said as the door opened. "I'm very pleased to introduce you to the head of the Favcom internship programme. The best of the very best. Your mentor for the next six months."

I think it was the scent. Or the size of the shadow. Or maybe that prickly sixth sense that gives you goosebumps.

My eyes moved up slowly, and my heart was racing. Thumping.

My heart knew.

Bay leaf green eyes were staring, wide, a steel jaw gritted hard. Killer angles. Tailored suit.

Those bay leaf eyes stared right at me, and I stared right back.

And I could have died.

"Carl," my father said. "I'd like you to meet my daughter, Katie." My father smiled at me, oblivious, entirely oblivious. "Katie," he said. "I'd like you to meet Carl Brooks. The best of the very best."

Oh fuck.

Chapter
TWELVE

CARL

I'm always direct, even in the most *awkward* of circumstances. And these were awkward circumstances. Really fucking awkward.

"We're already acquainted," I said, and David's eyes grew wide in perfect unison with Katie's.

There it was. The familiarity I'd experienced. Not one I'd have ever pinpointed, not without seeing them side by side in the flesh, but it was the eyes. The brows. The cheekbones, too, maybe.

She jumped in before I had a chance to expand, and I watched in morbid fascination as she flustered and blustered her way through an explanation.

A shitty cop-out explanation.

"I, um, I know Rick," she told David. "He's a designer. We're friends. We know each other, met online, and I met Carl, through Rick, because Rick is, um, Rick is Carl's..."

Don't say fucking friend. I despise it when people get all fucking wimpy and avoid calling a spade a spade.

David gave a little gesture, shook his head. "Yes, yes, Katie, Carl's boyfriend. I know Rick well."

Katie was a far deeper shade of pink than I'd ever seen her, even when I'd complimented her on taking two dicks in her tight little pussy.

I looked her up and down, and my professionalism was offended by the girl before me. If I hadn't known better I'd have dismissed her as a waste of time, a sulky child, just like her sister. Her fucking *sister*. A self-entitled little ratbag who expects an easy ride.

Bite me, baby. Her t-shirt was faded and shrunken, and I could see at least an inch of her belly, the curve of her hips heading into the top of some thoroughly tattered denim.

She looked away from me, folded her arms, and I registered her embarrassment.

She'd a whole case full of clothes back home at ours, I'd lugged them back and forth to the car enough to know, and every single item I'd seen her in would have been better suited to the office than the mess she'd chosen to rock up here in.

David was smiling. "Well, what a small world." His eyes met mine. "You didn't mention you'd met my daughter, Carl. This is a surprise."

Wasn't it just.

He laughed a little. "Didn't you realise? Did you two not... talk? Surely you talked?"

David wanted answers, I could tell, but direct has its limits. I couldn't tell the guy she'd called him a blank space on her birth certificate. Couldn't tell him that she claimed she *had* no father, *knew* no father, that she wanted nothing to do with her fucking father.

And yet here she was.

162

Large as life in Daddy's office.

My office.

And lucky number twenty on my internship programme.

"I guess I didn't put two and two together," I said, and my eyes were burning hers.

"I'm surprised *you* didn't realise, Katie," he said. "I've been working with Carl for twenty years. This is extraordinary." He handed me a batch of application paperwork, blank. "Katie hasn't officially applied yet, Carl. She'll need talking through the procedure."

"You're starting late," I said to her. "You'll have some work to do. A lot of work to do."

She closed her eyes, embarrassment practically steaming from her. And then she shrugged. "Sure, whatever."

Her nonchalance made me bristle.

David's phone started buzzing on the table top. "No rest for the wicked," he said. He checked out the caller ID before sighing and indicating the door. He slapped my back on the way past.

"I'll leave her in your hands, Carl," he said. "Take good care of my little girl now."

He could count on that.

"Sit," I said, and Katie sat.

I took David's seat and stared at her, and she stared at me.

"This is fucking awkward," she said.

"No fucking shit," I said. I reclined in my seat and weighed her up, piecing together the situation. "So, you're the love child?"

"Something like that." Her expression was sour. "I'm the love child and you're the sugar daddy. Brilliant. Just brilliant."

"You said he was a blank space on your birth certificate."

Her eyes were like fire. "He *is* a blank space on my birth certificate! He's an idiot, a prick, I don't know how you can even stand to work with him."

I couldn't comprehend her venom. "David's the best man I know, Rick excluded. The best man I've ever known."

"Poor you, then," she snapped. "Your standards must be pretty low."

"No," I said. "They're not."

I pushed the application form in her direction, but she didn't take it. "I'm here because he's blackmailing me," she said. "Holding Harrison Gables to ransom unless I do six months on this intern thing." I looked at her blankly until she continued. "Harrison Gables is a horse whisperer, from the States. The best."

"I see." I pulled the application form back. "In that case this *intern thing* isn't for you. I've already got one joyrider on my programme, I don't need another."

She pursed her pretty lips. "Verity?"

"Yes, Verity." I slid the paperwork back in the file. "I'll tell your father your application was unsuccessful."

"You'll what?!"

"I'm serious," I said. "I turned down over fifty worthwhile candidates for this year's scheme. Fifty people who wanted it, fifty people who'd have worked hard for it, fifty people who were devastated when they didn't make it. We have room for twenty on this programme, and right now I have eighteen who want to be here and one who doesn't. I doubt Verity will last another week as it stands, and I'm not taking on another timewaster."

"You'll fire Verity?!" she laughed a bitter laugh. "That'll be quite a turn up for the books. Princess Verity usually has the whole world fawning at her pretty feet."

"Not here she doesn't," I said. "Not with me."

"She won't let you fire her," she scoffed. "Not with Harrison Gables at stake."

"She won't get a choice, believe me."

Blue eyes looked at me and softened. "I don't like telling people about my father. I wasn't trying to lie, or hide anything, I just don't..."

"Surely you did due diligence?" I said. "When you were scoping out our profile, Rick and I, surely you... checked? Surely you recognised where I worked? Surely you knew? You should have known, Katie, rather than rolling up at some stranger's house without the most basic idea of who they were."

"I *did* check you out. I checked both of you out. I knew you worked for some swanky agency in Cheltenham, some tech thing. I didn't know you worked with the sperm donor. His office is in Stroud, not Cheltenham. Your company name isn't even the same as his."

"It's a subsidiary," I said. "Surely you'd have recognised it?"

She shook her head, but I found it hard to believe. "I'm serious," she said. "I've spent most of my adult life trying to *forget* about David Faverley and his stupid life and his stupid businesses. The last thing I'd have been interested in is which stupid companies he owns and which he doesn't. I couldn't care less."

I leaned closer. "Why hate him so much? I don't understand."

"Because he's an asshole! Because he's a judgmental prick! Because he ruined my mum's life! Because every time he's ever looked at me I felt worthless, because of him, because I've never been good enough for an asshole like him. And I don't want to be," she said. "I don't want to be good enough for him, not ever, he can go fuck himself."

This wasn't the Katie I knew, not that I really knew Katie at all.

"You seem surprised," she said. "Like he's a fucking saint or something."

"Not a saint," I said. "But David is a great man. A fair man. And he's not judgmental, I've never found him to be judgmental once, not in twenty years." I held up my hands. "I'm perplexed. I know the story, and I know they're always tougher in real life, when you're the one living them, but this, this *hate*, I struggle to match the venom to the man. Genuinely."

"He judges alright," she sneered. "Believe me. You've just never seen it."

I sighed, and thought through my options, figured honesty was the best policy. It usually is.

"David Faverley can't be judgmental," I said. "It simply isn't in his character."

"So you think."

"So I *know*," I continued. "And I know that, because if it was in David Faverley's nature to be judgmental, if he viewed people through some bigoted, egocentric, self-righteous view of the world, he'd definitely, not in a million fucking years, never *ever* have employed a loser like me."

"A loser?" I laughed, because it seemed so ridiculous. "You're not a loser, Carl. You wouldn't even know how to be a loser. Look at you."

"Not anymore," he said. "Your father saw something in me when nobody else would cast me a second glance. He took a risk on a kid with nothing but a big old chip on his shoulder, and he was patient,

166

and kind, and he persisted and tried, and put the effort in until I became something more."

"I'm sure you're being overly harsh on yourself." I *was* sure, too. Very sure. But he shook his head.

"A stint in juvenile detention. Petty theft. Carjacking. Vandalism." He paused. "Fighting. Fights I knew I'd lose. Fights I fought anyway, just because I was on the edge and didn't know how else to express myself." He clasped his hands together on the table top. "I had nothing. A couple of ex foster parents who'd already got the next kid in line by the time I left. Some friends not worth shit."

I swallowed, throat dry. "What did you do?"

He looked right at me. "I grew up, a little, just enough to know I had to get out. So I set myself up with a couple of tools, a bucket, anything I could get my hands on. *Legitimately* get my hands on." He smiled at some distant memory. "I washed your dad's car. He was at a junction in Gloucester one day, in his sparkling BMW, and I approached his window and asked him if I could clean his bumpers while he was waiting. He said no at first, but I was persistent, told him there was mud down there, that it would dry on and be a bitch to take off later. Told him I'd do a good job at a fair price, and then asked him again."

"And he said yes?"

He smiled. "He said yes. He pulled his car in at the car park up the street and he waited while I cleaned it. He said to give him the whole works, no expense spared, but the car was clean apart from the bumpers, and I told him so, charged him less when he offered me the cash, because I hadn't earned it. He asked me where I was from and where I was going, and I shrugged and told him I didn't know where I was going but I was from a block of flats just round the corner."

"And what? He gave you a job?"

"He gave me an opportunity in life where everyone else put the boot in. He gave me his business card and asked me to go to his office. He said he could do with people around him who are honest, and hardworking, and hungry for a chance to do better." He looked at the ceiling. "That was me."

I didn't know what to say, so I didn't say anything.

"Whatever issues you've had with your father, Katie, I've never seen anything to indicate he's a prick. Not a single thing in twenty years, not in the way you've said he is."

"He fucked my mum when she was his secretary," I said. "Got her knocked up and fired her and ruined her life. And then he didn't want to know her, or me. Not until he rolled up when I was ten years old, wanting another little trophy to show off at corporate event day, most likely, a little blonde kid to tag along with his *proper* children. Now do you get it? He ruined my mum's whole life. Ruined her. Used her and spat her out when she got pregnant, and me along with her." I stared at Carl and his eyes were shocked, and stern, and full of something. Pity, maybe. "What?" I said. "What's that face for?"

He shrugged. "I'm just taken aback."

"Why? Why taken aback? I told you already, the guy's a prick."

"I'm taken aback, because that isn't the story I heard, not by a clear mile."

"Well, he wouldn't have wanted to tell you the *actual* truth, would he?" I said. "Of course he wouldn't!" He went to speak but changed his mind, I saw him waiver, saw him close his mouth and check himself and turn the other cheek.

He looked at his watch. "I think we should wrap this up," he said. "Before this goes any further."

I shrugged. "But I haven't even filled in my form yet. When am I supposed to start?"

"My position still stands," he said. "Your application is unsuccessful. You're free to leave."

I couldn't believe it. He was actually serious.

"No!" I said. "I need to do this, for Harrison Gables. I'll do it!"

He shook his head. "You're not in it for the right reasons."

"So?"

"So, it matters," he said. "It matters to me." And I laughed, I laughed so hard he scowled at me. "What? What's suddenly so funny?"

"You'll pay me for sex, but you won't let me work with you, because I'm working with you for the *wrong* reasons. Have you any idea how fucking ridiculous that sounds?"

"I don't care how ridiculous it sounds, that's the truth of it."

"You'll be my sugar daddy, but not my boss?"

He nodded. "If you want to see it that way. I prefer not to."

I couldn't help but pull a face. "How do *you* want to see it?"

"Not here," he said. "This isn't a conversation for the office. I have things to do."

He stood to leave and plastered a smile on his face, and this was over, my Harrison Gables dream was over.

"Wait," I said. "Just wait a minute."

But he didn't wait. "I have to go," he said. "I've got nineteen people depending on my guidance in Cheltenham."

"And what about me?"

He shrugged. "Find some other way to fulfil your dreams, something that your heart is in."

"But I..." I blustered. "I'd be good. I could work hard. I could do really well."

He raised an eyebrow. "*Bite me, baby.* That's how you choose to attend an interview?"

I shook my head. "I didn't come here for an interview, I came here to tell my stupid father to get stuffed."

"By dressing like a petulant teenager?"

I tipped my head against the back of the chair. "Something like that."

He checked his watch again. "I really should leave, Katie. I have somewhere to be."

I looked between him, and the door, and the file he'd left on the desk, and I went for it, darted like a snake to the application form he'd put away, and fumbled around the place looking for a pen.

"What are you doing?" he asked. "It's already been decided."

I kept looking, but there was nothing, not even a crappy pencil. What kind of useless as shit meeting room was this supposed to be? I sighed. "Give me a pen, please."

He stood quietly for a few seconds, staring. I held my hand out, waiting.

And then he reached in his inside pocket and pulled out a pen. "This doesn't change anything," he said. "This programme is for people who really want to be there."

"Just button it a minute," I said, and my fingers were scrawling.

"This isn't going to affect my decision, Katie. I'm sorry."

But he was wrong.

Wrong about my dad, and wrong about me, too.

I continued regardless, scribbling and scrawling through all the questions, and he didn't move, didn't leave, didn't say another word to distract me.

I finished and closed the pen lid, handed him the form with a flourish of triumph.

I watched his face as he read it, watched his eyes. Watched the way he looked at me, and then looked at me again, over and over.

"So?" I said. "What now?"

He pulled out his car keys, held them up. "I'm going to Cheltenham, like I said. I have people waiting." He opened the door, swung it wide. And then he held it there, open. "It's where the internship is based," he said. "You'd better come with me."

"I'll check," he said. "I'll check everything on that form. I always check."

"Be my guest. I'm not a liar."

"I'd certainly hope not." His eyes dug into me, made my knees feel weak as we made our way through reception. Everyone looked. Everyone.

The automatic doors swooshed open and we stepped outside. He pressed his key fob and I heard the bleep of the Range. I'd walked straight past it on the way in without noticing, in prime position to the left of the main entrance. I can't believe I hadn't fucking noticed that. Idiot.

"I've got my car," I said. "I can follow you."

He shook his head. "Get in. I'm driving."

I didn't argue.

I watched his face as he reversed from the space, grateful for the opportunity to check him out when he was otherwise occupied. Scary hot. Scarier hot now I'd seen him in his natural environment.

"They are impressive stats," he commented. "Quite impressive."

"I needed the money for Samson's livery. The bonuses were

good." I leaned against the window. "I give my all. Always. You haven't seen it so far, not apart from when I was... well..." I smiled. "That doesn't count, but even with that. I always give my all. It's who I am."

"If you don't, you'll be out on your ear. That goes for everyone on my programme."

"Understood."

"You lied to your father, said you knew me through Rick."

"It's not a lie. I *do* know you through Rick."

"Misled him, then. Implied we're just casual acquaintances."

I smirked at him. "Aren't we?"

"Is that what you think?" He pulled a pair of shades from his pocket and slipped them on against the glare, and I wished he hadn't. He was impenetrable in shades. Unreadable.

"What did you want me to say? *Yeah, we've met. Hey, Pops, I took Carl and Rick in my snatch this weekend. Both of them at the same time. It was a hoot.*"

"You could have made it clear we were friends."

"Friends. That's what we are?"

"Aren't we?" He looked at me but all I saw was my own reflection.

"I don't know what we are," I admitted.

"Like we said before, Katie. That depends on you."

"And like *I* said before. Why on me? Surely it's your gig?"

He pulled the Range onto the main road. "Us working together, that won't affect our arrangement, no?"

I shook my head. "I'm not planning on it. It's separate. I can deal with that."

"I hope so."

It seemed funny suddenly — *fate*. What a dickwad. The universe sure had a sense of humour. "I'll be fucking the boss," I laughed. "How totally *rad*."

"It's not going to win you any favours, I promise you."

"Wouldn't assume for a second it would." I watched Stroud pass by the window as we headed towards Cheltenham. "What a crazy six months it's lining up to be. Six months with you and Rick, six months in this programme. Then Harrison Gables. Then my little yard. Definitely my little yard."

"You're doing this purely for some horse whisperer? Not for the money, or the experience? Just for him."

I nodded. "Just for him."

He steered around a bend, and I watched his hands on the steering wheel. Big fingers, long. He had great hands. "What if the programme had been a year? Two years?"

"It's not," I answered. "Luckily."

"But if it had?"

"I'd have had to think about it."

He tipped his head. "You'd have done it, wouldn't you? Sacrificed a year, maybe two, for what you wanted? Something that could change your life forever?"

I let out a breath. "I guess. Probably. Yeah, probably. I mean, for one shot like that, one chance at something. Harrison Gables doesn't normally take students."

We sped towards Cheltenham, and I looked at my tatty jeans. I was tempted to ask Carl if we could go back to my car, grab a change of clothes from my case. Should have thought. Should've. Should've.

Wouldn't do me much good now to think of should've.

"What about the yard? What if a couple of years could set you up in a yard of your own?"

I laughed. "I already told you, nobody is going to give me that kind of cash. Not even with your snazzy six month training programme under my belt."

"Don't be so sure," he said, and he sounded serious. His tone made my mouth dry.

"If you say so."

"What if they did? Would you take it?"

The car felt hot, stuffy. "I'm not sure. Depends on what it was. I'd have to think about it."

"A year out, maybe two, away from your dream in exchange for a yard of your own. Would you do it?"

I smirked at him, clapped my hands. "This is like the *would you rather* game. I knew you enjoyed it really." I laughed again. "I knew you loved it."

"I'm serious," he said, and I felt it in my gut. In my jittery knees. A sign zipped past us. *Cheltenham 5 miles*. Part of me wanted this day to be over, part of me didn't.

"Serious about what?" I said, and I was still laughing. "Serious about some random company giving me an unbelievable sum of money for two years in some undisclosed job role? How am I supposed to be serious about that? How am I supposed to even answer that?" I picked at the threads on my torn jeans, heart thumping and I didn't even know why. "Yeah, I'd do it. If I could, I mean, probably. Who wouldn't?"

"You'd do it?"

I shrugged. "Jeez, Carl, I dunno. This is the cruddiest *would you rather* I've ever played. Yours don't even make sense."

And neither did he. Not when he veered the car from the road and into a pull in. It was quick, last minute, throwing me around in

174

my seat while I gripped the arm rail.

"Shit!" I said. "What was that?"

The engine was still running, the car still rumbling as the traffic passed us by.

"Two years," he said, "and the yard would be yours. Would you take it?"

"The yard is worth over two hundred grand, Carl." I shook my head in disbelief. "Who the hell would give me two hundred grand for a couple of years? And what for? What would they even want me for?"

He pulled off his shades and leaned in, and my heart pounded, and I clutched the side of my seat and I didn't even know why.

"There's something they would want..." he said. "But it wouldn't be a job, Katie, not a nine to five. Not another internship programme."

"What then?! A kidney?" I laughed a nervous laugh.

He shook his head, and smiled a little. "No, not a kidney. But it's not too dissimilar... not really..."

"And you know these people?" I laughed to ease the tension. "These weirdos who'd buy my *not a kidney* for two hundred grand?"

He leaned further, reached out a hand, rested it on my shaking knee and squeezed. It sparked, and I wanted it. Wanted him.

"What are you saying, Carl? I don't... I don't understand."

I wanted to understand, but more than that I wanted to feel. Wanted to feel him. There was a brooding in his eyes. A darkness. A desperation. It made me feel all fucked up, all goofy and wired and desperate myself.

"Katie..." he said, and I was back on the Brighton balcony, when I thought he would kiss me, right before Rick came out.

And I was scared again, nervous again, needy again. Just like I had been in that moment.

"What?" I said. "What is it? What do you want me to do?"

He took a breath, and he swallowed, and cleared his throat.

And then the fucking Bluetooth rang through the speakers.

Chapter
THIRTEEN

CARL

Loverboy calling.

It flashed up on the dash, the bleep bleep bleep blaring through every bastard speaker. It connected automatically, and Katie's eyes were still wide, waiting for the words on the tip of my tongue.

"Hey, hot ass, where are you? Are you in the car? I can hear myself. La la la, ooh ah, I can hear myself..."

"Yes, in the car," I said, but he wasn't really listening, he was still chirping on to himself, caught up in his own echo. I could picture him in his loose jeans, tracking about the house with a hand down his boxers. He usually called then. "I'll call you back..." I said, but he continued on regardless.

"She stayed until almost lunch. And it's love, man, it's fucking love. I'm in fucking love with that girl."

I watched Katie's cheeks flush, they pinked in front of my eyes, and her mouth hung open.

"...She's incredible. She's so fucking funny, Carl. And she's sweet, and cute. And fuck, the ass on her. Seriously, Carl, she's the fucking dog's bollocks. Next weekend it's a double team, I'm potting the fucking brown and don't try and stop me. You can fill her pussy, and I'll take my time on her sweet little asshole." He laughed to himself. "Don't try and tell me you don't feel the same about our pretty lady. I know you fucking feel the same. She's it. Our fucking keeper. I just fucking know it."

I kept my eyes on Katie's. "She's here," I said. "Katie's in the car with me."

Silence. Then he laughed. "Nice fucking try, dickhead. Nearly gave me a heart attack."

"I'm not joking," I said. "She's here."

He laughed again. "Why the fuck would she be in the car with you?"

"Because she had a meeting at my office today. Because her father is David Faverley. Because she's in my internship programme, we're on our way back to the Cheltenham office now."

It took him a few seconds, and Katie grimaced. Screwed her eyes closed and pinched her bottom lip.

"Katie?" he said. "Katie, are you really there? What the fuck?"

"Yeah," she said. "I'm really here."

"Fuck!" he said. "Is this for fucking real? You're David's daughter?!"

"Yeah," she replied, and she looked horrified. "I'm David Faverley's daughter. Biologically."

He blurted out a laugh before composing himself. "Shit. This is like something from daytime TV. I fucked my boss's daughter, and so did my boyfriend."

"Thanks for that," I said, and my hand was at the dash controls, all set to cut him off.

"Look, Katie, I'm sorry for that a minute ago. I was just gushing, you know? Getting carried away, excited."

"It's ok," she said, but she had her palms to her cheeks.

"And the ass thing, that's only if you want to... I'm not gonna... Jeez, crap. You know what I meant."

"I know what you meant," she said. "It's all good. It's cool. I'm cool."

"David's daughter. That's mad."

Of course it's fucking mad, idiot. I tossed Katie a look. "Look, Rick, we've got to get moving. Time's getting on."

"Yeah, sure. Cool. Where are you, anyway? You parked up?"

"We were, but we're leaving now."

"Right, cool," he said. "See you later. Love you guys. Both you guys." He laughed, and then he hung up. A crackle on the line and then a bleep. I turned it off.

I rested my head back against the headrest. "He wears his heart on his sleeve, that one."

"I kinda gathered," she said and there was humour in it.

Her eyes twinkled as she stared at me, and I saw David again. Saw David Faverley's daughter in front of me.

Take care of her, Carl. Take care of my little girl.

"What were you saying?" she said, and she was nervous, I could see the tremor in her hands, despite the smile.

Give it a fucking minute, man. Give it a fucking minute.

I'm in love with that girl, Carl. I'm in love with her.

David's face. Take care of my little girl, Carl.

I took another breath. Stayed quiet.

"You said you needed something. Do you need me to do

something? What is it?"

My boss's little girl. As if things weren't complicated enough already.

I looked at her as I put the car back into gear, flicked the indicator.

And then I selected the audio control on the dash, smirking as the Rocky theme started up.

"I need you to sing for me," I said.

She was perplexed for a moment, trying to figure out what voodoo I was spouting. Trying to figure me out, her pretty mouth opening and closing as she wrestled with words.

"It's part of the programme," I said, pulling out onto the road. "Everyone sings for me, no exceptions."

"You're joking, right?"

"No."

"The Rocky theme?"

"Yes."

"You want me to sing the Rocky theme? Now?"

"That's right."

"Why?"

At least she asked. Most don't. "Music changes state, music changes mood, it's an anchor you can use for performance. Singing lowers inhibitions, makes those walls come down, pushes you out of your comfort zone. And that's what's needed, Katie, in a training schedule like ours. You need to be flexible, adaptable, confident, and immediate. Not afraid to push through barriers."

I didn't rule out that she'd baulk and show off, like Verity. Fully expected her to hum a little, sing in a little mousey voice that I could barely hear, but as seemed to be the case more often than not, little blue-eyed Katie Serena surprised me.

She launched into song, loud and clear, and she wasn't half bad.

She laughed when I joined in, and together we drowned out the stereo, and she was air punching, giggling through the vocals, and I air punched, too. One hand off the steering wheel, as other drivers stared in at us. I didn't care.

She was breathless by the time we'd finished, relaxing into her seat with a smile on her face. Tension gone, at least for the time being.

"That was fun," she said. "I love Rocky."

"You do?"

"He's the underdog, right? Rises up against the odds. Eye of the tiger." She flicked her hair from her face. "Yeah, I love Rocky."

"Did you hear the story about how Stallone wrote the script himself? Insisted on playing the lead role and the movie company said no?"

She sat forward, angled her to face me. "Yeah, I heard about that. He was offered quarter of a million or something, but not the lead. He said no way and turned down all that money, and had to sell his dog, just to buy food."

I nodded, smiling. "And then it came good, and he sold the script and got the part."

"And went straight and bought his dog back, paid a fortune for it."

"Yes."

"Amazing story," she said.

"One of my favourites."

I felt her eyes on me. "Slick subject change."

"Thanks."

"Are you going to tell me what you really wanted?"

"Yes," I said. "One day. When it's time."

Part of me wanted her to push it, insist that I stop the car and tell her what the fuck was going on with me, what was so important that I'd throw a few hundred grand at her, what the hell I wanted so badly that I'd veer the car off the road and stare at her like a wolf after prey.

But she didn't. She let it go.

I pulled into the business park, and Katie sighed.

"I feel stupid," she said. "Dressed like this."

"Treat it as a lesson." I pulled into my space, and a wall of glass reflected our car back at us. Our car? Katie peered up at the building. Five storeys of corporate hustle. "This is us," I said. "At least for the next six months."

She slipped from the Range and met me at the doors. I felt the strangest urge to take her hand, grip her dainty fingers in mine and parade her through the place. Parade her as mine. I put my hand in my pocket instead.

A sea of greetings. Afternoon, Mr Brooks. Afternoon, Carl. Hey, Carl, how's it going?

She waited until we were in the lift heading up before she spoke. "So, you're like the head honcho around here?"

"You could say that."

"Neat."

"Most of the time. Sometimes it's stressful, busy, frustrating." I smiled. "Sometimes it's incredible. Often it sits around the middle."

"I don't believe you," she said. "You love it all the time. It's written all over you."

"Tell me that when I'm having a bad day."

She nodded, and her smile was beautiful. "I will. Don't worry."

And I wasn't worried. I was strangely invigorated in her presence, her gentle manner both soothing and enlivening. Katie Serena was a strange and delicate little creature. A real beauty.

She took a breath as the lift pulled to a stop.

"Nervous?"

She nodded. "Yeah. Very."

"Don't be," I said. "You'll be fine. No pressure, just relax."

"Last time you said that you broke my ovaries."

My balls tightened at the memory. I laughed. "Yes, I did."

The doors opened and the floor was busy, heaving with people on headsets, people in glass-fronted meeting rooms, people everywhere, going about their business. Going about my business.

She followed with quick steps, nipping into my side as I weaved a path through the clusters of desks, and everyone looked at us, staring with nosey eyes. I pointed out a segment in the corner, away from the main floor. My power team, my group of nineteen, engaged in a presentation by our top telemarketer, Daniel Dawson. I stood to the rear once we approached, and Katie stood close. I could feel the heat from her, the press of her shoulder against my arm.

"So, that's rapport 101, in a nutshell. Carl will be able to give you the rest. Perfect timing." He smiled at me.

The heads turned, and my protégés looked at me, and then looked at Katie. I could practically hear the cogs whirring.

I stepped to the front and patted the speaker on the back. "Thanks, Dan. Great job." I smiled at the faces. "Good afternoon, all, I trust that was useful?"

A murmur of agreement.

"Good." I gestured towards the blue-eyed girl in tattered jeans, all so aware of the blush of her cheeks. "This is Katie Smith," I said. "She'll be joining the programme. I hope you'll all make her very welcome."

She waved and smiled and they waved back and said a motley collection of greetings. All except one.

Verity.

Her face looked like a slapped ass. Her shoulders were rigid and her eyes were glowering, her mouth paused somewhere between outrage and surprise.

I wasted no time in settling the group back to their places, paired up in call buddy teams while they listened to the more experienced callers on the main floor. I put Katie with Ryan, our most promising contender, the guy who'd stepped up and belted out the Rocky track on day one, and she fell into partnership with him easily. I watched her relax, her expression bright and friendly.

She'd do just fine. I could feel it in my gut.

I was happily walking amongst the group when a set of pincer fingers pinched my arm.

"A word," Verity said. "Now, Carl." Before I run to my daddy like a pathetic little baby.

She glowered at Katie some more, shooting her looks that could kill, even though Katie remained oblivious, lost in concentration with her headset on.

"If you insist," I said. "Lead the way, Miss Faverley."

Katie

A firm grip landed on my shoulder, and I pretended to be

184

surprised, looking around as though he'd come from nowhere. Like my eyes hadn't followed him everywhere, chasing after the man who'd bruised my cervix while he walked the room, the man who'd put three grand in my bank account and his monster dick all the way inside me. *The man I wanted.*

He gave me shivers in this place, and they were good shivers. I've never had much of a boss thing going on, but maybe I'd never had the right boss. This one was already tickling my gut, that flood of butterflies that comes when you really want to fuck someone. Like you're on a rollercoaster, dipping over the edge.

"We're going," he said.

"Now?" I looked around me at all the people still listening intently to their headsets.

"Now."

I put my headset on the desk. "Where are we going?"

Carl didn't answer, just started walking, and I shrugged and smiled at Ryan, who'd been so kind to me, who'd made me feel welcome. "See you tomorrow."

He gave me the thumbs-up.

Carl didn't answer me in the lift on the way down, nor on the way out through reception. He waited until we were back in the Range and out of the car park.

"Well?" I said. "Where are we going?"

"Town," he said, simply.

"Town? Like Cheltenham town?"

"Yes. Via the house." I looked at him clueless, and he looked right back at me, looked at the holes in my jeans. "What clothes do you have for the office? How many suits?"

I pretended to think about it, wondering if the old navy jacket in my wardrobe would still fit. "I have some blouses... a skirt or two... the trousers I waitress in..."

"Then we're going to town. We'll pick Rick up on the way."

I couldn't help but giggle. "You want to take me shopping? Like something from *Pretty Woman*?" He didn't laugh. "What are you going to do? Send me into one of those snooty boutiques with a handful of used banknotes?" I practised my Julia Roberts impression. "*Big mistake. Big.*"

That made him smile, just a little. "You need to dress the part to feel the part, Katie."

I can't say it was a sentiment I'd ever really bought into.

We pulled up outside the house and Rick was waiting ready to jump into the back seat. "Hey, pretty lady." He ruffled my hair over the headrest. "Gonna get you all dolled up. Good job I'm coming as lead stylist."

"Keep telling yourself that, Rick," Carl said. "We want corporate, not *trendy*."

"Trendy corporate," Rick said. "We don't want her looking like some power bitch from the 90s. Urgh. No."

"*I* want her looking like she's a serious sales candidate. No fucking polka dot, Rick. No neon-coloured beads and vintage cut-offs. I fucking mean it."

"Ruin all the fun, why don't you?" But Rick's tone was light. It made me smile.

"I can shop for my own clothes," I said. "You don't need to do this."

"I know," Carl said, but he kept on driving.

The boutique made me more nervous than the office. Super pristine sales assistants in fancy little suits, and me, looking like I'd been dragged through a hedge backwards and then some. They had bright white smiles, but their eyes were cold, weighing me up and finding me lacking. I could feel it.

The guys seemed oblivious.

Carl took my hand in his and practically handed me over to a woman called Greta, and Greta led us through to the display rails, but spoke with Carl and not me, flashing him the doe eyes.

"You're looking for daytime corporate or client-facing corporate?"

"Both."

"Traditional or modern?"

"Whatever Katie likes."

"And what kind of budget do you have in mind, sir?"

Rick laughed, guffawed a few steps behind.

Carl handed her his card. "Whatever it takes."

I could've died, not least when I caught sight of a price tag on one of the jackets.

I leaned into him, pulled a face. "You don't need to do this."

His brows pitted. "I'm quite aware of that."

Greta started pulling things from the racks, but Carl wasn't watching. He was too busy staring at mannequins, rooting through rails on his own little quest. Rick leaned against a mirror, checking out flouncy accessories, and I just stood, like an idiot, my arms folded over the stupid slogan on my chest.

That smiley woman was staring at me, her eyes slightly squinty. "Thirty-four, twenty-six, thirty-six?"

"Thirty-six, twenty-six, thirty-eight."

"Thirty-eight, right." She walked around me. "Horse riding?"

I nodded. "Yeah."

"Always leads to a generous rump," she laughed. "It's good," she added. "Gives shape."

She didn't have a generous rump, and it was clear she didn't want one.

She beckoned me through to a changing room, and Carl and Rick tagged behind, Carl with an armful of clothes of his own choosing. He made me take them.

I pulled the curtain closed behind me and stripped down. My pale flesh was luminous under the changing room lights, and I felt vulnerable, naked. *Inferior.*

I could just imagine Verity shopping here on Daddy's gold card, laughing with the assistants like they were long lost buddies.

I started dressing with a sigh, expecting to hate every moment, expecting to see a stupid pasty fraud staring back at me from the mirror, a silly girl who didn't belong here.

But I didn't.

The clothes I tried on fitted perfectly, hugging me in all the right places. The blouse fastened perfectly over my tits without gaping, and nipped in at the waist to accentuate my curves. The pencil skirt rested just above my knees, hugging tight to my thighs without being slutty, and the jacket. The jacket was wonderful. A little height in the shoulders, but not too much. A smooth flare over my hips. Jet black with the tiniest satin trim around the lapels, and I was in love.

I stepped out from behind the curtain.

"Whoa," Rick said. "Hey, sexy lady."

But it was Carl who looked the most impressed. His eyes didn't stop moving, up and down, from my eyes to my toes and back again. "Yes," he said. "More of that. That's perfect." He stepped forward and ran his fingers down my sleeve. "You look perfect."

I look perfect.

I was prickling under my suit, my heart pounding, but I wasn't nervous anymore. My shoulders were high and my smile was genuine, and I knew I could do this, any of this.

"I'll try the rest," I said.

I tried not to think about the bags in the back, or the figure missing from Carl's bank account. It made me a little queasy.

"I'll pay you back," I said for the tenth time. "I have money, now."

"No," he said. "You won't."

I'll pay you in kind, then. The prospect made my pussy clench, and I was still aching there.

It thrilled me that I could still feel where they'd been, as though they'd marked me somehow. Made me theirs.

"Can you stay?" Rick said. "Go with Carl to work in the morning? Makes sense, doesn't it?"

I thought about my case full of clothes, slung in the passenger seat of my old rust bucket. Of my lack of toothbrush, and hair products. But mainly I thought of Samson.

Jack could take care of him, just for one more night. The weather was good enough for outdoors, and Samson would like that. He'd definitely like that. I could ask Jack the question, at least.

I sent off a text message and the reality of my situation came pouring in. Nine to five in Cheltenham. How would I fit in any riding? How would I fit in my waitressing evenings? How would I work my notice period with Benny?

"If you don't like the clothes, we can take them back, try another boutique tomorrow," Carl said, and I realised I was scowling.

"No," I said. "It's not that."

"What, then?"

"Just... logistics," I said. "I wasn't expecting a job when I walked into that office this afternoon. I have... commitments."

"Samson?"

"And work, and life, and things."

He shrugged. "We'll make it work, the stuff that matters."

We will? I hoped so.

I did what I had to do. I made the calls, I explained the opportunity, letting down the people who'd been so good to me, offered me work when I'd needed it, standing by me through university when my shifts had to fall all over the place to accommodate my studying. They were kind and encouraging and that only made me feel more guilty, more unsure.

I called my mum, too.

"I'm so glad you saw sense!" she said. "Show them what you're made of! I'm so proud of you, Katie. So proud."

I told her I was staying with friends. Maybe even a *special* friend, and she was pleased about that, too. I wish I could have told her how things really were, how I was holed up in heaven with a double whammy of gorgeousness, how they were sending me crazy, making me giddy, making me feel so *alive*.

But no. What kind of girl dumps a confession like that to their mother?

"Samson," I said, finally. "I'm just worried how all this will affect my time with my baby."

"Samson will still be there in six months," she said. "Samson will

190

be just fine, waiting. He's had all of you, Katie, for long enough. It's time."

I was missing him so much it hurt my tummy, desperate to mount up and canter through the woods until my soul soared, but by the same token I really didn't want to leave the guys. Especially not when Carl opened up a bottle of champagne and handed me a flute.

"To new opportunities," he said, and we toasted. "You've a fair amount of prep work to catch up on, but I can help. We can work through the technical slides over the evenings. Come Monday you'll be as geared to start live calling as the rest of them. An even playing field."

And then I hit him with it, the topic I'd let slide all day.

"What did Verity want with you?" I focused my eyes straight on his. "I saw you leave the room with her."

He shrugged. "Verity is always wanting something. She's a complainer."

"She doesn't want me there, does she?"

He took my shoulders and squeezed, stared down at me with smouldering eyes that turned my legs to jelly. "It doesn't matter what Verity wants, Katie. Not to me."

"That's refreshing. The whole world normally revolves around what Princess Verity wants."

"An even playing field, like I said." And there was meaning in the words he left unsaid, his tone heavy and lingering.

An even playing field. The same starting point, she and I. Both of us with our toes on the same line, competing on the same track, and this time there'd be no fancy outfits that would give Verity the upper hand, no special coaches in the wings to up her game and set her out of my league.

No special treatment. No biased scholarships. No wad of cash set to raise her to a higher platform.

Just us, like for like, waiting for the bell to ring. *Round one!*

My brain raced through the times I'd felt inferior and she'd revelled in it. The posh birthday parties, just for her, even though her birthday was just five days before mine, where I'd been the poor girl, the useless half-sister, the odd one out. How she'd laughed at me with her friends until I'd cried all night to Mum.

Look at my ponies, Katie. All of them, all mine. You *don't have a pony, do you?*

Look at my dolls, Katie. All of them, all mine. You *don't have dolls like mine, do you?*

Look at my daddy, Katie. He loves me, not you. Why are you even here, Katie? Nobody likes you here. Nobody wants you here.

Just go home to your own mum, Katie, where you belong.

I hate you, Katie. You're not my sister. You're nobody. Just an ugly girl without a proper daddy.

I'd struggled to pay for one horse, she'd had ten. I'd begged and bargained to get lifts to local eventing circuits with Samson, she'd had a tailor-made horse wagon with sleeping quarters. I'd taken two jobs to support me through a business degree from Worcester University, she'd waltzed through Oxford without the burden of tuition fees, taking International Business, French and Latin with extra time coaching.

I learned to sew to repair tired items in my wardrobe to extend their usefulness, she'd had a whole new wardrobe every season. Every fucking season.

But now, for the first time, we were matched. Even.

None of it mattered, not really. I'd learned to accept it and take pride in my own accomplishments a long time ago, but this... this, *promise* felt warm in my belly.

The promise of fair treatment. The prospect of taking on Verity without all the fanfare and the glamour and the hype that usually follows her around.

Maybe, just maybe, I could go up against Princess Verity Faverley on an even playing field and win.

I could win.

And maybe I wanted to. The feeling felt alien, cold and scaly but surprisingly compelling.

"What are you thinking?" Carl said, and he was still staring at me, his eyes eating me up.

I put my champagne on the side. "Let's start on those technical slides," I said.

I soaked it all in, everything he told me. Went over the slides again and again until they made sense. I wanted to please him, wanted to get it right.

Rick hung out with us, playing retro arcade games on his tablet while we crunched sales statistics. His hip was pressed to mine, the tickle of his beard against my shoulder as Carl and I talked work. He didn't hurry us, or try to interject, just kept himself amused in his own little bubble while we worked away right next to him.

I imagined he was used to it.

Carl split the remaining champagne between our three glasses. "Don't get too caught up in the technicalities," he said. "It's about forming relationships, not about selling technology. You just need enough of the framework to add value to the client."

I nodded. "Can't hurt, though, right? Knowing the details?"

He raised an eyebrow. "You'd be surprised. Sometimes a little knowledge does more harm than good."

"Score," Rick announced. He showed us his tablet, a new personal best on Frogger. "Piss and smoke calling, think I'll bail while I'm winning."

I watched his ass as he walked away, and Carl smirked at me.

"Our lovely Richard has a mighty fine derriere."

I smiled. "He does." And I imagined Carl fucking him. The thought sent tingles through my tits. This champagne was certainly loosening me up. I stretched out my legs as Carl closed down his laptop, watching his fingers dance over the keyboard. He shut the lid and pushed it aside.

"So," he said. "Was that worthwhile?"

"I hope so."

"Quite a turnaround, considering you planned to tell your father to get stuffed a few hours ago. I'm impressed."

"It's an opportunity," I said. "For something special, something I really want. Might as well make the best of it."

"My sentiments exactly."

He was still in his suit, still cutting a professional edge even though he was at ease on the sofa. I dared to reach out, ghost his cheek with my fingers. His eyes met mine and stayed there.

"Thanks," I said. "For everything today."

"You're welcome. Just get me some decent results next week."

"I'll do my best."

He draped an arm across my shoulders, curling his hand around to point at my tits. "*Bite me, baby.* I could have done without seeing such an invitation plastered across your tits all day."

194

"Don't," I groaned. "I don't know what I was thinking. I'm never wearing these clothes again."

"Not ever?" He feigned horror. "But I quite like them."

"Whatever, Carl."

He put a hand on my thigh, squeezed. "We'd better get ready to wrap up for the night," he said. "Early start."

He was pulling away when I stopped him, gripping his wrist before he could leave, and he paused, his eyes questioning. "Wait," I said. "Please."

I was a bag of nerves as I took hold of his tie and pulled his face to mine. He moved slowly, his breath on my lips for long seconds before they made contact.

"You don't have to…" he whispered. "You don't owe me anything, Katie…"

"I know," I said, and kissed him.

I may have made first contact, but Carl led from the front. He kissed me deep, his body angling towards mine, pinning me back against the sofa, his fingers at the hem of my stupid top.

He groaned against my lips, pulling away only to clear a path for my t-shirt as he yanked it up and over my head. He tossed it to the side and I took his hands in mine, put them on my tits. "Touch me. Please, Carl, touch me…"

He squeezed me, pushed his thumbs inside my bra to rub at my nipples, and it tingled, made them hard. I squirmed in my jeans, hitching a leg to stretch the denim tight against my pussy, and his hand went there.

"Horny girl," he growled. "Are you still sore? Does your pussy still remember how hard we fucked you?"

I nodded.

JADE WEST

He ground his palm against my mound, and the denim was so stiff against my clit.

"We'll take it in turns tonight," he said. "Over and over."

His knuckles rubbed the seam at my crotch and made me squirm, and he lowered his head to suck my tit into his mouth, taking as much as he could fit. I loved the noises, the slurp of his mouth and his soft grunts, the rub of his hand between my legs.

My eyes met Rick's as he appeared back in the doorway, and he smirked at me, his fingers at his shirt buttons. "Nice," he said. "I'm gonna leave you two alone more often if this is the shit I come back to."

He ditched his shirt at the side of the sofa and knelt up alongside me, his eyes on Carl's mouth as he slurped at my tit. Rick took my knee and tugged my legs wider apart, and he brushed Carl's hand away, pulling down my zipper and squirming his way inside my jeans. He found my clit and pressed hard, circling it in long slow motions.

He lowered his face to Carl's. "Share," he said, and he poked his tongue out, hunting after the same nipple.

Share. Fuck, how I wanted them to share.

Carl plopped my nipple from his mouth and guided it to Rick, and Rick sucked where he'd been, sucked hard. I groaned and pulled my bra down fully, arched my back, loved the sight of Rick sucking me, and Carl's open mouth as he latched onto my other nipple. I placed my hands to the backs of their heads and pulled them into me. Closed my eyes to it as they sucked hard. They bit. They nibbled. And I moaned like a bitch and held them there, pressed them into me until they pulled away, gasping for breath, mouths wet, eyes drooling.

I couldn't speak, breaths too heavy, nostrils flaring. My hands went to my tits, squeezed them, loving the wetness two hungry

196

mouths had left on my skin. "Oh God," was all I managed, my ass squirming of its own accord.

Between them they pulled down my jeans, yanking them down my thighs and pulling them off over my feet, and there was only the wet cotton of my knickers hiding my pussy from them.

Two sets of fingers rubbed at me, two thumbs aiming for my throbbing clit.

"Yes," I hissed. "Make me come... I need to come..."

I was still aching inside, a dull pain as my clit fluttered and my muscles clenched, but I wanted them. I wanted to be taken. I wanted to be fucked hard enough that I'd feel them all the way through tomorrow.

Carl dropped from the sofa, and the warmth of his mouth pressed wet and breathy to the inside of my thigh. He scraped his teeth and kissed his way up my skin, nudging my clit with his nose as he breathed in my scent, and fuck I pushed into him. He took the fabric of my knickers between his teeth and he sucked, tasting, and I pushed some more, writhing against him. Then he moved the fabric aside and his fingers spread me, his tongue hunting out the throbbing little nub of my clit, and I moaned for him, heard myself saying his name over and over as his fingers searched inside me.

Rick shifted at my side, pulled my hands from my tits, and his smile was so beautiful, just for a few seconds before he lowered his mouth to my nipple and sucked me in. Sucked my tit all the way into his mouth – at least that's what it felt like.

Carl's tongue darted and lapped at my clit as Rick's tongue bar flicked at my nipple. His fingers grabbed at my other tit, and pinched and rolled and squeezed and it was fucking heaven.

I took Carl's hair in one hand, Rick's in the other, held them in position.

"More," I said. "Suck... suck me..."

I bucked my hips against Carl's mouth, and his tongue squirmed and teased. His fingers scissored the tender flesh around my clit, gripping me for his tongue, and he worked me hard, his tongue quickening into tight little circles right where I needed them.

"Fuck, I really need to come now..." I moaned. "Please..."

Carl sucked. He sucked hard. He sucked on my clit until I arched my back and curled my toes. He sucked until I lost my mind and hissed out words that made no sense. He sucked until my grip on his hair loosened, and my breath was deep and fast and evening out.

And then Carl became consumed. He pushed Rick aside and took hold of my shoulders, forced me down onto my back and tugged my knickers off. My hands were reaching for him, hot for the sight of his naked body, the feel of his skin, but he seemed too urgent for that. He loosened his belt and pulled out his cock, thick and dark and heavy as he thumped it against my thigh. He pressed it to my fluttery mound, and Rick raised my head so I could stare at it, the way its length rose to my belly button when his balls pressed to my slit.

Carl ground against me. "Deep," he said. "I'm going to fuck you deep."

I nodded, and held my knees to my chest.

Rick laughed, and his voice was thick and horny.

"Open her up," he said. "Fuck her so deep you're in her fucking womb, Carl."

The thought made my clit hiss.

I wanted him in that fucking deep. I wanted him all the fucking way.

Rick moved behind me and lifted my head into his lap, and I

198

could feel the swell of him. He leaned forward and loosened Carl's tie, unbuttoning his shirt, and I watched Rick's hands run up Carl's chest, loving the hunger in his fingers.

I stared up at the two hot guys above me and I wanted to see them together.

"Kiss," I whispered. "I want to watch you."

Rick took Carl's face in his hands and flicked his tongue over Carl's lips. I saw the glint of his piercing before Carl sucked it into his mouth and they kissed hot and heavy and wet. It was delicious. It was beautiful. It set me on fucking fire.

Rick groaned against Carl's open mouth, and his fingers dropped to his own belt. He fumbled in his jeans and I felt his cock against my cheek, slapping gently as Rick worked himself. "Fuck her," he groaned in Carl's face, and it was only just audible. "Fill that gorgeous little cunt, fill her up."

And Carl did. His cock pushed inside, and he was a battering ram of hard fucking meat, stretching me as I squirmed. It stung a little as my tender pussy took him in, enough to hitch my breath, and then it ached. Oh it fucking ached. But I wanted it, needed it, craved it. "Fuck me," I said.

I cried out as he pushed deep, but I didn't move. My knees were still tight to my chest, my pussy unguarded and willing... and his. My pussy was *his*.

The boys kept kissing, and Rick was working his dick, and Carl was so fucking deep inside me. Rick guided the head of his dick to my lips and I opened wide. He pushed himself inside my cheek, stretching my lips as I tried my best to suck him, his Prince Albert clipping my teeth as he went.. He took my knees and yanked them towards him, and my weight shifted onto my shoulders, my ass hitching up and into the air.

Carl shifted, too, and he was deeper in this position, I felt him thump against something tender inside me, as far as he could go. And the feeling was surreal. Beautifully surreal.

"Let's fill her," Rick hissed. "Fill that pretty little cunt full of us."

Carl nodded. He nodded and kissed Rick's lips, full and hard, then he smiled and pinched Rick's cheeks, sucked on his bottom lip.

And then his attention was on me. He dropped on top of me, his weight bearing down, and his eyes were fierce, hungry for mine as I sucked and slavered and licked at Rick's shaft.

Carl fucked me, and stretched me, and it ached all the way inside.

"Take her," Rick said. "She wants it. She fucking wants it all."

I did want it all. Whatever that even meant.

Carl slammed me, his hips thrusting hard, his skin slapping against mine, each thrust sending waves of horny pleasure through me. It felt like he was right inside my fucking belly, and I loved it, couldn't get enough of it.

"Yes," I groaned but it came out so muffled against Rick's cock. "More. Fuck me."

Carl growled in my ear. "I'm so fucking deep. I'm all the way inside your hungry little cunt." I nodded as Rick slapped his dick across my open lips, and Carl thrust hard. I felt his cock reach a dead end, and it ached, oh fuck it ached so fucking beautifully. "This is what I need," he groaned. "*This*." His voice was ragged, strained with his thrusting. "Need to fill your cunt, need to come inside."

My belly lurched and tickled, and I nodded, let out a gasp.

The ache was building, my pussy clenching and tightening and driving me insane.

"Fuck me hard," I moaned. "I want you to come, I want to feel you come…"

"Good girl," Carl growled.

And I was away, delirious, rambling. "I want your cum inside me at work tomorrow, I want to feel you, I want to know you've been there…"

"Fuck," Rick said, and his hand was slapping away at his dick, his balls bouncing against my cheek.

"…I want to be full of you, both of you… I want to be dripping… I want to be all filled up…"

I didn't know what I was saying, didn't know why I wanted it so fucking badly. Didn't know why I wanted Carl's cum dripping from my pussy all the way through tomorrow.

And Rick's, I wanted Rick's, too.

But it was Carl that was grunting and heaving and slamming into my cervix. It was Carl who was on the edge, fucking me hard and fast while I whimpered and squirmed.

It was Carl who rammed all the way inside and groaned as he came, his eyes closed and his abs tense and tight, his whole body tight as his thick cock spasmed inside me.

"Yes…" Rick said, and his hand was working fast. "My turn next, my turn…"

Carl pulled out slowly, but held me in position, shifting to the side to let Rick take his place.

Rick slammed inside in one thrust, and he fucked fast, his hips a fucking piston, his thumb on my clit, and all I could do was shudder and gasp beneath him as he pumped me.

He was already half gone, his eyes glazed and needy. Carl put a hand around his throat, and Rick liked that. I liked it too. The horn just grew horns. Carl squeezed Rick's throat. *Fuck.*

"Gonna come," Rick's voice was raspy and strained. "Oh, Jesus..."

His thumb sent me over the edge as he lost control, and I cried out loud as he unloaded inside me. A shuddery climax ripped through my body, made me throw my head back against the leather, gripping at the armrest and thrusting back at him until he was spent.

Until *we* were spent.

I smiled as I caught my breath. "That was fucking amazing... my fucking God."

Rick pulled out and gave my clit a final flick, and he was grinning. "Our pleasure."

He kissed Carl on the lips, and leaned in to kiss me next, and I pulled him close, wrapped my arms around his shoulders. I squeezed him and breathed him in, and held him until he dropped to my side on the sofa.

And then I was reaching for Carl, too. I wanted to hold them both.

But Carl didn't want to be held.

A thump against my clit made me moan, tender. He was hard again, and his eyes were fierce again, desperate again.

Oh shit. My poor aching pussy.

"Round fucking two," he said.

Chapter
FOURTEEN

Katie

A spring in my step and that *fucked last night* ache between my legs and I was all ready to hit round one of Katie versus Princess Verity. I'd selected one of my new blouses with care, the lightest teal blue, cute but subtle, professional without being too brash. My hair was up in a messy bun, to show off the tailored lines of my new swanky suit jacket. My pencil skirt hugged my ass, and my heels made a satisfying clack as I walked. Yeah, I felt good. I felt ready for this.

I had a lovely little flutter in my belly as we arrived at the office. It was gooey and warm and far too squishy, and although I knew it was a potentially dumbass move to get all gushy over a guy who was A. my boss and B. paying me to fuck both him and his boyfriend, I couldn't help myself.

I liked pulling up to the office in Carl's Range. I liked walking through the office at his side. I liked borrowing his toothbrush in the morning, and sleeping in his bed at night. I liked taking his cock, once, twice, three times over, only to take him again the next morning.

I liked the fact that the part of him he'd spilled inside me was still dribbling its way back out again. I especially liked how dirty that made me feel.

And I liked his boyfriend. I *loved* his boyfriend.

Carl dropped me at the desk next to Ryan, who I'd been working with the day before, and that felt good, too.

Ryan seemed a genuine guy with his head screwed on. Everyone else was jabbering on about their evening, or where they were headed for lunch, or who was likely to get voted out of the latest piece of reality TV show crud, but Ryan was having none of it. I recognised the presentation slides he was staring at, the same ones Carl had talked me through the evening before, and pulled up a chair.

"Early morning cramming," he said. "Want to get a head start."

"Ditto," I said, and he smiled and angled his screen in my direction.

"We can be study buddies," he offered.

I nodded. "Sounds good to me."

And so it began.

I listened to the morning training sessions so intently that my brain fizzed. I made notes until my fingers cramped and my writing became all but illegible. I asked question after question that made Carl smile and Verity scowl, and I committed the answers to memory. I thrilled as Carl marked up the whiteboard with our names all ready for the sales results table to kick off the following Monday, and for every look of disdain Verity shot in my direction my resolve grew a little more steely.

I could do this. I could come out top and show that snotty little cow I was far more than the loser sister she'd chalked me up as.

I expected Carl to distance himself from me at work, to draw the *boss* line and pretend I was just another minion on his training programme, but it seemed Carl doesn't work that way. He tapped my arm as we were breaking for lunch and he had his car keys in his hand.

"I'm heading out for coffee and a bagel. Want to come?"

Of course I did.

We ate at a little cafe at the far end of the business park and he watched me so intently that I could only take tiny mouthfuls of sandwich.

"So," he said. "What's with you, Katie? You seem different."

I shrugged. "If something's worth doing, it's worth doing well, right?"

He took a hearty bite of his bagel. I watched as he chewed and swallowed. "I looked into the stats you put on your application form."

"And?"

"They were impressive, if not entirely believable." He paused. "And they checked out."

"Of course they did. I'm no liar."

His eyes looked so green under the fluorescent lighting. "I spoke to your old boss, from the insurance agency."

"You spoke with Colin Wilkins? What did he say?"

"He said you were dedicated, talented, hardworking. He said you had one of the best track records across your region. He said you were a faultless new business developer, and he'd offered you a spot on their management training scheme but you turned him down."

I felt myself burning up. "I did pretty well there. It was only part time."

"He told me I'd be an idiot not to cultivate your talent and push you into management."

I laughed a little. "Management? I just did a bit of telemarketing, no big deal."

He leaned in and I felt the charge from him, felt the tingle. "I don't think you're the simple little horsey girl you play at being. I don't think that's you. I think you want more than that, even if you don't know it."

I pushed my plate aside. "I don't play at being anything. I just want different things than you. Just because someone *can* do something doesn't mean they *want* to do it. I'm really not such a dark horse, Carl."

He smirked. "And yet here we are, suited and booted, grabbing a bagel before heading back to the office." His voice lowered. "I watched you all morning, and you want this. I saw it in you. You've got the calling for it, even if you refuse to acknowledge the fact."

I shook my head. "No," I said. "I've got the calling to win my little trip to see Harrison Gables and earn some decent cash towards my yard."

"It's more than that."

I met his eyes. "It's not."

"Fine," he said. "I'll transfer you for the six months, I could do with someone to help manage my diary. You can check out of the training programme and work alongside me." My face must have dropped before I could stop it, the prospect of a Katie-Verity sales smackdown slipping through my fingers. "And there we have it." He smirked. "*Busted,* as Rick would say. So, tell me. Why do you want this all of a sudden?"

I hesitated. "Maybe it's a calling, like you said."

He shook his head, and I felt like he was boring his way into me. Only into my brain this time, not my pussy. "No," he said. "It's something else. Is it about your father?"

I nearly spat my coffee. "About the sperm donor?! *No*. I couldn't give two shits about him."

"Then it's about Verity?"

I raised an eyebrow. "Why does it have to be about anyone? Maybe I just like a hard day's work?"

"I've been around the block a few too many times to buy into that, Katie. I know when someone's out to prove something, there's a steel to it, an edge. You've had that edge since we sat down to look at slides last night."

"Why does it matter?"

He shrugged. "I like to know what I'm working with. It helps me get the best out of you."

"I'll get the best out of myself," I said. "You don't need to worry."

"I'm not worried." He was quiet as he finished up his bagel. Big purposeful bites without any self-consciousness. I couldn't take my eyes from him. He dabbed his lips with a napkin, left a single crumb behind. I wanted to pull him close and lick that crumb right off. "Just use that motivation in the right way," he continued. "Competition can be healthy, it can also be destructive."

"Sure thing, *Daddy*." I laughed at his frown, and it was quite a frown. "Jeez, Carl. I'm joking, just playing around."

His frown relaxed. He raised an eyebrow at me, and couldn't help smiling. "Let's get back," he said.

I followed him out, watching his firm ass all the way back to the car. He slung an arm behind my seat as he reversed out of the space. "I told him," he said. "Your father, I mean. I told him what Colin Wilkins said about you. I gave him a copy of your performance stats, as well."

The thought gave me shivers. "And what did he say?"

"He said *that's his girl*."

I folded my arms. "I'm not *his* girl."

"I told him as much. I said he can relinquish whatever ideas he has for a hold on you, because there's a new *daddy* in town."

I gasped at that. "You didn't."

He laughed. "No, I didn't." He met my eyes as he turned back onto our section of the estate. "But I would, if it called for it. I don't believe in pussy-footing around for the sake of the status quo, Katie."

The thought thrilled and petrified me in equal measure. "That would be crazy," I said.

"Maybe."

"Definitely." I unclipped my seatbelt as he pulled into his space. "And I'd lose all respect from the team. Nobody likes someone they think waltzes around getting special treatment, Carl, especially not one they think is in bed with the boss."

"And there we go," he said. "You're all in, even if you don't want to be. You already care what they think of you." He grabbed my wrist as I made to open my door, and I flashed back to the weight of him over me, pinning my wrists as he pushed his way inside my sore pussy while the birds chorused the dawn outside. "Will we see you tonight?"

My mind turned blank. "I don't know... I, um... Samson..." I took a breath. "I need to see Samson." *And my pussy needs a break.*

He nodded, let go of my wrist, and I immediately regretted my answer. "Of course, yes. Sorry."

But I wasn't sorry he'd asked. Wasn't sorry at all.

I tried to say it, but he'd already opened his door.

I left Carl's side on the way back through the office, and headed to the toilets to freshen up. My skin felt clammy and flushed, and my pussy felt battered and hot. *And needy. Again.* I washed my hands in cold water and splashed some over my face, opening my eyes in time to watch that bitch Verity walk in.

She didn't pick a cubicle, just stared at me in the mirror.

"What?" I said, finally. "What do you want?"

She shrugged. "I was wondering the same thing about you."

"I'm here for the same reason you are," I said. "Harrison Gables. Not that it's any of your business."

"It's *all* of my business," she said. "*I'll* be the one inheriting it."

"Whoopty doo. Like I care." I didn't care, either. Not one shit for the pile of stuff she'd inherit from that fucking idiot. She was welcome to it.

"Dad only wants you here because he thinks it's the *right* thing to do. You're just his little charity case. His embarrassing little secret."

"Sure, whatever," I said, pretending it didn't sting. Not even a little.

"Don't think you can show up here and make me look bad. I won't let you make me look like an idiot, Katie, no matter how hard you try."

"I don't need to make you look like an idiot," I said. "I'm just here for Harrison. How you choose to make yourself look is completely up to you."

"I heard you did well at some shitty job once. Don't think that will make you better than me. A shitty job around shitty college won't make you better than me."

"I didn't say it would." I glared at her reflection.

"No, but you *think* it."

I laughed. "You're paranoid. You've always been paranoid." But she wasn't paranoid, not this time. That steely hard little part of me did want to think it would make me better than her, just this once. I was counting on it.

She tutted. "You'd be paranoid, too, if some little bitch was always after what was yours."

I turned to face her and I could feel my cheeks burning up. "Since when have I *ever* been after what's yours? I've never given two fucks about what's yours."

And she hissed, she actually hissed at me. She jabbed a pretty little manicured fingernail in my direction and her face was contorted by rage and jealousy and maybe a little bit of fear, too. "I won't let you take what's mine. Not my friends, not my company, not my fucking dad. You can just fuck off back where you came from, you should never have come here!"

It took me aback, and for a moment I was a little girl again, unsure of my own footing. "I didn't *want* to come here. I didn't *want* to know any of you. I wish I'd never even known I had a fucking dad, alright? I wish you people didn't exist to me."

"Feeling's mutual," she said.

I turned back to the sink, washing hands that were already clean and splashing more water over my face so she wouldn't see the angry tears pricking.

"You can take your greedy eyes off Carl, as well," she said. "He isn't going to fall for your shit, either."

"Sorry?" I snapped.

"*Carl,*" she repeated, as though I was a dullard. "I've seen the way you gawp and drool, and he's gay. He's got a boyfriend." She folded her arms, so smug. "He's just not going to be interested in a little skank like you, *sorry.*"

Oh God, how I wanted to tell her. The urge to gloat about how he'd taken me over and over and over again while his boyfriend rammed his gorgeous cock in my mouth was almost too much to bear. The words were in my throat, burning me, desperate to spring out and slap the little bitch across her spoiled little mouth, but I didn't. I couldn't.

She smirked a vile smirk at me. "Of course, the fact that he's already with someone probably wouldn't stop you. Like mother like daughter, after all. Adultery probably runs in your skanky DNA."

"Or yours," I said. "Probably yours, too, since it's your lovely *daddy* who couldn't keep his dick in his pants."

"Your mum chased him, your mum made him do it."

"You can shut your mouth about my mother," I snapped, and I meant it. My blood was boiling, pulse racing.

"My mum says your mum was nothing but a gold-digging slut. A cheap-rate whore."

"Your mum is a bitter, twisted bitch if she thinks that. My mum wasn't even twenty years old. Younger than we are now, just think about that."

"Old enough to know better."

"Young enough to be taken advantage of by a seedy, arrogant, disgusting old prick."

"A prick who's paying you money to be here! So shut your nasty little mouth!"

"I fucking won't!" I snapped. "I don't even want to be here, you can stick your nasty little fucking family up your spoiled little asshole, Verity. You're all fucked up. All of you."

I made to storm out, but the bitch lost it. She grabbed my hair with her talons and pulled my bun loose, dragging me back across the toilets, and she screamed and hissed and spewed venom while I wrestled against her grip. I wasn't going to hit her, that's not my style, but the bitch was a psycho, slapping my head and tugging at my hair, and one of her little bitch slaps landed on my cheek and her stupid fake nails scratched me. And that was it.

I launched myself backwards until I slammed her into the wall, and it winded her. She dropped her grip and I spun in a flash and pinned the stupid cow by her shoulders while she spluttered.

"Listen up, bitch," I hissed. "I'll give you that one for free, but if you ever, ever touch me again, you're not going to get a hall pass. I'm not ten years old anymore, and I'm not taking your spoiled little rich girl shit. Understand?"

She didn't answer, and I didn't really need her to. She was still catching her breath, eyes wild and spiteful.

I shoved her again for good measure and then I let her go.

I had work to do, and the job satisfaction of wiping the floor with her bitchy, self-entitled little ass would be a sweet balm for my bitter soul.

CARL

Two empty seats as the afternoon resumed, and the sight made me a little uneasy. I looked at my watch and was contemplating sending a search party to the toilets when Katie made her way across the room.

She looked like shit, scraping back hair that was clearly dishevelled and twisting it back up into a bun only to find her hair tie was missing. She checked her wrists for another, and I saw her curse under her breath. She abandoned her efforts and let her hair fall free, and someone had clearly had a go at it. It didn't take a genius to work out who that someone was.

I didn't see the scratch on her face until she took her seat, and the sight of it knocked me for six.

Verity appeared just a moment later, and I shot her a look that could sour milk. She walked with the same Verity swagger, but her eyes were dark and wired. Unlike Katie, she still looked immaculate, her hair still hanging in a perfect plait, her makeup pristine without so much as a smudge.

"Prepare some notes," I said to the group, deviating entirely from my plan for the afternoon. "Upselling opportunities — list any you can think of. See what ways you can envision maximising value on an introductory call."

I waited until the thrum of activity was in sway before I approached Katie. She turned away from me and pressed her palm to her cheek, as though that would cover anything.

"What happened?" I whispered.

"Nothing," she said, and her smile was big and fake.

"Bullshit," I hissed. "Did she hit you?"

"You don't sound all that surprised at the prospect," she said. And I wasn't. I'd known Verity long enough to know she was a tantrum-thrower. A little madam who lashed out when she didn't get her own way. Katie sighed. "I'm fine," she said. "Don't make a scene."

But it was too late for that, I was already headed for Verity's desk. I grabbed her by the elbow and pulled her to her feet and was already frogmarching her out of the room by the time I beckoned Katie to follow. She shook her head, but I continued regardless, relieved when she shrugged and followed in our wake.

I led Verity into one of the meeting rooms and virtually forced her into a seat.

"You're out," I said. "Dismissed."

She shot me a look full of hate. "What? Why?!"

Katie opened the door and I pointed straight to her face. "How about assault?"

Verity laughed. "It was an accident, I slipped. Didn't I, Katie?"

Katie's eyes were like fire and her jaw was gritted. "Something like that."

"You're out," I repeated. "You can get your things and leave. Now."

"You can't fire me!" she snapped, and then she laughed. "This is *my* dad's business! It's *mine*! Or it *will* be!"

"Not yet, it isn't," I said. "It's my call, and your father's."

"He'd never fire me!"

I picked up the telephone extension on the desk in front of me. "Let's see, shall we?"

I pressed for David's extension, but Verity reached out and pressed call cancel. "This is stupid! It was a stupid accident."

"I've seen plenty of your accidents over the years, Verity, but not on my watch. I want you gone."

Her mouth flapped like a fish. "But you can't! I'm not leaving!"

I went to grab hold of her again, but Katie reached for my arm. Her touch was light and delicate and stilled me instantly.

"Don't," she said. "Don't make a martyr out of the little bitch. I can handle her."

"She's out," I said. "She assaulted you, on work premises, on *my* watch."

"Yeah," she replied. "And I slammed her into the wall and now we've got each other's measure. I can handle her," she said. "She doesn't need to leave, and I don't want her to, not when I'm about to

214

outperform her spoiled little ass."

"Outperform me?!" Verity sneered. "As fucking if."

I looked at Katie and the scratch on her pretty skin gave me the rage, deep inside. I was all set to ignore her and throw Verity out regardless, but I noticed the fire in her eyes. There it was. Resolve, and hunger and drive. The drive to win.

And she could win this.

It would be blissfully fucking sweet to see her win this.

"I mean it," she said. "We're cool now, we've clocked each other's form."

I glared at Verity as though I could burn her alive. "If this *ever* happens again. Ever. If I hear so much as a peep of any kind of incitement, or abuse, or physical violence, you'll be out on your ear and straight into a fucking police car, understand me? I don't care who your fucking father is."

"Yeah, whatever," she said, and I could have slapped the bitch.

I leaned over the table, until we were eye to eye. Her brows flew high and her composed facade broke down enough that I could see right through her, and all I saw was a jealous, vindictive, spiteful little cow.

"I'm disgusted by you," I said. "And I will be telling your father. I'll be telling him exactly what a nasty, violent little cow you are."

"Tell him!" she said. "I don't care!" But she did care, it was written all over her face.

"I should take this further," I said to Katie. "You should report this." But she was already shaking her head.

"It's a scratch," she said. "Bad aim, that's all." Her eyes pleaded me. "Let us go back to work, where it matters."

"This matters," I insisted. "This matters a lot."

"Let me do this," she said. "Please, Carl. Just leave it be."

And Verity saw the familiarity between us. Her mouth twisted into a sneer and she glared daggers at me.

I was glad she saw it.

I was proud she saw it.

I wanted to show the bitch a whole lot more.

I weighed up the situation. I weighed up Katie's injury and her composure. I weighed up how adamant she was that she wanted to take Verity on. I weighed up how I'd keep an eye on the situation, every single word that spewed from Verity's mouth. How I'd tell David all about it and make damn sure it wouldn't ever happen again.

I weighed up how steely my little blue-eyes was becoming and how confident she was, how sure.

And I noticed the feelings rising up in me. The venom and the anger. The impotence I felt at failing her, at not keeping her safe.

I wanted to keep her safe.

But I wanted to see her fly, too. I wanted to see her take on the nasty little cow and win.

"This isn't over," I said to Verity. "Not by a long fucking shot, madam." She stared, mute. "Get back to your desk," I said. "I'll deal with you later."

She didn't need telling twice, and Katie breathed out a sigh of relief when she was gone.

"Thank you," she said. "For not firing her."

"I should have fired her," I snapped. "I still should. She should be gone."

Katie smiled. "I'm used to it, seriously, it's just a scratch."

I took her chin in my fingers, angled her face so I could see. I ran a thumb over the cut, and it was just a scratch, hardly a break of the skin. "I hate this," I said. "I hate that this happened on my watch."

"In the ladies' toilet," she said. "What were you supposed to do? Armed guard me?" She sighed. "I'm used to Verity bitch face, I can handle her shit."

"I don't want you to handle her shit," I said, and the words tumbled out. "I want to keep you safe."

Her eyes widened and her cheeks blushed. "Thanks... but, I, um... I'm tough. I'm alright..." She reached out and touched my arm. "I'm good, Carl, really. It was nothing."

But it was something.

It was something to *me*.

She was something to me.

Chapter
FIFTEEN

CARL

David was uncharacteristically quiet as I gave him the lowdown. I didn't pull my punches and he didn't interject. I watched as the man I'd grown to know so well grew old before my eyes. He rubbed his temples as I recounted the aftermath of toilet-gate, and then he put his face in his hands.

I poured him a scotch, shunted it across his desk, but he didn't even notice.

"It needs sorting," I said. "Seriously, David, I'm not having this shit going down on my watch."

He sighed. "So many years of trying. I tell you, Carl, I just can't get it right."

I leaned back in my chair. "Why do Verity and Katie hate each other?" I asked. "What's the story, David? The real story about Katie."

I tried to convince myself this was just professional interest, that I needed to safeguard my employees and do my job. But my palms were clammy and hot and my stomach was itching inside.

He shrugged. "The story of my fuck-up, you mean?"

It needled me to think he was referring to Katie as the fuck-up. The umbrage was in my throat, about to let loose before he clarified his stance.

"The affair was a fuck-up," he said. "It was before your time, back when we were still expanding hell for leather. I was working long hours, Olivia was busy with the boys. I was never there, not how it counted, and she was always so bloody bitter, Carl. Seb and Dommie were boisterous kids, they took it out of her. She was tired, I was tired. It was shit."

"Sounds like life," I said.

"Debbie was everything Olivia wasn't. She had so much energy, so much enthusiasm."

"Debbie is Katie's mother?"

He nodded. "My secretary. Nineteen years old. Less than half my age." He smiled, noticed his scotch and took a sip. "Should've known better, Carl. Should've known to keep it in my pants."

I shrugged. "You aren't the only man who can't keep his dick to himself, sure as hell aren't going to be the last."

"We got close. I know they always say that, but it's true. She listened. She was always listening, *actually* listening, you know? She had the most amazing laugh, the most genuine smile." He tipped his glass in my direction. "Katie has her smile. You can see every emotion on her face, that girl, just like her mother. Same freckles, too."

I felt a knot in my stomach. Something uncomfortable and vulnerable and exposed. "Katie's a beautiful girl."

He nodded. "I loved her mother, Carl, she wasn't just a fling. I used to watch her across the office, and I'd dream of a different life. I'd wonder what it would be like to wake up with her in the morning, how we'd spend our evenings, what our home would be like. What our kids would look like."

My stomach panged at the honesty in his confession.

"Had it bad, then?" I said.

He didn't answer, just stared beyond me. "Six months we were seeing each other, and then I cooled it off. Olivia was at breaking point, and I felt so bad for the boys, Carl. The guilt crippled me. I talked myself into giving it another go, one last shot. Stupid. It was stupid." He laughed a sad laugh. "I wanted to be with another woman, and still I convinced myself to stay."

"Understandable," I said. "For the boys."

His eyes met mine, and they were so blue, just like Katie's. "We had sex. Just once. Just to try and get the spark back."

I held up a hand. "You don't need to tell me the details, David, not if you don't want to."

He waved my words aside. "Once, Carl, it was just once, and I knew then. I knew my heart wasn't in it, would never be in it. I loved Olivia, she'd given me two beautiful boys and made a home for them, she'd been there when I was a nobody and was still right there when I wasn't. She's a good woman, Carl, she's still a good woman, but I was in love with Debbie."

"And then?" I prompted.

"I told Debbie I was leaving Olivia. She was so happy, Carl. So fucking happy. I can still picture her face." He rubbed his forehead. "We talked about how things would be. We made plans, so many fucking plans. All I needed to do was tell Olivia it was over. I psyched myself up to it over a couple of weeks. We were busy, they went quickly. Two weeks, three weeks, a month. Debbie was getting edgy, I could see it in her eyes, so one day I just bit the bullet. I drove home and waited until the boys were in bed and told Liv we needed to talk."

His eyes were so pained when they looked at mine. "She agreed, said we very much needed to talk." I knew before he said it, but I didn't stop his flow. "She was pregnant, Carl. Fucking pregnant."

I nodded. "Verity."

"Our little princess." He finished his scotch. "Olivia knew about Debbie. I hadn't been all that quiet about it. She wanted her gone."

"What did you do?"

"I broke Debbie's heart." He sighed. "Gave her a good severance package, told her I was sorry, told her I didn't have a choice." He looked me in the eye. "I didn't know she was pregnant, too. Fucking hell, Carl, what were the fucking odds? Five days apart, Verity and Katie. Five fucking days."

"That's... virile." I smiled.

"That's a fucking nightmare," he said. "Debbie left, wanted nothing to do with me once I'd chosen Olivia over her. I found out she was pregnant through a friend of hers, girl in the office called Maggie. I went round to her parents' house and confronted her, but she said it was already done."

"Done?"

"Abortion, she said. She was nineteen years old, she said, no partner, she said, no prospects, she said. She was angry, and hurt, and hostile. Leave and never come back, she said."

"So that's what you did?"

"That's what I did. Felt easier that way, for both of us." He leaned towards me. "I swear I didn't know about Katie, Carl, not until the girl was just shy of ten. I was coming back from a meeting in Hereford, supplier up on the Three Elms Trading Estate, took the road through Much Arlock, and there she was, my Debbie, walking up the street as I stopped at the lights. She had a girl with her, in her school uniform.

My window was open all the way down, and I heard Katie's voice. *Mum*, she said, and I knew, I just fucking knew."

"Shit," I said. "That's a head fuck."

"Never felt so fucked up in my life," he said. "Shocked, and angry, and disgusted at myself. And then sad, so fucking sad."

"What did you do?"

"I looked up Debbie's new address, went round there when Katie was at school. She looked like she'd seen a fucking ghost, and so did I. She denied it at first, said Katie wasn't mine, but I demanded to see her birth certificate. I was a blank fucking space, Carl, a nobody, but dates don't lie. Debbie cried then, cried and begged me to stay away, said they didn't need me, neither of them, said they'd been coping just fine."

"Shit."

"She was a care worker, still is. My bright little Debbie wiping up old people's shit to support my daughter while I lived the life of fucking Riley a few miles away."

"What did you do?"

He shook his head. "Acted impulsively. Went straight home and told Olivia, told her I had another daughter and she'd be coming to stay with us. Insisted we tell the kids, insisted we invite Katie into our home. I forced my wishes on Debbie, threatened legal action, DNA testing, all that. I thought it would be easy. I was angry, Carl."

And I knew the story from here. "I remember."

"I didn't tell anyone much about the backstory, I was too ashamed and Olivia was fucking mortified. I kept quiet but insisted that Katie was my daughter now, told Debbie that the past didn't matter, that what counted was what we did from there." He groaned. "I thought I could make it all right, thought if I pushed hard enough people would accept it, learn to love it. I met Katie for the very first time as she climbed into my car for her first day at ours. I was such a fucking prick, Carl, handled it all wrong. The girl didn't get a chance to find her feet, I just wanted her to meet her brothers and sister, wanted her to see what a nice house we had, how much fun she could have. But she hated it, and Verity hated her. The whole thing was a fucking disaster."

"Must have been hard on the kids, all of them."

He nodded. "I thought they'd adapt, slowly, learn to get on. I thought we'd be alright."

"But it wasn't alright?"

He shook his head. "No, it wasn't alright. Katie hated me, hated the house, hated the kids. She didn't want to come there, used to cry to her mum that she wanted to stay at home, but I'd turn up anyway, try and make it work. Bull-headed, Carl, I was bull-headed. When she got to thirteen she didn't want to know me anymore, and when she got to sixteen she told me she'd had enough of the whole fucking lot of us. Wouldn't take a penny from me, not for anything, didn't want to know."

"You let it go?"

"No," he said. "Not really. Kept trying, kept pushing. It's her mother, though, she's so close to her mother. Wouldn't even let me speak her name, still won't now. She said I had no right to speak about her mother after what I'd done to her, no right to even think about her mother."

"And what about what Debbie did to you?" I said. "Katie knows presumably? That Debbie lied to you?"

He sighed. "I dunno, Carl. I really don't know what she knows. I've never rocked the boat far enough to bring it up with her, communication is tough enough as it is without that can of worms springing open. Katie doesn't want to know me, no matter how hard I try, and Olivia and Verity kick off if I try too hard to make inroads, so I don't, for an easy life. Not for me, for all of them."

"Then why is Katie here?"

"Because she's my daughter," he said. "Because I love her. Because I want what's best for her. Because I hope that Verity and Katie can find some common ground in adulthood, something to bring them together. I hoped it would be this Harrison Gables guy."

I shook my head. "There's animosity there, David, real animosity. What happened today was unacceptable."

He sighed. "I'll sort it."

"How?"

"Maybe I shouldn't have insisted Katie came here. Maybe it was a mistake."

"That's ridiculous," I said. "It's not Katie that's the problem. Katie is mature and hardworking and committed to the programme. The issue is with Verity."

He nodded. "It usually is. I'll talk to her."

I couldn't hide my frustration. "Verity shouldn't be here if she's incapable of controlling her temper, David, regardless of who she is."

"She'll control her temper," he said. "I guarantee it."

I wasn't convinced. "Verity is too used to getting her own way. She's got no commitment to the training programme. She's rude and sarcastic and does whatever she pleases."

"Tell me something I don't know." He groaned. "You know what Verity is like, Carl, you've known her long enough."

He had that right. I looked at my watch. "I've got to go," I said. "Shit to do."

I felt a pang of guilt at the realisation I was racing back home for Katie, just in case she decided to turn up again, even though she likely wouldn't.

He stood and held out a hand. "Tell me you'll do your best for them, Carl. Tell me you'll try to build bridges between my two girls."

I shrugged. "You think I can do that? I wouldn't hold your breath, David."

"Please," he said. "I'll bring Verity into line, but just... just try your best to get them on the same team, will you? It would mean everything to me." His eyes were so fucking honest.

"I'll try," I said. "Although I probably stand more chance of herding cats." I picked up my file and my phone. "You need to start communicating with Katie, David. The girl doesn't seem to have any idea you're not the bad guy in all this, not entirely. She needs a father who can support her, who wants to be there, if she doesn't believe that's you and you want it to be, then you've got some serious work to do."

"I know," he said. "I know I've got some work to do."

I shook his hand. "I'll see what I can do about building bridges, but it may take some time."

"You've got six months." He smiled. "Six months is the only time I can buy with Katie. She'll be gone as soon as she's done, I'm certain of that."

"A lot can happen in six months," I said.

"I'm counting on it," he said.

As was I.

Even more so than he was.

"We need to talk," Rick said, his eyes glinted as he stared at me from across our dining table. "Something has to be said. Things are escalating real fucking quickly."

I paused, my knife halfway through buttering my roll. My stomach tensed. "Couldn't agree more. I'm more than happy to say something, Rick. In fact, I'm dying to fucking say something. It's you who insisted on waiting six months."

He looked blankly for a moment, then gave me a sigh. "Not *that* something, I mean something between *us*."

The disappointment panged. "What something between us?" I dipped the bread in my soup. Homemade a la Rick. Vegetable medley. "Things are fucking sweet, no?"

He nodded. "Yeah, they're sweet. Sweet as fucking daisies."

We both agreed on that. Another few days of Katie in our bed at night, another few days of Katie in my office through the day. A couple of days of Rick taking her to the stables while I finished up work.

A couple of days of fucking like fucking rabbits.

She was at home tonight, spending time with her mother. The first night in several, and it was quiet. So fucking quiet. She'd left a Katie-shaped hole in our life here, and it itched like a fucker when she was away.

I tried to convince myself it was always like this, that we always fell this hard. But it was bullshit. Total fucking bullshit.

"Spit it out, then," I said. "What's the problem?"

"The inevitability." He stirred his soup. "Things are bound to happen, sooner or later."

"Things? What *things*?"

He shrugged. "You two at the office all day, for instance. Or me on stable-boy duty with the prettiest girl of all the time while you work late... someone's gonna break, Carl."

I stared at him. "We come together or not at all, that's what we decided."

He folded his arms. "And I'm saying it needs rethinking, it's not sustainable."

I hated to admit he was right. It'd been bothering me for a few days now, those lingering looks in the office, the hard-on in my pants as I watched Katie at her desk. The way I was jacking off in the toilets when it got too much.

"Are you saying you're going to fuck her, Rick? A tumble in the hay, so to speak? Literally?"

"I'm not saying that." He held up his hands. "Katie's more into Samson at the yard than she is me, way fucking more. I'm just saying it's a fuse waiting to spark, all ways round. Better to address it now, I think. Save a fucking hoo-hah down the line when someone fucks up."

"So, what are you suggesting?"

He put his hands in his hair. "I'm not sure. Maybe just an option to call? Before it happens? For permission?"

"Like a courtesy call? *I'm about to plough Katie's tight little cunt over a hay bale, is that alright?*"

"What would you say if I called you with that?"

"I was fucking joking, Rick." I thought about it while I took another bite. "What could I say? I'd say yes, I guess. What else could I fucking say?"

He shrugged. "I'd say yes, too." He smirked. "And then I'd want to listen."

"It's dangerous," I said. "It's always dangerous."

"Yeah, I know." He sighed. "Always a fucking minefield, Carl. I dunno why we put ourselves through it." But he was smiling.

"We're strong," I said. "We'll cope."

He nodded. "I hope so."

"Hope?"

"Alright," he said. "I know so."

"I'll probably have to have one of those angry fucking wanks while I think about it, then come home and take it out on your sorry little fuck hole."

"Sounds even better."

"You say that now." I stared at him, and my dirty Rick was looking so fucking hot. His t-shirt was tight and stretched across his chest, his hair was messy at the back, like a bird's nest, just asking to be grabbed and pulled as I fucked his tight little asshole.

"What?" he said, taking a swig of beer. "What's that look for?"

I finished up my wine. "I want to fuck you."

"I love how direct you are, Carl Brooks."

I got to my feet. "Now," I said. "I want to fuck you now."

He held up his phone. "Maybe we should test out our new rules? Call Katie and ask if she minds. Maybe she could listen. Maybe she'd want to listen?" His eyes were hopeful. Sparkling. Horny.

I shook my head. "No fucking phone, Rick. Just you and me."

I watched his breath catch. "You're so fucking hot when you get all bossy." He pushed himself from the table, rubbed his palm in the crotch of his jeans. "Where?" he said. "Where do you want me?"

I knew just what I wanted.

"This way," I said.

I wanted to fuck him where she'd been, where the sheets still smelled of her. I pinned him at the bottom of the stairs, kissed him hard, until he grunted into my mouth and fumbled at my belt.

228

"Feels like ages since it was just us." He snaked his fingers inside my boxers, gripped my cock. "Feels good to know you want me."

"Of course I fucking want you," I said, and it was more than that. I thrust against his fingers. "I fucking *need* you." My mouth pressed to his, and my words were muffled, but he heard them well enough.

We stumbled upstairs with wet kisses. With frantic fingers and hard cocks and short breaths. I kicked the bedroom door open.

"Where she's been," I whispered. "I want to fuck you there. Want to fuck you where she sleeps. Want her to sleep where I've taken you. Want to love you where we've taken her."

He groaned into me and kissed me hard.

I took off his clothes and he took off mine, and I pulled him onto me, falling to the bed as he straddled me, his hands on my thighs and his back arched.

He was so fucking beautiful. That gorgeous fucking man with his cute smile and his messy hair and hungry eyes.

I lubed up my cock, and he eased himself down, exhaling one long breath as my cock filled him up.

And then he rode me, slowly. So fucking slowly it fried my fucking brain.

I watched him intently. Watched the rapture on his face as I worked his dick with my fingers. Watched the way his eyes glazed and his mouth dropped open.

And I felt it all, felt him.

"I love you," I said, and his eyes snapped into focus.

"I fucking love you, Carl, so fucking much."

We stared at each other, through each other, and there was so much unsaid.

The unspoken hung heavy, thick and deep. The need that never left, that never eased, that never relented.

"I love her," he said. "She's the one." His voice was barely a whisper.

I nodded, and then I pulled him down onto me, his chest to mine, and I held his face and kissed him while my cock twitched deep inside.

"I love her, too," I said.

Chapter
SIXTEEN

Katie

I'm not enough of a dreamer that I could ignore the inevitable. I'd known when I took the sperm donor's offer that my summer plans for Samson would be largely kicked to the kerb. It's not that I didn't care. I did care. We'd worked hard, Samson and me, months and months of training and trust to get his form up enough to compete in cross country events this season. He was in good condition, but with the reduction in hours at my disposal, my ambitions would have to drop a gear.

I was ok with that. We'd have another year. Samson wasn't young, but he was still in his prime. We'd get our time, he and I, so I'd shoved my eventing timetable in my dressing table drawer back at home, and pushed it out of my mind.

Until Verity pinned up the Cheltenham Chase cross country leaflet on our team noticeboard that Friday.

She'd formed a little gaggle of horsey girls around the office, and there they'd stood in a thrumming little huddle before work kicked off, enthusing over who was competing and how they were going to smash it. I'd kept my distance, pretending to be busy on my phone while they gushed over their horse's form and who was signing up and who had the edge. Verity was competing her latest acquisition, a 16.2HH warmblood competition mare called *Fleetwood Fancy*. Fancy was right, over fourteen grand's worth of cold hard cash after negotiation by all accounts, but that was nothing for the Faverleys. Pocket change.

I should have let it go, I mean, who cares what stupid fancy horse Princess Verity is dicking about on for the summer? She'd be bored of the mare before the season was out, and I'd normally have let it go. Normally.

But right there, with my coffee in one hand and my phone in the other, watching those horsey bitches mouthing off about who'd be kicking whose ass around that course at the end of August, I found I cared quite a lot.

Fleetwood Fancy had form, but Verity wasn't as dedicated as she liked to think she was. She was all about the image, not about the substance. She didn't take the time for the foundation work, didn't want to put in the hours of warm up and preparation. Why would she? She had people to do all that shit for her. As a result, she'd be riding a horse that was still new to her, and sure, that horse had the scope to carry her through almost anything, but she'd never hit peak, not in time.

And that gave me a shot. Not a big one, but enough to send a thrill up my spine.

I mean, we'd never win, Samson and I, not the whole event, but that didn't matter, just so long as we beat that arrogant little cow. Just so long as we had a chance.

There was that cold scaly feeling in me again, and my heartrate picked up as I watched her. She thought she had it in the bag, that she'd hop up on Fleetwood Fancy and the mare would carry her to victory without even breaking a sweat. I doubt I'd even crossed her mind, not with my budget auction horse that she'd never have given a second glance. She had no idea how far we'd come, Samson and me, no idea that we'd hit that sweet spot where we worked as one, trusted each other, knew each other by heart.

She'd never had that. She'd never stuck with a horse for long enough.

I'd been keeping my money safe towards Jack's rent, but I clicked onto *Horseclub* and checked out their cheapest horse trailers. There was one locally for just under a thousand. It would get me there. My rust bucket would tow it just fine, and sure, it wasn't slick or special, but it would do the job. There was a niggle in me, a niggle that I should be saving and focused, not running away with some stupid quest of pride to get one up on Verity. Like kicking her ass in the office wasn't going to be enough already.

But I never spent money, not on me, not really. And I'd never had a trailer before, not one of my own, and I'd use it, definitely, when I had the time again. It was an investment. A useful investment. A sensible investment, even.

So, I bought it.

PayPalled the cash without even viewing, and it felt good. It felt really fucking good.

And then I signed Samson and I up for the Cheltenham Chase.

It was becoming comfortable so easily with Rick and Carl. I'd fallen into a routine nothing short of heaven, travelling to the office

233

and back with Carl every day, lunching at the bagel joint, then zipping over to Samson with Rick of an evening while Carl spent his hours on extra work shit. We'd eat and laugh, drink sometimes, then shower and fuck and suck and fuck some more until I fell asleep in my spot between two hot bodies in their kickass bed. *My* spot. Yeah, it was my spot. How fucking sweet.

I'd almost forgotten our arrangement — the fact that they were paying me for my time — because in truth, it didn't feel like that. Not anymore. I would have been there anyway. I'd have told them as much, and I considered it, but I still had a dream to pay for, and with Jack up against it and the yard on the line, that three grand a month was money I needed. It didn't sit easy, but it was the truth, and come the weekend I was conscious that this was my billable time, as per our arrangement.

It made me feel like shit when I threw on my crappy clothes to go pick up my new trailer, and I aimed to play it down, say I was nipping out for a couple of hours but would be back before they knew it. Only it wasn't that simple.

Carl was frying bacon when I stepped into the kitchen, and Rick was pulling a face at the smell, wafting his hands around his nose and fake retching.

"Firemen don't eat bacon," Rick told Carl. "You know why?"

"Enlighten me," Carl said.

"Smells like burning human flesh."

Carl turned to face him, spatula in hand. "An advert for cannibalism if ever I heard one. Yum yum fucking yum." He saw me in the doorway and looked me up and down. "Morning, Miss Horsey. Fuck me, I do love a woman in jodhpurs."

"Hey, pretty lady." Rick smiled. "Carl's cooking pig. Want some?"

I took a seat at the island, and Rick leaned in to kiss my neck over and over. Wet sloppy kisses that made giggle, and then he blew a raspberry and I squirmed, poked my tongue out at him.

It felt so shit to say it, but I said it anyway. "I've got to go out. I won't be long, I promise."

Carl turned and stared at me, but he didn't look pissed off. "Samson?"

I shrugged. "Kind of. I bought a trailer, need to go pick it up." I pulled my hair into a pony and fastened it. "Enjoy your breakfast, I'll be back before you know it."

I made to scoot off without fanfare, but Rick grabbed my wrist. "Whoa whoa whoa," he said. "Not so quick."

And I thought it was time for the chat, the one where they reminded me that this was a Saturday and I was on their time, the one where they reminded me that I had a fat wadge of cash in my bank account and two fat cocks to service. But it was just my guilt. Of course it was.

"Kept that quiet," Rick said. "Where's this swanky new trailer of yours?"

"Hartpury," I said. "Not far. It's not exactly swanky..."

Rick looked at Carl, but Carl wasn't looking at Rick he was looking at me. "We'll come," he said, just like that. Just like it was the most normal thing in the world. "Just eat your bacon first."

Carl bleeped the Range as we stepped outside but I shook my head.

"What?" he said. "I've got a tow bar, we can take mine."

"But I need to be able to hitch it on mine," I said. "I'll need to do it for shows. I can do it."

He looked at my shitty car, and back at me. "If you're sure."

"I'm sure."

He shrugged. "Alright then."

And so Rick and Carl piled into the cruddy Katiemobile. It was funny to see them in there, amongst the grooming kits and the saddle soap and the bits of old tack.

"The height of luxury," I laughed, and cranked the old brute into gear. I looked at Carl at my side, and he was dressed too nicely for this, as usual. His shirt was expensive and far too clean, his jeans had never seen mud in their life. And his shoes. His poor posh shoes.

"Don't think I can't see you checking me out," he said.

Rick leaned between the seats, and my skin did that lovely little shiver it does when he's close. "You're so not dressed for this shit, Carl." he said. "You're never dressed for this shit."

"Says Mr fucking Outdoors. A bit of time at the stable and you think you're Farmer bastard Richard."

"I've ridden," Rick said, and I saw his grin in the rearview mirror. "It's getting serious."

Carl raised his eyebrows. "You've been on a horse?"

"Samson," he said. "Katie gave me a lesson."

It wasn't a lesson, but I didn't butt in. It was hardly more than a donkey ride, a bit of a walk up and down the yard but I didn't want to piss on his parade.

"You didn't say," Carl said, and I swear I caught a whiff of jealousy. It made Rick laugh.

"You got your cock out when we walked back through the door. It slipped my mind."

"You can have a go, too," I said. "If you want."

But Carl pulled a face. "Horse hates me," he said. "He'd buck me

236

off, then trample me."

"He loves me," Rick gloated. "He came when *I* called him yesterday, knows I give him mints."

"He'll do anything for a mint," I said, but Carl didn't say another word.

The trailer was pretty shit, and I knew it. But it was mine. I couldn't stop smiling.

Carl gave it a bit of a kick, scoped it out with critical eyes. "This is safe, is it?"

I nodded. "Yeah, looks sound."

Rick opened up the back. "Samson will love this, his own personal chauffeur service."

Carl jumped on the floor inside until it clanked and echoed. "You're sure this is safe?"

I rolled my eyes. "Yes, it's safe. It's rough round the edges not a total bag of shit."

"I'll take your word for it," he said.

Rick jabbed him in the side, then grabbed him in a headlock to ruffle his perfect hair. "Don't knock it, grumpy face. It's fucking awesome."

Carl pushed him off and aimed a foot at his ass, gave him a healthy kick. "I'm not knocking anything, I'm just safety conscious. Better safe than fucking sorry, Rick."

It made me laugh. They always made me laugh. "I'm good," I said. "I'm happy. I've wanted one of these forever."

"Fine," Carl said, and held up his hands. "Then I'm very happy for you."

I checked the fixtures then fetched my car, reversing it back with bated breath in case I made a tit of myself, but I didn't. I lined it up just right.

I waved them aside as I fastened it up, determined to do this shit myself, and I was grinning like a lunatic as we rumbled away with a trailer in tow.

"You're a kickass chick, Katie," Rick said. "She's kickass, isn't she, Carl?"

"I'm impressed," he said. "Kickass, indeed."

It made me feel on top of the world.

We rocked that trailer up onto the yard, and I wanted to show it off to Jack, but he was nowhere to be seen. I hadn't seen him for days in fact, the van was rarely there. I tried calling him but it rang through to voicemail.

"It's Katie," I said. "Just checking in. Got a trailer, parked it up by the barn. Hope you're alright. Catch you soon."

"Check this out," Rick said to Carl, and he was off, jogging on past the stable block to the field.

My heart fluttered as Carl stared back at me, and there was a look in his eyes. A heaviness. A *need*. "You don't have to," I said. "We can head back."

But he shook his head. "Let's go see the furry boy."

Rick was up on the gate, waving his arms and yelling Samson's name. He was funny, Rick. Everything about him was so funny. I climbed up beside him and joined in the call, and the thump of hooves came thundering. Samson pulled to a halt later than usual, and I swear it was just to make Carl nervous. Samson gave him the eyeball and a bit of a snort, and it made me cringe, and maybe smile a little.

"I told you," Carl groaned. "He fucking hates me. He'd trample me, I'm telling you. That beast wants my blood."

"He wouldn't!" I giggled. "He'd be fine."

But he tossed his head away when Carl tried to pat him, nipping around Rick to root in his pockets instead. Rick had mints, an unfair advantage.

"You can ride if you want," Rick said. "We have plenty of time."

I was tempted. I looked at Carl and he didn't seem impatient. "If you want," he said. "You're driving anyway, I believe that puts us at your whim, unless we plan on hiking back to Cheltenham."

I looked at my furry boy and the urge to leap onto his back and go galloping across the common was strong, but there were other urges, too.

My tummy was tickling. It felt scratchy and strange and panged a little. Panged with something hard to place, a throb of something that wasn't entirely sexual. I stared at the two guys in front of me and admired them, their easy manner, their kind eyes. Their patience, both of them. The time they had for me, and Samson, too. Their care.

Rick had mints in his pocket especially for Samson, and Carl cared enough to check my trailer.

They cared enough to slum it in my rusty old banger, and trudge through mud to see my baby.

They cared.

And so did I.

The tickly pang warmed and spread right through me, all the way to my toes.

"Let's go home," I said.

"Home?" Carl said, and looked at Rick, and Rick smiled. They both smiled.

And I smiled, too.

"Home," I said.

I smelled of horse and hay and I knew it. I nipped for a quick shower while the guys listened to tunes downstairs, and my belly was fluttery and my pussy was hot.

I chose one of my best dresses and I wore it without a bra. It was flared and floaty and a little bit short. A pale blue halterneck that my nipples poked through without underwear. But that didn't matter.

I shaved everywhere and fought the urge to bring myself off. The real deal was waiting just a floor below, hot and horny and so much better.

I spritzed myself with perfume and brushed my hair and decided against knickers, just because.

Just because I want them to know I wanted this. Just because I'm so horny I can't think of anything else.

Rick had made a light lunch. A big bowl of salad with some fancy dressing. The guys were already plated up at the island and ready to eat, waiting for me.

Carl stared at my chest, and I knew my nipples were standing proud.

"Nice dress," he said.

I took a seat on the end between them, and Rick leaned over to wrap his arm around my waist. He ran his tongue up my shoulder, and my pussy clenched at the thought of his piercing against my clit. "I could eat you up." He smirked, and took my hand, placed it between his legs where his jeans were swollen. "I'm starving," he said. And then he grinned, forked out some salad, crunched on a tomato.

Carl poured me a wine, and I glugged some back.

He raised an eyebrow. "Planning on getting a little tipsy?"

I nodded. "It's been a long week, maybe just a little." He topped me back up, then poured Rick a glass and held up his own.

"To a long, successful week and Katie's new trailer," he said. "Cheers."

"Amen to that," Rick said and knocked his back.

"Amen." I smiled.

The tension was so fucking hot it was palpable. It smouldered between the guys, lingering glances as they ate, and I got the feeling they were in mind meld, talking without words and I was the topic. It made me jittery, with nerves and want and the heady thrum of anticipation. I ate a little, and then I drank. The wine was crisp and fruity and it warmed me. The warmth bloomed in my belly, spread between my thighs, and I was clenching them on my stool, shifting in my seat at the thought of what was brewing.

My heart did a little stutter as Carl put down his cutlery. He patted his mouth with a napkin and it was sexy as fuck. It always was.

"That was delicious," he said to Rick.

"Not as delicious as dessert is gonna be," Rick said.

And they stared at me, they both stared at me.

"Chocolate." Rick licked his lips. "I've been craving chocolate for a while now."

Oh. Oh fuck.

"What do you think, Katie?" Carl asked. "Do you think Rick has been good enough for chocolate?"

My nerves were in my throat, but my clit was sparking and buzzing and desperate. I nodded.

Carl took my plate and stacked it on his, and Rick's eyes were glinting and dirty.

This side of Rick always took my breath. It would appear

unbidden, rise up like a cobra, fast and hypnotic.

Rick was a dirty boy. Rick was rough, and filthy and absolutely insatiable.

He turned in his stool and spread his legs, and then he beckoned me, patted the top of the island at his side.

I slipped down from my stool and went to him, a rabbit in the headlights as Carl cleared away the salad. I shivered as Rick got to his feet. He stepped behind me, the heat of his chest against my back, and then he folded me at the waist, his hands on my shoulders as he pressed me flat to the island.

He pulled my halterneck loose and tugged it down, and it slipped from my breasts, baring them to the chill of the marble. He hitched my skirt, throwing it up over my hips, and he groaned to discover I was knickerless.

"That's our girl," he growled. "That's fucking hot."

I felt his hands, warm on my ass, and he dropped to his knees and teased my thighs open. I started as his tongue lapped at my slit, digging forward to my clit as it curled. I kept my eyes on Carl, and he was staring right back. I could see the outline of the monster in his jeans, straining to come out.

My breath was quick and raspy as Rick licked at my slit. I reached out my fingers and gripped the edge of the island, pressing my cheek to the marble as Rick dipped two fingers inside my pussy and twisted. I moaned when he found the spot, and he worked it, hard, so hard I thought I could pee. I doubt he'd have cared.

And then he stopped. He stopped and left me panting.

His hands gripped my ass cheeks and spread them wide, and the air was cool, and I was exposed. I felt so fucking exposed.

I cried out as he licked me there.

Carl stepped towards me and put his fingers under my chin. He tipped my head up and his eyes were hungry and dark.

"Look at me," he said.

I nodded.

I felt so bare, my eyes on Carl's as Rick tongued my asshole. It was squirmy and tickly and absolutely fucking wonderful.

His fingers worked my clit as his tongue worked its way inside me, and my thighs were quivering so hard Rick shunted me forward so the island took more of my weight. It shunted my face right into Carl's crotch. My lips pressed against the denim, and I could feel the shaft of him. He hissed under his breath and moved his hips and I nuzzled him.

I opened my mouth in invitation but kept my eyes on his.

Rick got to his feet, and reached to the side of me. I turned my head instinctively to see him pick up the olive oil, and my belly clenched.

Carl turned my face back to him. "Me," he said. "Keep your eyes on me. I want to see you."

"Yes," I said.

He smoothed my hair and it felt nice, and so did the drizzle of oil in my ass crack. It tickled, and I gasped.

Rick's fingers were warm. They rubbed the oil all over me, all the way round to my clit, and I felt so slick, so slippery.

I heard his belt opening, and then his zipper, and the soft sound of his palm as he lubed himself up.

He pushed his thumb inside my ass and I gasped again.

And then I groaned.

Loud.

I fucking loved it.

I fucking wanted it.

"Dirty girl," Carl whispered, and he was smiling.

I pushed back on Rick's thumb. "Please," I said. "More."

"Don't worry." Rick's voice was heavy. "You'll get more, baby. So much more."

He gave me more. Two fingers at least, and I sucked in my breath as they slid inside. He circled his knuckles, and I felt myself loosening, stretching, and it was dirty and fucking gorgeous.

Carl loosened his belt and I groaned.

"Yes," I said. "Give it to me…"

I could only take the head and a bit. It was hard to fit him between my teeth, but I was getting better. I relaxed my jaw and he wrapped his fingers in my hair, held me tight as he thrust in further. He hit the back of my throat and I breathed through the gag reflex.

He groaned his pleasure.

"Relax," he said. "Don't fucking bite."

I wondered what he was referring to, until Rick pulled his fingers from my ass. I felt empty and open, and then I felt the thick head of him, pressing to my open hole.

Carl kept his cock in my mouth, and I squirmed a little, squeaked around his dick.

"I've been looking forward to this," Rick groaned, and then he pushed.

He pushed and grabbed at my hips and levered himself inside me as I tensed.

Oh my God, it was big. Oh my God, it was sore and tight and sharp. Oh my God, it felt so fucking good when he pushed all the way in.

I knew I loved anal. I fucking loved the way it felt.

I closed my eyes, sucked on Carl.

Squeaked again as Rick pulled out for another thrust.

"Your ass feels fucking divine," he hissed. "Oh sweet fucking Christ."

Carl's dick twitched in my mouth. "Fuck her," he said. "Fuck her, Rick, loosen that tight little hole." His hands reached under me, slipped under my tits to pinch at my nipples.

He pushed into my throat until I retched.

"Good girl," he rasped. "Suck me."

I did suck. Sucked and moaned and writhed a little as Rick took my ass.

It hurt, and then it didn't. It hurt until it didn't hurt at all.

I spread my legs wider, pushed back at him, and he liked that.

"Fuck," he laughed. "Fuck, Carl, look at our sweet little Katie. She's fucking loving it in the ass."

"Something you've both got in common," he said, and his words made my clit tingle.

He pulled out of my mouth and I panted. "Harder," I said. "Fuck me hard, Rick."

"My fucking pleasure," he groaned and slammed in all the way.

Carl stepped aside, and then he left us. My heart dropped to see him walk away, but Rick just picked up pace. He pressed his hand to the back of my neck, held me firm. "Fuck me with your asshole," he hissed. "Work it."

I wriggled my hips, bucked back at him, cried out as his fingers wrapped under my thigh to strum at my clit.

And then Carl came back, with one of those floor standing mirrors. He positioned it in front of me, checking out the view from my angle.

I saw Rick's face, saw his smile, the lust there. It set me on fucking fire.

I met his eyes and I begged him for more, begged him for harder, begged him to fuck my fucking ass, and I didn't care how dirty it felt, I wanted it all.

My eyes widened as Carl appeared behind the both of us. I caught sight of him in the mirror and so did Rick, and Rick jolted in shock as Carl pushed him forwards.

Rick's weight pushed down on me, and it felt good. His chest pressed against my back, and he moved from his hips, circling and grinding while I groaned under him. I watched Carl's eyes as he tugged at Rick's jeans. I felt them come down, the denim rough against my bare thighs.

"Fuck," Rick hissed, right in my ear.

Carl picked up the olive oil, and he dribbled it from high. Rick kept fucking, kept pumping me, but he was groaning.

"Yes," he grunted. "Fuck me, Carl. Fuck my ass."

I saw Carl's arm pistoning, and Rick cried out, his body tense against my back, and he went still, his cock deep in my ass, and Christ it was heaven.

Carl shifted position, tipping his head back as he pressed up against Rick, and I felt the extra weight, the extra pressure.

It felt amazing. It felt dirty and delicious to be pinned so tightly under two.

Rick cried out as Carl pushed inside, and I felt it, I felt his pain. His mouth was hot against my neck, his breath ragged. He clenched his teeth for the second push, and I felt that one, too.

And then Carl fucked Rick, hard and deep as he grunted and groaned. Hard and deep as his balls slapped against Rick's underneath him, and Rick's balls slapped against me. I could hear it all.

Carl fucked Rick and Rick fucked me, and the image in the mirror was amazing.

And we all groaned and grunted and bucked and writhed and breathed in jagged breaths.

My God, it was everything.

Carl took Rick's hair in one hand and mine in the other, and he met our eyes in the mirror.

He smiled a dirty smile, and Rick smiled one too, and I laughed, delirious, gritting my teeth and then begging for more.

Rick gave me more. He fucked himself hard on Carl's dick as he fucked me, and his cock tightened, started twitching. I felt the strain in his breath.

"Gonna come," he said. "I'm gonna come, Carl."

Carl grunted.

"Fuck, Carl, I'm gonna fucking come!"

Carl's hips slapped harder, faster. He closed his eyes.

"Come," he groaned. "Now..."

And I felt them, I felt them both. Spasming and thrusting and losing their fucking mind. Carl emptied his balls into Rick as Rick emptied his into me, and it was beautiful.

It was so fucking beautiful.

A pile of heaving, hot bodies, and I was sweating and breathless, pinned to hard marble, but I never wanted them to move.

I didn't want to be released.

Not now, not in six months.

Not ever.

Chapter
SEVENTEEN

CARL

"Relax," I said. I reached over to the passenger seat and angled Katie's back until her shoulders were mine for the grasping. She was tense, her muscles knotty under her suit jacket. She hunched as I worked my fingers, and then she exhaled, loosened up a little. "It's your first calling week. It takes time to find your feet."

"I just want to do well," she said.

Maybe that's all it was. Maybe the niggle in my gut was wrong, and Katie was just all in with the training programme. Maybe there was a tough little saleswoman deep inside Katie that craved the thrill of the chase and close, and this had nothing to do with pitting herself against her snotty sister.

I got it. Hell, I fucking got it. Sales is a performance-based career, and the pressure builds and fills you up. I'd always been ambitious, consumed by the fire of topping the leaderboard, bringing in bigger deals, better deals, more impressive clients.

But Katie seemed different these past few days. The carefree girl who'd rocked up at ours with that breezy countryside smile on her face wasn't the one sitting in my car. This Katie was steely and resolute, consumed by the desire to win.

She was changing before my eyes, sacrificing stable visits to listen through her call recordings and pick holes in her performance.

I want to improve, she'd say. *What's the point in giving less than your all? What's the point in not striving for the top of the pile?*

I got that, too.

Still, despite the kinship, I couldn't help feeling a sense of loss for her somehow, a tainting of innocence. I couldn't shake the feeling that my training programme had stolen the sparkle of sunshine from her eyes and replaced it with grit and embers.

Katie wasn't the only one affected. The atmosphere in the training suite was tense enough to blow. Everyone had some measure of fire in their belly, everyone was chasing the win.

Even Verity. *Especially* Verity.

Whatever words David had shared with his little princess had done the job. She'd been quiet and compliant in the aftermath, her eye on the ball. Grit and embers, another one.

I'm all for healthy competition, but this felt deeper, verging on the unpleasant.

"Today's the day," Katie said. "I want a tick by my name on that leaderboard. Katie Serena Smith, ten points, top of the class."

"And Verity none? Am I right?"

She shrugged. "Why should I care what Verity does?"

I didn't need to see her face to know she did care. "Forget about the tick on the leaderboard," I said. "Just focus on the person at the end of the line. Ask the right questions, have a conversation. That's all you need to do."

She nodded. "Sure thing, boss."

"That's my girl."

I gave her shoulders a final squeeze and she opened the car door, flashed me a smile.

"Today's the day," she said again. "I can feel it."

It turned out it was Ryan, my early bet, who put the first tick up on the leaderboard. He made a cracking call mid-morning, the right pitch at the right time to a frustrated tech director looking for greater business insight. His face was a picture, pure bliss as he took the winner's walk up to the whiteboard and made that tick next to his name. I was pleased for him. A young kid at home, his first real shot at a career above minimum wage. I shook his hand and gave him a pat on the back, and the lad looked like he could cry.

It's a strange phenomenon that things really kick off once that first tick is made. His was followed by another, a sharp girl called Leanna, a smaller opportunity, but a good one, and then another, a long-term opportunity with a logistics company up north, discovered by our eldest trainee, Nick, who'd been working in tech support since he left school.

Katie was quiet as we ate our bagels. I could feel the cogs whirring, the tightness of panic twisting in her belly.

"Don't let it eat at you," I said. "It's far too early to judge anything."

She stared at her plate. "I just wanted it to be me."

"It *will* be you, anytime now."

But she didn't look convinced.

She let out a sigh as we pulled up outside the office.

"What if I can't do this? This isn't insurance, Carl. This is hard. Complicated."

"That's where you're falling down," I said. "You're *expecting* it to

250

be hard. You're picking up the phone with fear. Maybe a little desperation."

"What can I do?" Her eyes were piercing and beautiful. They hit me right in the chest. "What would *you* do?"

"I'd breathe. Find my zone. Make sure I was in the right headspace before that call connected. And then I'd have a conversation and see where it went." I smiled. "No pressure, Katie. The pressure is all in your head."

I unclipped my seatbelt, but she put her hand on my arm. I stilled, watching her as she reached for the dash controls.

"Don't laugh," she said, and there was a blush on her cheeks.

I smiled as I realised what she was doing. "I'd never laugh," I said. "Never."

She took a breath and closed her eyes as the opening bars sounded. "Will you do it with me?"

"Always," I said, and I took her hand.

We sang the Rocky theme in the car park until she was giggling too hard to get the words out, until her tension was gone and her eyes were bright and her breath was ragged but free.

And then my blue-eyed girl nailed it. She found her groove, delivered the right call at the right time, and got her tick on the leaderboard just five calls in after lunch.

I couldn't have been more proud.

Half of the trainees had a tick on the board by Friday afternoon, and those that hadn't were getting close. Verity was one of those getting close, but there was still an empty white space next to her name.

Conversations were getting slicker, more skilled. The atmosphere was buzzing as everyone pushed for that final result before end of play, and Katie was on fire, animated and smooth-talking with one eye on the clock.

I thought we had a winner for the week when Ryan ticked his second lead up on the board, but I was ahead of myself. I was sitting at his desk to transfer his lead details when Katie's call connected with the CTO of a big Welsh agricultural supplier. I heard the whole thing play out, from her faultless introduction, to the merry dance of questioning and rapport building, and finally through to the close.

I watched the excitement sparkle in her eyes, the bright smile of someone who knows they're onto a winner.

It thrilled me.

Intoxicated me.

Made my heart thump in my chest.

"I did it!" she said as she disconnected. "He wants a meeting! They have budget allocated and everything!"

She shot like a rocket to make that second tick, the one that put her in joint first position and marked her as a real contender. Ryan took it well, congratulating her with genuine pleasure at her success. It made me like him even more.

Katie could hardly contain herself as I got to my feet, she did a little jump on the spot and her hands were gripped in victory fists. I took a step towards her to shake her hand, but she bypassed that completely, forgetting our surroundings long enough to throw her arms around my neck.

"I did it!" A breathy giggle right in my ear.

I put my hands on her waist to guide her back to a professional distance, and she looked around at the other callers, her eyes wide as she registered her over familiarity. But it didn't matter, because nobody was looking at us.

They were too busy looking at David Faverley.

He stood at the front of the training suite, flanked by two senior members of Human Resources, his eyes roving the whiteboard and soaking in the scores.

A hush descended as he prepared to address the group, the chatter of calls easing off as people wrapped up their conversations and took off their headsets. Big boss man had an aura about him, he was dressed in navy with a dark maroon tie, and his silver hair was slick and styled. He nodded his approval as he totted up the totals, realising, as I had long since done, that our team was on track to be a solid performer.

And so was our sweet little Katie.

I pulled her to my side, be damned with professional distance, and her body had become tense, her excitement drying up to nothing.

"Good afternoon," David said to the room. "My apologies I haven't been around sooner, but I assure you I've been hearing a great deal about your progress from Carl. I hope you've enjoyed your first few weeks with us, we know the learning curve is intense, and the adjustment is hard, but I promise the effort will pay off."

He did the usual introductions, a bit of a company overview, a talk about opportunities post the training programme and a motivational speech about how proud he was of the work everyone was putting in. He was well-practised, his eyes moving steadily across the desks, making eye contact to convey his sincerity, but I knew him too well. Well enough to realise that he was fighting the compulsion to stare in our direction, stare at Katie, at his little star performer.

I was glad he fought it, because Katie's eyes were narrow, her lips tight, her gaze anywhere but on him. I brushed her fingers with mine, hooked them gently and pulled her hand behind my back out of view where I could hold it properly. I squeezed and she squeezed, pressing that little bit tighter to my side.

It felt so wrong to hide the way I felt from her father, even in the heart of my corporate surroundings. I wanted nothing more than to wrap my arm around her waist and hold her, encourage her to broach the distance and speak with him. I'd hold her hand and I'd tell him how wonderful she was, how hard she was working, how great she was doing. How proud I was, how proud he should be.

How she'd wrapped her dainty little fingers around my heart and stolen it. Rick's too.

I wanted to say all those things, but when David pulled a handful of golden envelopes from his pocket and called the first of the star performers up to claim one, I said nothing, did nothing.

Katie pulled her hand from mine when she realised the inevitable, and I expected her to bail before he called her name, turn tail and disappear to sleight him, leaving him standing with a golden envelope in his hand and egg on his face. She didn't. She stood still, stern-faced and tense, but rooted to the spot.

I started up an applause when Ryan's name was called, and his smile lit up the room as he collected his envelope. David shook his hand, congratulated him on an exceptional result, two sterling leads in the first stage of training was impressive, he said, very well done indeed, he said.

And then he turned his attention to Katie with one remaining envelope in his hand.

His smile was bright, and his eyes were warm and proud. It

pained me somewhere deep to see the chasm of disconnection between father and daughter.

"Katie," he said, and he beckoned her. "Please, come and get your prize."

There was so much emphasis on the *please*, a quiet desperation, the tone of a man eager to bridge a divide and make it right. Katie didn't move, and my heart was in my throat, my hand on her back to encourage her forward. She resisted, but only for a moment, taking slow steps in her fancy heels, looking mature and professional in her suit as she made her way to him.

Her smile was stilted and her hand was tense and awkward as she shook his. I saw the flash of emotion across his face as she dropped her eyes to the floor.

My heart broke a little for him, and it broke for her, too. For the love waiting right there for her, imperfect love from a man who meant it, a man who'd made his mistakes and lived to regret them, a man who was good and kind in the heart of him, a man who wanted to be there.

A man who'd tried to be there, and failed.

I thought he would admit defeat and let her go with nothing more than an awkward handshake, but I should have known better than that. He handed her the envelope, and took advantage of the moment. My breath choked as he wrapped his arms around her shoulders and pulled her to him, even though she was stiff as a board. The applause erupted, but his words carried, just loud enough to hear.

I'm so proud of you, he said. *I'm so very proud.*

And then he let her go.

She dithered for a moment, clutching that envelope in her fingers, a flicker of emotion on her face before her guard came back up. She nodded and thanked him, and then she backed away, retreating to her desk to a fanfare of congratulations from her colleagues.

David made his exit with a final thanks, and I took the floor, reiterating everything he'd said about their hard work and how impressed I'd been with their attitude and dedication over a tough start to the programme.

I sought out every pair of eyes, every eager smile, thanking all of them personally and individually, finding something worthwhile to say for every one of them.

Until I came to Verity's empty chair.

I scanned the desks, back and forth, trying to locate her amongst the others, but she was nowhere to be seen.

I set everyone the task of grabbing a coffee and an informal discussion amongst themselves before the week wound up early, and I headed out to the kitchen, and further to the toilets. Still there was no sign of her. Her bag was still in the footwell of her desk, her scarf still draped over her chair, and a glance through the front window showed her sporty little Audi still in her parking space.

A couple of admin girls were chatting by the photocopier in the corridor outside, and I asked if they'd seen her.

About ten minutes ago. They pointed to the stationery storage and server rooms. *Went that way.*

I found little princess Verity behind a stack of envelope boxes, crouched on the floor with her face in her hands, sobbing her heart out like the whole world was ending. I dropped to a crouch beside her, and she let out a ghastly wail.

"Go away!" she said. "Please, just go away!"

But that's not my style.

I waited until the sobs eased off a little, waited until she pulled her hands from her face and stared at me with puffy eyes.

"Do you want to talk about it?"

She shook her head.

I dropped to my ass, indicating I wasn't going anywhere. "If this is about the leaderboard, you needn't be so hard on yourself. You've had some great conversations this week, I've heard you. You'll get your lead any day now, you just didn't get your break today."

"I can't do it!" she cried. "I just can't!"

"You can," I said. "I know you can. You've worked hard, you're doing well. Sometimes the results don't come in, it can be bad luck, pure and simple."

Her face crumpled like a scared little girl, and Verity's bluster was all gone. She looked like a child again, the girl I'd seen in her pigtails all those years ago. "She's going to ruin my life!"

"Katie?"

She nodded. "He loves her more than me!"

Her words took me aback. "That's not true," I said. "Your father loves you very much."

"Not like he loves her!" She wiped her tears on the back of her hand. "*Be nice to your sister, Verity, share your things with your sister, Verity. Make sure Katie has a good time, Verity. Let Katie choose which horse she wants to ride, Verity. Make sure you give her first choice, Verity. Why don't you wear your hair like Katie, Verity? Katie's so pretty, Katie's so nice, Katie's so fucking clever and cute and sweet and blonde and fucking wonderful, Verity.*"

"I'm sure things weren't like that," I said. "I'm sure that isn't how your father intended them."

She shook her head. "She turned up and it was all about Katie, sweet little Katie. He was working too hard to spend time with us, but when it was time to pick up little Katie he was always right there, driving over to get her and bringing her back like a little doll. *Katie, Katie, Katie.* Did Katie have a good time? Did you play nicely? Did you share?" She scowled. "And what about me?! What about *me* having a good time?"

The idea that Verity was shunned in favour of a younger sister she hadn't known of until she was ten was quite ridiculous, I was certain of it, but Verity's eyes weren't lying. Her outburst was raw and real, and full of bitterness.

Whatever the real situation was, this was how she'd seen it. How she still saw it.

"Now she's better than me at the office, and Dad will love her even more!"

I shook my head. "No. He won't. He loves both of you."

"I wanted to do better than her! That way he'd know I was better than her! Even if I'm not the pretty one with blonde hair! Even if I'm not the cutest one! The sweetest one!" The tears came thick and fast. "She's... she's... she's better than me!"

So much I wanted to say. So many things to put her outlook in perspective, but I decided against it. The girl was wired and hysterical, far too worked up to be rational.

I couldn't talk sense into her about her childhood post Katie, not just like that, but I could help her make the best of things now.

I took her elbow, pulled her to her feet, and for the first time in my life I reached out to Verity Faverley and wrapped my arm around her shoulders while she cried.

"Nobody is better than anyone," I said. "We're all just people."

"She is…"

"She probably feels the same about you, have you ever thought about that?"

She shook her head. "She doesn't. She wants all my things, my dad, too."

I smiled. "I know for a fact that isn't true," I said. "She's just trying to do her job so she can go and meet that horse whisperer guy, just the same as you are."

"You would say that," she said. "You love her, too. It's obvious. You can't stop staring at her." Her lip went again. "Even gay men love perfect little Katie."

I didn't attempt to explain or deny, just let out a sigh, and hugged her a little bit tighter. "I'll help," I said. "Monday morning we'll do some extra coaching."

"We will?" she said.

"We will. But this has to stop, all this hate and bitterness, for both of you."

"But she…"

"No," I said. "It has to stop." I met her eyes, forced her to meet my gaze. "Say you'll try."

"I don't think I can…"

"Try, Verity, you just have to *try*. That's all. Just *try*. Give it a shot."

She held off for long seconds, halfway between scowling and sobbing, and then she sighed, her lip trembling.

"Alright," she said. "I'll *try*. Just make sure I sell something so Dad doesn't hate me." Her tone softened. "Please."

I held out my hand. "That's a deal," I said.

Chapter EIGHTEEN

CARL

"Aren't you going to open that?" I tipped my head towards the golden envelope she'd tossed on the dashboard like junk mail.

She shrugged. "Dunno. Probably not."

I turned out of the business park, pulling into the traffic queue. Rush hour. Gridlock. "You earned it, you should open it."

"I don't want *anything* from him. Except my Harrison Gables trip. That's the only reason I'm here."

"The *only* reason?" I shot her a smile. "You're telling me you didn't enjoy today just a little bit? Didn't enjoy putting your ticks on the board?" I paused. "Don't you enjoy our little lunchtime chats?"

She tutted at me. "Alright, *yes*, I enjoy *some* things. I still don't want his shitty envelope, though."

"Fine," I said, and reached over to take it. "I'll save it for Monday, give it to the next person to get a tick on the board." She shot me a look and it said it all. I laughed, dropped it in her lap. "Open it," I said.

She poked her tongue out, and then she opened it.

"Well?" I prompted.

She cast it back onto the dash. "Vouchers. Some posh clothes shop I'll never visit in a million years."

"Why won't you?"

"It's not me."

"Why isn't it?"

She shrugged. "It's just not. I'm not Verity. I don't do all polished and preened and pompous."

"You don't do pompous," I agreed. "Polished and preened, however. You do those very nicely."

"Thanks." She smiled. "I'm still not going."

I didn't push it, just smiled to myself as she took the voucher from the dash and slipped it into her bag. "He's very proud of you." I looked over at her. "As am I."

"My second call was lucky."

I shook my head. "No, it wasn't. I heard it."

"You did?"

"I did." I reached over and squeezed her knee. "I mean it, Katie, I'm very proud. You should be, too."

"You helped me," she said. "A lot. Thanks."

"I helped everyone, but it was you who put those ticks on the board. *You.*"

Finally, for the first time since the awkward hug with her father, she gave me a proper smile. It started at her eyes and went all the way down to the fingers that squeezed mine. "I did it, I really did it, didn't I?"

"You did, yes."

"And Verity didn't."

The warmth in my gut turned cold. "This isn't about Verity, this is about you."

"I know," she said. "But still. *I* did and *she* didn't. I bet she's seething. I bet she can't believe the *idiot* sister nailed it and she didn't."

I edged the car forward as the traffic lights changed up ahead, debated how much to say. "Verity has her issues, Katie, but I don't believe for a second she's written you off as an idiot. Far from it."

"Oh, she has," she said. "It's all she's ever said to me. *Stupid, pathetic, nobody wants you. Idiot.*"

"Plenty of people have a front. It's often the most insecure of us who lash out the hardest."

She laughed. "Verity?! Insecure?! No way. She's so full of herself I'm surprised she fits her pouty little head through the door."

"She didn't seem so full of herself this afternoon, Katie. She was quite upset."

I watched her reactions, watched her shoulders tense up and her lips tighten. "Good. Maybe it brought her down a peg or two."

"Stop," I said. "You aren't a bitter person. Don't let success make you someone you're not. You're so much better than that."

She looked like I'd struck her. "I didn't... I'm not... that's not what I meant..." She turned her shoulders towards me. "It's just her, Carl, she makes me like this. I'm not gloating. I'd never gloat."

I didn't say a word, just waited, watching the cogs turning behind her pretty eyes.

"She was upset?"

"She's taken it hard, not getting a lead this week. She worked for it, just the same as everyone else did. Just the same as you did."

"That's what she said? That she's upset about not getting a lead in?"

"Amongst other things."

She turned her attention back to the road in front. "She's manipulative, game playing, spoiled. She's never sincere. She'll say whatever she wants you to hear."

"I'm a bit long in the tooth to be taken in by all that, Katie. Give me some credit."

"I know," she said. "It's just her. I know her."

"As do I."

She sighed. "I know. Sorry."

I'd ruined her mood. I could see it in her posture, in her eyes. It was the last thing I'd wanted. I reached out, smoothed a stray tuft of hair behind her ear. "Enough of all that," I said. "It's your special day. What do you want to do to celebrate? I'll take you anywhere, do anything you want. My treat."

Her smile came back. "You will?"

"It will be my pleasure."

I should have guessed her response a clear mile away.

"Samson," she said. "I'd like to see my furry boy. I've missed him so much." My stomach panged to see the emotion in her eyes. "I could get some riding in, if we're quick."

"As the lady wishes," I said.

We called Rick to see if he could join us, but he was still on his way back from a client sign-off in Weston.

Fuck, he groaned. *One day out and it's the day I have to miss the big celebration.*

"We'll celebrate later," Katie said. "No biggie."

It will be a biggie, he said, and his voice was dripping dirty. I watched her shift in her seat, and it made my dick hard.

I smiled as the call wrapped up.

263

"Just us, then."

"Just us." She smiled back. "Hope you won't be too bored."

"I'll be far from bored," I said. I indicated to change lanes, aiming to cut out the Cheltenham traffic seeing as we didn't have to swing by the house for Rick. "Do you have some clothes, at the stable? It'll save time."

She grinned as the traffic eased off, our route clearing. "We can stop at mine, it won't take a minute. I can grab some jodhpurs. I have another pair of boots there." She paused, stared out of the window. "Mum will be home."

"Is that a problem? I can wait in the car."

She shook her head. "You don't have to. Unless you want to."

The idea of meeting her mother gave me a strange thrill. I shot her a smirk. "Will I do? Am I dressed well enough to impress?"

She smirked back, reached over to smooth my tie. "Always."

Katie lived on a regular little street in Much Arlock. A row of terraced houses with matching front doors and little front gardens. Hers was on the end. Another old Ford was parked outside, but this one was smaller. Her mother's I guessed.

My hands were surprisingly clammy as I parked up behind it.

Katie unclipped her seatbelt and jumped out. "I'll be a minute," she said, grinning at me through the open door. "Are you coming?"

Yes, I was coming.

I followed her to the front door, looking all around me as she fumbled with a jangle of keys. She pushed the door open with a creak.

"Mum, it's me, just grabbing some clothes!" she called. She kicked off her heels and dumped the keys on the side.

It was a nice enough place. A worn green carpet along the

264

hallway. A couple of kid's paintings in frames on the wall. *Katie Smith, age 7. Katie Smith, age 9.* One that was just a tiny handprint. *Katie Smith, age 3.* There was also a framed photograph, *Mum and Me,* the frame said. Katie, smiling in a crocheted cardigan, one of those colourful threaded braids in her hair. Her arm around a woman who looked just like her. I knew the place. I'd been there myself, my only holiday. I recognised the waterslide in the background.

Katie climbed a couple of stairs, shouted up. "Mum, are you there?"

I had the strangest urge to snoop around, track my way upstairs and look at her bedroom. I had another urge, too. The urge to bury my cock in her on her own turf. Make her mine in her own bed. Sleep in her bed, amongst her things, amidst her regular life.

I heard footsteps on the landing. "I was in the shower, won't be a minute."

"I've got a visitor," Katie called, and she was smiling.

"A visitor?" the voice called. "Holly? Is that you?"

A little blush on Katie's cheeks. "No, Mum, it's not Holly." She turned to me. "Friend from school," she whispered.

We waited what felt like an age until the footsteps started up again. I took a breath, prepared the smile.

The woman who came down the stairs was a real stunner, just like her daughter. Her blonde curls were still wet, and she was wearing nothing but a simple t-shirt over jeans. No makeup, but she didn't need any. Her eyes were blue and her smile was broad. Same freckles.

She held out a hand. "Debbie," she said. "Katie's mum."

"Carl," I said, and left it at that. I shook her hand firmly.

Katie looked at me, eyes wide and a little unsure. "Carl's my

265

boss," she said, and my heart dropped a little. "And a friend."

Her mum raised an eyebrow at her. "Friend?"

"Friend. Close friend."

"Your daughter's doing very well," I said. "Two leads today, topped the leaderboard."

That made Debbie Smith smile with her eyes. "Well done, Kate," she said, and squeezed her tight. "I'm so proud." She turned her attention back to me. "So, friend-boss Carl. Has Katie offered you a drink?"

"No need," I said. "I think we'll be off soon. Quick change of clothes."

"Samson," Katie explained.

"How awfully nice of your boss to take time out to go and see your horse on a Friday evening." Her eyes were suspicious, and there was an edge to her gaze.

"Friend," Katie said again. "Good friend."

"I'm glad Katie is doing well at the office," she said. "I'm glad she has the opportunity."

"She's excelling," I told her. "Working very hard, and it's paying off."

"And you're Katie's direct boss are you?"

"For the duration of the training programme."

She was weighing me up, I could feel it. I ignored the niggle in my gut.

"I'll get changed," Katie said, and my urge to follow her up came to nothing. I felt rooted to the spot.

Both her mother and I watched her climb the stairs, I heard a door open and then close at the top. And then her mother cast her verdict.

"You're the *special someone*," she said, and it wasn't a question. "The special someone *and* her boss. In my experience the two don't mix, and Katie needs this opportunity. She deserves the opportunity to do well for herself."

"Katie is doing very well for herself, I have no intention of that changing."

"All good intentions," she said, and it was barbed. "Do you have kids? Married? Divorced?"

"No," I said, and my throat was dry. "And neither."

She gave me a little nod. "Ok, Carl. That's good to hear." Her eyes seared mine. "You know Katie's Dad?"

"I know David very well."

"Then I trust you'll help Katie make the best of the situation. For her sake, not his."

"I'll help Katie make the best of whatever situation she finds herself in. In this instance, for David's sake as well as hers. He cares very much for her."

"Yes," she said. "I'm sure he does." Her smile was back at full radiance by the time Katie made her reappearance, and I made sure to smile, too. I held out a hand.

"Pleasure to meet you, Debbie."

She shook my hand and it was firmer this time, pointed. "Same to you, Carl."

But I wasn't so sure.

"Let's go," Katie said, and she seemed oblivious. "I want to hit some jumps, it's been a while."

She led the way, and I followed without a backward look. It felt so much more airy outside. I breathed it in, bleeped the Range, feeling Debbie's gaze burning into my back.

267

Katie jumped in and waved her mother goodbye as we pulled away. I held up a hand, gave a smile, nothing too bright.

"Sorry," she said. "I didn't know what to say. Boss came in my head first, then friend."

"Is that the order you think of them?"

She laughed. "No, definitely not."

My stomach was niggling again. "And that's what we are? Close friends?"

"Aren't we?"

"I'm asking you."

"I don't know what we are," she admitted, and there was an awkwardness to it. "I mean, we're friends, I know that. You're my boss. You're Rick's boyfriend. And you and Rick have a thing, a *proper* thing. I'm not sure what that makes us."

"What do you want it to make us?" I pulled away from Katie's street and felt so much better.

She shrugged. "That's a question and a half, Carl. I don't know how you want me to answer that off the cuff."

"With honesty," I said. "It's not a hard question, you must know how you feel."

"I like you, if that's what you mean. I like you both, a lot."

"You *like* us?"

"Like you, enjoy your company, enjoy your dicks," she laughed but I didn't. She stopped. "I really like you guys. You're funny and you're smart, and kind, and different, and great in bed."

"But you're in it for the cash," I said. "It's alright, I get it."

Her eyes burned me. "No," she said, and there was fire in it. "I'm not just *in it for the cash*. I hardly think about the cash." She sighed. "If I didn't have a dream and no way to pay for it, I wouldn't even *want* the cash."

"So, what *do* you want?"

She pointed out the sign for Woolhope. "I want to see my baby boy," she said. "That's what I want."

"Fine," I said. "I can take a hint." I reached for her knee and her hand was waiting. "Onwards, to the furry beast. We'll pick this conversation up another time."

The furry beast seemed bigger without Rick there too. Bigger and clumsier. He threw his head up, ears pricked as he followed Katie along to the stable block. I nipped ahead of him, avoiding his clomping feet, playing it cool even though the brute made me uneasy.

Katie could tell my unease regardless. "Relax," she said. "He's totally fine." She offered me the lead rope. "Take it if you want, you'll see."

"I'm ok as I am for now," I said.

"So am I," she said, and leaned in to kiss my cheek. "That's what I should have said in the car. I'm happy, Carl, with everything. For now."

"For now?"

She nodded. "For now, yeah. We're good. All of us. I like it."

I wanted to say so much. Spill my load in more ways than one. The need to lay it all out slept uneasily in the pit of me. I could wake it with just a touch, and it would spring into life and come rolling out. And it would plough into her, and maybe she'd run. Just like the others.

"I like it, too. Very much."

"Good," she said. "Then we're good, right?"

I wrapped my arm around her waist. "We're good."

She tethered Samson to a loop of twine outside his stable door. "Surely he could break that?" I asked.

"That's the point," she said. "If he got freaked, or spooked or whatever, he could break the twine. He wouldn't hurt himself."

"Nice to know," I said, imagining that flimsy bit of nothing doing sweet fuck all if the brute decided to go for me.

He was still eyeballing me, still hostile. Even chomping on hay he was eyeballing me. She picked up his feet one by one, held them between her thighs as she scraped the mud out of them. Rather her than me.

I wished Rick was with us, making her laugh with his easy conversation. He'd know what to say, what to do. He'd do this *what's going on* conversation so much more casually than I could. Probably because he wouldn't do it at all.

Katie saddled up, fastened up her helmet. She was all smiles.

"Do you need a leg up or something?" I asked, but she shook her head.

She hoisted herself up easily, swinging a leg across his back and mounting up without a second's hesitation. She shortened her stirrups, and took up the reins, and they were off, pacing back the way we'd come.

"Could you get the gate?" She pointed to the side of the wood-chipped arena. "That one."

I dashed in front of them and did what she asked. She trotted on through, rising and falling in the saddle, her thighs so toned I could see the definition of her through her jodhpurs.

She pointed at the jumps laid out around the field. Poles of red and white, yellow and white. Some high, some doubles, some just poles on the floor. One of the arrangements had toppled.

I ran to it before she asked, propped it back up to height.

She thanked me. My suit definitely didn't.

I leaned against the fence at a safe distance and watched. I watched everything, soaking her in. Samson's easy gait as she warmed him up, long loops around the outside, figures of eight through the jumps. I watched the way she moved, the sophisticated freedom in her posture. The smile on her face, the concentration as she turned him, guided him.

She was a picture.

A swan on water, in her element, bursting with joy.

I could watch her forever.

My heart thumped as she took the first jump, but the horse leapt it easily. She rose and fell, freeing up the reins as he needed them, then patted his neck, squeezed her legs to his sides to encourage him onwards. They took another jump and it was magical. A third and I was addicted. Feeling the rhythm in his hooves, the duh-duh-duh, duh-duh-duh, duh-duh-duh, and then the silence as he leapt, the thump of his landing, and back to the duh-duh-duh.

I was smiling as they jumped a double, two in quick succession. Willing her forwards, loving the way they moved as one.

I could love this, watching her.

I could fall in love with this.

She gave Samson a big pat when they'd done enough, and her cheeks were rosy as she walked him around the field, his head hanging low, reins long and loose in her hands. He was sweaty at the neck, and smelled of leather and beast as she walked him close by. I opened the gate for them, and they passed me close enough that I could feel the heat of him, heading back up to the stable block.

I followed, and she stared over her shoulder, leaning back on his rump.

"What do you think?" she asked. "Were we good?"

"Amazing," I said. "Seriously. It was amazing."

"It's taken a long time." She smiled. "He was green when he arrived, jumped too big. Nervous."

"He didn't look nervous today."

"He's not anymore," she said. "He trusts me. He knows me."

"The beauty of experience," I said. "In becoming comfortable with each other."

She dismounted and tethered him, taking off his saddle as he rummaged in the hay net. "We're competing in the Cheltenham Chase in August," she said. "The only course this summer."

"I'm sure you'll do very well," I said, and I meant it.

"I hope so." Her eyes met mine. "Verity is doing it, too, on some posh fancy horse her daddy paid a fortune for."

"And that's why you're doing it?"

She shrugged. "Maybe a little. I want to win."

"It's a slippery slope," I said. "Competing with just one person. It never ends up pleasantly, even if you win."

"Still," she said. "I want to win." A rumble of a truck sounded in the distance and she dashed along the path. "It's Jack," she said. "Finally! I haven't seen him in aaages!" She picked up Samson's saddle, handed it to me with his bridle. Sweaty leather slammed into my suit jacket, but she didn't notice, she was too keen to go. "Can you put this in the tack room, please? And keep an eye on Samson? I won't be long."

I nodded, but I doubt she even saw me. She was already rushing away.

She was gone a while. Long enough that the furry brute finished up his hay, even the scraggly bits that had dropped to the floor. He blew out a sigh and looked around the place, straining on his rope as he looked towards the farmhouse.

"Steady," I said. "Don't go breaking that twine." As though the beast would understand me.

His eyes met mine and they were dark and curious, and hostile. Still hostile.

His ears flicked about, this way and that, his tail swishing idly at the flies.

I dared to take a step forward. "Hey, boy. Good boy."

I reached out a hand, but he tossed his head away. It freaked me out enough to step back again, but the action pained me, frustrated me.

And then it hit me.

I wanted the animal to like me.

Ridiculous, but true.

I wanted him to like me, so that she'd like me. Because he was important.

"Hey," I said again. "Who's a good boy?"

His eyes bored into me. I took a breath and a step forward, and this time I kept my hand out, even when he moved his head away. "Who's a good boy? A friendly boy?" I kept my tone light. "Hey, boy, please don't savage me, hey? Don't trample me."

I placed a hand on his neck and he was hot and sweaty, but soft. My heart thumped.

"Good boy."

I patted him, as though I knew what I was doing. He didn't move, just stared.

Please, I willed. *Please, just like me. Please.*

I took deep breaths, gentle steps, until I was close to his side. His ears kept flicking, his weight shifting on his feet.

"Good boy, Samson, that's a good boy."

He tossed his head again as I placed a hand on his face, and I pulled away but only a fraction.

"Please," I whispered. "Please just give me a chance, boy."

When I put my hand out again he stayed still, and my heart leapt in my chest. I placed my hand on his nose, and he snorted, snuffled. He snuffled me, his nose in my pockets. And then he butted me, like he'd butted Katie.

And I wasn't scared.

"Good boy!" I said, and wished I had fucking mints. I wished I had a whole truckload of fucking mints.

He butted me again, and I rubbed his ears, and he didn't mind.

I felt the connection, beast to man, man to beast. He'd taken my measure and I'd done alright. I'd passed whatever horsey paces he'd put me through.

"Good boy, Samson, that's a good boy."

I stroked the white stripe on his face and he didn't flinch.

Didn't move when I wrapped my arms around his neck and gave the beast a hug, caring fuck all for my suit.

"That's it," I whispered. "Friends now."

It felt seriously fucking good.

I was still petting the brute when I heard Katie's footsteps on the path. I turned to face her with a smile, patting the horse like we were best fucking buddies.

My stomach was tight and tickly, and a little bit excited, and my heart was full of life.

"He likes me," I said. "He actually fucking likes me!"

My eyes met hers, hoping for approval and joy and excitement to match mine, but there was nothing of the sort.

Katie's eyes were puffy and sad. Her cheeks reddened from tears.

"What?" I said, dropping the horse hugs and heading straight for her. "What the hell happened?"

She struggled to speak at first, just took my arms and gripped them with tense fingers. She shook her head and another tear fell.

"Talk to me," I said. "What is it?"

She took a gulp of air that sounded like a sob.

"It's Jack," she said. "The bank... the bank are repossessing, threatening to close the business..." Another tear, and a proper sob this time. "He's selling the land, he's got no choice. He's got to sell it, the stables, the yard. All of it."

"Ok," I said. "It's alright."

But she was shaking her head. "It's not alright," she said. "My dream is over. It's gone. It's all fucking gone."

And then she cried.

She really fucking cried.

Chapter
NINETEEN

CARL

She didn't let me hold her, just brushed her tears aside and busied herself with Samson. I helped as best I could, helping her brush him down before putting his rug on, opening gates, holding a hosepipe while the water trough was filling, but I don't believe she even noticed. Her thoughts were far away, eyes brimming with tears as they stared into the distance.

I could feel her dreams breaking.

And mine were in my throat, desperate to reach out and grab hers and hold the cracks together.

I watched Samson make his way back down the field, calling out to his horsey friends before he took off into a run, but for once Katie didn't linger. She was already off, head collar in hand, trudging back across the yard towards the car.

I caught her up, but she said nothing, just hung the collar on its hook by Samson's stable and gathered up the hosepipe.

"Home?" I said, and she nodded. She climbed up into the Range and clipped her belt, and her breath was shallow and ragged. I pulled away from the yard, keeping slow along the lane.

The silence was loud. Too loud.

"It's that bad?" I said. "No room to negotiate? They won't give him any leeway?"

She shook her head. "They've given him all they were willing to give. I was too late."

"Too late?"

"I hoped I'd have enough money to pay six months' rent up front. Jack needed the cash for the bank."

"But that's no longer an option?"

Her lip trembled a little. "I think it was always a longshot. Wishful thinking, both of us. He couldn't make the business work on his own. I just hoped…" Her voice trailed off.

Wishful thinking, maybe, but the girl looked broken. She chewed on her knuckles as the car rumbled on, and the need in me boiled over, exploded. I pulled into a turning, *Haugh Wood* the sign read. A parking area virtually empty. I pulled up, turned off the engine, and Katie stared at me.

"What are we…?"

"It's your dream?" I asked. "This place? This *particular* place? This yard?"

She nodded. "Stupid really." She was breathy, her voice a wisp. "I have it all planned out, everything. I know where I'd put the field shelters, how I'd fix up the school, where I'd set up a proper jumping course. I know this place, I know the people. I've got a list of kids who want lessons, a list of kids who can't afford it but want to help out anyway." She met my eyes. "I wanted it so bad. I *want* it so bad."

"What about other yards? You could rent somewhere else, no?"

She shrugged. "Maybe. I dunno. I guess. It's all the unknown." Her eyes welled up again. "This place just feels special to me. The place I had my first horse, the place Samson and I found our feet." She pointed to a track at the far end of the parking area. "We hack through these woods all the time. I know every path, every hill, every turn. I love it here. I love everything about this place."

I sighed, my hands on the steering wheel. "How much does he need? How much is he selling the land for?"

She laughed a sad little laugh. "Too much. I don't even know, a couple of hundred grand. Too much to worry about."

And I said it. I just fucking said it. "I could buy it."

Silence. Then a laugh. More like a snort. "You what?"

"I'm serious," I said. "I could buy it for you. A couple of hundred grand, I could do that. It could be an investment, the land wouldn't lose its value. I have enough capital."

Wide eyes stared at me. "Why would you buy it? You don't even like horses."

"No." I turned to her. "I don't like horses, but I'm here anyway. I don't even like the outdoors, I don't like mud, I don't like the smell of animal shit, the thought of trekking through open fields really doesn't turn me on. But I'm here. Because of you. Because I like *you*."

"I like you, too," she said. "But you can't buy Jack's land, that's... that's insane. I couldn't pay you back. I have no idea when I could pay you back. Probably never." I could see the thoughts piling up behind her eyes, her head shaking as she worked through them.

"You wouldn't need to. I wouldn't expect you to."

"Then why? Why would you?" She held up her hands. "And at the end of six months, what? What even happens? What if we call it quits and move on? What happens then, when you own my yard and you

278

don't want it anymore?"

"That wouldn't happen."

She raised her eyebrows. "How do you know? Anything could happen. And then you'd own a yard you never even wanted and I'd owe you everything."

"Or you'd be happy, and I'd be happy, and Rick would be happy. We could be happy, Katie. How about that?"

She took a breath. "A couple of hundred grand for a few years, you said. The other week, in the car, what did you mean?"

I felt a shiver down my spine. "That doesn't matter now. That has nothing to do with this."

"It has everything to do with this," she said. "You're offering me a couple of hundred grand, just like that, you say it's so I can be happy. So *we* can be happy. What does happy even look like to you, Carl? What do you want from me?"

I sighed, gripped the steering wheel. "It's just an offer. You want the yard, I can buy it. That's all."

She shook her head. "People don't just go around buying hundreds of thousands of pounds worth of gifts to be *happy*, Carl. In the car, you said a couple of years, you said it was an option. That's what you wanted from me, that's what you implied. Is that still what you want? Because if that's on the table, if that's really what this is about... a few years in exchange for the yard... I mean, I dunno... if that's what it meant... maybe I could..."

I closed my eyes. "Don't do this, Katie. It was a simple offer. This isn't the right time for this."

"For what?" I heard her shift in her seat. "What isn't this the right time for?"

Six months, Carl. Just give it time, man. Chill the fuck out.

Katie's breath was loud. "I mean, if you want me to guarantee this... *arrangement* we have, for a couple of years... I could do that... I wouldn't even mind..." I listened to her breathing, listened to her thinking. "But even at the current rate... two hundred grand... that's like six years or something..." She sighed. "Anything could happen in six years. How do you know you'd even want that? *Do* you want that?"

I shook my head. "I don't want to pay you to be in a relationship with us for six years, Katie."

She laughed, but it was nervous. "I know, I mean, that would be stupid. Six years, that's crazy. That's like... silly, right?"

I opened my eyes. Looked at her. "I want you to be in a relationship with us because you *want* to be in a relationship with us. I hope that lasts six years. I hope it lasts longer. I hope it *lasts*, Katie."

She was quiet. So quiet.

"I want..." I fought for the right words. "I want us, all three of us... to work... I want." I sighed.

"Just say it," she said. "You always just say it, right? Why not now?"

Because of Rick.

Because you'll run.

Because I don't want you to run.

She shrugged. "How can I know what you're offering if you won't tell me? I can't think straight if I don't know what I'm thinking about! This is... it hurts my brain... I just can't..."

"Just think about the yard," I said. "Do you want it, or not?"

"But it's not about the yard, is it? You want something from me. You've always wanted something from me."

"It doesn't matter," I said. "It's not about what I want. It's about your dream."

"Tell me," she insisted. "What's *your* dream? What does *happy* mean? Just tell me, Carl!"

"A baby," I said. "I want you to have my baby. That's what *happy* means." I sighed. "I dream about being a father."

Her eyes widened. Like they always do. I kept talking. Like I always do.

"I'm forty in December, Katie. I'll be a forty year old man in a gay relationship with no family in sight." I sighed again. "I want what most people want. I want a home, I want a family, I want to watch a little person grow up, I want the school visits, and Christmas mornings, and family holidays. I want to watch kids TV until it drives me insane. I want to know the words to all the crappy cartoon songs." I stared at the trees. "I want to be a dad. I want Rick to be a dad. That's what I want. That's *my* dream."

"A baby in exchange for the yard? A couple of hundred grand for me to... breed for you?" I could hear the disgust in her voice, the undertone of horror, even though she tried to hide it.

I spun in my seat, met her eyes. "Christ, no! I'm not some fucking human trafficker trying to buy a fucking baby through *Sugar Daddy Match Up*. I've looked into surrogacy, *we've* looked into that. *Actual* surrogacy. We could do *that*. *That* isn't *this*. *This* isn't *that*."

"So, what is *this*?"

"This is me saying I want a proper family. An actual family, for the long haul. I want to love someone who can love us, *both* of us. I want to pick out nursery wallpaper with the mother of my child, I want her to live with us, I want to hold her hand at the birth, I want to go to bed with her every night. I want to watch my baby grow up with her, with *us*." I paused. "I want that someone to be you, Katie."

"And you'll buy me Jack's yard if it is?"

I shook my head. "I'll buy you Jack's yard because it's your dream, not because you'll give me a baby in return."

"But that's the hope, right? We swap dreams? You buy me mine, I'll give you yours?" Her eyes were piercing.

"No. That's not how I see it. That's not how I mean it."

"But that's how it is. You said a couple of years. That's for what? Conception, pregnancy, birth... breastfeeding, I guess... then, what? It doesn't work out? What's your plan then? I leave the baby with you and Rick? Disappear? Or I end up stuck as a single mother? You swing by every weekend, maybe take it on holiday, buy it a new bike, whatever..."

"I really don't have it planned out like that."

"But you have *everything* planned out," she said. "That's who you are. You must know how the story goes, Carl. You must have known before you even met me. This is why they didn't work out, right? The others? They didn't want the baby thing, just the sex?"

"Amongst other things." I stared at her. "They didn't work out because they weren't right."

"But I am?"

"I hope so." I smiled, but she didn't smile back. "Katie, you turned up and you were everything we'd hoped for. More than we hoped for. More than *I* hoped for. Maybe with the others... maybe I was more..." I shrugged. "One track minded. Maybe it was less about them and more about the dream... maybe I wanted it beyond all other things. Maybe I wanted it so much it consumed me. Maybe that scared them."

"And this time?"

Please believe me. "This time it's about you. *Us.* This time it's about *your* dreams, what you want, what will make you happy. I'll buy you the yard because I *can*, because it's what *you* want. Because I want a future, with you and Rick. Because you're important."

Her lip trembled. "But I don't want a baby, Carl. I don't think I can give you that. I've never wanted a baby."

"I know," I said, and smiled. "We saw. On your Facebook profile. Some stupid quiz, *how many kids will you end up with? Katie Smith, none. Thank fuck for that*, you said. *I never ever want kids*, you said. *Horses over babies, always,* you said. Rick showed me, printed it out."

"And that's how I feel."

I swallowed, throat tight. "That could change…"

She shook her head. "I want a riding school, I want to ride, I want to event. I can't do that with a baby. Unless… unless you're talking ten years away… I just don't know…"

But I wasn't talking ten years away. I wasn't talking about being a dad approaching retirement age while his kid is still in nappies.

It must have shown all over my face.

Her eyes were so big. "You really wanted this straight away, didn't you? That's what you wanted?" She sighed. "Oh God, you want it now. When were you going to tell me?"

"Six months," I said honestly. "Rick and I agreed six months, until you knew us, until you stood a chance of knowing what you wanted."

"I want what I always wanted," she said. "A yard, a riding school, time with Samson…"

"And that's it?"

"No," she said. "I love being with you guys. I think about it sometimes, when I'm alone. How this could work, whether it could work. Whether I could be with two men. Properly, I mean."

"And what was your conclusion?"

She shrugged. "It doesn't matter now. You want a baby. That's what you want, Carl, don't pretend it isn't."

"I want you and Rick," I said. "I want you to be happy. I want us to be a family."

"With a baby, Carl. With a baby. That's what you need to make you happy."

I couldn't argue with that.

She leaned forward in her seat. "This is all too much. The yard... all this work stuff... my dad, Verity... you and Rick... a baby... it's too much to think about."

"I didn't mean to force this on you right now," I said. "I just wanted to buy you the yard, that's all I wanted."

"I couldn't take the yard. Not unless I could give you what you wanted in return. Maybe not even then."

"This has nothing to do with what I want. It has everything to do with how I feel about you." I reached out a hand, but she flinched as it landed. "We both adore you, Katie. We think you're incredible. Kind, and beautiful, and funny. Smart."

"Please stop..." she said. "I just can't..." She rubbed her temples. "I need to think this through. I'm upset about the yard, upset for Jack. I just need some space."

Space.

"I can give you space," I said. "Let's go home. I won't mention it again, any of it. You can think. We can watch some movies, eat, get an early night... whatever you want."

She shook her head. "Space, Carl. I just need my own bed. I need to talk to my mum. Probably cry a bit, get it out of my system. You know?"

I knew. Of course I knew.

I made myself smile. "Sure. I'll take you home."

I drove in silence and my heart was thumping. So many words I wanted to say, but I'd already said too much. Way too fucking much.

I pictured Rick, waiting at home, waiting for us. He'd be excited, ready to congratulate Katie on an awesome week, and I'd show up alone.

Because I'd blown it. Again.

Because she needed *space*.

Because, no matter what I said, she was equating my offer of a yard with the need to give me a baby. She was adding it up, working it out, wondering how often I looked at her and saw a womb for sale.

And the answer was I didn't. Not at all.

Not anymore.

We were outside hers so quickly.

"I could pick you up in the morning," I said. "Your car is at ours..."

She shook her head. "I can get a lift with Mum to the yard. I can sort out the car later."

She didn't unclip her seatbelt, and I almost wished she would, just to get this over with.

"I'm sorry, Carl."

They always are. Maybe they can see the desperation. Maybe that's why they're always so sorry.

"The offer of the yard still stands," I said. "You could rent it from me, just like you would Jack. That's what I was thinking. That's all I was thinking."

She leaned over and kissed my cheek, and her eyes were wet.

"You're so much nicer than I ever thought you would be."

"I don't know if that's a compliment."

She smiled. "It is."

"The same applies," I said.

She squeezed my hand. "Thank you. Your offer was very generous."

But you don't want it.

"Goodbye, Katie," I said.

She unclipped her seatbelt. Opened the door.

"Bye, Carl."

My heart fucking pained as she walked away. Pain and fear and panic at the thought of Rick's face as I walked through the door alone. His face as his calls rang to her voicemail, all because I'd spoken too soon.

Because he was right. He always is.

It was way too fucking soon.

I took a breath. Closed my eyes. Waited for my heart to stop fucking pounding.

She was staring at me as I opened them. Her face to the driver's window. It made me jump.

She tapped on the window and I lowered it.

"You said goodbye. Not bye, or see you, or catch you later. You said goodbye."

"Isn't it?"

She pulled a face. "Do you want it to be? Is that how you work? No baby, no more Carl or Rick?"

I shook my head. "No, of course not."

"Then it isn't goodbye," she said, and once again my blue-eyed girl surprised me. "I said I needed my own bed, to talk to my mum, maybe cry a bit. That's exactly what I meant."

"I hope so, Katie."

She ran a finger down my cheek. "You're quite a sensitive guy under that scary hot exterior, Carl Brooks."

"Is that a compliment, too?"

"It is," she said. "This isn't goodbye, it's see you later."

I put the car in gear, forced a smile.

"Then I'll be seeing you later, Katie."

"Yes," she said. "You will."

Chapter
TWENTY

CARL

I tried to hold on to her smile, cling tight to her *see you later*, but I'd been here too many times before. Every time I'd convince myself I wasn't gutted inside, that I wasn't feeling the clock ticking against my dream, that I wasn't aching at the thought that it might never happen for me.

But I couldn't convince myself this time.

She'd been right there, the one for us. I'd seen it in her smile. I'd heard it in her laugh. The way she'd fit so easily between us, so snug, so *there*. The way my heart raced when she called my name. The way her fingers felt for mine when no one was looking. The way I was so proud of her. So fucking proud.

Those moments I was deep inside her and wanted to stay there, with Rick, both of us together. Fill her up with my baby, *our* baby, and watch her grow big and beautiful, swollen and glowing with the new life inside her belly.

The way I looked into her eyes and saw a future. A future for all three of us, and the baby we could make together.

And I'd blown it. No matter what she said now, I'd truly blown it.

She'd be running scared, and who could blame her? What kind of desperate weirdo throws a few hundred grand at a young woman half his age and practically begs her to have his baby?

That's how she'd see it, no matter what I said. *Desperate*. That's how she'd see me. Because I was. I was desperate.

And it hurt so much more for loving her. For wanting *her* baby, not just *a* baby. Katie wasn't just a womb, wasn't just a pretty face and a smile. She wasn't like the others. She wasn't just a *Never mind, Carl, we'll try again, Carl. Just don't fuck it up next time, Carl. There's someone out there for us, Carl. We just have to find her, Carl. Keep your cool, Carl. Trust me, Carl, she's out there. She's fucking out there.*

Keep my fucking cool?

We'd found her. And *I'd* lost her.

I'd fucking lost her.

I gripped the steering wheel tight, and kept my attention on the road. I felt sick as I drew closer to Cheltenham, the prospect of telling Rick rolling around my gut. The sky turned grey and heavy, the road dull as it stretched ahead. And I stank, of horse and hay and the bitter stench of failure.

I took a breath as I parked up on our driveway, fumbling in my briefcase to delay the moment I'd have to step inside. I took another long breath as I turned the key in the front door, bracing myself for the inevitable.

Rick was already waiting. He was still suited and booted from his client meeting, his hair slick and trendy and his smile bright. A bright purple tie over a pale pink shirt. Matching purple brogues. He had a bottle of champagne in one hand and a balloon on a string in the other. The string was bright pink, the balloon a huge daisy. *Well done* it said on one side. *Good job* on the other. It twisted and bobbed against the ceiling, taunting me with the irony.

Rick glanced behind me, eyes sparkling, waiting. His smile dropped as I kicked the door shut.

"Where's our pretty lady?" he said. "I thought we were celebrating?"

I dropped my keys on the side. "She, um." I couldn't look at him. "She had bad news, about the yard."

He took a step forward, I could feel his eyes burning. "Shit! What bad news? Is she ok?"

"Yard is up for sale, bank repossession, or close to." I slipped off my jacket, hung it over the bottom of the stairs, fiddled with my cufflinks.

"So she can't rent it from Jack anymore? Bummer. That fucking stinks, man." He shook his head. "Talk about a shit end to the day. I bet she's fucking gutted."

The thought hit my belly, and it hit hard. "She was upset."

Rick paced a bit, dropped the champagne next to my keys. His hand was on his forehead, rubbing. "She should have come home with you, we could've talked about it, worked something out. There must be something we can do." He stared at me. "Maybe we could talk to the bank? With Jack, I mean. Find out what's owing. Back Katie up with the rent money, let the bank know he has the cash coming in to clear some debt. That could work, right? It's worth a shot." He pulled his phone from his pocket. "Is she still with Jack? I'll call her, tell her to come home."

He'd pressed the call button before he registered the truth. His phone to his ear before his eyes met mine and stayed there.

"Except she's not there, is she? You'd never just leave her there..." He cancelled the call, walked past me, opened the door. "Her car's still here. Why would she stay at the yard without a car, Carl? What's going on?"

I braced myself. "She needed space..."

And he knew. He fucking knew.

"What did you do?"

"She was upset. I tried to help."

He let go of the balloon, I heard it bop against the ceiling. "*Help*?"

I walked through to the kitchen and uncorked a bottle of red. He followed me, hands open wide, demanding.

I poured a glass, downed it in one. "I offered to buy the yard."

"You what?!"

"I offered to buy the yard, for her."

"How much?"

"Couple of big ones."

He shook his head. "Big ones? What the fuck does that even mean?"

I took a breath. "Couple of hundred grand."

His eyes were wide. "You offered to spend a couple of hundred grand on a riding yard? Just like that? Fucking hell, Carl. And what did she say to that?"

I shrugged. "She said no, said it was too much. Said it was crazy. She didn't understand why I'd offer, wanted to know why."

"No fucking shit. And what did *you* say?"

I didn't answer.

"Please tell me you didn't. Not like that. Not when her dreams have gone to shit and there's an offer of a crazy fucking bankroll swaying over her head. Please tell me you didn't fucking do that, Carl."

I had no words. I refilled my glass.

His face turned pale, a hand over his mouth, pacing back and forth. "You told her, didn't you? Fucking hell, Carl, you fucking told her."

"She wanted to know why. She wanted to know what I wanted. She wanted to *know*, Rick."

"And so you just told her. Great. That's fucking great."

"I'm sorry," I said, and I was. "I should have waited. I should have given it more time."

He slammed his palm on the island. "Too fucking right you should have waited, Carl! Too fucking right!" He let out a sigh that sounded more like a wail. "We had it *good*, Carl. She was *good*. She was amazing. She was everything we fucking wanted, everything *I* fucking wanted." He clenched his fists against the marble. "I fucking *love* her, Carl."

There were tears in his eyes and an ache in my stomach, a horrible pitiful pang of regret. "So do I."

He shook his head, eyes closed. "Tell me everything. Every fucking thing you said."

And so I did. I told him everything.

Rick listened and shook his head all the way through my sorry recap. His face said it all, reinforced what I already knew. I'd fucking blown it.

"She said it's not goodbye," I said. "She said it was a *see you later*, not a goodbye."

"She's going to say that, isn't she?" He grabbed himself a beer from the fridge, chugged it back. He pulled his tobacco from his pocket, rolled a cigarette. "I can't believe you did it. After everything we said."

"You can believe it," I said. "Of course you can. She asked, I answered."

He held up a hand, waved me to shut the fuck up. "I need a fucking smoke," he said, and left me. He let himself out through the back door, and the security light came on, illuminated him as he paced up and down the path. He smoked one and lit up another, and I watched, sipping wine in misery while he fumed.

He was outside for an age, pacing and smoking.

I'd moved to the living room by the time he came back in, my stomach paining worse than ever as reality set in.

He propped himself in the doorway, his face stripped of its easy charm. I sat forward in my seat, forced out the words I'd been churning around my mind.

"Her issues are with me, Rick, not you. It was all about what *I* wanted."

He shrugged. "So? What does that matter now?"

I met his eyes, holding the gaze even through the anger in his. "My point is you could... be with her. You two could still... without me... *I'm* the problem, Rick, I know I'm the problem. She knows it, too."

His lips were tight, eyes hollow and wide. "What the fuck are you trying to say?"

"I'm trying to say I'm sorry, that I don't want to ruin this for you, for either of you." It hurt so fucking bad to say it. "I'm saying you could be with her. You and her." I clasped my hands in my lap. "I'd understand, Rick. You shouldn't have to pay the price for my

293

mistakes."

I didn't want to look at him, turned my head away as he stepped towards me.

"Hey," he said, dropping to my side on the sofa. "What the hell is this?"

"I fucked up," I admitted, and my words came out choked.

"Probably," he said. "But we're together, you and me. We come together or not at all. That's never gonna change, Carl, no matter what." He pressed his hand to my cheek, turned my face to his. "Look at me."

I looked at him, and I felt defeated. Empty. Guilty.

"I'm pissed off, and fucking gutted, and think you're a dick for running your blunt fucking mouth off, but you're still the best fucking man I've ever known. You're still the one I want to be with. Christ, Carl, I still fucking love you."

I leaned forward, pressed my forehead to his, and his hands clasped my face, held me there. I closed my eyes, and breathed, just breathed. "It hurts," I said. "This one hurts so bad. I thought this one..."

"I know," he said. "I'm right fucking there with you." He sighed, long and deep. "Come here." He folded me in strong arms, pulled me close. He kissed my cheek, held me tight, and I held him back. I felt weak, exposed. Open. The dull ache in the pit of me making me nauseous. "You're so fucking strong," he said. "Like a bull. Always so fucking unstoppable." He kissed my mouth, his lips firm. "You've got to stop sometimes, you've got to learn to ease up on the fucking reins."

I didn't have any words left. I just nodded, just enough for him to see.

"We make decisions together, we're supposed to be a team."

"I'm sorry," I said again.

I squeezed him tight, my arms around his muscular shoulders, and he was rigid and strong, and there. Rick was right there with me.

Rick was always there.

And I loved him so much I thought my heart would burst.

Chapter
TWENTY ONE

Katie

Samson picked up pace as we headed up through Haugh Wood, his hooves churning up the track as he broke into a canter. We were early, the sun still climbing through the trees to the east. I squeezed Samson on, driving him faster, and he put his head down, ears forward and alert, breath steady. I gave him free rein and he extended himself, a snort and he was away, galloping up the main incline.

I loved it here so much. So did he.

We belonged here. I'd always known we belonged here.

Only we didn't.

Not anymore. Not now.

I fought the lump in my throat, blinked away the tears that threatened. Like I hadn't cried enough already.

A night in my own bed sucked bad. I'd never realised it was lumpy on one side. Lumpy and a little too soft. Cold, too. It was cold in bed without Carl and Rick.

Everything was cold without Carl and Rick.

SUGAR DADDIES

Losing the dream of Jack's yard was shitty enough, and I'd cried, a lot. But Carl's big revelation had hit like a car wreck, a big-arsed truck ploughing into my small town dreams. A big splodge of *what the fuck* on my cute little life plan.

What life plan?

Plan A — rent Jack's yard, Katiefy it and make it pretty and smart, fill it with happy kids wanting riding lessons. Smile and congratulate myself on completing life plan at age twenty-two.

Plan B —

There was no plan B. There had never been a plan B.

Samson slowed on the brow of the hill, stretched out his neck and snorted. I gave him a pat, ruffled his mane, and he slowed further, his hooves clop-clopping as he dropped to a walk. I leaned back in the saddle, listening to the songbirds. I really fucking loved it here. I could stay here forever, Samson and me.

My phone bleeped and I dug it out of my pocket. My heart did a little stutter at the prospect it was one of the boys, but it wasn't. It was Mum.

I'm sorry about the yard, Katie, but maybe it's for the best. You've got a real shot at making something of yourself at your dad's, an actual career, Katie. It's not so bad, sweetheart. Really it's not. x

Her words were nothing new, I'd heard them last night already as I'd cried until I was a sniffly mess.

It really was so bad.

I shoved the phone away.

She just didn't get it. Couldn't possibly get it.

I turned Samson off the main track and headed deeper into the woods, where the undergrowth was wilder and the trees were thicker. We explored those hidden areas of the woods we'd conquered like

297

explorers back when he was fresh and green, and it was all so exciting. I felt it all over again. I loved it all over again.

It's amazing how that happens, how something feels so much sweeter when it's hurtling towards the end of its time. Bittersweet.

Were Carl and Rick like that? Is that why life around them felt so powerful? So all-consuming?

Did I love Carl and Rick so much because it was supposed to be temporary? Nothing but a six-month foray into a life between two men?

"What are we going to do, boy?" I said, and Samson's ears flicked in my direction. "Just what the hell are we going to do?"

Eat a big bit of hedge was his answer.

That would have to do for now.

We trekked for hours, reliving our early days, following every path and every turn, cantering along every straight. We waved to the cyclists we'd come to know so well, listened to the same old dogs barking as their owners called their names.

I soaked it all in, as though this one ride could sustain me for all time, its memory enough to stave off the pain of losing this place I'd come to know so well, love so much.

Acceptance. Maybe this was the beginning of acceptance of a cruel sleight of fate. Pipped to the post by a bank who couldn't wait just a few cruddy months longer. Assholes.

Samson was loose-limbed and happy as we headed back onto the yard, but me not so much. A few months from now and this would really be over. New people here, people with their own dreams for the place, probably so different to mine. I felt defeated as we walked past the farmhouse, defeated as I stared at Jack's empty parking space, already a morbid omen of what was to come.

The lump in my throat was back, eyes hot and a little itchy, stomach twisting and empty.

Until there was Rick.

His car was by my trailer, silver and shiny against the dull metal shell of the barn. I squeezed Samson on, headed over to it, but Rick wasn't inside.

My heart was thumping at the thought of him, the unmistakeable fizz of excitement overriding my misery. But I was nervous, too. Really nervous.

"Hey, pretty lady."

My belly fluttered at his voice. I turned in the saddle to face him, shielding my eyes from the glare of sunlight, and he looked nervous, too.

He was wearing a green checked shirt over jeans, a pair of old boots on his feet. His hair was messy and stylishly unstyled, his smile warm and bright. The nerves were all in his eyes.

"Hey, sexy boy." I smiled.

"Not such a boy," he said, and walked over. He ran a hand over Samson's neck, gave him a pat. "Good ride?"

I nodded. "Saying my first goodbye to the woods. I hope it takes ages, I hope I get to say hundreds of goodbyes."

"I hope so, too," he said. "Final goodbyes suck like shit." He gave Samson a mint. "Who's a boy, Sammy?"

He walked at our side as we headed to the stable block, his arms waiting as I dismounted. He didn't linger, just gave me a squeeze and fastened Samson's head collar around his neck. I loosened Samson's girth, took down his saddle, and Rick was already in action, filling up a bucket and sponging down his back as I took off his bridle. We didn't speak, our eyes making fleeting contact as we carried on with horsey business, and the tickle in my belly was so strong it made me squirmy, shifting my weight from foot to foot as I brushed Samson down.

I fastened up his rug and Rick loosened the lead rope. He led Samson to the field and I walked at his side. I watched Rick's face as he let Samson free, his eyes full of genuine affection for my furry boy. He pulled the gate closed and stood to watch Samson away, arms folded on the top bar. I stepped up alongside him, breathed in the country air.

"I'm so fucking sorry, Katie." His voice was quieter than usual. "I'm sorry about the yard. It's such a fucking shitter." He paused. "I'm sorry about..." He sighed. "I'm sorry about everything."

"Where's Carl?" I said.

"Working." He sighed again, then he looked at me. "No, he's not working. He's at home. I asked him not to come."

Tickly belly. Tickly everything.

I tried to find words. "Are you... um... is it what you both want?"

"A baby?" He looked back at the field. "Yeah, it's what we both want. Carl is more... impatient." He took out his tobacco, rolled a cigarette. "Carl's older, more single-minded. It's more urgent for him." He lit up. "He's sorry. He knows he fucked up."

"He didn't," I said. "He offered me everything, Rick, offered me my dream. I just... I can't take it. I can't give him what he wants."

"You're sure? Not ever?"

I shrugged. "Shit, Rick, I don't know. Forever's a long time. Yesterday I was celebrating kicking Verity's ass and planning to do it again at the Cheltenham Chase. I was planning what I'd do with this place, once I was officially renting. I was thinking about you guys, spending the weekend with you, chilling out and having fun, probably drinking too much wine and taking more cock than is good for my riding." I pulled the hair back from my face. "I wasn't thinking about losing all of this. I sure as fuck wasn't thinking about babies and dirty nappies and bringing up a kid with two men I barely even know."

"You know us," he said. "There's nothing much more to see than you've seen already."

"I like what I've seen already," I said. "I just... a baby, Rick. That's so... big."

"Too big." He took a long drag. "Too big and way too soon."

"But I'm glad he told me, I'm glad I know. This kind of thing doesn't get any easier down the line, people just get more invested. I'd have been more invested in six months."

"And maybe that would've made all the difference."

"Maybe." I shrugged. "I never really wanted to do the kid thing, Rick. I never felt it."

"I know," he said simply.

"Mum tried her best but it was hard. I watched her sacrifice everything, as soon as I was old enough to get it. She was young, her friends were going out, she was always home, always with me. Working loads of crappy hours to keep me in uniform and shoes and school dinners." I shook my head. "That's not what I want. Not for me."

"It wouldn't be like that for you."

"Maybe not."

I could feel his eyes on me. "Definitely not."

I laughed a little to myself. "It's funny. When I was a little girl I used to wonder about my dad. Used to dream about who he was and where he was. Used to conjure up all these crazy fantasies about how he was a soldier, or a faraway prince, or a pirate even, that he couldn't be there for me because he was on some adventure somewhere he couldn't get out of. I'd plan it all out, imagine how I'd feel when he turned up one day, and he'd be like *Katie, I'm your dad, I've been thinking about you your whole life*. Only then I realised my dad wasn't a soldier, or a prince, or a pirate. He was just some douchebag who knocked up my mum and abandoned us both."

Rick didn't say a word.

"I used to wish for a dad, every birthday, every Christmas. Eventually I got one shitty half rate one." I smiled. "And here I am, with the offer of two good dads for a baby I may never have. Isn't fate weird?"

"Yeah, it is."

"It's the riding," I said. "Maybe more than anything else. I've worked so hard with Samson, and he's nearly ready. We're both nearly ready. He'll be in his prime for another couple of years, and I want to make the most of them. I want to event, compete, show the world how far he's come."

"And after that?"

I shrugged. "I've no idea, but even if I didn't event again I couldn't guarantee I'd want to knock out a baby and do the mummy thing."

"But you might?"

"I don't know."

He stubbed out his cigarette. "Sorry, of course you don't. This is such bullshit. How can you possibly make a call on something like this so soon."

The thought of Carl pained me, made me feel fucked up inside. "He wants it *now*, Rick. I can't. Not with Samson. Even though my dreams are going to shit, I still can't."

"He's just jaded and scared, that's all."

The thought hit me in the belly. "Scared?"

He nodded. "Scared it won't happen for him."

"Why wouldn't it? He's a gorgeous guy, you're both gorgeous guys. Kind and funny and successful. You should have a queue of potentials."

He shook his head. "No. Nobody that fits. Nobody that really wants us, not for keeps. They want the sex, and the money. They want the fun and games. The baby, not so much." He sighed. "Carl's pretty cut up, thinks we won't see you again, not properly."

"And what do you think?"

"I dunno. I'm holding out a little hope here." He smiled. "You've knocked our socks off, both of us."

"Ditto," I said. "You guys are awesome."

"But you don't want us, right? Not like that? Is this just... money? I get it, if it is. I wouldn't blame you."

My eyes widened. "Shit, no. No way. This isn't about the money. It was about the money for about a week."

"So what is it about? What do you want from us?"

I smiled. "You sound like him."

He laughed. "Sorry. I just... we're a bit lost. A bit fucked up. Flailing around trying to work out whether we've blown it or not."

"He won't wait, Rick. I could see it in his eyes. Maybe if he had ten years... maybe if he could just hang on and see..." I closed my eyes. "Why can't he wait, Rick? Why now, why so breakneck? What's so important that it has to be right now?"

He ran his fingers through his hair, eyes fixed on Samson in the distance.

"I think it's time I told you about Carl," he said.

Chapter
TWENTY TWO

Katie

I dropped to my ass on the wood-chippings and so did Rick. I crossed my legs and my stomach tightened in anticipation.

"I grew up lucky, really fucking lucky," he started. "I always knew it, but it took me meeting a guy like Carl to realise just how good I had it as a kid. I had everything, everything that mattered. And Carl, poor fucking guy, he had nothing."

"He mentioned a hostel, when we were in Brighton..."

Rick's eyes met mine and they were so sad. "Children's home. Shithole from what I gather. A whole lot of kids needing love, not enough people to love them. Not enough people to take care of them, even."

"What about his parents?"

Rick shook his head. "His mum died when he was really young. Bit of a party goer, so he says, but it's all hearsay really, bits of memories, scattered information from people who didn't really know. They found her in a pool, face down and in nothing but her knickers.

Accidental death officially. I don't know much more than that. Carl was only six at the time. They found him in filthy clothes at one of her loser mate's flats."

My stomach lurched. "Shit."

"He doesn't talk about it much."

"And then what? What happened to him?"

He sighed. "A load of shit. Life in care, like loads of other kids. Not enough attention, not enough love. They didn't manage to find his dad, so they said. Only then this loser rocks up when Carl's about thirteen years old. Says he hasn't got space or money to have Carl come live with him, but he loves him, misses him, thinks about him all the time, yada fucking yada."

"He wasn't genuine?"

Rick shook his head, and his face was stony. "He was a fucking asshole. Used to get Carl to do *favours* for him. Piece of fucking crap."

"Favours?" I felt sick inside, but Rick shook his head.

"Nothing like that, not that I know, but I wouldn't swear on it. Drugs. *Hold onto this for me, Carl, it's a present for a friend. Don't tell anyone, I want it to be a surprise. I'm working on a place for us, Carl, me and you, won't be long now.*"

"Fuck."

"Yeah. Of course Carl did whatever the asshole wanted. He was a teenage lad hoping someone actually gave a shit, you know? Thought he could be something to somebody, finally. Makes me so fucking angry."

"What happened?"

Rick tipped his head back, squinted at the sun. "A carer found one of the parcels hidden behind a skirting board by Carl's bunk. Along came the police, social workers, a million questions. Bye bye,

Dad."

"His dad went to prison?" My heart was in my throat.

"Part of a bigger investigation, I think. Yeah, he went down for it, good fucking riddance. Carl ate himself up with guilt, sent letters, never heard back. Not a fucking thing. Never has. I mean what kind of cunt even does that to their own kid? Sets them up and then just fucking bails? Doesn't even fucking reply?" Rick shook his head. "Poor kid went off the rails. Started vandalising shit, fighting, stealing. He says it was like he was filled with this... tar, all black and thick, just this... rottenness. Says he felt like he was worth nothing, didn't deserve anything, didn't even want anything. Ended up in juvenile detention, then back in care. A problem kid." He paused, picked at the woodchips. "It's not really my place to tell you this shit, but I think you should know. So you understand."

My eyes felt sore and full of tears. Too much, all at once. Jack's yard, and baby talk, and Carl. Mainly Carl.

"Shit," Rick said. "I know this is fucked up, I know it's sad, believe me, it breaks my fucking heart, but please, whatever you do, please don't look at him like that."

"Like what?" I asked, and my voice was crackly.

"Like you're looking at me, now. Like you pity him, like you feel sorry for him. He'd hate it. It's the last thing he wants, that isn't who he is."

"But I do," I said. "Feel sorry for him, I mean. I don't pity him, he's not the kind of guy you could pity." I looked away. "He seems so strong, so grounded, so... together."

"He is. He's all those things. He's the best man I know. The strongest man I know."

The lump in my throat threatened to choke me. "How did he...

how could he... who even comes back from something like that?"

"A guy like Carl does." Rick smiled. "Don't ask me how, but he did. Pulled his shit together, made a better life for himself. Carl's steely and determined, serious... motivated. You've probably noticed," he laughed, "He can seem... unapproachable. But that's just the grit he uses to push himself forward, and underneath that, despite everything, all the shit he's been through, all the times he's been let down and fucked over, despite *all* that, he's loyal, and kind, and generous. He wants the best for people, he gives his best for people, always his best." He paused, looked right at me. "He credits your dad for a lot of that."

My belly panged. "I'm sure my father can't take the credit for much of that."

"Maybe. Maybe not." He looked at me. "I always speak as I find, and I've always found your dad to be a top guy. No bullshit, no games. Sees the best in people, just like Carl does."

"That's not how I've found him," I said, and my voice was prickly. *I* was prickly. "Not ever. Not at all."

Rick didn't linger on it. "Anyway, this is just background. The real heart of the matter, this baby thing, that's been brewing for years. Carl told me there was this park about twenty minutes' walk from the hostel, a better park than the rundown piece of shit one by theirs. He used to take himself off there, and sit and watch. There were families, he said, nice families. Proper mums and dads with happy kids, just having a good time. He used to sit outside the fence and watch them, and pray that he'd have a family like that of his own one day. People to love." He sighed. "Kids to love." He picked up a bit of woodchip, turned it in his fingers. "When your dad gave him a shot he threw himself into work, to get ready for the future, to make something of himself. That's what he says. Didn't meet Melanie until his late twenties, but thought she was the one. She claimed she felt the same. Who wouldn't with a guy like Carl? He's gorgeous, successful, smart..." His voice trailed off. "But the woman was a wild thing, believe me. Couldn't imagine her doing the school run, to be honest, couldn't imagine her with a couple of kids, not in a million years. But he could."

"She was the woman with him when you met?"

He nodded. "Yeah, on some seedy website. You know the drill. Turned up at theirs and hit it off. I thought they were cool. Nice couple, great in bed. Adventurous. They seemed pretty solid, until they really weren't."

"They split up?"

Rick's eyes met mine, and he was wary of telling me. I could see the hesitation.

"You don't have to tell me..." I said, but he shook his head.

"I do need to tell you." He tossed the woodchip from hand to hand. "Carl thought they were serious. He thought they were for keeps. They talked about it, he says, about settling down, having a family. It was all he ever wanted."

"She didn't want it?"

"She said she did. Stopped taking the pill, made all the right noises, said all the right things. I mean, they'd been together ages. Years and years without any real commitment, any real signs of her being ready, but he waited. He finally thought she was ready, she said she was ready."

"She didn't get pregnant?"

He sighed. "Apparently not. She kept telling him to give it time, said it would happen."

"But it didn't?"

He flicked the woodchip away. "She was lying."

"Still on the pill?"

"No," he said. "That would have been easier." He closed his eyes. "Two abortions."

Fucking hell. "Two?"

"At least two. A slip up from a friend who'd had too much to drink, mentioned it in passing, like he knew."

"Oh my God."

"He was fucking devastated. His whole life he'd wanted a family, months, *years* probably of trying. Imagine that, all that waiting, all that trying, just to find out the woman you think you want to spend your life with has decided to terminate two of your kids without you knowing. Broke his fucking heart."

I felt cold. Cold and sad. My stomach ached for him. "That's horrible."

"Yeah, it is. It really is. They split up over it, she walked away without really breaking a sweat. She never loved him, not really. I think she loved the idea of him, which is crazy to me, really fucking crazy, he's *everything* to me." He took a breath. "For a while we were just mates. A couple of beers at the weekend. Then a couple of beers in the week. We'd talk, a lot. Laugh a lot. We just fit together. We found other women when he was up to it, just casually." He smiled a big smile. "I knew I loved him, even back then. I thought he was amazing. It took him a little longer. I guess it was the family thing. Or maybe he just wasn't that into me." He laughed a little. "I guess I wormed my way under his skin. Eventually."

I smiled. "Did you always know you were bi?"

He nodded. "My family were awesome, taught us kids that love

309

is love and that's all that matters. It didn't seem like a big deal to me, I just wanted who I wanted. They love Carl." His eyes twinkled and it gave me butterflies. "They'd love you, too."

I didn't know what to say about that, so I said nothing. "Was Carl always bi, too?"

"I think so, maybe. For me my sexuality was no biggie, I just liked what I liked, loved who I loved. For Carl I think it was more of a take comfort where you can kinda thing, that's how it started. I guess he found some solace in some of the other kids when he was headed off the rails, a bit of physical closeness through dark nights. An outlet for the urges, I dunno. He says he was grateful for any kind of love no matter where it came from, and that stuck, although now I think it comes from a much healthier place inside. For him it doesn't really matter whether that love is from a guy or a girl, or both. He doesn't always say it back, the magic little love phrase — a hang up from Mel, I guess — but he shows it, he *feels* it. Carl's all about people, the people who care about him, people who want him. I wanted him. I *really* wanted him."

I gave him a nudge. Squeezed his elbow. "And he wanted you. He loves you, that's obvious."

"I fucking love that guy. I love him so fucking much." He sighed. "But we always wanted more. We wanted a family, right from early on, especially Carl. We figured we could have a polyamorous relationship, find someone on our wavelength, only it wasn't so simple." He paused. "Sex, yeah, that was simple. Money in exchange for sex, even easier, on the face of it. But something genuine? That evaded us."

I didn't speak, just listened.

"It's hard for people, I guess. Threesomes are fun, hanging out as a threesome is fun, but to settle down? Do the whole poly thing long-term, with a kid, with a family, with funny looks from the other mums at the school playground?" He shook his head. "Sends people running. We're like Saturday afternoon cocktails, me and Carl. Easy enough to get people to the bar for the buy-one-get-one-free, but they invariably guzzle enough to have a good time, then head off home for the night."

"That isn't how I see it," I said. "Not now, I promise."

"I hope not," he said. "I really fucking hope not, because we're in pretty deep with you, Katie. We think you're amazing."

I felt the blush. "Thanks."

"I mean it. We think the world of you. Always will, no matter how things pan out." He scratched at his beard. "Carl's turning forty this year, and he's feeling it. He's worried it's never gonna happen for him, for *us*, and that even if it does he'll be too old to enjoy all the things he's spent his life dreaming about. Too old to enjoy his grandkids, knocking on retirement's door before his kid's even flown the nest. It makes him... demanding."

"How could it not? If he wants something that bad..." I thought of the yard, the disappointment of my dream slipping away from me. It hurt like a motherfucker, and I was just twenty-two, hardly any age. I still had Samson, still had my mum, still had my whole life ahead of me to find another dream.

"He's a stronger man than I am, holding out for a dream for that long, having it thrown in your face and still keep going, still keep hoping. It can make him difficult, but Carl is a little difficult, especially at first."

I got a tickle in my tummy at the memory. "Scary hot," I said. "Intimidating. Blunt, too. But I like that."

"I like that, too." He got to his feet. "He'd have bought you this place, you know, if that's what you wanted. He's generous, wants to see you live your dreams. Always wants the best for people."

He held out a hand and pulled me up, watched me as I brushed the dust from my jodhpurs. "I could never have taken it. It's too much. Unless I could have..." I shook my head. "Probably not even then. I don't think I could swap dreams like that, not when mine's worth a cool couple of hundred grand." I held my hands up. "I mean, fuck, that's massive."

"So is having a baby. The whole thing is massive, and way too fucking soon, like I said."

I leaned back on the gate, looked at him, at the way the sun turned his hair chestnut, the deep brown of his eyes. He was so beautiful. "What's the deal with you, Rick? You know all about Carl's dreams, his shitty upbringing, mine, too. What's your story?"

He shrugged, stared out at Samson. "Like I said, I've been lucky. My story is a good one." He smiled. "Had a wild stint at university though, smoked a bit too much weed and spent all my money on slot machines." He brought his finger to his lips. "Shh, don't tell anyone, I'm a good boy now." He smirked. "Seriously, my lot is a good one. Dicked about with a load of randoms, had a lot of sex and it was fun, but not fulfilling. Made it in graphic design, which is all I really wanted, to be creative." He stepped up onto the gate, leaned over. "I have my faults. I waste way too much time. Carl's a doer, I'm a procrastinator. I get addicted to things so easily, weird food, stupid games, getting inked. Everything. But I can live with that." He laughed. "I'm really not that exciting or that special. I'm just a guy who tries to look on the sunny side, appreciates what he has."

But he *was* exciting. He excited me. *Everything* about Rick excited me.

"I think you're pretty damn special," I said. "Pretty damn exciting, too."

It took him aback, I could see it in his eyes. "Wow. You do? That's sweet."

"I do."

He grinned. "That's mighty fucking cool. Thanks."

I stepped up on the gate beside him, kissed his cheek. "Thanks, Rick. Thanks for coming. I was feeling shitty, you brightened my day."

"I'd be feeling shitty too if all this was being taken away from me." He sighed. "It's fucking ace here, I can see why you fell in love with it." He stepped down. "Sure you're not tempted? Take Carl up on his offer, live the dream?"

I shook my head. "I wish I could. I'd love it if this place was mine, more than anything." I met his eyes. "But it's not mine, and it isn't going to be mine. I'll just have to accept it, move on."

He raised his eyebrows. "That's fighting talk. I think you're a tough little cookie, pretty lady."

I laughed. "Not really. I still feel like my dream's been wrenched from my heart, chewed up and spat out at my feet. But I'm feeling inspired." I looked at my furry boy in the field. "I mean, if Carl can go through all that, lose all those dreams, and still come out the other side, I can take this little knockback on the chin, right?"

He wrapped an arm around my shoulders, kissed my head, pulled me close. "Carl's a mystery to me, some kind of superhuman. But if anyone else can do it, take a setback and turn it into fuel to do better, I think it's gonna be you. You've got fire, little miss horsey. Fire and passion and sunshine sparkles. Don't ever lose that."

"Don't ever let me lose it," I said.

313

"I'll try my best."

We walked back through the school, up past the stable block where Rick hung up Samson's head collar like he'd been doing it a hundred years, and it felt so good to be at his side. It felt perfect.

If only I could be that person, the person they needed. The person they wanted so badly.

Chapter
TWENTY THREE

Katie

I hovered beside Rick's car. Wondering where this left us, wondering where any of this would lead. Wondering where I even wanted this to lead.

"So," he said. "Where to now, pretty lady? Need a lift?" He opened the passenger door in invitation. "I can put the roof down, travel in style. Wherever you want to go."

I slipped into the seat, and the answer became obvious. So obvious.

"Home, please," I said. "Yours."

He reached over and took my hand, pressed it to his lips and kissed me, kissed my knuckles, every single one. And he smiled. He smiled and it lit up the world.

"Let's go home," he said.

He lightened the mood on the way back to Cheltenham, tuned into a cheesy radio station and sang along. He put the roof down, and it felt amazing, the wind catching my hair as we picked up speed. I loved the way his fingers drummed to the beat on the steering wheel, the way he danced in his seat so easily, so freely. Even though we were exposed — on show to every passing motorist without the privacy of the car roof — Rick had no reservations, no sense of self-consciousness, and I loved that about him. It was something I loved about both of them, the way their company felt so liberating, so free from the pressure of following any kind of status quo.

"I like this one," I said, as one of my favourite tracks came on.

Rick turned up the volume. "Sing it, baby," he said in a stupid voice.

And I did, I did sing it. My sad little heart picked up, and I laughed and sang the high bits even though my voice squeaked like a chipmunk when I lost the note.

He clapped when it was over, turned the volume back down.

"Man, we really need a night out," he said. "Drinks and dancing and a huge fucking blow out."

"Yes," I said. "That sounds good." I sighed, letting the tension of the stable disappointment fall away. "That sounds really great."

"We still need to celebrate. You still did fucking ace this week, remember that. We need to party."

I'd all but forgotten my triumph at work, a little thrill zipped through me. "It's early days."

"Early days, but you aced it. Carl said you were awesome. He's so proud." He squeezed my knee. "So am I."

It made me blush. Maybe I was a just a little proud of myself, too.

The nerves started up as Rick turned onto their estate. The thought of facing Carl both excited and terrified me. Would he be cold again? Intimidating again? Closed off at the thought I couldn't be the one they wanted?

Couldn't I be the one they wanted? Was this inevitably doomed? The idea hurt.

Rick pulled onto their driveway. He turned off the radio and triggered the roof, and I fiddled with my seatbelt as we waited.

"Don't look so scared," he said. "We're home. It's all good." He squeezed my hand. "There's nothing to worry about, Katie, for real. No pressure."

"I know... I just..." I let out a breath, unclipped my belt. "Let's go."

He opened the front door with a big smile on his face, ditched his keys on the side. "Honey, I'm home!" he called, and his voice was so warm, so silly.

I followed him through to the kitchen, and there was Carl, leaning against the island with his tablet in his hand, a mug of coffee by his side. His attention was on what he was doing, some work business, no doubt. I'd seen the same expression often as he crunched figures for sales meetings and client calls. But there was something else there, too. Maybe it was the grit of his jaw, or the uncharacteristic ghost of stubble, maybe even something more, something untenable, some kind of... sadness.

He was wearing a shirt, black and simple, over dark jeans. His hair was styled differently, slightly less slick than usual, probably towel dried, and he had no shoes on. I don't know why that affected me so much, I don't know why the sight of his bare feet on the tiles gave me flutters inside. I don't know why seeing him so casual and off guard made my breath catch, made me feel hot and breathless.

He put his tablet down as he caught sight of Rick, his eyes full of questions.

And then he saw me. There was shock as his gaze met mine, a long moment of amazement as I stepped into the kitchen. And then there was a smile, a nervous smile that made my heart do a weird little flip.

"Katie," he said, as though I'd been gone a million years.

"Surprise," I said, and it sounded so dumb.

Rick slapped his arm as he walked by, gave him a playful smile. "Couldn't keep her away. I tried to ditch her in Much Arlock, but she was having none of it." He flicked the kettle on and gave me a wink. "I guess we'll just have to put up with her."

"Guess you will." I poked my tongue out. "Tea for me, please."

"*And* she expects hot beverages." He mock groaned. "So demanding. I don't know why we put up with it, Carl."

But Carl wasn't listening, wasn't buying into our stupid banter. His gaze was intense and constant, green eyes eating me alive. My heart did another weird flip, and I felt like I was falling. I stood still, watching him right back.

"Hey," I said, just like that. One stupid little word and I felt my cheeks burning.

I didn't know what he'd say, but he didn't say anything at all. He put down his mug and closed the distance between us in a couple of quick strides. He folded me in his arms, and kissed my hair and held me tight. He smelled of bodywash and citrus, and him. My cheek pressed to his chest, his heartbeat against my ear, and it was warm there, safe there. Everything felt so right there.

His chin rested on my head, his arms solid as they gave me a squeeze.

"I'm sorry," he said. "I'm sorry for what I said, I'm sorry about the yard." He breathed into my hair, kissed me again. "I'm so glad

318

you're here."

I felt as though I was melting into him, my body sinking into his. I held him right back, my arms around his waist, squeezing him just as hard as he was squeezing me.

"Thanks for coming back," he said, and there was such sincerity there it caught in his throat.

I wanted to say so much, but the words were catching in my throat, too. I couldn't shake the sadness, the pain in my heart at Rick's story.

"I stink of Samson." I tried to laugh, but it came out all goofed up, and there was a pathetic little sob, one I couldn't stop, and tears pricked even though I didn't want them to.

"I like the stink of Samson," he said, and sniffed me.

I fought him a little as he took me by the shoulders, prised me away enough to look at my face. I tried to blink away the sadness before he noticed, but I was too late.

"What is it?" he said. "The yard?" He sighed. "I'm so sorry you're losing the yard. We can still try and rent... we can talk to Jack..."

But I was shaking my head. "I'm fine," I said. "It's not the yard. I'm ok with the yard. It's not even that important, not in the scheme of things. It's just some land."

Carl's eyes dug into mine, and I looked away before he could dig my thoughts right out of me, but I was too late, he'd already seen.

He looked towards Rick, a half-smile on his face. "Had a little chat, did you, Richard? Spill all my dirty secrets?"

Rick stepped over, handed me a mug. "Don't even think about telling me off for blurting out shit I shouldn't, mister." He jabbed Carl's shoulder with a finger, but he was smiling. "Pot fucking kettle springs to mind." He pulled his tobacco from his jeans, rolled a

319

cigarette. "Smoke time. I'll leave you two to do your little kiss-and-move-the-fuck-on."

He stepped in the direction of the back door, but Carl gripped his arm. He yanked him close, wrapped an arm around his neck, pulling him into a headlock which didn't look altogether comfortable. And then he kissed him, a big wet kiss, right on the cheek.

"I love you, Rick," he said, and my heart thumped.

Rick stayed put, snaked his arm around Carl's waist before Carl let him go.

"Urgh," he protested, wiping his cheek. But his eyes were sparkling, they said so much.

I waited until the door closed behind him before I went to speak, but Carl cut me off.

"You don't need to say anything," he said. "I was wrong to put you under pressure. There is nothing to talk about, nothing you need to say."

"But I want to..." I sighed. "I wanted to say thanks, for the offer."

He held up his hands. "The offer stands, no conditions. It's there if you want it, Katie."

I shook my head. "No," I said. "But thank you."

"If you change your mind..."

"I won't," I said. "Not about the yard."

His eyes widened. "And about everything else? Are you planning on staying with us? For the rest of the six months? Is that what you want?"

I sipped my tea. "No." I shook my head. "That isn't what I want. Not for six months."

His face dropped instantly, his shoulders heavy. "I see." He paused. "I do understand."

"You don't," I said, and then I waited, watching Rick pacing and smoking through the window. "I don't know what I'll want forever, but I know what I want right now."

"And what's that?"

I smiled. "Let's wait for Rick."

We moved to the living room, and I took the armchair. Carl took the sofa, and Rick took the pouffe between us both.

"So," Carl said, ever the straight-talker. "Where do we go from here? What do you want from us?"

I took a second to organise my thoughts, still not entirely sure where they were heading. "Our arrangement is off," I said. "I don't want any more payments, I don't want any more money." I looked between them. "I don't want any three weekends out of four stuff, not that we've ever had that yet. I don't want *sugar daddies*, I don't *need* sugar daddies. Not anymore. Not now the yard is off the table."

Carl nodded, and so did Rick.

It was Carl who spoke next, predictably. "Alright," he said. "If that's what you want. What now? Friends?"

"I hope we're a little past that." I smiled. "I want to see how this goes. I love being with you guys, I love spending time with you, I love what we have."

"I think it's safe to say we all feel like that," Rick said. "You won't get any arguments from this end."

I sighed. "I'm not saying I can be that person, the person you want. I'm not saying I'm going to change my opinion on wanting kids, or that if I ever do, that it'll be soon." I looked at Carl and he looked right back at me. "I'm sorry, but I just can't promise that. I just don't know."

"That's ok," Carl said. "We understand."

My hands twisted in my lap. "But I *do* want *this*. Whatever this is we're doing. I *really* want this." I looked at Rick. "I love the way you guys love each other, and I love the way you've been with me. I love the way you're so supportive of me and Samson. I love the life we have here." I smiled. "And I love having sex with you. I love that a lot."

"Amen to that." Rick smirked.

"So, what I'm asking," I began. "What I'm asking is that you give me the six months you were planning on. Before we make any long-term decisions, I mean. I'm not sure I'll even know then, not for sure, not what I want. But we'll have had time to try this out, to see how it goes."

"Sounds fair," Carl said.

"Sounds really fair," Rick said.

"I'm not having the yard now, so I'll have to relocate Samson. I might not have a riding school, but I've still got a horse I want to event for the next few summers." I sighed. "I'm gutted about the yard, I really am, but my dream was about more than that. It's about Samson, it's about how far we've come. I just don't think I can sacrifice that."

Carl held up his hands. "You don't need to justify anything, Katie. It's ok. We understand." He paused. "We support you, with Samson, with whatever you want to do."

My heart was beating so fast. "I know," I said. "That's part of the reason I'm not sure what I want anymore." I looked at my hands. "It's always seemed so simple, what I wanted. Samson, riding school, no kids, nothing to hold me back, just me and horses and a dream."

"Things change," Rick said. "Just give yourself a break, see where things go. No pressure, pretty lady. I mean it. We both mean it."

"Ok." I let out a breath. "So, we do this? No sugar daddies, just us, just seeing where this leads?"

Carl nodded. "We see where this leads."

Rick smiled. "We do this."

The relief flooded me, relief and happiness. "Great," I said. "That's really great."

The guys looked at each other, then Rick spoke. "Are you gonna... move in? Is this... official? I dunno... are we... *in a relationship*?"

I shrugged. "I guess so, if that's what you want."

"It's what we want," Carl said. "Official. We're official." His eyes were intense and it made me blush. "As for the future, we'll decide in six months."

Rick shot him a look. "Or whenever Katie's ready to decide."

Carl held up his hands. "Yes, whenever you're ready to decide."

"Six months," I said. "I'll know. I'll make sure I know."

"Fine," Carl said. "That's all we can ask for. All we'd ever ask for."

I smiled. "I don't know how my mum is going to react to all this." I caught myself. "I mean... if that's ok... if that's what we're planning? That this is official?"

Carl nodded. "It's official. You can tell your mum when you want to tell your mum. We'd like that."

Rick grinned. "I want you to meet my folks, they'll love you. And my sisters."

Carl shrugged, smiled a little. "I don't have anyone. There's nobody for you to meet."

"You do. You have my dad," I said, voicing the unspoken. "I couldn't give a shit what he thinks about anything... but you..."

His eyes crashed into mine. "I would like to tell your father, yes. I don't do secrets, and I respect David. He's important to me. I'd like to be honest with him."

"I don't know him, I don't know how he'll react. He probably won't give a shit," I scoffed.

"He'll give a shit," Carl said.

"He'll definitely give a shit," Rick said. "You're his little girl."

"I'm his *mistake*," I said. "What difference will it make to him?"

Carl shook his head. "You're not a mistake, Katie. David would never call you a mistake, I can assure you of that."

It made me feel sick inside, sick and small, and fragile. *Weird*. It made me feel weird.

I shrugged it off. "Maybe hold off from telling him, just until this internship thing is over. To be safe."

"That's a long time," Carl said. "I'm not sure I can wait that long. People will find out, he may ask me directly. If he asks me, I'll answer. It's how I work."

"Don't we pissing know it," Rick groaned, but he reached out a hand, squeezed Carl's knee.

"Ok," I said. "If he asks, you tell him, but if he doesn't, we just wait awhile, just until... it's time. I dunno." I shrugged. "Does that work?"

"That works," Carl said. "For now. Anything changes, I'll let you know before I tell him, give you the chance to do it for yourself. He's your dad. It's your call."

"He's not my *dad*," I said. "Not like that. He's never been a *dad* to me."

Neither of them spoke. It sat uncomfortably in the air, our difference in opinion about David *Mr Perfect* Faverley.

Rick slapped his knees, called us to attention. He got to his feet, held out his arms. "Group fucking hug," he said. "Seal the deal."

I took his hand, pulled myself up, and as my body moved towards theirs, their bright smiles, their kind eyes... the way they were so happy, the way they wanted me... I felt my skin prickle, from head to toe, this *need* in my belly, lower than that... this *want*...

I wanted them. Both of them.

I wanted them both so much I couldn't stand it.

They pulled me close, wrapped me in strong arms that held me so tight, and I said it. I just said it. Because I *could* say it, because I could say whatever I wanted now. Off the script, a proper *relationship*.

They weren't paying. Not anymore.

"I was hoping for a bit more than a group hug," I said.

Chapter
TWENTY FOUR

Katie

"Wait." I laughed as two sets of hands came straight for me. "I didn't mean right this second. I stink of horse. I'm muddy!"

"But we love it when you're dirty." Rick grinned. "That's how we like you best."

He hooked his fingers inside the waist of my jodhpurs, and I shunted towards him as he pulled. He kissed my neck, slowly, softly, tickling me with his tongue bar as Carl's hands snaked around my waist from behind.

"I've really missed this," I said. "I think I'm addicted. It's official, I'm a sex addict. Good job I have two of you to give me my fix."

Carl's breath was hot against my cheek. "Twice the pleasure. For all of us."

I reached back for him, pulling him closer, until I could feel the swell of his cock against my ass. His hand slipped under my t-shirt, climbing my ribs, and I held my breath as he felt his way inside my bra. He found my nipple, rolled it between his thumb and forefinger.

I closed my eyes and moaned into him.

Ricks palm pressed between my legs. "Gonna take you," he said. "Carl's cock against mine as we open you up."

My clit pulsed and sparks danced through me. "Fuck yes," I said. "That's what I want. Both of you inside me."

"That's our beautiful girl." Carl hitched me against him, grinding against my ass, and I groaned as Rick pinned me there, his fingers working at my jodhpurs. He tugged them down roughly, and Carl wriggled my top off over my head. Between them they stripped me as I squirmed and gasped as warm hands explored me, squeezing at my tits, pulling at my nipples. Rick's fingers slipped between my pussy lips, pushed their way inside and my head fell to his shoulder. I bit into his skin and his fingers fucked me.

"Dirty wet girl. She's so fucking wet, Carl. She can take more. Give her more."

Carl trailed his hand down my belly. He worked two fingers in next to Rick's, and I grunted and worked my hips, and moaned as I heard the wetness. Their knuckles stretched me, pressing the spot inside that made me squirm. Heat travelled through me. Sweat on my brow. And the smell, of horse and mud, of two hot men. I just wanted fucking.

"How do you want us?" Carl whispered.

"I don't fucking care. Just fuck me."

"How?" His hand was at my throat, squeezing, and shit I could almost come right there.

"Both at once. Both holes. Fill me and fuck me."

"Good girl," he said and kissed me.

"In the shower," Rick said. "All hot and steamy."

They pulled their fingers from me, and it squelched. My thighs were slippery as Carl walked me backwards, Rick's fingers wet in mine as he positioned my hand on his belt. I undressed him as we moved, pulling his belt loose and unzipping his jeans. He kicked them off as I unbuttoned his shirt, following Carl's lead into the hallway.

I turned to face him as we reached the bottom of the stairs.

"You have too many clothes on," I said.

"Far too fucking many," Rick agreed.

Rick took Carl's jeans as I took Carl's shirt, and we stripped him a heartbeat, casting his clothes back along the hall with ours. His cock stood proud, and I took hold of it along with Rick's, worked the two of them in tandem with greedy hands.

I dropped to my knees, gave them both a lick, one after the other, feeling like some kind of porn star, opening wide for two big dicks. I just needed some pigtails and false lashes. I found myself grinning as I worked those dicks.

"Our little miss is getting demanding." Rick took hold of my hair, guided my mouth to Carl's dick. I sucked him in, and Rick was rough, pushing me onto Carl's cock until I gagged and spluttered. "Take him," he said. "Swallow him down. All the way."

But there was no way. It hit the back of my throat and I retched a whole load of saliva down my tits. It made Carl groan, made his cock jerk. I wanted it more. Wanted to swallow it all the way down.

"Upstairs," Carl growled. "Both of you. Before I shoot my fucking load down someone's throat."

He pulled me to my feet, sent me ahead, and I squealed as he slapped my ass hard as I went. He slapped Rick's, too, chased us both up. And I was giggling by the time we reached the top, heady and horny and desperate for cock.

Carl turned on the water and we stepped under the torrent before it had even warmed up. I didn't even care, just let out a squeak as cold water hit my skin and my nipples pulled to instant hardness. Too cold, and then too hot, but it didn't matter. Rick's mouth was open wide on mine, his hand straight down to thumb my clit, and Carl was behind, his hand reaching between my legs, his big fingers opening me up.

The water temperature evened out, and it was bliss, raining down on my skin as the guys brought me to climax between them. I wrapped my arms around their shoulders for leverage, working myself up and down on their fingers, and my clit tightened and pulsed, quickened and sent me over the edge. I tipped my head back and came for them, a wriggling mess of moaning breath and a host of expletives. My legs felt weak as I came down, but it didn't matter, they had me.

Carl grabbed a tube of something from the toiletries rack, and I figured he was going to soap me, but he didn't. "It's lube," he said as he squeezed some out into Rick's hand. He did the same in his own, and I watched him work it all over his cock. He took me from Rick, guided my arms around his neck and lifted me by my waist. I knew what was coming. I gripped him with my legs, holding myself up as he positioned his cock against my pussy. I lowered myself slowly, taking him an inch at a time.

"Good girl," he said, and his hands were under my ass, hitching me up and down. He filled me up, thumped deep, and I leveraged myself, gripping hold and working that gorgeous dick, wanting it deeper and rougher and harder.

I was getting used to this, used to two, used to taking it and wanting more more, always more.

I felt Rick at my back, his chest against my skin. I cried out as wet fingers pushed their way inside my asshole, working in sync with

Carl's thrusts. I groaned as he opened me wider, leaning back to rest my head on his shoulder. "More," I said. "Fuck me."

He pulled out his fingers and rubbed his cock between my ass cheeks, and I readied myself, took a deep breath.

I let out a groan as he pushed inside. It took a few slow thrusts, Carl slowing to a standstill to let Rick work his way in. I hitched down on Rick carefully, so carefully, gritting my teeth as I went, groaning as he pushed past the tightness. He pressed his lips to my ear.

"I'm in," he said. "We're both fucking in."

"I know," I hissed. "I can feel you. It's deep. It aches. It really fucking aches."

"Want to stop?" he asked, but I shook my head, consumed by the joy of having these guys as mine.

They were mine. They were really mine.

"Don't stop," I said. "I never want you to stop."

Slowly we moved, slowly they fucked me, alternating strokes, one in one out, until I loosened, until I stretched enough to squirm, wanting more. They changed their timing, matching thrusts, grunting as one and fucking me deep, two big dicks inside me.

"Fuck," Rick said. He kissed Carl's mouth over my shoulder. "I can feel you," he said. "Your cock feels so fucking good, Carl. So fucking good."

I could feel them thrusting, could feel Rick's piercings as he pressed tight against Carl's cock.

"Harder," I said. "Fuck me harder!"

They fucked me harder. They fucked me rough. Slamming into my holes as they grunted and jerked and worked me into a quivering mess.

Carl braced himself against the wall, and Rick slammed in, and it really hurt, but it was a perfect hurt. I could feel the pressure in my belly building, nerves tense and achy, the need for release backing up in me. It was coming. *I* was coming.

I let out quick moans, levered myself up and down, over and over until the guys started grunting, their balls slapping wetly together. And it was fucking heaven.

"Fuck," Carl said. "You're so fucking tight, Katie, perfectly fucking tight."

"Gonna come," Rick groaned. "Need to fucking come."

"Do it," I hissed. "I want to feel you."

I was crying out as they came, lost to the pleasure as they jerked and grunted and dumped their loads inside me. I stilled, my arms around Carl's shoulders, catching my breath as they caught theirs.

I let out a groan as Rick pulled out, and my ass felt empty and sore. He pulled my ass cheeks apart and self-consciousness ate me up.

"Fuck," he said. "That's fucking beautiful." He pushed his fingers inside and they went in so easily.

I groaned again as Carl lifted me from his dick. He kissed my lips, then lowered me, and my legs felt weak and bandy as I took my own weight.

He reached another bottle from the rack, and he smiled.

"Body wash this time," he said, and lathered me up.

It felt like bliss.

One hot shower, two hot guys. I soaped them, and they soaped me, and then they soaped each other for good measure. I giggled as they washed my hair, too many suds, far too close to my eyes, but it didn't matter. None of it mattered.

Finally, they held me, and held each other, and I breathed in the comfort of the moment. Three bodies skin to skin, breath to breath.

I loved these guys.

I loved this place.

I was home.

I sipped my cocktail, peering out of our booth at the empty dancefloor.

"Dance?" Rick asked. "Just say the word and we'll hit the floor."

I shook my head. "Later."

Carl pressed closer to my side. "Whenever you want. It's your celebration." He clinked my glass. "To Katie's excellent success."

"To Katie acing the fuck out of sales," Rick added, and clinked my glass, too.

I smiled, happy, bopping my head to the beat of the music. They'd picked a good spot, close enough to boogie, far enough to talk. And I wanted to talk.

I guess it was the alcohol making me brave.

"How would it work?" I said. "The... the baby thing."

The guys looked at each other for a long moment before Carl answered my question with another question.

"You really want to talk about this now?"

I nodded. "I just want to know. So I can think properly."

He smiled. "Whatever works. No pressure, Katie. If this isn't for you, it isn't for you."

But it was for me. *They* were for me.

I looked at the people in the club with us, the couples going about their business, having a good time. I looked at the group of women at the bar, laughing and joking, casting glances in our direction. And that's when it hit me.

If I wasn't the one for them, they'd need to find someone else. They'd need to find someone who could give them what they wanted. Give them a family.

I thought about it being one of those women, the women flashing glances our way, wondering which guy was mine and which was free game. I thought about another woman having Carl's baby, Rick's baby, bringing up a family with these two amazing men at their side.

And it made me feel sick as a fucking dog.

I didn't want someone else to have their baby. I didn't want someone else taking my place in their life.

I took another sip of cocktail.

Drunk. I was drunk.

"So," I said. "Tell me. How would it work? You must have plans."

Rick cleared his throat. "We, um... we've given it some thought."

"A lot of thought," Carl added. "We come together or not at all, that's the rule."

"I know," I said. "I get it."

"But you don't," Carl said. "We wouldn't want to know, not for certain."

I raised my eyebrows.

"Who the father was," he continued. "The *biological* father. We'd rather not know."

Rick leaned over, took my hand. "We'll love a baby the same either way, it doesn't matter. Why complicate it by knowing?"

I looked from one to the other. "So, you just... share... and then don't know whose baby it is?"

"Exactly," Carl said. "That feels right to us."

"And then we'd live together? Bring it up?"

We. I said we.

333

Rick nodded. "I only work part time, it makes life a bit easier."

"And how would you explain it to the baby? Daddy one and Daddy two?" The thought made me laugh and it shouldn't. "Sorry," I said. "This is just surreal."

"It's alright," Carl said. "And we don't know yet. We don't know what the baby would know us as."

"Daddy Rick and Daddy Carl," Rick said. "I like that." He smirked at Carl across the table. "I really like *Daddy Carl*, it suits you."

"You can stop that train of thought," Carl said, but he was smiling.

"And what about school? What about general life?" I continued.

Carl shrugged. "There are plenty of poly relationships out there. We'll be honest with people, honest with our child, make sure they know how much they're loved. Believe me, Katie, it could be a lot worse."

"I know it could be a lot worse, I'm just... won't they have trouble? I mean kids can be so cruel..."

Rick cleared his throat again, and his eyes were serious. "Kids are cruel to anyone who's different. I had my fair amount of crap growing up. I mean, I'm bi, always have been, and some kids didn't like that. But you know what? It didn't bother me, not really. I had a great family back at home, who taught me I was worth much more than some cheap bullying. I had confidence and self-esteem and I was happy in my own skin. Words bounced off me. I know they don't bounce off everyone, and I know it might not be as easy for our kid as it was for me, but in general terms, we'll do our best, we'll love them hard, and I think we'll be alright. That's my gut instinct on it."

"There are worse things," Carl added. "Much worse things. We'll love them, and we'll make sure they're confident enough to make their own path, whatever that may bring."

I leaned back in my seat. "Them? How many children do you want?"

The guys looked at each other.

"Sorry?" Carl said.

"You said, we'll love *them*."

"Ah."

"So, how many?" I repeated. "I mean, this isn't going to stop at one, right? You'll want more?"

Carl's eyes widened. "We haven't really thought that far. We daren't even hope..." He sighed. "We thought about adoption. Should we be lucky enough to have one of our own, maybe we'd adopt as well. Plenty of kids need a home. Don't I know it."

"And biologically?" I prompted. "You'd be happy with just one? How many would you really want?"

Carl took my hand, and he looked at me, looked through me. "However many you'd be willing to give us, Katie. That's the truth of it."

I laughed, shook my head. "I can't believe this is happening to me. I can't believe I'm even talking about having kids. I never wanted kids."

"No pressure," Carl said. "Like we said, it's your call."

I held out my hands, struggled with drunken thoughts. "It's like asking someone if they want ice cream when they watched their best friend drown in a vat of the stuff."

Rick smiled. "Sorry, am I drunk? Does that even actually make sense?"

"It makes a little sense," Carl said. "And you *are* drunk, Rick."

"I mean my mum had it shit," I said. "I watched her struggle, watched her suffer, listened to her cry at night. And that was my fault. Because she had me. And we had nobody else to turn to, nobody else to make it better." I sighed. "My grandparents live way up north, and they weren't that great to my mum, to be honest, I think they'd rather not have had her, either." I finished my cocktail. "So, the bottom line is that I *know* kids fuck things up, like I fucked things up for my mum. Not intentionally, just because that's what kids do, they take your whole life and make it about them, that's what has to happen."

"You didn't fuck things up for your mum," Rick said. "And it would be different. There's three of us. Mum, Daddy Rick and Daddy Carl."

"Stop it with the *Daddy Carl* thing," Carl said. "You're enjoying that too much, Richard, don't think I can't fucking hear it in your tone."

"And what if Mum, Daddy Rick and Daddy Carl didn't work out? What if Mum ended up stuck with all the kids while the Daddies only popped in at weekends? What about Mum's riding and Samson and stable dreams?"

"It *would* work out," Carl said, and his eyes burned. "We'd make it work out. We'd never walk away from our kids. Never, Katie, not ever. Not in a million years."

I sighed. "Then you'd be a better *dad* than I've ever seen."

They didn't speak, and I knew. Yet again the great David Faverley was bamboozling them with his stupid nice guy act.

It upset me again, the thought of him. That weird unsettled feeling I'd been getting since I'd taken his stupid Harrison Gables bargain.

I stared at the dancefloor, watching the lights change and dance, letting everything slip away apart from the alcohol in my veins and the beat of the track.

Rick interrupted my thoughts. He took one hand, squeezed it tight, and Carl took the other. "Enough of the baby talk," he said. "I think it's about time we hit the fucking floor."

Chapter
TWENTY FIVE

CARL

I tried not to think about it too hard, tried not to hope, tried not to make plans that might never happen. We had our beautiful Katie back, in our home, in our arms, in our bed. She'd weathered my fuck-up, stayed the course through the big *baby* reveal, and we were still going strong. This was as far as we'd ever made it. Our gorgeous, vivacious, infectious girl was still with us, still loving us, and that was enough.

For now, that was enough.

Besides, the topic wasn't up for discussion. One drunken conversation at the side of a club dancefloor, and Katie closed up about the whole subject.

Babies were very much off the agenda those next few weeks, not so much as a peep about *Daddy Rick* and *Daddy Carl* and what the fuck that could mean for the three of us. Babies were off Katie's radar entirely as far as I could read it, but Verity Faverley was very much on it.

It wasn't so much what Katie said, or even what she did, that made me uneasy about the dynamic between those two young women. On the face of it, Katie was happy and gracious, smiling without gloating as she marked up her sales leads on the whiteboard. There was no arrogance in her. She was calm and collected, dedicated without being obsessive. In truth, the girl had it nailed. But I couldn't shake it. That *something*. That gut instinct that says there's trouble brewing in paradise.

Strangely enough, the animosity that bristled my senses didn't seem to be coming from Verity's direction. I'd coach her for long afternoons, as promised during her back office meltdown, and she barely even gave her sister a second glance.

But of course she wouldn't. Verity had a much bigger game plan. She was all out to get better, to prove her worth. Her grit had been tested and found lacking, and she'd come back with steel in her gut for round two.

Verity Faverley fucking nailed round two.

She soaked in everything, every little piece of advice, every scrap of feedback. She took sales materials home at night, and be all the wiser for it next morning.

She impressed me in a way I'd have never expected. Brat comes good. Who'd have ever thought it?

Seemingly not Katie. She refused to acknowledge Verity's existence, certainly not as a contender. Not on the face of it.

Katie and Ryan topped the sales leaderboard with ease over the first few weeks. They'd finish up ahead of everyone else without breaking a sweat, every day without fail. Sometimes Katie would take the day, sometimes Ryan, but their relationship was full of easy camaraderie, content in the knowledge that they were the two to watch. They were smashing targets, producing sales leads that were progressing into real opportunities for the field based teams. They were developing a solid pipeline, networking with the right people in the right target organisations. They were good. Really fucking good.

They made me so proud.

But so did Verity. Her steely resolve as she learned the trade from the ground up. She wasn't a firework, one of those bright burners that shoot across the sky. She was a submarine, cruising under the surface, unnoticed until she was in the right position. Then, BAM, one day she hit her zone. She made her calls with confidence, armed with product knowledge that would have put most field reps to shame. She asked the right questions, with a framework to understand the answers. She hit the phone, making those calls steadily, without blips or slumps, and she started bringing those leads in.

What Verity Faverley lacked in natural communication skills she made up for in effort.

She crept up through the ranks, a couple of leads at first, the odd one here or there which morphed into a clockwork performance of one a day. Then more. She consumed data, ate through calling records on her quest to hit the top echelons, and one day, as we reached the middle of the telemarketing phase of the internship programme, she was hot on the Katie-Ryan superteam's tail.

Once she had their tail, they couldn't shake her off. However many leads they generated, she was always right there. She'd clock one up on the board for almost every one they did, and once she had the bug it possessed her, consumed her.

She was in early every morning, picking up the phone to catch those targets unavailable in office hours. She was working through lunch, to the point I'd have to turf her from her seat to make sure the girl was eating properly. She was staying late to listen through her call recordings.

"She's doing well, your sister," I said to Katie in the car one night. "Really well. She's really put the work in."

All I got was a shrug. "Good for her."

"Is that really what you think?"

"I really think I couldn't care less how the bitch is doing. And she's not my sister, Carl, she's made that perfectly clear."

I opted to push it. "Have you considered talking to her? Swapping some tips? Verity has her data management sales points nailed right on, she might have some useful info you can use in the big pharma vertical."

And that's when I knew for sure. It was the look in Katie's eyes when she shot me a glare. It lasted no longer than a second, a momentary slip of her guard that revealed the powerhouse of resentment burning behind the scenes.

"I've got nothing to say to Verity," she said. "Swapping tips with her really doesn't interest me. I don't *need* her tips, and she sure as fuck won't want mine."

"Don't be so sure on that," I said. "She's a dedicated learner. I'm certain she'd appreciate your guidance." I looked at her. "After all, you are top of the leaderboard, Katie, you have nothing to prove and everything to give."

"I have *everything* to prove." Her voice was edgy and raw. "*Everything.*"

Her tone made me pull the car over. I indicated into a shopping arcade, parked up in one of the empty spaces.

"What?" she said. "Why are we stopping?"

"We're stopping because I want to say something. Because it's important." I turned to face her. "You have nobody doubting you, nobody trying to knock you down, or see you fail. The only person you have to prove anything to is *you*, Katie."

She shook her head, scoffed at me. "Me, right. Sure. And Verity, and David sperm-donor Faverley and their whole fucking family, Carl."

"Why so?"

"Because they expect me to fail," she said. "They *want* me to fail. That's why I'm even in this internship programme." I raised my eyebrows, but she shook her head. "Don't look at me like that, it's true. Not for you, who wants the best for everyone, but for them. For them it's all a stupid game. One silly gold envelope and an awkward hug doesn't change the facts, Carl. He's laughing at me, I'm a set up to prove *she's* better than me. Just like always."

"That really isn't true, Katie."

"That's why my idiot father wants me here, just so Verity does better. Just like she *always* does better. So I can be the useless crappy sister again, and she can take all the glory. But not this time." She smiled. "This time I'm coming out on top. Fuck them all." She folded her arms. "I'm good at this shit, I know I'm good at this shit. Verity can fuck off if she thinks she's going to be better than me at this shit."

"She doesn't," I said. "She's said nothing of the kind."

She shook her head again. "She wouldn't, would she? Not to you."

"Has she said anything of the kind to anyone else? Anything you've heard?"

She shrugged. "I don't need to hear anything. I *know* her."

I squeezed her knee. "Sometimes people can surprise you, Katie. Maybe Verity is one of those people."

"Nice try," she said, and put her hand on mine. "I appreciate the sentiment, and the psycho-analysis, but those people are toxic, and I'm going to come out on top, just because I can. Just because this time, in this arena, I'm better than she is."

"This will eat you up." I looked at her but she wouldn't look back. "Believe me, Katie, it'll eat you up. Do this for you, not for other people, not to prove a point. Nobody is waiting for you to fail, there is no ulterior motive here, not for anyone."

"Not for you, Carl, not for you."

I sighed. "That first week on the phone, when you got your gold envelope, I found Verity sobbing her heart out in the stationery cupboard."

"Good," she said. "That'll be a first. I had enough years of being the one crying, she can have it fucking back."

I shook my head. "You know me, Katie, I'm going to just put this out there, what I think."

"Mr Direct, yes, I know. Shoot." She met my eyes. "Go on, tell me. What is it you think?" She sighed, softened her voice. "Go on, Carl. I'm listening."

I squeezed her knee that little bit tighter. "I think it's a two way street. I think she felt as rotten as you, *feels* as rotten as you did, as insecure as you, as inferior as she made you feel. I think she was lashing out, because underneath it all, Katie, underneath all her bullying and her bluster and the *I've got more horses than you have* bullshit, underneath everything you wanted and everything you tried and all the times you said you didn't want to know your father and his posh snooty family, I think there were two very scared little girls who just wanted to feel loved by their dad. Who just wanted to feel good enough."

343

She didn't say a word. Didn't even breathe.

"Am I right?"

She shook her head and there were tears there.

"Talk to me," I said. "Katie, I'm right here. You can talk to me, I get it. I get all of it." I willed her to let me reach her. "I know what it's like to have someone turn up out of the blue, someone you've dreamed of your whole fucking life. The magical father, the guy you dreamed would show up on a big fucking chariot and whisk you away with declarations of love and devotion and finally make you feel like someone who matters. I get what it feels like when it all turns out to be bullshit, when he turns out to be someone who doesn't give a shit, not really. When it turns out your dreams were all for nothing, and you're still the same sad kid without a dad."

"Stop," she said. "Please stop, Carl."

"But your dad *isn't* that man, Katie. Not like mine was. He's just a guy who fucked up, who didn't know what to do for the best, who doesn't know how to make things right between two daughters he thinks the fucking world of."

"Stop!" she said. "This isn't how it is, Carl. This isn't who he is. He didn't want me. He never fucking wanted me!"

Her lip was trembling. It broke my heart.

"I thought he would be someone. I thought he would have a million answers, a million sorries. He didn't even say sorry, Carl, not once. He came and dragged me out of my home, just to show me how wonderful his fucking life was, how wonderful his other fucking kids were, and then he'd drop me back again with a few poxy words about *see you next time*. Every fucking week, over and over, one long cycle of gloating and disappointment. I cried every weekend, Carl, every fucking weekend." She stared out of the window, eyes glistening as a family with two young kids passed us by with a shopping trolley. "The guy's an asshole and I want nothing to do with him. I want nothing to do with any of them."

"But you're doing it, Katie, you're right there. I'm so proud of you, you have no idea how proud I am, that the spirited young woman in her *bite me, baby* t-shirt turned out to be such a talented, mature, dedicated, professional member of our internship programme." I sighed. "And David's proud, too. I promise you, Katie, he's so proud of you. He's always been proud of you."

Her shoulders turned rigid. "No! He hasn't! He's not!"

"He is," I said. "I've known him for twenty years. He's the only person who ever gave me a shot. The only person who took the time to get to know me when I was a nobody. I know him, Katie, he's like the father I always dreamt of."

"*You* have him then! He didn't do shit for me! Didn't take *any* time for me when I was a nobody! He wasn't there, Carl, he ditched my mum and abandoned her, abandoned *us*, just to rock up again like the big fucking I am and parade me around a life I wasn't good enough for! He didn't want my mum and he didn't want me. Rubbing my face in a life I could have had if I was *good* enough just makes him a cunt, Carl, it doesn't make him a fucking messiah. I know he gave you a shot, but he's still an asshole who messed my mum's life up, still an asshole that didn't give a shit about me."

"That's what you think?"

She glared at me, and the first tears spilled, rolling down her cheeks as her breath caught in her throat. "That's what I *know*." She let out a little sob and it panged in my gut. "Why are you doing this? Why can't you just let sleeping dogs lie? A couple of months and I'm out. Harrison Gables and I'm done. I never have to see him again. Any of them."

"Because *my* dad was a cunt, Katie. Because even when he'd fucked me over, gone to prison and cast me aside like I meant nothing, I still wrote to him. Every week I wrote to him. Every week I prayed he'd write back. Even when I knew he was an asshole, that he didn't give a shit about me, even then I still wrote to him and still cried every night because he didn't write back."

"We both have cunts for fathers." She tried to laugh through the tears. "Maybe we should join a support group."

"But you don't," I said. "That's what I'm trying to tell you. You have a father that made mistakes, but he loves you. *Your* father loves you."

"He didn't want me, Carl." She let out a sob. "How can he love me if he didn't want me?"

My heartbeat was in my stomach, my temples thumping as I wrestled with the words in my throat.

But I had to say them.

I always do.

"He didn't even know you existed, Katie."

Chapter
TWENTY SIX

Katie

Carl pulled up outside mine, and the car wasn't even stationary as I opened the door.

He took my wrist, held me back. "Katie, wait. I'm sorry, maybe I shouldn't have... we could go home, talk about this... think things through..."

"Stop," I said. "I have to ask. I have to know."

I took a moment to stare at him, and he was worried. Scared. His mouth was tight and his eyes were sad and lost and nothing like the Carl Brooks I worked with all day. But I didn't have time for that, not right now.

"I have to do this," I said. "Please, let me go, Carl." I tugged my wrist from him.

"This is becoming a habit, me spouting my mouth off and sending you running home."

"This isn't the same," I said. And it wasn't, it wasn't the same at all. "I'm running for answers, not running away. I'm all in, with you and Rick, whether you spout your mouth off or not. Ok?"

He nodded but didn't smile. "I'll wait for you," he said.

"You don't have to..."

"I'll be right here. I'm not going anywhere, Katie. Take as long as you need." He put the car in neutral and turned the engine off. "Take all night, I'll still be right here."

I managed a weak smile, but my head was already spinning, churning through memories and reflections, my heart in my stomach, all twisted up.

All through the drive back here I'd been grasping for evidence that Carl's revelation couldn't possibly be true, struggling to recall the moment I'd first found out my dad didn't want to know me. That he'd abandoned my mum as a pregnant teenager and said he didn't want to know either of us. That he knew I was a kid, growing up just a few miles away, that he hadn't cared enough to want to be there. I knew that, right? I'd known that for as long as I could remember.

And that was the problem. I couldn't remember ever *not* knowing that. I couldn't recall a single conversation from my past that confirmed anything, not for definite, not a single one.

I'd always just known. Just like I'd known how to breathe. Just like I'd known how to walk, and eat, and go to sleep at night. I'd had fantasies that it wasn't true, that my father was lost or incapacitated, on some adventure somewhere far away rather than being a straight out asshole, but I'd *known* they were fantasies.

And then one day he'd just shown up. And I'd been angry, upset that he'd taken so long, upset that he hadn't wanted to know me.

But I'd never *said* that, not to him. I didn't know him well enough, didn't *know* him at all. I hadn't sought answers, because I already knew every part of the story I cared to know, and he was too

348

much of a bragging asshole to stoop low enough to apologise, even if I'd have wanted him to.

That's what I'd thought. *Known.* That's what *happened.* It *happened.*

"There must be a mistake," I said. "Mum will probably wet herself when she realises how stupid the question is." I let out a laugh that sounded fake enough to make me cringe. "I just can't remember the details. That's all this is." I sighed. "I'll be back as soon as I can."

His eyes pierced mine. "Forget I'm here, Katie, just concentrate on you."

I nodded, and then I left him.

Mum was watching TV, some crappy weeknight quiz show after dinner. Her half-finished bowl of pasta was still at her side.

"Hi, sweetheart. Have you eaten? There's some pasta on the hob." She turned back to the screen. "Edison! Thomas Edison! He made the lightbulb!" The team on screen got it wrong and she let out a sigh, shook her head. "Dimwits. Where do they even find these people?"

I could only stare at her, at the mum who'd raised me, who'd loved me, who'd always been there. I took a seat on the armchair next to her, perched on the edge like a dithery little bird.

I felt so stupid, so angry at my thumping heart for even considering the need to ask the question. But I did need to.

"Mum, I need to ask you something, and I need you to tell me the truth, ok?"

She shot me a glance, and her eyebrows lifted. "What is it? My God, Katie, you look like you've seen a ghost." She paused the TV, turned in her seat to face me.

I took a breath. "He knew who I was, didn't he? The sperm donor.

349

He knew we were here, that *I* was here. He knew, right?" I smiled, waiting for her laughter, her look of surprise.

But it didn't come. She looked like she'd seen a ghost, too.

"What did he say?" Her eyes were so wide. "What did he tell you?"

I shook my head. "Nothing. He didn't... he never told me anything..." I fiddled with the hem of my skirt. "He did know, right? He knew about me?"

She was quiet.

"Mum, tell me." I fought the panic. "Did he know about me? He did, didn't he?"

"It'll change everything." Her voice sounded pained and I felt it. She sighed. "We said we wouldn't dwell on the past... we agreed..."

Her eyes welled up, and I felt horrible. I felt terrible. Guilty and nasty and ungrateful.

"Just tell me," I said. "Please, Mum, just tell me."

She shook her head. "He didn't... I didn't..."

"You didn't what?"

She breathed slowly, deeply, closed her eyes. "I couldn't. I couldn't tell him."

My mouth turned dry. "About me? You couldn't tell him about me? Why not? Why couldn't you?" My thoughts tumbled, rolling and lurching through my brain. "You mean he didn't know? He really didn't know I existed? Didn't know who I was? Didn't know anything? Mum, I don't understand, I don't..." I swallowed my panic. "Why?"

"Katie, I..."

"Why?" I repeated. "Why couldn't you tell him?"

She took a moment. "Katie, please try and understand. I was nineteen years old. I was just a kid. I was out of a job, without anyone, without *him*. I was hurt, and I was scared. *That's* why I didn't tell him."

The horror. It knocked me right in the gut. "You lied? To me? You lied *about* me? You lied to him?"

"I didn't lie to you, Katie..." She looked at me, looked into me. "I just hid the truth. You were young. It didn't seem right. It never seemed right to tell you."

"But I knew... that he fired you... I knew he left you..."

She shrugged. "You picked bits up, eavesdropping, bits of conversations. Telephone calls with friends when I thought you were playing. You were like a sponge, sweetheart, taking everything in, but I never told you. I never lied to you, but I never told you, not about any of it. And you stopped asking, when you got a little bit older, you stopped asking."

"But you lied to *him*! You lied to him about *me*!"

"Because I was scared!" she said. "I was so scared!"

I held up my hands, astounded. The shock ricocheting around my brain. "Scared of what? What were you scared of?"

"Scared of him." She cleared her throat. "Not *of* him, not like that. Scared of what he could *do*."

"What could he do?" My voice sounded so pathetic, so small. "What could he possibly have done?"

"He's David Faverley! He had money, connections, lawyers. He had a big house and a couple of kids of his own, he had a family!" She took a breath. "I was scared he'd take you away from me. Scared he'd fight me for you. Scared he'd win."

"How could he win?! You're my mother! I belonged with you! Anyone would've seen that, Mum!"

"Christ, Katie, I know that now!" she said. "But back then, when

I was struggling to sort my shit out, trying to prepare for a baby to come into a life that wasn't prepared for one, back then it didn't seem nearly so obvious." She looked at her hands. "Your father was a great man, a powerful man. He'd already spat me out of his life and sent me reeling, he'd already taken everything from me. I couldn't have him take you, too. And I couldn't trust him, not after how he treated me. What if he did the same to you? What if he hurt you like he hurt me? I couldn't, Katie... I just couldn't..."

"So he didn't know? He didn't even know I was born? You didn't tell him I existed?!"

She shook her head. "He knew I was pregnant. He found that out on his own." She brushed her tears away, and my stomach pained again. "He found me, early on, before I was even showing. He demanded to know if it was true, what my plans were, and I was angry. I said the first thing that came into my head. I told him he was too late, that I'd had an abortion."

My skin froze. "You told him you'd got rid of me?!"

She nodded. "Don't think I did it lightly. It didn't feel good, Kate. Not one bit did it. He looked so hurt, when I told him. But *I* was hurt, too."

I blinked the tears away. "Is that what you were planning? To get rid of me? Did you want to get rid of me, Mum?"

She reached for my hand, squeezed it hard. "No, of course I didn't. I wanted you so much, Katie. You were everything to me, from the very first moment I knew I was pregnant." She smiled, but it was a sad smile. "I didn't want to need him, not when I was pregnant, not when you were a baby. I thought I'd tell you when you got a bit older, but it never felt right. We were happy, sweetheart. Weren't we happy?" Her tears fell. "We were happy. *You* were happy. We didn't

352

need anything from him. Not a single thing."

I shook my head. "No, we didn't need anything. I was happy. But Mum, he was my *father*. He was my *dad*."

She nodded. "I know. I know, Katie. Believe me, I know."

"I thought he didn't care. I thought he didn't want me!" I put my head in my hands, fought the urge to be sick.

"I'm sorry," she said, like it was so simple.

I felt my lip tremble. "That's it? You're sorry? That's all this comes down to?"

Her eyes were so blue, like mine, her freckles across her nose, just like mine. "You hated it there, right from day one. You hated their house, and you hated his kids. You hated going with him, I'd have to convince you every single weekend."

"So?"

"So I didn't tell you. I didn't want to make it worse."

"How could it have made it worse?! How could knowing he didn't hate me from birth make anything worse?!"

She calmed her breath, steadied herself. "I was afraid you'd hate me, too. Hate that I'd lied to you..."

"I'd *never* have hated you!"

She took a breath. "...Two parents who'd let you down, two parents you couldn't believe in, two parents you didn't want to be around. How good would that have been for a little girl who was already hurting?"

"But he was my *dad*," I said again. "Maybe if I'd have known..."

"Maybe it would have been different? It wouldn't have been different, Katie, you hated being there. You hated all of it."

"But if I'd known, Mum... I'd have had a choice..."

She shook her head. "Verity was spiteful, so was her vile mother.

353

You said you didn't want a dad, didn't want *that* dad. You said you were happier just us."

"I was ten! I didn't know what I wanted!"

"And *I* made a call. Maybe it wasn't the right call, but it had already been so long, Katie." Her voice broke. "I'd brought you up so differently to them. We had nothing much, they had everything. You were gracious and kind and polite. You appreciated everything we had, and they appreciated nothing. You didn't want his money, you wanted nothing of theirs. I didn't see anything he could offer that you wanted, that would make it worth the pain and the heartache, not back then."

"A dad," I said, and my voice broke, too. "I wanted a dad."

"Not *that* dad," she cried. "You didn't want to be there with them! If I'd have told you the truth it wouldn't have made any difference, not by then, Katie. It was too late!"

I had nothing to say, no words would come.

She let out a sob. "Don't hate me, Katie. Please don't hate me. I was just a kid. Younger than you are now."

"I couldn't hate you, Mum! Not ever! I'm just…"

"I know it's late in your life to find this out. I know it is…"

"I just…" I shook my head. "I'm so confused. I don't know what this means. I don't know what it would have meant. I don't know if it would have changed anything… I mean, you're right, there was Verity… and Olivia… and I didn't even like the boys…"

"You weren't like them… they're so different to you…"

"But maybe if I'd known the truth, if I'd have been younger, if I'd have given him more of a chance…"

"You still wouldn't have been like them," she said. "Katie, you're nothing like them!"

I fought back a sob. "I know, Mum. And that's because of you. Because you taught me to be kind, to enjoy the things we had, not miss the things we hadn't." I brushed my tears away. "But *you* could have had more, too! You could have had more time, more money. You didn't have to work so hard, Mum, you worked so hard. All the time! And it made you sad, *I* made you sad, and he could have helped you! He could have helped us!"

Her eyes met mine. "My God, Katie, you *never* made me sad. What on earth makes you think you made me sad?"

I had to take a moment. "I used to hear you cry, Mum. Every night, sometimes for weeks. I used to listen to you get upset and know it was about me, because you had to do everything for me. He could have stopped that! He could have helped!"

She took both of my hands, pulled them to her. "I cried a lot when I was younger, Katie. I cried a lot over many things. Missing your father, even though he left me high and dry to go back home to his wife. Missing the life he promised me, all the things I thought we'd have together. I cried for the people in the care home, sweetheart, the people who had nothing, no family to visit them, no reason to get up in the morning. I cried for the people I watched die alone, the people reaching the end of their lives and having nobody to share it with. I cried with frustration that I couldn't help those people more, that I couldn't do more hours to help them, that I couldn't just walk away at night and forget the things I'd seen. I cried for many reasons, so many reasons I can't remember them all, but not one of them, not once, not ever did I cry about you."

My tummy hurt. It hurt like it hurt when I was a little girl. "I thought..."

She shook her head. "You're the best thing that ever happened to me, from the very moment I knew I was having you, you were the best thing in the world. I'm so proud of you, and I always was. Every minute of every single day."

"Don't..." I said.

She looked so scared. I'd never seen her look scared before.

"Don't hate me, Katie, please don't. I may have made some bad choices, but I made them with the best intentions. I did my best for you, and sometimes it wasn't good enough, I know it wasn't good enough, but I did my best anyway."

"It was *always* good enough!" Her pain hit me in the stomach, and I felt it, I felt it as my own. "You taught me to be strong and have faith in myself. You taught me a person's value is on the inside, in their heart and soul. You taught me to focus on what's important and not give a crap for the things that aren't. You taught me to work hard, and put in the effort if you want the result." I squeezed her hands. "I'm everything I am because of *you*, Mum. How could I hate you? You believed in me, no matter what."

"But I kept you from a father who could have offered you so much." She let out a sob. "All the opportunities that could've been yours, just like Verity had them. Schools, and holidays, and horses. I hate myself for that. How could I have let you go without? Just because I was scared? Just because it was too much of a risk? Because you seemed so young?"

"And I didn't want it, any of it. That isn't why I'm sad." I closed my eyes. "I'm sad because I spent my whole childhood thinking he never wanted me. I'm sad because maybe I didn't give him a chance to get to know me, not because I missed out on some *things*. Things mean nothing."

"I'm sorry, sweetheart, I'm so sorry."

I shook my head. "I'm not angry, Mum. I can't be angry." I sighed. "This isn't just your fault. *He* should have told me, too. He didn't tell me anything, just took me to his house and tried to jam me into a square hole. He could have told me. He *should* have told me."

"We *both* should have told you."

"But it's gone now. It's done. You taught me that, too, how to concentrate on what's important. How not to cry over spilled milk or things we can't change."

"I tried to teach you whatever I could. Not that I had much to teach, kiddo. I wasn't all that wise myself, you know." She brushed the hair from her face and she looked so defeated.

"But you were! You taught me to be who I am. I'm strong, I'm happy, I try my best. Always. Like you taught me."

"But I wasn't honest! I didn't teach you that." She was still pale. Still sad. "We shouldn't have had any secrets, Katie. Secrets always come out, they always rot people from the inside out. Secrets tear families apart, cause rifts that never heal, and that might happen here, and it's all my own fault. It's what I deserve. It was always a ticking bomb, waiting to go off one day. I just got complacent. It felt safe after all this time."

Secrets.

Sometimes they're so much easier to keep that way.

"What now?" Mum said. "What happens now?"

I shrugged. "I think. I think some more." I sighed. "I dunno, Mum. I'll work it out."

"I'm so sorry, Katie. Maybe you can build bridges... maybe it's not too late."

"I'm in shock, Mum, but I still think he's a wanker. This doesn't change anything. He still treated you like shit. His kids were still vile to me. He still made me feel like a nobody on his posh, fancy property."

"Don't hate him, sweetheart. He's not a bad man, not really. He's never been a bad man, life is just... complicated sometimes. Things don't go to plan, things don't turn out as you expect, or as you want... Things aren't simple. *People* aren't simple."

I cleared my throat. "Secrets," I said. "So many secrets."

She nodded. "Too many. Far too many. No more, though, I promise. No more. I'm through with secrets. I'm through with hiding, being afraid of the truth. It's always better to know, even if it's difficult. Even if telling the truth makes you scared."

I looked out of the window, at the bulk of the Range through the drapes, and my heart suddenly started thumping.

The words just came out.

"Talking of secrets," I said. "It's time I told you one of my own."

Chapter
TWENTY SEVEN

CARL

I kept an eye on their living room window, even though I could barely make anything out through the blinds. My palms were sweaty and my throat was dry, and I was scared my revelation had done more harm than good. And yet, I couldn't argue with my gut, with that unyielding part of me that insists on speaking the truth, on telling it like it is, damn the consequences.

Damn my big fucking mouth.

I closed my eyes as I called Rick, preparing to face the music. His voice was breezy, blissfully cheerful, until I told him what I'd done.

A long sigh, and I could picture him shaking his head, pacing, cursing my name under his breath. "Mr fucking Big Mouth strikes again. Jesus, Carl."

"She needed to know. It wasn't fair, not on anyone. Not on her."

"I fucking hope she sees it that way."

I rested my head back against the seat. "So do I."

"What now, hmm? What's your grand master plan?"

I shrugged, even though he couldn't see me. "I wait, I bring her home, I listen. *We* listen. She decides how she wants to handle the situation from here on in."

"You make it sound so simple." He sighed. "Let's just hope you haven't messed things up for her. She was happy, Carl. I'm not so sure she's gonna appreciate your good intentions, not in the short term."

"She will," I said, and I was sure. "Katie's strong, she's grounded. She's got her head screwed on tight." I glanced back at the window, still no movement. "She can handle this, Rick, I know she can."

"You haven't given her much choice." He groaned. "Just tread gently, will you? No more grand revelations, my nerves can't fucking take it."

"My cards are all already on the table," I said. "There's nothing left to reveal. I'm all done."

"Thank fuck for that." I heard him light up a cigarette. "Do you want me to head over?"

"No need," I said. "No point us both sitting out here. I caused the mess."

"Just bring our pretty lady home when she's ready. We'll clean it up together, all three of us."

"I will."

"Take care of her, yeah? And make sure you take care of you, too."

"Alright, *Mother*." I took a breath, and made myself say another truth. One that never usually comes so easily. "I love you, Rick."

I could hear the surprise in his tone. "I love you, too." He laughed a little. "Even your big fucking blabbermouth."

"Don't pretend loving my mouth is a hardship for you, Richard." I smiled. "We'll see you later."

I busied myself with work emails, but my efforts were half-arsed. My motivation was lacking, and my nerves were heightening. An hour turned to two, and two turned to three. The warm evening drew on and still there was no sign of my blue-eyed girl. I just hoped she was alright in there, hoped she was getting the answers so long denied. I'd abandoned both my phone and tablet by the time Katie reappeared, enjoying the last of the sun as twilight closed in. She hovered on the doorstep, exchanging parting words with her mother, and they seemed ok. Smiles. A big hug.

I sat up in my seat, watched her approach the car with my heart in my throat.

She slipped into the passenger seat, and her cheeks were puffy and tear stained, even though her eyes were dry.

"Alright?" I asked.

She nodded. "Let's go."

Her mother waved as I pulled the car away, and Katie held up a hand in farewell.

I waited until we were away from her estate before I considered talking, but Katie beat me to it.

She sighed, long and loud, then slumped further into her seat. "My head is fucked," she announced. "Fried. Totally fried."

"I'm sorry," I said. "This is my doing."

"No. It's not." She reached out a hand and took mine. "You told me the truth, thank you. I mean, it sucks, but thank you. It seems it's something I've been lacking, people who'll tell it like it is."

"Always," I said. "I'll always tell you the truth."

I could feel her eyes on me, even though mine were on the road. "I was a long time. Thanks for waiting."

I smiled. "I'll always be waiting if you need me, Katie. That's another thing you can count on."

She squeezed my fingers. "I can count on *you*," she said. "And I'm grateful. I'm really grateful."

"Even though I just triggered the switch that fried your brain?"

"*Especially* because you just triggered the switch that fried my brain." She took a breath. "I don't know what happens now. I mean, what can possibly happen now? What do I do with this stuff? Where do I take it? But at least I get a shot, right? I get a shot to make my own choices, know things for what they really are." She laughed a strange little laugh. "Shit, Carl, I don't even know where to start. The whole thing feels crazy. Everything I've ever known feels... unsteady."

I shot her a look, and the urge to stop the car and crush her in my arms threatened to possess me.

"Why don't you take it from the top? And we can work it out together."

She nodded, sighed again. Breathed deeply, steadily, her eyes on the road ahead as we left the Much Arlock bypass and turned towards Cheltenham.

And then she took it from the top.

I listened intently while she spoke. Listened to the tale of a young woman who'd been cast aside by the man she'd loved. A young woman who'd been afraid and lonely, fearing the powers that be would deem her an unfit mother because she couldn't afford the trappings of a more affluent lifestyle. Fearing her baby's father would take her for his own, and take her away, another dream stolen. One she couldn't bear to lose.

A young woman who should have told the truth, but didn't have the courage. A young woman who'd worked hard to give her daughter everything, but couldn't face opening the can of worms it would take to give her a father.

"I don't think she'd ever have told me," Katie said. "If he hadn't found about me, I mean. I don't think she'd have ever told him, either."

"How do you feel about that?"

She shrugged. "I don't know what I feel. Part of me thinks I should be angry, but I'm not. I mean, I get it, why she was scared, why she lied. I'm sad she did, but I get it." She paused. "I love my mum so much. She's everything to me, she's always been everything to me. She was always there, always seeing the best in me, always trying her hardest. I know she meant the best."

"And how do you feel about your father?"

She shrugged again. "That's harder. I just don't know." She sighed. "I mean, he's still a dick. He still left my mum, still fired her. He's still the guy with the spoiled annoying kids who were really fucking mean to me, he's still the guy who tried to make me something I wasn't, tried to shape me into part of his family rather than get to know me as myself."

"Is there a but in there?"

She nodded. "But he didn't abandon me. Not like I thought he did. He didn't even know I existed. So, how could he have been there? How could he have tried? How can I feel angry for the way he rocked up into my life at ten years old? He came as soon as he could." She stared out of the window. "I didn't get to know him, I didn't want to. I didn't want to know him because I didn't think he wanted to know me. But I was wrong. I just don't know where this leads, how this changes everything. It's all so... big... all so... fuzzy..."

"It's a lot to get your head around, Katie. Give yourself a break."

"What do you think I should do, Carl? What would you do?"

"That's a big question."

"I know it is... but I..." She paused. "I trust you."

"I'm glad, but that doesn't mean I have the right answers. *You* have the right answers for you, Katie."

"It doesn't feel like it."

I pulled her hand to my lips, kissed her fingers. "You're smart, you're strong. You have a good heart. You'll make the right choices."

"All the choices I've ever made have been based on lies."

I shook my head. "That isn't true. Your heart is your heart, your soul is your soul. This shit with your father doesn't change who you are inside, who you've always been inside."

"Ok, so *most* of the choices I've ever made have been based on lies."

"Maybe, but that matters little now. You made the best decisions for you at the time, with the facts you had available. Now, in the future, you may make different choices, based on new information."

"A whole new world..."

"If that's what you want."

She sighed. "I don't know much of what I want right now."

"So start with the things you *do* know, work from there."

I felt her tug at my sleeve, and it made my breath hitch. "Pull over," she said. "There's a truck stop up ahead."

I indicated left, rumbled the Range off the road. I put the car in neutral, turned to face her. "What?" I said. "What's the matter? What is it?"

Her eyes twinkled in the last rays of the sun, expressive and confused. "I don't know what I want, Carl. I don't know if I want to know my dad, or if I'll be disappointed to find out he's still the same prick I thought he was. I don't know if I lost out on being a kid because my mum was scared to let me love someone who didn't love her, and I don't know what that means for my future. I don't know if I clipped my own wings because I learned it was ok to be content not to push myself, not to challenge myself, because I was rebelling. Rebelling against a family I was against from the very beginning. I don't know if I'd want the same things, know the same things, have done all the same things if I'd have known better, known I wasn't an unwanted daughter."

"So, what *do* you know?" I stared at her. "Why are we here? Parked up in the middle of nowhere?"

"Because I know *you*." She unclipped her belt, and my belly flipped. "Because I know I want you. Because you're the only thing that makes sense to me, right now, you and Rick." She reached for me, and I closed my eyes. "Because you're so straight, Carl. Because you don't shy away from what's ahead. Because you're always *there*."

I smirked. "I'm rarely called *straight*, Katie. That makes a novel change."

"Rick's right about you, when he says you're the best man he's ever known. You're the best man I've ever known, too. The best *men* I've ever known, you and Rick."

"Stop," I said. "You don't have to say all this."

She smiled. "You'll be the best dad, Carl. You're everything a good dad should be. Loyal, and honest, and strong. Kind. Hardworking. Supportive."

Her words made my skin tingle. I had to change the subject. I couldn't take it, not even the thought. Just in case. Just in case it was false hope.

"Your dad isn't all that bad, Katie, I promise. I really think you should consider giving him a chance. A fresh start, right from the beginning. The start you should have had."

She was close, so close. Her knees up on the seat, her breath on my cheek. "Kiss me," she said. "That's what I want. That's the one thing I know."

"Rick's at home," I said. "He's only minutes away..."

She shook her head, and then her lips were on me, soft against my cheek. "Please," she said. "Kiss me, Carl, right here."

Katie

My heart was racing, my stomach all chewed up. My legs were wobbly and my throat was dry, and life felt unsteady and raw.

And all I wanted was him.

The man who laid everything on the line, who walked the road of truth and honour, no matter where that took him.

"Please," I said. "Kiss me, Carl, right here."

He turned his head and his lips were so close to mine. "We come together or not at all," he whispered. "That's how we are."

I stroked his face. "But we're a three now, right?"

"Yes. That's right."

"So, things have got to change, no? Move forward? Evolve?"

"What do you mean?"

His breath was hot on my lips, and I breathed him in. "I love you, Carl."

He stopped breathing, and his eyes turned wide.

"I love you, and I love Rick. I love both of you. I love both of you together, and both of you as just yourself. Sometimes I'll want to love

Rick, and sometimes I'll want to love you, and sometimes, most of the time, I'll want to love you both together." I let him digest my words. "And sometimes I'll want you to love each other without me. That's how three should work, Carl. That's how I want it to work. Naturally, however it feels right."

"Katie... I don't know..."

I put a finger to his lips. "Do you love me, Carl? I know you don't like to say it, but I'm asking you. And I'll know you'll give me the truth because..."

He moved my hand from his mouth, and his lips pressed to mine. He took a breath, took my face in his hands, and he kissed me. He kissed me like he loved me.

And then he said it.

"Yes, I love you, Katie." He paused. "And so does Rick, and he's waiting for us at home."

I pictured Rick, his kind smile, his beautiful body. The way he loved so easily.

I nodded. "Ok," I said. "Let's go home."

His fingers were in my hair before I could move, holding me tight, holding me still. His mouth was urgent this time, his tongue hunting mine, his breath ragged. He let out a low moan, and pulled my body close to his, the warmth of him burning me up.

And then he let me go.

"We'll talk about this," he said. "All of us. We'll make this work as a three, together and separately. It's time."

He pulled away from the truck stop.

"It's real," I said. "I told my mum about us."

He raised his eyebrows as he worked up through the gears. "You really did cover a lot of ground this evening. What did she say?"

I laughed a little, remembering the moment. The shock, the surprise, the awkward questions. *Do you... with both of them? At the same time? And do they...? Are they...? How does this work, Katie? How does it ever work?*

And what about the future, Katie? What about marriage? What about kids?

And then my shock, my shock at the realisation I wasn't repulsed, wasn't armed with my usual *I don't even want kids* announcement, that I'd been using right through my teens, right off the cuff.

I cut a long story short.

"She said she wants to meet you. Properly." I smiled. "She wants to meet you both."

"That's something," he said. "At least she didn't run screaming." He smirked. "And where does she want this to happen? We could take her out, a nice bite to eat, somewhere tasteful. Impress her with culinary delights."

"We already decided." I looked at him. "The Cheltenham Chase. I mean, you are coming right? You are coming to see me and Samson?"

He squeezed my knee. "Of course we're coming. Wouldn't miss it for the world."

And so it was settled.

Mum would meet my boyfriends at the Cheltenham Chase.

Right after Samson and I had kicked Verity's nasty little ass to the kerb.

Chapter
TWENTY EIGHT

Katie

It was that same snooty receptionist at the Stroud office, the same one who'd judged me on interview day and found me severely lacking in my *bite me, baby* t-shirt. She didn't give me any such look this morning, not in my posh little suit and my posh little heels.

"David Faverley," I said, and my tone was confident, demanding.

She dialled him without hesitation. "Mr Faverley, your daughter for you." A pause. "No, sir. Miss Smith…"

She gave me a smile as she disconnected.

"He'll send someone right down."

"I'll find him."

She didn't even try to stop me.

I checked out my reflection in the elevator mirrors, so different than the girl who'd stared back at me last time around. Had I really changed so much? Inside as well as out?

I wasn't sure anymore. Wasn't sure of anything. I took a breath and willed my heart to calm itself the hell down as the doors pinged open, and I was back on the executive floor, back amongst director's offices and board level meeting rooms and all that crap.

Another of the neck scarf brigade was heading down the hallway. "Miss Smith, I was just on my way. Your father is right down the hall, on the left. I'll take you."

"No need," I said, and I was off.

I found his office right on the end. *Mr David C. Faverley. CEO.*

I knocked once before I opened the door, took one last deep breath before I pushed my way into his office like a bull entering a china shop.

He didn't even have time to stand. No time to greet me.

"I know," I said. "I know my mum lied. I know she told you I was... aborted. I know you didn't know about me."

His face turned pale, so pale.

Just like I imagined mine had.

Just like my mum's had.

"Katie... good Lord, I..." He gestured for me to take a seat. Picked up his phone, dialled out with a cough. "Cancel everything for today... yes everything... I don't care, he'll have to wait... thank you." He put the phone down.

I stared out of his window, and the sky was blue. Just a smattering of cloud. Just a nice normal summer's day.

He coughed again. "Was this... your mother? Did she..."

I shook my head. "Carl."

He nodded, just a little. "Carl, yes. Of course."

"Why didn't *you* tell me?" I asked. "*You* could have told me."

He held out his hands. "Your mother was worried about the effect it would have on you. She didn't want to dwell on the past, she was adamant, right from the off. She said we should start afresh, so as not to confuse you any more than absolutely necessary." He sighed. "I respected that."

"*Why* did you respect that? She lied to you, for more than a decade."

"Because I respected your mother, Katie. I respected her judgement. I still do."

I couldn't hold back a laugh. "Is that why you fired her? Cast her aside like a stray dog? Was that your *respect*?"

"It was never like that." He looked right at me. "I made mistakes. I didn't do right by your mother, Katie. Lord knows I didn't, and Lord knows I regret it, but with you…" He paused. "I would have been there for her, I would have been there for you. But it was too late. I'd already done the damage." He put his head in his hands. "I loved your mother, with God as my witness, I loved your mother dearly, but I'd lost the fight. It was over for her."

"You didn't fight very hard, *Dad*. Not for *love*. Not for the baby she was carrying!"

"She told me it was too late." His eyes were so sad. "Told me she wanted nothing to do with me."

"And you accepted that?" I tried not to glare at him.

"Things were difficult enough at home. I had the boys and Olivia was carrying Verity. I tried to make the best choices, but everything I did was wrong, Katie. I was wrong to try again with Olivia, I was wrong to cast out your mother, I was wrong to accept her word about the termination, knowing she'd already lied to me once about you."

I raised my eyebrows.

"She left without telling me she was pregnant. Not a single word on the subject. I found out through a friend of hers."

"And she told you it was too late?"

"Yes, she told me it was too late. And I believed her."

I met his eyes, and he was telling the truth. I could feel my own emotions, bubbling around, but I kept breathing, kept my cool. "Mum loved you."

"And I loved her."

"But you were still sleeping with your wife? You must have been."

He shook his head. "It was once. One last ditch attempt at salvaging something for the boys."

"Convenient," I scoffed.

"I don't expect you to believe me."

"I don't know *what* to believe." I took a steadying breath. "I thought I knew everything, thought I understood everything, but I didn't. I don't."

"I'm sorry."

I smiled, fought back the tears in my eyes. "Yeah, you and everyone else."

"I should have told you."

"Yes, you should. Maybe things could have been different. Maybe we'd have had more of a chance." I sighed. "I never gave you a chance. I never had *reason* to give you a chance."

"That's my own fault," he said. "I handled it all wrong. I know that now." He looked straight at me, eyes glassy. "I was just so… overwhelmed. I treated the situation like I treated everything in life, just dived right in, tried to make the best of it, but it was the wrong call."

"I didn't belong there… not with you… not ever…"

"You did, Katie," he said. "I just handled it so badly you didn't *feel* like you belonged there."

"Maybe *you* think so," I scoffed. "But not Verity! Not Olivia! Not the boys!" I wiped away the threatening tears. "They hated me!"

He held up his hands. "And that was my fault, too. I didn't prepare them, didn't warn them, just tried to throw you all together. They were as shocked as you were, as shocked as I was."

"But I wasn't mean! I wasn't spiteful and nasty and cruel."

"I didn't know how hard they were making things," he said. "Not until it was too late. By then you didn't want to know them, didn't want to know me." He reached out his hands. "I couldn't reach you, Katie."

"You didn't try!"

"You wouldn't let me."

And he was right, I wouldn't let him. It would have been too little, too late.

"This is all fucked up," I said. "The whole sorry fucking thing."

He sighed. "No, Katie. It only feels like that. This could be the beginning. The new beginning." He reached his hands further across the desk. "That's what I want. More than anything. It's what I've always wanted."

"We don't know each other..."

"We can get to know each other. Slowly, this time. Like it should have been, Katie. Just you and me."

"I don't know..."

"You're here aren't you? That's a start..."

I shrugged. "So much bad feeling... so much unnecessary bad feeling."

"It doesn't matter now. It doesn't have to matter now."

"You could have been with my mum," I said. "If you loved her."

He sighed again. "Love is complicated, Katie. I loved your mother so much it took my breath, but I loved Olivia, too. She was the mother of my boys, a good woman, a woman I could depend on." His shoulders were tense. So tense. "I know you may not see them like that, but Olivia and Verity are good people. They are just very insecure, very highly strung. They have a more prickly heart. Not like your mother, and not like you, either."

"Is that a compliment?"

He smiled. "You've always made me so proud, Katie, from the very first moment I saw you. I just regret you never got to realise."

Tears pricked, but I didn't let them fall. "This has to be slow," I said. "I just... I don't know how this could even work... after all this time..."

"However you want it to. You call the shots. Not like last time, this time it's all at your pace, Katie, whatever you want."

"I didn't think you gave a shit last time."

"You have no idea how much I gave a shit. No idea at all." His words were raw and choked.

I felt awkward again, scratchy in my suit, small in the big leather swivel chair. "I'd better go," I said. "I told Carl I'd only be an hour."

He smiled. "I hear how well you're doing. I check in every day."

"I know," I said. "He tells me."

"He does?"

"I'd better go." I got to my feet, held out a hand, and it felt stupid. He took it anyway. "I'm sorry," I said. "For my part. For not giving you a chance."

"You have *nothing* to be sorry for. Nothing. The apology is all mine." He squeezed my hand so tight. "I'm sorry, Katie."

My breath was sore in my chest. I nodded. Smiled. Shook his hand.

And then I pulled away, walked to the door, brushed aside a tear before I stepped into the corridor, but there were footsteps, a hand on my arm.

"Katie..." he said, and then he didn't say anything at all. He pulled me into him, and held me tight, and I was so rigid, so scared. "I am so sorry. I'm sorry about your mother, I'm sorry for what I did, I'm sorry I wasn't there."

I nodded, held my breath to stop the tears.

"I love you, Katie, you're my daughter. I always loved you."

And I couldn't say it back. No matter how much I wanted to, no matter how much I wanted to believe him, wanted to believe I had a dad, and that that dad loved me, had always loved me. No matter how much my heart thumped in my chest and my stomach pained with all the hurt and all the forgotten dreams, I just couldn't say it back.

I didn't know him enough to love him.

Didn't know him at all.

But maybe one day.

I wrapped my arms around my father's shoulders, and I stayed there, just long enough to count.

And that would have to be enough.

For today.

The tears pricked again as I pulled up outside the Cheltenham office, and underneath them my thoughts were all fucked up. Sadness, and shock, and a glimmer of hope.

And anger. There was anger there.

Not at my mum, who'd done her best despite a few wrong calls. Not even at my dad, who'd let her down and made a few wrong calls of his own. Epic style.

My anger was at Verity.

375

The cold steely determination in my belly turned hot, and it spat and spluttered. Maybe if she hadn't been so cruel. Maybe if she hadn't made me feel so worthless, so unwelcome. Maybe then, I'd have been able to stay, just enough to get to know him, just enough to know he didn't hate me.

Maybe things would have been different.

I sighed to myself. What did that really matter now?

I breathed out all my hurt, all my anger, breathed out all the bitterness and confusion, and fear. And what was left was me, just me, the same me I'd always been.

Except now I knew the truth.

Finally, after all this time, and all this hurt, I knew the truth.

Carl pulled me aside on my way in, but I shook my head.

"I'm alright," I said, and brushed his hand from mine. "I'm good."

"What did he say?"

"Lots," I shrugged. "Nothing. Everything."

"Want to go talk?" His eyes were so hard on mine.

I shook my head again. "I want to work, Carl. I need the headspace."

He nodded. "Alright, Katie, whatever you want. I'm right here."

"I know," I said, and I did know.

I hammered the fuck out of my calls that afternoon. I was on a mission, consumed by nothing other than the desire to forget it all and fly high on the leaderboard. I chased up all my prospects, closed everything I could into an opportunity, and those leads clocked up for me. Even Ryan looked confused.

"Who put the steam in your kettle today?"

I shrugged. "Just my lucky day, I guess."

He reached out to me, pretended to bathe in my glory. "I hope it's contagious."

"If this is luck, you're welcome to it," I said, and gave his arm a friendly slap.

I was making a coffee when Verity clacked her way into the kitchen behind me. My skin prickled. Wondering what she knew. Wondering what she'd heard. Wondering if she knew anything at all.

She appeared at my side, reached up for a coffee mug, and she was stewing, I could tell.

"Hey, Katie," she said, like she ever made casual conversation. She turned around, leaned against the counter, looking anywhere but at me. "I know we don't... speak."

No shit.

"...but I just wanted to..." She sighed. "Good leads today. So many of them."

"Yes," I said.

"I've been meaning to say. For a while. You, uh, you sure know how to make those calls."

I didn't even know how to reply.

Her earrings sparkled under the florescent light, and so did her lip gloss. She was so preened, so perfect, so stylish and groomed and well-fucking-educated.

But she was nervous, a little bit hollow. She felt like glass. I could tell.

"Look, Katie, I, um..."

"You, *um?*"

She shot me a half smile, like she was crazy and she knew it.

"Ruth and Sharon and I are meeting up at Cheltenham Chase, before the event kicks off. I was wondering if you would... if you wanted to... I dunno... meet us? I have a spare trailer, if you..."

"I have my own trailer," I said.

And she looked disappointed, like I'd lashed out and stamped on her olive branch. It felt so surreal.

She pinked up, and shrugged. But she wasn't hostile. She didn't attack.

"Ok," she said. "Well, I guess we'll see you there. Dad's coming. Seb and Dommie, too. And Mum."

I watched in silence as she made her coffee, dumbfounded beyond coherent speech. She dropped the teaspoon in the sink and shot me a final look before she walked away.

"Hey, Verity," I managed, as she reached the open door.

She turned, stared right back at me.

"Thanks," I said. "For the offer."

She shrugged, offered me a small smile. "No problem," she said.

Chapter
TWENTY NINE

CARL

Bagels were off the lunch menu today. I felt uncharacteristically nervous as I gave the training suite a final onceover.

It had come around so quickly, the end of the telemarketing phase of the internship programme. As of Monday, my group of twenty would be fractured into smaller teams, assigned to different departments of their own choosing. Some into the account management teams, some into back office support, Ryan was heading for the field sales division, shadowing one of our Northern Territory sales managers.

Katie and Verity had both opted for the marketing team, and there would be just four of them heading in that direction.

Maybe it was their shot to find some common ground, without the background noise of a busy calling regime.

I hoped so. As much as Verity Faverley had been a self-righteous, bitchy little pain in the ass for the vast majority of the time I'd known her, I still hoped they'd find some way to forge a relationship of sorts.

Verity had surprised me, and as much as Katie hated to admit it, she was surprising her, too.

I'd seen it for myself, the little olive branches Verity was holding out. Little comments in the team meetings, a genuine smile as Katie claimed the leaderboard for the day, an offer of a trailer for the Cheltenham Chase by all accounts.

I didn't push it. Partly because fragile flowers need space to bloom, and partly because I doubted poor Rick could take another round of my brutal honesty.

I'd done more than enough of that for the time being.

David and our senior management team were due at our Cheltenham office for the Friday afternoon festivities. We had champagne and celebratory cake, and a buffet from outside caterers. Hell, we even had balloons.

I suspected we'd also have a fresh round of golden envelopes, but that wasn't my call. I'd presented the final leaderboard figures with my recommendations, but the final decision on bonuses would be down to David and the finance team.

"It looks amazing in here," Katie said. Her smile was bright and her eyes were happy. She took a seat at her old desk. "I can't believe this is the last time I'll be sitting here, it's come to feel so comfortable, you know?"

"You can always come back and pick up the phone, for old time's sake. It's only over if you want it to be."

She shrugged. "I dunno, Carl. Maybe I'll lose my touch." She looked up at me. "Maybe I'll be a marketing whizz instead, have you thought of that? Maybe I'll join Rick in his little design empire and have my own ads up on the kitchen wall."

I put my hands on her shoulders, gave her a squeeze. "The world is your oyster, Katie. Nothing would surprise me."

"We could give ourselves a cool funky name. *Kat-rick*, it's a bit like hat trick, no? Three in a row. That could be us." She laughed. "You'd have to join then, though."

"Unlikely." I smiled down at her. "Anyway, Rick would want something abstract. Indigo Trout or some crap like that. You know what he's like. Any excuse for a hip rebrand."

"I like Kat-rick."

"So do I," I said, and tipped her face up to mine.

"Smooching in the office is a no-no, Mr Brooks, very unprofessional." Her eyes mocked, but her lips were open.

I leaned in further, until I could feel her breath, and she blushed.

"Carl, seriously. What?"

"It's a celebration," I said, and kissed her.

I kissed her like we weren't at work, like it was just us, alone, like it had become so natural to do. She wrapped her arms around my neck and pulled me close, and moaned into my mouth as I moaned into hers, and it was perfect, so perfect.

But it was a mistake.

A cough from the doorway doused us with cold water, and my eyes crashed into the stare of Evan Michaels, Finance Director.

"I apologise for the... interruption," he said, and there was a barb in it. "I was hoping for a word, Carl, about next month's projections."

I nodded, gestured to our meeting room. "Of course. Be my guest."

I flashed Katie a smile as I went, mouthed *it's ok* in response to her horror.

But the clock was ticking.

It seemed my brutal honesty would likely get another outing

after all.

It came even sooner than I expected. The buffet was in full swing when David's hand slapped on my shoulder, and his expression was friendly but serious.

"We need to talk."

I nodded. "Yes. We do."

Katie's eyes followed us as we left the training suite, and this time it was for another meeting area, far away from inquisitive ears. I closed the door behind us, and David remained standing. I did, too.

"I know I don't need to ask you for honesty, Carl."

"No," I said. "You don't."

"I've heard a rumour..."

"Yes," I said. "Katie and I are in a relationship." I met his eyes, held firm. "I wanted to tell you. I'm sure you understand why I didn't. The secrecy didn't rest easy with me, I can assure you."

He paced. Nodded his head. "How long?"

The admission was the only thing that made me uncomfortable. "Before she joined the programme. Before I knew she was your daughter."

I could see the shock in his face. "That's quite some time, Carl."

"I know," I said. "I'm sorry this is the first you're hearing about it. Genuinely, David. But with Katie being your daughter, with your relationship being as it was, and her participation in the internship programme complicating matters, I felt it best to let time... take its course." I sighed. "I wasn't hiding things with any subversive intent, David. I'm not ashamed."

"I had my suspicions," he said, and his eyes pierced me. "Is it serious?"

"Very."

He nodded again. "You're a good man, Carl. I have nothing but respect for you, and under the majority of circumstances I would wholly support your relationship with my daughter."

Such a mix of emotions churned in my stomach, but his praise hit hardest of all. "Thank you," I said. "That means a lot." I paused. "What do you mean by the majority of circumstances?"

He didn't sugarcoat the issue. "Rick," he said. "Where is Rick in all of this?"

I didn't sugarcoat the issue, either. "Exactly where you'd expect," I said. "Rick is very much in all of this."

He raised his eyebrows. "What is this? Some kind of... *orgy*?"

I shook my head, unable to resist a smirk. "It's no *orgy*, David. We're a polyamorous couple, Rick and I, have been for years." I stared at him. "You know that."

"Yes, I know that." He sighed. "But I didn't... she's my daughter, Carl."

"I'm aware of that." I didn't break eye contact. "I always felt you supported mine and Rick's relationship, David. We both count you as a friend."

"And I *am* a friend, of both of you." He took a seat, and I followed his lead and took one, too. "You know I like Rick, Carl. I've always liked Rick. I like both of you."

"But?"

"But I'm not sure..." he sighed again. "This isn't what I imagined for my daughter. It makes it..."

"Different?" I raised an eyebrow. "So, you support our relationship just so long as it doesn't involve a member of your close circle, is that what you're saying? That it's conditional, David? *Do what you want, just so long as it's not in my backyard?"*

"No," he held up his hands. "That's not what I'm saying."

But he was saying it, that's exactly what he was saying.

"We love Katie very much," I said. "Both of us."

"And she feels the same?"

I smiled. "I would hope so. I certainly believe so. Feel free to ask her for yourself."

He fixed me in a stare. "Would you not consider making a choice, Carl? If you chose to be with Katie, I'd be very happy about the situation."

I stared right back. "I'm not even going to grace that question with an answer, David."

"You must understand," he said. "She's my daughter, Carl, she's my little girl."

"And she's very happy. We're all very happy."

He sighed. "You'd understand," he said. "If you had a daughter."

"With all due respect, I wouldn't," I said. "Love is love, David. Commitment is commitment. Integrity and consideration and communication, honesty and genuine care, compassion, support... those are the things that make a worthwhile relationship, whether that's two people, or three people, or ten people." I willed him to listen. To understand. "We have all of those things, so no, David, I wouldn't understand the preference of the status quo over a situation where three people have found genuine happiness. I'm sorry if our relationship disappoints you, honestly I am, your opinion matters to me very much, but I am not ashamed of loving your daughter, and I'm not ashamed of loving Rick. I'm not ashamed, David, and I have no intention of leaving either one of them."

He pointed a finger in my direction, smiled. "This is why you'd make such an excellent partner for my daughter, Carl. You have such integrity, such honour. I've always respected that in you."

"I hope I *do* make an excellent partner for your daughter. Maybe you should ask her before you come to any conclusions about our situation."

"Maybe I will," he said.

"Please do." I got to my feet. "We have a celebration to attend, if we're done?"

He waited, staring up at me. "I can't say I'm alright with this, Carl."

"So don't. Don't say anything until you know what you *can* say."

He rose from the table, and I looked at the man I'd come to respect to highly. He was still a strong man, still proud. His grey hair was thinner than it once was, but he was still an attractive man, still a charismatic, dynamic, driven leader. He held out a hand and I took it.

"Please don't feel this is a reflection on my feelings towards you, Carl. I respect everything you've done for me, not least for building bridges between Katie and I. I know that was you, I know what you did for me."

"I did that for both of you," I said. "And maybe that's where you should be putting your attention. We're really no threat to Katie's happiness, Rick and I. We'll do the right thing by her, always."

"I know," he said. "I just need some time, to make sense of my outlook."

"Take all the time you need, David. We'll all be right here when you want to talk."

He nodded, and I opened the door.

"Psst," Katie said. She had a party hat on her head, a golden crown with garish glitter stars. I raised an eyebrow and she smiled. "Ryan brought them in. Mine's the queen one, isn't it cool?"

"Very."

She took a breath. "What did he say? My dad, I mean. What was all that about?"

"He knows," I said, and her eyes widened.

"And...?"

"And it's a lot to take in. I was honest, he knows the situation."

"Shit," she said.

"No," I argued. "It's not shit. It's a relief."

She shrugged. "Honesty's the best policy, right?"

"Always, Katie." I smiled. "Always."

"He's still here." She looked over at him. "That's got to be a good sign."

"He is indeed, and I hope so." I pulled her close, took her hand in mine. "And a little birdie told me you may well have an envelope to match your crown. Maybe you'll even appreciate it this time."

"Maybe I will," she said.

I handed her a champagne and we raised our glasses to David across the room.

He only hesitated a second before he raised his in return.

We stayed on late to clear up, the least I could do for the cleaners. We'd made quite a mess of the buffet, and someone had been thoughtful enough to bring party poppers, the whole room covered in coloured strings.

Katie mucked in, and she was giggling, happy on champagne.

"When am I going to spend my vouchers?" she said, casting

386

paper plates into the recycling bin. "I'll be able to buy a whole winter wardrobe at this rate."

I gave her a smile. "Whenever you want. Rick will love that."

"And you," she said. "Mr Suave."

I gathered up the last of the streamers, dumped them in the bin. Finally the place looked respectable, respectable enough for a regular clean at the weekend.

"Weekend calling," I said, and Katie downed the rest of her drink, tossed the plastic flute in the recycling.

She moved back to her old desk, dropped into her seat, and spun around and around as she laughed.

"That's probably not the wisest move," I said, and stopped her.

She stared up at me with a grin. "Spoil sport. I'm just saying goodbye."

"I don't want a sick-splattered car, thank you very much." She poked out her tongue and I pinched it. "This isn't the end," I said. "You'll be back on Monday, the marketing suite is only downstairs."

"But it's the end of all this." She gestured to the room. "Of us working together."

I shook my head. "I'll still be involved, Katie, this is still my programme."

"Yeah, but still," she said. "You know what I mean."

I did know what she meant, but I didn't say so.

She reached up for my tie, smoothed it down. "I won't be able to perv over you anymore."

"You'll have to get your fix in the mornings."

Her eyes twinkled. "Do they have any hot studs in marketing?"

I pretended to think about it. "Maybe one or two. If you like redheads in heels."

Her fingers wrapped around my tie, pulled me down as she smiled.

"What?" I said.

"We were interrupted. I didn't get the rest of my kiss."

"You can get it at home."

But she shook her head. "It's a celebration, I want it here, where we're celebrating."

I kissed her quickly, but her fingers tangled in my hair, and her breath was warm. She held me to her, and her lips opened against mine, her tongue needy and demanding.

My resolve crumbled, and I kissed her back. Between us the chair was pushed away, and she was in my arms, hitched onto the desk, her ankles hooking my legs, her fingers on my belt.

"Wait," I said. "Rick."

"I want you in the office," she said. "I've wanted this since day one. I've wanted this every day from day one."

And so had I. Fuck how I'd wanted to take her at her desk since day one.

"We shouldn't," I said, but her lips were still hungry for mine, her fingers already inside my boxers to wrap around my cock,

"We'll make it up to Rick when we get home," she said. "We can suck him off together, you and me. He'd like that."

So would I. My dick twitched.

"It's not right... behind his back."

She took her hands from my cock and I groaned, but she was only reaching for my phone. She took it from my pocket, worked my cock in one hand as she scrolled through my recently dialled list.

"Call him," she said. "Ask him if he minds."

My breath hitched. "This is a line we haven't crossed, Katie."

She shrugged, worked my dick a little bit harder and it felt too fucking good. "Call him, Carl. If he minds, we'll stop."

"And if he doesn't?"

She smirked. "If he doesn't, I want you to fuck me, right here, right now. Over my desk with my knickers around my knees and my skirt hitched around my waist. Just like an office fuck should be, Carl. Just like I dreamed of."

"Shit," I groaned, but I was dialling. The tone was ringing.

Katie dropped to her knees as Rick answered, sucked my cock into her mouth as he said hello.

"Rick," I said, and my voice was ragged. "I've got to ask you..."

"Fuck," he said. "Fuck, Carl, are you fucking her?"

I closed my eyes, tried to still my thrusting hips. "No... yes... we can stop..."

He was quiet for a second.

"We can stop, Rick. Just say the word."

But he didn't.

"Don't fucking stop!" he said. "I was just getting my fucking cock out."

I smiled, took a fistful of Katie's hair.

"Loudspeaker," he said. "I want to hear everything."

I put him on speaker and dropped it in the IN tray, and Katie let out a little squeal as I pulled her from my cock and onto her feet.

I hitched up her skirt, and pushed her back against her workstation, toppling her onto the desk as I dropped to my knees.

I pressed my mouth to her sweet cunt and she was wet. Her knickers were soaked through. I pulled them down slowly and she moaned for me, moaned for Rick.

And then I licked her, long strokes of my tongue until she was bucking. Until her clit was a hard little bullet, and she was spread wide open. I sucked her between my lips and grunted my approval, and her pussy ate up my fingers as I pushed them inside. Three, straight to the knuckle, and she squirmed and begged for more.

I could hear her sweet little murmurs, and I could hear Rick's breath through the speaker.

My cock pulsed, and I wanted in, all the way in.

I sucked and grunted and ploughed her wet little pussy with my fingers until her drink-relaxed limbs tightened up for me, until her hands were in my hair and she was crying out, begging for more.

Until Rick was grunting, too, his breath ragged.

"Make her come," Rick groaned. "Make her come, then fuck her, Carl. I want to hear you fuck her."

I curled my fingers, and she grabbed my wrist. "Fuck," she hissed. "Right there."

She wouldn't let go, guiding my hand as my fingers worked her from inside. She tipped her head back and arched her spine, and her cunt made such lovely wet noises.

"Come for me," I said. "Rick wants to hear."

"Yes..." she rasped. "Oh fuck..."

I picked up pace, and circled her clit with my tongue, and the girl was delirious, all limbs and gasping breath, her leg resting over my shoulder, her heel digging into my back.

She came like a banshee, and it was beautiful. She came loud enough that she drowned out Rick on the loudspeaker, and the world was only Katie and her gorgeous wet slit in my face.

And then I fucked her. I flipped her onto her front and I fucked her before she'd even caught her breath.

She grunted and groaned as I slammed my way inside, and I was grunting, too, and my phone was dancing around the IN tray.

"Fuck me," she hissed, gripping on to the edge of the desk. "Fuck me hard, Carl. I want it fucking hard."

"My fucking pleasure."

I took her hair and twisted it in a braid, then wrapped it around my hand and pulled, enough to tip her head back.

"Tell Rick how it feels."

She let out a little whimper.

"Tell Rick how it feels," I repeated, and licked up her face, angled my breath to her ear.

"It feels... deep..." she said. "Oh, fuck, it feels... hard, so hard... it aches... it aches so fucking good..."

"Fuck her." Rick's voice was raspy.

My flesh slapped against Katie's, her body shunting into the desk with every thrust.

"Fuck her, Carl. Fuck that sweet little cunt."

I changed angle and she cried out, but she was wriggling, bucking her hips right back at me.

"I'm about to shoot my fucking load," I growled, and she moaned for me.

"Fuck her, Carl," Rick repeated, and I could hear the edge in his voice, his own ragged breath.

"Shit..." I growled. "Oh, fuck..."

I came hard, pulling Katie's hair tighter than I should have, but she didn't care, didn't even let out a squeak.

I slammed balls deep and pumped my load right the way inside her, as she tightened and bucked and milked me fucking dry.

I rested my forehead on her shoulder, and she leaned back at me, kissed my temple.

"You still there?" Rick asked, "I just jizzed all over my desk." He laughed. "Fuck, guys, that was fucking something." He paused. "Told you that was a good idea, Carl."

"Arrogance isn't becoming, Rick. Nobody likes a smart arse."

I pulled out of Katie and she moaned, giggled.

"You'd better be ready for round two," I said. "We're on our way home."

"Just hurry the fuck up," Rick said.

Chapter
THIRTY

Katie

I used to think dreams were constant and unchanging, that they'd last a lifetime. Maybe some dreams do. Maybe others ebb and flow, dull and fade to be replaced by others. Maybe some dreams return from the ashes.

The dream of a father who loves you, for instance.

I took a breath, cherishing the moment, head collar in hand as I made my way across wood-chippings to fetch my furry boy. Our big day. The day we'd been training for. The day I'd been waiting for.

I tried not to let Jack's words dampen my spirit, ignoring the sadness in my belly. I now knew with certainty my dream of this place was really over. I'd seen the letter, in black and white, the bank's intention to repossess in twenty-eight days should a buyer not be found. The little girl in me cried out that I should take Carl's generous offer and have this place as my own, but I'd never do that. I'd never swap my dream for one of his I may never be able to fulfil.

I called my boy, and he came running. I slipped on his collar and led him to the yard, and there were butterflies in my tummy to cancel out my hurt.

"Just us, Samson," I said. "Our special time on our special day."

I'd wanted to do this alone, determined to do it all under my own steam. My trailer was ready, all hitched up to the battered old brute, and his tack was soaped up and gleaming to perfection. I shampooed and brushed him down and braided his tail, fastened up his travel boots and loaded him up ready to go. He chomped on his hay, his ears pricked, and I bolted up the doors, taking just a moment to plant a kiss on his furry nose.

"I love you," I said. I stroked his blaze and he butted me. It made me smile. "This is it, boy. Our big moment. It'll be fun, I promise."

He butted me again like he understood.

I took the drive slowly, but we still arrived with plenty of time to spare. I pulled up amongst all the other trailers, and there were riders everywhere in their fancy gear. I spotted Verity's right at the end of the row, a huge gleaming lorry with the Faverley crest on the side. I caught a glimpse of Fleetwood Fancy — Verity's prize mare — through the other horses warming up. Her mane was all braided, and she was in high spirits, restless as one of Verity's minions walked her around. The prospect of beating her time seemed much more untenable here, a ridiculous pipe dream, but fuck it, we'd be going for it anyway.

I was unloading Samson when the guys arrived, and my mum was with them. She looked great — in a rich peach lipstick and a dark green summer dress, her hair bouncy and light. And so did, Carl and Rick.

In fact, they looked really fucking great.

"It's not the races." I laughed as I looked Carl up and down. His suit was impeccable, his hair too styled for a cross country course.

394

"Thought I'd make the effort. No law against looking smart, is there?"

I shook my head. "No, no law."

"Only social conventions." Rick elbowed him. "But we've never really taken much notice of those."

"Thanks for coming," I said, and kissed them both. I gave my mum a hug and she was quiet but smiling. "You've met, then?" I asked, and she nodded.

"Carl and Rick kindly picked me up this morning, so I can have a glass of bubbly when you come in first."

I laughed, gestured across the field to Verity's camp. "I doubt we're up to that, but we'll give it our best."

"You can do anything," Carl said. "Just give it your all."

"Go Sammy!" Rick said, and gave Samson a hearty pat. But he was more interested in mints than encouragement. He dug his nose straight into Rick's trouser pocket, and left a smear of horsey drool. "Cheers for that, boy."

He wiped it down, tried to hide it with his shirt, but it made me laugh. "Teach me for dressing up," he said.

"Teach you for bribing the horse with treats," Carl said. He took a step forward and Samson didn't flinch. "The beast likes me for me, Richard, not for cheap mints. We have a mutual respect."

I rolled my eyes at my mum. "Horse rivalry."

She didn't say a word, but her eyes were happy. Maybe she liked them.

Maybe she even approved.

I could hope.

Verity was up in the listings early. I kept my distance as she took her position at the start of the course, nervous as I saw the Faverley posse out in force to see her off. My dad looked smart, almost as smart as Carl, and Olivia had a stupid purple hat on. Seb and Dommie were in slacks and jumpers, their hair all posh-boy ruffled. I made sure they couldn't see me, ducking out of view as Verity's name was announced over the tannoy.

Miss Verity Faverley riding Fleetwood Fancy.

Her brothers gave a cheer as she prepared to ride. The horse was already warmed up, she was raring to go, dancing on the spot, her head up high in Verity's face.

They didn't know each other, not really. Verity looked slightly awkward, her shoulders way more tense than they should have been.

A sliver of hope warmed me. *Maybe, just maybe.*

They took off like a rocket, the mare charging at a gallop right from the start. I held my breath as she took her first jump, a simple brush fence, and they cleared it easily. The horse had a beautiful pace, and a beautiful jump. She landed with ease and motored along and my heart dropped a little. I pushed it aside.

Rick wrapped an arm around my shoulder. "How you feeling, pretty lady?"

I squeezed his waist. "Excited. Nervous."

Carl appeared at my side, kissed my hair. "You'll be great."

I stood happily between them, pulled them both close, and Mum looked curiously, but didn't comment.

"There's David," Carl said, and he held up a hand before I could stop him.

My father approached, with his *proper* family in tow, and my stomach tightened. Olivia and my mum faced off, and you could have cut the air with a knife.

"All set?" my dad asked regardless, and I nodded.

"I hope so."

Olivia looked twitchy, she took his arm. "We should get going, darling. We can catch Verity at the water jumps if we're not tardy."

Urgh.

Seb and Dommie looked at me, and looked at Carl and Rick. They didn't say a word.

"You could go ahead," my father said to his wife. "I could catch you up."

She looked like he'd slapped her, and the shock hit me, right in the belly.

"But we should go together..." she said.

"I'll stay with Katie awhile. I'd like to meet Samson."

"But David," she hissed. "Verity is riding."

I smiled at my father. "Go," I said. "See Verity. I'll introduce you to Samson later, after we've ridden."

"I can stay..." he said, but I shook my head.

"It's cool, I'll see you in a bit."

"If you're sure."

"Very," I took hold of Rick and Carl's hands. "I have chaperones."

He grunted, but smiled. "So I see." He patted Rick's arm. "Good to see you, Rick." He shot Carl a grin. "As for you, I see too much of you already." He slapped Carl on the back as he left, and Carl was smiling.

"I think that went well," he whispered.

"Hope so," I said.

And maybe it did. Even Mum didn't look too bothered. She was more interested in the riders coming onto the final straight than she was in my father.

Maybe, just maybe, things would work themselves out after all.

I was nervous as our time slot arrived. I fastened myself into my body protector and tied my numbered bib, put on my helmet and mounted up for the warm up. I worked Samson through his paces, walk then trot, loosening him up in a slow canter, and slowing him back down again. Carl, Rick and Mum looked on, and I tried to appear more confident than I really was. We'd done a few courses before, Samson and I, but nothing quite like this. Not competing.

Verity's time came in. It was good, but not great, not really.

Just shy of twelve minutes.

My spirits soared.

I waved to the guys and Mum as I took up position at the start, and the officials counted down from ten and we were off. Samson opened out into a gallop, ears pricked forward as we charged towards the first fence. We cleared it easily and the spectators let up a cheer which made my heart sing. I gave him a pat and tried to relax, keeping his pace fast but steady as we headed for the first of the water jumps.

He didn't falter, jumping right through and galloping up and over the bank the other side. He took a solid looking triple and his pace was perfect, and he gave his all on the straight as we made our way to a coffin jump. He cleared it big, but it didn't matter, straight into another gallop and I was loving it. We were both loving it.

I felt the thrum of my body, my concentration on my posture, on the hands that guided Samson, and we were as one. I moved with him, felt the thump of his hooves on the ground, and this was everything, everything I wanted.

Halfway through the course and I realised we were in with a shot, maybe not of coming top, but certainly of beating Verity's time. I'd heard she'd had an awkward jump, a ditch right at the end of the course, and she'd gone in wrong, almost sending her mare tumbling, only to recover with just a lagging pace to stumble over the finish line.

We could take her.

As long as we kept it up.

I encouraged Samson on, through water and over a wide table jump, over a fallen tree fence and over another bank, and he was doing so well, so fucking well. The spectators were cheering and the commentators were saying good things, and I was smiling. Really smiling.

My heart started thumping as we came to the final third, and my adrenaline picked up. I knew our time was good, I just knew it. A quick glance at my watch told me we were in the game to beat Verity's time, but it would be close. Her mare was faster than we were, more skilled, but we were doing it, a solid effort, giving it our all.

I urged Samson on, and he did me proud, even though I felt he was tiring. I pushed him over the final straits, and he put his heart into it, tearing along to the final hurdles. The biggest fence of the course and he jumped it with ease, landing a little hard but he recovered well, back into another solid gallop. His ears were still forward and his heart was still all in it, and so was mine.

I dared to dream, dared to hope, my heart bursting with pride as we curved on round to the final section.

I knew Rick and Carl would be waiting there at the final jump, Mum, and my dad, and probably even Verity, too.

It would be our moment. Our moment of victory.

Please let us win, just let us win.

Samson saw the jump coming and I saw Rick and Carl, Mum and my dad, too. I tried not to look at them, zoning out of the gathered crowd and focusing back on the fence. The drop was quite big, and Samson wouldn't see it, I angled him into position, but our time would be close, so I gave him a squeeze encouraged him onwards, and I was so happy, knowing how solid we looked, how in sync we were.

This would be our victory, our sweetest moment.

I tried to be smart, aiming for the far edge to give us a couple of paces advantage on the final stretch. I tried to look our best, tried to show off, tried to prove how great we were, how perfect we were, how great my Samson was.

And I took it wrong.

I made a mistake.

I gave Samson mixed signals, and he turned awkwardly, taking the fence mid-way. He was off balance when he took off, and I was, too. I couldn't adjust my position quickly enough to compensate, couldn't guide him for the drop, and in my hesitation he'd lost some height.

A moment of horror as I realised the inevitable, my breath leaving me as I felt Samson's rear hooves clip the top rail. I didn't loose the reins quickly enough, and I was too far forward in my saddle. He hit the ground heavily on his front legs, and I couldn't sit back to rebalance him.

We toppled, and I felt it in slow motion. Felt him lurching forward and taking me with him.

His front legs went from under him, his unbalanced rear end crashing forwards to send us both tumbling, and the bank was unyielding, unforgiving.

I heard a gasp from the crowd, and my own heart in my ears.

The whistle of the wind.

A weird stillness.

And then a thump as we landed, a terrible sound as we skidded. And pain. In my leg. Pain as his weight rolled onto me, and pinned me.

My head bashed into the ground, and the world felt far away, my vision blurred.

And everything hurt.

People and screams, and Samson's breath.

And then it all faded away.

Chapter

THIRTY ONE

CARL

That horrible moment when time stands still. When you see the inevitable, the horror unfolding right in front of you, but you are powerless to do shit about it.

I couldn't tell you the moment my breath caught in my throat, when that instinctual sense of dread enveloped me and chilled me to the bone. Their jump just didn't look right, didn't feel right, and had me pushing through to the barrier before they'd even fallen, helpless and petrified as our beautiful girl went tumbling.

Samson's legs went from under him, and he went forward, and Jesus, they landed so hard, both of them, and there was a scream, a horrible scream as she took his weight, a horrible thump as they landed and slid.

And then she was still. Our beautiful girl was still.

Samson writhed on the floor, and there was blood. His eyes were wild and frantic, his instincts raging as the officials rushed over.

And so did we. Rick and Debbie, and David, too. All four of us piling over the rope.

Katie's eyes fluttered as she regained consciousness, her gaze flicking around before the horror came rushing back. Her face contorted with pain, her leg still stuck under Samson's shoulder, and she was ashen, so ashen.

"My leg!" she screamed. "It hurts! It hurts so bad!"

The officials were trying to stop Samson struggling, but he was wild, his legs flailing. He couldn't get a grip against the slope of the bank, trying desperately to get enough leverage to take his own weight and failing. Both of his front legs were bloody, but one looked worse, his hoof hanging awkwardly as he flailed.

I felt sick. So fucking sick.

Not so much at the injury, but at the expressions on the faces of the people who knew this kind of shit. The people calling for medical assistance on their walkie-talkies.

They hitched Samson enough to free Katie's leg, and she screamed a terrible scream as they pulled her out, and pulled her clear. Her mother was at her side, and so were we, trying to tell her it would be alright, that she would be alright, but she wasn't even listening. Her eyes were fixed on Samson and were streaming with tears.

"Help him," she said, and her hand clutched at mine. "I don't care about me, just help him! Oh God, Carl, don't let them hurt him. Please don't let them hurt him!"

She pushed me towards him, and I moved, a tentative step towards the fallen animal. And I was impotent, for the first time in my adult life I didn't know what the fuck I should do.

The paramedics arrived, and gave Katie some oxygen, painkillers, too, talking in calm voices as they tried to examine her leg. They made her lie flat and fastened her into a neck brace, splinted her leg as she cried into the oxygen mask, and I was scared, so fucking scared. I shot Rick a pitiful look and he was ashen, too, crouched at Katie's side while she death-gripped his forearm, her mother on the other side of her with tears in her eyes.

I closed the distance between me and Samson, and David appeared at my side. He gave me a look that said this was futile, and his knowledge of eventing horses filled me with absolute dread.

"We have to save that horse," I said under my breath. "Whatever it takes, David."

He nodded, patted my shoulder.

A guy who was clearly a vet was crouched at Samson's forelegs as a couple of stewards held the animal down, and his face was stern.

"How bad is it?" I asked. "Please tell me you can fix him."

My heart was in my throat as he tipped his head from side to side. "We need to get him up, he fell awkwardly, I hope he can stand."

"And if you can't get him up? If he can't stand? What happens then?"

David gripped my elbow, and I knew. And so did Katie.

"No!" she screamed. "Carl, don't let them! Whatever it takes, Carl! Please don't let them hurt him!"

It broke my heart to see her there, in so much pain, with so much fear. The paramedics busied themselves preparing her for the ambulance, and Rick and Debbie looked so helpless, as helpless as I felt.

"He has to be able to support his weight," David said, his voice so low. "If they can't get him up, Carl…"

I shook my head. "I can't even begin to tell you how much this horse means to that girl. We have to get him on his feet."

He nodded.

"Clear some space," the vet said, and they gave Samson some room. He braced his forelegs on the ground, even the mangled one, and attempted to push himself up. I held my breath, willed fate to give him a break, but the poor brute slipped and fell, collapsed back against the bank, his sides heaving. I cursed under my breath.

The vet shrugged, shot me a fatalistic glance.

"He just needs some help," I said. "Let's give him some help. Come on David, help me." We joined the stewards, and as the poor brute strained for a second attempt, I put my hands under his flank and lifted, pushed him upright with all my strength. "Come on, Samson," I hissed. "Come on boy, get on your feet. There's a good lad."

David pushed and I pushed, and we gave it everything we had to help that horse back to standing. He braced his weight on one of his forelegs, and he wavered just a moment as he struggled for grip. We gritted our teeth, held him steady, and his weight shifted as he lurched and heaved. His leg held, took the weight, enough for his back end to come up and under him.

A big lurch, and a shove from us at his side, and he was on his feet. The boy was on his feet.

I was breathless, heady, my forehead pressed to Samson's sweaty neck as he struggled to limp forward on his battered legs.

"Tendon damage," the vet said. "Extensive, I'd say." He looked at me, looked at David. "This horse is unlikely to work again."

I shook my head. "It doesn't matter. None of that matters."

"His recovery will be expensive."

I waved my hands and so did David, and for that one moment our thoughts aligned in perfect sync.

"Whatever it takes," I said.

"Fine," the vet said, and got to work.

They limped Samson from the course, and applied cold compresses as the horse ambulance arrived.

I let them do their job, let the experts take over.

And I begged fate for mercy.

"You saved him," Katie whispered as they lifted her into the ambulance. Her voice was muffled and fragile, her eyes so sad.

Our beautiful girl looked so broken, so weak, all trussed up on a stretcher.

I leaned over her. "No," I said. "I just helped him up." I gestured towards David. "We both did."

"Good job, Carl. David," Rick said, and Katie's hand was still clamped tight to his wrist.

"I want to ride in the ambulance with her," Debbie said. "Can you follow us?"

"There's room for one other," the paramedic said, and Rick looked at me.

"Go," I said. "I'll meet you there."

Katie tried to move, tried to lift her head to me, but Rick and Debbie held her firm. "Don't leave Samson!" she cried. "Please don't leave him, Carl! Don't leave my boy!"

"I won't," I promised, dipping my face to hers, and she relaxed, her eyes fluttering as they took her away.

I watched the ambulance pull away, sirens blaring, and my heart dropped through the floor.

"I'll go with Samson," I said to David. "Wherever they're taking him."

He looked across at an ashen Verity, a shocked-looking Olivia at her side. Seb and Dommie looked sullen, and I realised we were all feeling it, every one of us. Olivia took a step towards David, beckoned him over, but he didn't move. He held up a hand, indicated she should stay put, that they should all stay put, and then he turned to me, his eyes on Samson as they tried to load him into the truck.

"I'll come with you," he said.

We followed the horse truck, thoughts heavy as I kept the Range close behind. My legs were shaky and my nerves were shot, my mind veering between the poor brute in front of us and my poor sweet Katie on her way to the hospital. I hoped they'd stabilised her, hoped to God she wasn't in too much pain.

"I'm having Samson directed to our vets," David said. "They're the best, Carl, we use them for Verity's show breeds. They'll do their very best for him."

I nodded. "I'll take your guidance. I know fuck all about horses."

He sighed. "Poor girl. Poor, poor girl."

"Just so long as the horse lives, David. She'll be ok as long as Samson's ok. She's tough."

"Like her mother."

"And her father," I said.

I could feel his eyes on me. "You were right there beside her. You looked as damn well rotten as we did, Debbie and me."

"We love her, David. As I said."

His hand landed on my arm. "I can't say it's the situation I'd have opted for my daughter, being with two men. I can't say the revelation filled me with joy, Carl. But despite my initial reservations, having thought things through, having known both you and Rick long

407

enough to know the kind of men you are, you have my blessing." He laughed gently. "For all that's bloody worth."

"It's worth a lot," I said.

"I've never been much of a fan for the path well-trodden, Carl. You know me. I make my own route, go my own way." He sighed. "I should have expected Katie would share my lack of respect for mindless convention."

"We work well, the three of us. You'll get to see that. Hopefully."

"Hopefully," he said. "I'd like that." He shifted in his seat, exhaled a long breath. "I'd love to get to know my daughter, Carl, that's what I've always wanted."

"You'll be impressed. She's really something."

"So many years to make up for."

"Better late than never, David. Tomorrow is a brand new day."

We followed the truck to Cirencester, parked up alongside as they pulled to a stop at an equine facility. It looked the business. I felt the tension ease just a little.

He was in safe hands, efficient hands. A team of vets and assistants got to work, unloading him with care and supporting him through to their treatment suite.

We took a seat in the waiting area, grabbed a coffee, just like we were at a regular hospital.

"Thanks for this," I said. "I wouldn't have had a fucking clue."

David sighed, took a sip of coffee. "I knew she loved the horse, Carl. Even I knew that. But seeing her on him, the way they rode, before the fall. She was incredible."

"She loves him." I smiled. "And he loves her."

"So much I don't know," he said. "So much I need to know. Need to learn."

"You won't go far wrong by starting with Samson. He's her greatest joy. Her dreams revolve around riding, revolve around him."

"Harrison Gables was a chance call, because of Verity. I figured Katie would enjoy the same trip."

"You got that right."

"We'll be here a while," he said. "Before we get the prognosis. You could go, I'll stay."

"I'll go as soon as I can, but not until I know the situation with Samson. She'd never forgive me for turning up without answers."

"Who'd have ever thought it, Carl. What a twist of fate, you ending up loving my daughter, building bridges for a sad old man who'd give anything to get to know her. And finally us, ending up here, waiting for a horse's salvation."

"Life is strange," I said.

He turned to face me, eyes warm. "Another favour for a sad old man, Carl, if you'd be so kind."

"You're not so sad, nor so old, David. But fire away."

He smiled, a wistful smile. "Tell me about her. Tell me about my Katie. Tell me about her life, Carl, the big things, the little things. Tell me about the things that make her smile, the things about her that make you smile. Tell me what she dreams of."

I took a breath, and settled into my seat, taking a moment to listen to the hustle and bustle of efficiency all around us.

And then I told David about his daughter.

Chapter
THIRTY TWO

Katie

The words no rider wants to hear. *A tibial plateau fracture.* I mean, I'm no fool. I knew it was bad. I knew as soon as I landed, I even heard the crack. It sounded like a twig breaking, the most surreal sound.

And then there'd been pain.

So much pain.

Fear, too. Fear for me, but mainly for Samson.

My poor furry boy.

I was delivered to some posh hospital, courtesy of my father, and for once I didn't argue about taking something from him. I just wanted to walk again, wanted to ride again one day, and if he was my best shot, then I'd take it gladly.

I was kept in for over a week. The first days were the worst days. Confined to my bed, in agony every time a muscle twitched, every time I shifted in half-sleep. They brought me a wheelchair after three days, but getting in and out of it was an ordeal, all for the reward of

Rick, Carl or Mum wheeling me up and down the corridor awhile. One day we made it outdoors, just to the hospital's twee little garden, but I didn't want to be there, didn't want to smell the grass or feel the breeze on my face. Knowing my furry boy was likely shut away inside somewhere, scared and alone, made my gut churn.

I'd dream about him constantly those first few days, picture him every time I closed my eyes. Reliving those horrible moments over and over, wishing I'd have taken more time, wishing I hadn't been so reckless, so bloody stupid.

I asked so many questions, about where he was, about how he was doing.

Torn tendons, in his right foreleg. Both superficial and deep digital flexor tendons. They were treating him with cold compress therapy, realigning his hoof with support braces. The rest would be rest. Plenty of rest.

It was doubtful I'd ever ride him again.

It ripped my heart into pieces.

They hardly seemed worth it, the wheelchair excursions, nor the visits Rick, Carl and Mum insisted on daily only to find me doped up or morose, but I made myself smile, made myself say thank you, made myself keep going. Dad stopped by, too, with flowers and a big bright *get well soon* card. But it wouldn't be soon. Not by a long way.

The surgeon waited for the swelling to go down enough to operate, and then there were pins, screws, and a big jagged scar running down my calf.

I tried not to look at it. Tried not to think about it. Tried not to let the gloom swallow me up.

The regime was intense and the days were long. Physiotherapy on my knee, drugs for the pain, scans and examinations and consultations.

And then finally, after the longest ten days of my life, they allowed me home.

I cried when I saw the effort Carl and Rick had gone to. They wheeled me inside with a *'tada'* and the dining room was no more, replaced by a downstairs bedroom. They'd moved their bed, *our* bed, all the way from upstairs and set up a chest of drawers for my things. They'd even put some photos up, me and them, and me and Samson, me and my mum, too.

"To keep your spirits up," Rick said. "Cool, eh? The Katie recovery suite. There'll be masseurs, and cocktails... the full luxury experience..."

"You didn't need to do all this," I blubbed, but Carl kissed my head.

"We *wanted* to, Katie, we both wanted to."

"Don't think we haven't missed you, pretty lady," Rick said. "It's felt so empty here without you around. Guess you've got us pretty hooked."

I smiled through the tears. "Yeah, well, you've got me pretty hooked, too."

We had to be careful. My position between the guys was no longer tenable, and I was relegated to the outside edge while the two of them slept at a safe distance, their fingers reaching out to touch mine. It was a comfort. They were a comfort.

They became everything in the world to me without even breaking a sweat.

You have no idea how much you take for granted until every little thing is an impossible task. Moving out of bed, getting dressed, taking a pee. Reaching for a drink, showering, grabbing some food.

Any semblance of modesty or personal space I'd ever enjoyed was smashed into oblivion. They bathed me, they dressed me, they wiped my shitty ass. They brought me meals, kept me comfortable, and entertained me.

They made me smile when I didn't feel like smiling, made me laugh despite the pain. They made me forget my sorry situation when they were around me, when they were loving me just as much as they had before.

And how I loved them for it.

I loved them so much it made me cry at night, when they were asleep, crying for my luck at having them, even though everything else had turned to shit.

I loved them for everything they did, but I loved them most for taking me to see Samson, even though they didn't think I was ready.

"Where is he?" I said, as the car turned in the opposite direction of the equine hospital. "Is he not in Cirencester anymore?"

Carl shook his head, and he looked wary, shifty.

"What?" I said. "Where is he, Carl?" The panic engulfed me. "They can't send him back to the yard! It's being repossessed! There'll be nobody there! Nobody who can take care of him!"

"He's not in Woolhope," Carl said. "He's not far."

"Where's *not far?*"

Carl looked right at me as he answered. "He's at your father's house. They have facilities, Katie."

I can't deny my heart pained. "Who's taking care of him? Who's going to be there for him?"

"Verity," he said, just like that. "Verity and a team of equine physiotherapists. He's doing well, I promise you."

"Verity?!" I could hardly comprehend it. "*Verity* is taking care of my Samson?"

He nodded. "You'll see for yourself."

They wheeled me through the stalls, the ones I'd hated so much when I was a kid, and I could feel my heart pounding, nausea threatening to make me vomit.

Rick and Carl were so quiet, the whole yard was so quiet. A couple of horsey faces peered out to say hello, but none of them were my Samson.

They pulled my chair to a halt at the stall on the end. I held my breath. Hardly daring to look.

And there he was.

He poked his head over the door, and his ears pricked forward, and I could hardly see him through the tears. Relief and guilt and love, all mushed together.

"Help me up," I said, squirming in my chair, and even though Rick and Carl protested, they helped me stand, held me tall and balanced while I threw my arms around his neck. "I'm sorry," I cried, my face in his mane. "I'm so sorry."

I leaned over the door to look at him and his forelegs were still bandaged, still swollen and sore and messed up. But he was still him, still happy, still snuffling around for mints.

"He'll be alright," Carl said. "He's doing well."

"I did this," I cried. "It was my fault. All my fault."

"Don't be daft," Rick said. "You were amazing, you were both amazing. It was just an accident, that's all. Just one of those fucking awful things."

I shook my head. "I wanted to win, it was all I was thinking about.

I was stupid, and selfish and reckless."

"It was a split second," Carl said. "One split second of bad luck. Everyone on that course wanted to win, Katie. *Everyone*. It wasn't your fault."

"Look at him." Rick's voice was so warm. "He's doing just fine. Snug in his stall with an endless supply of hay and mints. He probably thinks he's on fucking holiday."

The thought made me laugh, and it was snotty and wet and no doubt thoroughly unattractive, but those guys held me tight and kissed my hair and made it feel alright.

"You'll ride him again," Carl said. "Just give it time. Don't give up Katie, not on him and not on you, either."

"I'd never give up on him," I said.

"Not your dreams, either. Never give up on your dreams."

"My dream was to event with Samson. And to have Jack's yard." I sighed. "Both of those are gone now."

"For the time being," Carl said. "But it's not permanent. It's not the end."

"Harrison Gables, the internship, the yard... Samson... it's all gone."

They didn't say a word.

What could they say?

They lowered me back into the chair and I was already tiring, but I didn't want to leave.

"Can I have a minute?" I asked. "I just want to sit with Samson awhile."

"Sure," Carl said, and both of them ruffled my hair, gave me some space.

I spoke to my boy, told him how much I'd missed him, how happy

I was he was safe. Told him I'd find him a new home, somewhere nice to recover at pasture, somewhere with other horses and people who could help me take good care of him.

I told him I loved him, how much I'd always loved him, how proud I was that he'd tried so hard for me on the course.

I blushed as I heard footsteps behind me, unable to turn in my seat far enough to see if it was Rick or Carl coming back for me.

"Hi, Katie," a voice said, and my skin prickled, my heart thumping.

I held my breath as my sister stepped into my eyeline, ready for the big I am to come out and start gloating.

But she didn't.

She didn't do anything like that at all.

Verity launched right into an explanation of Samson's current medical state. She told me how they were treating him, what painkillers he was on, and what the plan was for his improvement.

She leaned against his stable door as she spoke, and my furry boy nudged at her like she was someone he cared about, someone he knew.

My mind could hardly compute it.

She rubbed his ears, and smiled at him. "He's a really good lad," she said. "He's so good natured, Katie, and he has such good manners." She looked at me. "You've done so well with him. He's a testament to a good handler."

I shook my head. "He's always been like that."

She cleared her throat. "You were great out there, on the course. You were doing so well."

The tears pricked. "No. I wasn't. I was reckless."

"Unlucky," she said. "You were unlucky. That's all."

I shrugged, changing the subject. "I can't believe he's here, that you're taking care of him. Thank you." I met her eyes. "I know we've had our differences..."

She laughed. "Yeah, well, you could say that."

I laughed a little, too. "A few differences." I paused. "But thank you. He's so important to me."

She smiled, and it reached all the way to her eyes. "No problem." She shifted from one foot to the other, and I was jealous, just wished I could be on my own two feet. "Katie, I just want to say. I need to say I'm sorry."

"For what?"

She shook her head as though I was crazy. "For everything. I was just a kid... but I was..."

A mega bitch. A psycho from hell. A horrible little cow who ruined every chance I had of getting to know my father.

"...scared," she said. "I was scared."

"Scared?" The thought was strange. Alien. She'd never seemed scared. Not once.

She shrugged. "My mother always taught us that attack is the best form of defence. No mercy, go get' em and all that." She sighed. "Then there was you, and it was all anyone talked about. All Dad talked about. *Katie's so lovely, Katie's so pretty, so kind. Play nicely with Katie, look after Katie.*"

My blood turned cold.

"And I was scared. Scared he'd like you best. Scared you'd take my things. And you were so lovely and pretty and kind. Everything I wasn't. I hated it. I hated you."

"You made that pretty clear," I said, but it wasn't hostile.

"I just wanted to say sorry. I mean, at work you were so much better than me... you could have gloated... I wouldn't have blamed you, wouldn't have blamed you for humiliating me or rubbing it in... that would have been fair..."

"I wanted to," I admitted. "Some days."

"But you didn't."

"No, I didn't. That isn't who I am."

She laughed. "I wish I could say the same thing about myself."

"Maybe you can," I said. "Every day is a fresh start."

"That's what I'd like," she said. "One day, I mean. A fresh start." She looked so nervous. "It put things in some perspective for me, seeing you at work. And then with Samson, you rode so well on that course. Really great. I had a horse who carried me through, but you, you really rode... you and him." She gave him a pat. "I just wanted to say sorry, not that it'll be worth anything, not after everything, but with Samson being here, and you and Dad making amends, I just thought I'd say it."

"Thanks." I couldn't think of anything else to say. "I really appreciate your help with Samson. I really do."

"You'll ride him again," she said. "Give him some time out."

"A *lot* of time out."

She didn't argue. "And your leg, it will get better..."

"Eventually." I was smiling, though, because she was right. It would get better. "It could have been worse. He made it. We're both still here."

"And you'll still do things together, and if you want to ride, when you're better, I mean, you could always ride one of mine, just until Samson's..." She took a breath. "I'd like that."

Too much, too soon, but I kept smiling. My emotions were piling up in my belly, and I felt small again, and weak. But strong, too. I felt it all at once.

I tried to lighten the mood.

"I'm so bummed about Harrison," I said. "I mean talk about a shitter. You'll have to take me some photos. I'll want to know *everything*." I laughed. "You'll have to think of me, hobbling around on my crutches while you're learning secrets from the best handler that ever existed." I flipped her the finger, but it was good-humoured, as good-humoured as I could make it. "Lucky cowbag."

She didn't seem to think it was funny, and I felt strangely guilty.

"But I..." She cleared her throat. "We cancelled Harrison. *I* cancelled Harrison. Not permanently, just until you're better."

The blood drained from my face, my jaw loose. "You did?"

"Yeah." Her eyes twinkled. "Not just for you, of course." She tutted loudly, but it was in fun. "I'm planning on staying on at the office, after the internship. I think I might specialise in marketing. I'm enjoying it."

I'd forgotten all about the internship. It felt so far away.

"That means a lot," I said. "About Harrison. I really wanted..."

"I know," she said. "It's my dream, too."

I felt choked up and awkward. "You must be busy, with all that at work and looking after Samson... a lot on your plate..."

"A little, but I have people to help, too. I can't take all the credit."

I smiled. "I'll find him another yard, get out of your hair as soon as I'm back in action enough to sort something out."

She tickled his nose, but her eyes were on mine. "Won't exactly have to look hard," she giggled.

I stared at her. "Sorry?"

She looked at me so strangely, as though I'd taken some kind of knock to the head. "Woolhope..." she said. "Surely he'll be going back to Woolhope? Eventually, I mean, he can stay here as long as you want."

I took a breath. Prepared myself to say it. "The yard's been repossessed. Up for sale." It still pained. "He won't be going back there."

She looked confused, properly, seriously confused. And then a smile crept across her face. "You don't know, do you? Fucking hell, you genuinely don't know."

"Don't know what?"

"It's a great place, by the way, loads of potential. I see why you wanted it so much, I see why it was your dream." She sighed, but she was grinning. "Shit, I really shouldn't say. I really shouldn't."

I shook my head. "Sorry? I don't..." And then it dawned. Of course it did.

But I daren't even.

"Carl," I said, and I was already looking around for him. "Are you telling me Carl bought the yard?" And I knew. Of course he did. Of course he bought the yard. "My God... oh my God..."

I was reeling. Part euphoric, part giddy at the thought, part scared, overwhelmed. Angry that he'd done it.

But so grateful I could hardly take a breath.

I wheeled myself back towards the car, my fingers tingling and my heart pounding, but Verity jumped in front of me. "Wait," she said. "It wasn't..."

"What?" I said. "Is it mine, or not? I just don't..." I took a breath. "I don't know what to think. I don't know what to do..."

"Oh, it's yours," she said, and her eyes were bright and happy. "Only it wasn't Carl who bought it for you. It was Dad."

Chapter
THIRTY THREE

Katie

Life is so weird.

So good and so bad all at once.

Verity was right about the yard. It was mine. Signed, sealed, and delivered.

"I was going to tell you," Carl said. "I would have bought it myself, but your father wouldn't budge on it." He paused. "I wanted to let him tell you, when you were ready to hear it. Ready to see him."

"But why? How did he?" I stared, and he met my eyes, just one short glance before he pulled the car onto the main road, and I knew. "How much did you tell him?"

"Enough."

"I see." I smiled. "Did you tell him about my cruddy music taste? About my silly rabbit slippers?"

"Oh yes," he said. "I told him the lot. I told him how you eat your eggs in the morning, how you'll only watch horror if you can watch kids' TV straight after, how you insist on leaping three stairs at a time when you're in a rush in the morning."

"Not anymore."

"You will again. You've just got to believe it." He reached out for my hand. "Oh, and I told him how you read the backs of shampoo bottles when you're about to take a dump."

"You didn't!" I could feel my cheeks burning.

"No," he said. "I didn't, but it would have been funny."

"You do know he's ruined your little *get to know Dad* plans," Rick said from the back seat. "He's already told him everything. There'll be nothing left to say. *Boring.*"

I laughed. "I'll have to come up with some new material then, won't I? Keep him on his toes."

And I did.

I did come up with new material. Brand new dreams.

It was slow. Like roots taking hold under the soil. So slow I didn't feel them, those dreams growing in my mind.

Woolhope was there for keeps, whenever I wanted it, Dad made that perfectly clear as he handed over the paperwork.

I've never hugged anyone so awkwardly for so long, but he didn't seem to mind.

Jack was staying on to mind the place, keeping the farmhouse and work units on low rent until his business was back on its feet, and the rest of it waited for me, with a bit of livery income from the other horses on the yard.

It would take some time. A lot of time.

It took an age before I was even allowed on crutches, and even then I could do virtually nothing, not without spare hands.

Luckily there was Rick, my constant companion, and actually my stupid *Kat-rick* thing wasn't so crazy after all. Rick let me shadow what he was doing, giving me an outlet to replace the marketing internship I'd had to leave behind, and I loved it. I loved working with him, loved throwing ideas around and watching them take shape before my eyes.

Some of them were shit, and some of them looked so much better in my head than they ever looked in reality, and I know Rick was humouring me through a lot of it. But even so, some of them were alright. Some of my ideas were even good. And I was smiling, enjoying it. Happy.

Crutches made it easier to see Samson, easier to do everything, especially as my broken leg became more weight-bearing. Ten percent at first, then twenty. Fifty seemed to take an age, and then one day I was back up to full capacity. I could stand.

Only then I had to learn to walk again, and it was harder than you'd think. So much harder.

Learning to fuck again came a lot more organically.

I don't think my muscles ever let me forget that.

Even when my leg was still useless, back when I'd be propped up in bed with no inclination to move, even then, in my darkest moments, when everything felt like shit, I still wanted those beautiful guys.

I couldn't have them, but I wanted them.

I just had to make do with watching them have each other.

Such hardship. Such terrible hardship. Life sure sucks sometimes, right?

There's one real thing that struck me most about the whole sorry reality of my accident, through all of it — all the pain and the humiliation of being unable to do anything for myself — those two incredible men didn't once falter, didn't once grumble or snap, or call time out.

They didn't once look at me as though I was anything less than the girl they'd fallen in love with.

They didn't love me any less, they didn't want me any less.

And they didn't take me any less. Not once I was up to it. Slowly, very slowly, but surely.

And maybe that's what began to change everything for me.

We were into winter when I first felt the reluctance to pop my contraceptive pill in the morning. I tossed the thought aside and took it anyway, figured it was a stupid hormonal blip and the urge would pass right by again.

But it didn't.

It really didn't.

Maybe it was largely circumstantial. A hole in the timeline of my dreams. An enforced hiatus while I got better and Samson took his pasture rest. I mean, I had no interest in filling my yard with new horses, no interest in replacing Samson with another, even if I could have. My dreams for a riding school were strong, but far away, just for the time being, and maybe *that* had something to do with the reason I first thought seriously about babies.

Maybe it had a little to do with my changing relationships with my own family. My own thoughts about family, and how it could have been for me under different circumstances. What life could have been like. What life was becoming like with both a mum and dad I could believe in, without any lies festering under the surface. With a sister and two brothers that I was coming to know just a little, just a tiny bit better every day.

But mainly I think it had everything to do with Carl and Rick.

To do with the way they were there for me, the way they loved me, and cared for me, and came through for me when I needed them.

Maybe it was to do with the way they always put me before themselves, my schedule before their own.

Maybe it was the way they were so strong. The way Carl had come through for Samson when I couldn't, stayed at his side when I couldn't, the way Rick had held my hand so tight in the ambulance and hadn't let go, not once.

Maybe it was because Carl's birthday was looming, and I knew, I knew how much he wanted a family, knew how badly the clock inside was ticking for him. Knew how much it meant to him.

I'm certain it was to do with the way he held me tight when his birthday finally arrived, told me I meant more than any of it and had done for some time, more than his dream, more than being a dad at forty, and being young enough to enjoy all the things that younger dads do.

The way he told me we were in it for the long haul, the three of us, baby or no.

Me before his dream.

He put *me* before his dream.

It made it so easy to want to put him before the tattered remnants of mine.

But despite all of this, all this pondering, all the reasons that could have contributed to why, I think it was really quite simple when it came down to it.

I have a body and a heart and a mind, and at least two of the three of those overruled my decision to avoid babies my entire life.

At least two of those three wanted Carl's baby. Rick's, too, and

425

the other part, my stickler of a mind? Well, that came round, too.

My ovaries began to combust every time they'd walk in the room, every time they'd smile and laugh, and tell me this was it, that we were it. For keeps.

Forever.

I'd feel an ache in my belly at the thought of holding their baby in my arms, *my* baby. Our baby.

At the thought of being a family of our very own.

So one day I didn't pop that contraceptive pill in the morning. I put it right back in the box, and I didn't take one again.

I kept an eye on my periods and plotted one of those fertility planners out on my phone, and kept quiet until I was ready to talk about it.

Until my leg was up to it, to taking them both, at just the right time.

I slapped Rick's hand aside as he tried to help me upstairs.

"I can do it," I said, and poked my tongue out. "I'm back on my feet now."

"Busted," he said. "It was just an excuse to grab a feel, you know that."

"Sure it was."

Carl was already in the en suite, already naked for bed, his cock already at half-mast as we stepped into the bedroom. He gave us a smile as he brushed his teeth, and my belly did a weird little flutter. I joined him in the bathroom, and so did Rick, washing up happily in silence as the tension thrummed between us.

I cast aside my clothes, and raised my leg carefully, examined the fading scar as I did every evening.

But Rick and Carl weren't looking at that, they were looking at me, their eyes all over me.

"How are you feeling?" Carl asked, and it was pointed.

I smiled. "I'm good. I'm *well*. Same as I've been *well* enough the last twenty times you've asked me."

"Just wanting to be sure," he said. He washed his face and towelled dry, and I was waiting, my hands on his waist as he turned.

"Both of you," I said. I looked at Rick, at his easy grin. "I want both of you, at once. Like we used to do."

"Used to do?" Rick said. "I thought we'd been doing plenty of that."

I shook my head. "Not one by one, not turns, both at once."

"You're sure you're up to that?" Carl asked.

"I'm sure." I took them by the hand, both of them, led them through to the bedroom where I grabbed my phone. I called up my app and my palms were clammy, heart racing.

I held up my calendar, and it took them a moment. Carl looked at me, and then at Rick, reached out for the handset and stared at my little notes on screen.

"You mean you..."

"A baby," I said. "I want a baby."

I thought he'd faint, thought they'd both faint. A beautiful moment of shock as the realisation set in.

Carl sat down on the bed, pulled me down next to him, and I knew what was coming.

"You don't have to do this, Katie, like we said. This isn't a condition, we're past all that. *I'm* past all that."

I shook my head. "This isn't just about you," I said. "It's about me, too. It's what *I* want."

He raised his eyebrows. "You want this?"

I nodded. "I've thought it through, for ages and ages, this isn't some whim... I'm sure, I made sure I was sure, definitely sure, before I said anything..."

"You want to have a baby, for real?" Rick asked, and he was grinning. "We're really gonna do this?"

"Really," I said. "Really really. *Really* really really."

"I don't know what to say..." Carl said.

"So don't." I kissed him. "Don't say anything." I smiled. "Just give me a baby."

I hitched myself up carefully, making sure not to jolt my leg, and the two of them just stared awhile, long enough to make me blush and giggle.

"Come on," I laughed. "I'm only fertile for like three days tops, I'm never going to get pregnant if you two just gawp at me."

Carl looked at Rick, and Rick shrugged. He came to my side, and he was already hard. His gorgeous pierced cock was against my hip, his mouth hot against my neck as he slipped his fingers between my thighs.

"She's not joking," he said to Carl. "Believe me, she's all in. Pussy doesn't lie, and this one's absolutely beautifully fucking sopping." He pulled my pussy lips apart, slipped two fingers inside, and I moaned for him, looked right at Carl as Rick hooked his fingers and found the spot.

"Please," I said. "Come on, Carl."

He moved slowly, until his eyes focused, snapped into life as they fixed on mine. "I won't need asking again," he said.

He took position on my other side, pressing himself so carefully against me, so tenderly against my leg, but I was fine, I hooked my knee over him, pulled him closer.

I took a cock in each hand, worked them slowly, loving the way they felt, loving the way they moved back at me, the way they thrust in my grip.

I was smiling as they kissed me, one by one, wet kisses, until they were blurred, all three of us together, hot mouths and breath as Carl's fingers joined Rick's in my pussy.

It made me groan, made me work those dicks harder, faster, made the bed creak under us as we all shunted for more.

Carl pulled his fingers from me, and they were wet. He squeezed my tit, flicked at the nipple, then lowered his head and sucked me in.

"Fuck yeah," Rick said, and took Carl's hair in his hand, and then he whispered, he whispered such filthy words. "Suck and imagine those big milky tits she's gonna have, won't that really be something? That'll be fucking something, Carl." He climbed down the bed, until his breath was against my pussy. "Gonna fill you up," he hissed and his voice was so filthy. "Gonna put a baby in your belly, Katie. Gonna watch you get all swollen and big, and you'll be so beautiful, you'll be so fucking beautiful. Everything we ever wanted."

I couldn't find words, just breath, just quick shallow breaths.

Carl licked up from my nipple, right the way to my open mouth. "You're so beautiful," he said. He reached down for Rick, pinned his neck as he sucked on my pussy. "Both of you. You're so beautiful."

I wrapped my arms around his neck and kissed him, and I wanted him, wanted both of them. Wanted them to take me and fill me up with cum and give me a baby. *Their* baby.

"Please," I said. "Make me ready."

I groaned as Rick slipped another finger inside, then two, then more.

"Relax," he said, and Carl handed him the lube. A squelch and cold, and then such wet noises. I felt the stretch and I groaned again, spread myself wider.

Carl's hand was on my stomach. "I can't wait to see you grow," he said. "It will be the most beautiful thing."

And I couldn't wait either. My belly tickled and lurched, hormones exploding.

"Give me a baby," I said.

Carl nodded. He squeezed my fingers around his cock, and he was so big, so fucking big.

I kept hold of him as Rick picked up the pressure, his tongue on my clit as my pussy squelched around his hand. I felt so full, so wet, and it felt amazing. Felt perfect.

The pressure built, and my breath turned ragged. I moaned against Carl's mouth as he kissed me, as he tugged at my nipples.

I came with my fingers around Carl's dick, jerking him as I squirmed, letting out little squeals as Rick stretched me wide.

They didn't waste any time. There was a fervour in them, a hunger in their eyes.

Rick lay on his back, and between them they guided me, carefully, helping me up onto Rick's waiting cock. I shuddered as he slipped inside me, smiling as he wrapped his arms around my waist and eased me back, my head against his shoulder, his chest to my back. He thrust underneath me, circled his hips, pushing deep, so deep.

And there was Carl, my beautiful Carl, his big thick cock in his hand as he positioned himself between my legs. He slipped his fingers into me first, alongside Rick's dick, and it felt so good. Rick felt it, too.

"That's nice," he grunted. "That's so fucking nice, Carl."

"Not as nice as this," Carl said, and he eased my legs up, careful to keep them steady. I felt the head of him against my pussy and I held my breath, waited for the stretch, and when it came I groaned, my body rigid until I adjusted to the sensation.

He sank in so slowly, all the way, and I'd forgotten how this felt, how full it made me feel, forgotten how sweet the sensation was of being pinned between two gorgeous men, *my* two gorgeous men.

"Together," I whispered. "Come together."

Carl nodded. "Don't you worry about that."

He shifted his hips and thrust, and I squealed. "Yes!" I hissed. "Like that! Fuck me!"

"Fuck," Rick groaned. "Oh fuck yes." He bucked from underneath, and his breath was in my ear. "Gonna fill your sweet cunt up with cum, all the fucking way, don't you worry."

Carl thrust against him, and I could hear their balls slapping, feel Carl's flesh slapping mine.

"Yes! Give it to me!" I cried. "I want it all!"

God, how they fucked me. They stretched me and filled me and fucked me deep, grunting and thrusting and holding me tight. And I knew what they were thinking, knew what we were all thinking, three people focused on making us a beautiful baby.

The thought made me heady, almost feral.

And they were feral, too, all instinct. Primal drive to spill their seed, cocks thrusting and twitching until they were on the edge.

Carl tipped me as he exploded, rocked me back so my pussy was open and ready to take that cum. Rick was rigid underneath me, muscles tense as he unloaded, too.

"Don't move," I rasped. "Don't pull out, I need it all."

They held firm, all the way inside me as they unloaded. I felt

431

them twitching, knowing I was full of them, full of their cum as they gave me what I wanted, what we all wanted.

They pulled out carefully, and slipped me from Rick so gently, and Carl grabbed some pillows, propped them under my ass.

"Stay still," he said. "Give it the best chance."

I could hardly breathe, praying they would give me a baby.

They fucked me slowly, all night long. Filling me up, the words unspoken. Carl first, as Rick grabbed some sleep, coming deep inside before he slipped his hand over to Rick's side of the bed, took his cock in hand.

Rick groaned and shifted in his sleep, his eyes fluttering open as he began to thrust into Carl's hand.

He didn't need prompting, taking Carl's position as soon as Carl pulled out, and Rick took me next, crying out as Carl pushed his fingers in his ass.

I was lost, delirious in the sensations, taking everything they had to give me, everything they could give me, my pussy clenching tight as I spiralled towards another climax of my own.

I couldn't stop smiling as Rick came, couldn't stop the euphoria as my pussy took a fresh load of cum.

I pulled them both close as we caught our breath, and they were smiling too, I could feel it.

"I wonder," Rick said, his fingers on my tummy. "I wonder if it's happening."

"Time will tell," Carl said. "But we can hope."

"Screw that," I laughed. "We've got another forty-eight hour window. We'll be going again in the morning."

There wasn't any argument from their side.

It took me four months to conceive. Four months of trying. Of popping the vitamins and checking the dates, and waiting with bated breath.

Oh, and four blissful months of taking cock. Lots of cock.

I didn't tell them at first, and they didn't ask. They didn't voice the obvious, our wall calendar making it perfectly clear for everyone to see without tempting fate.

One day late, two days late, three days late.

I took out the pregnancy test, placed it on the kitchen island after dinner.

"It's time," I said.

You could have cut the tension with a knife.

"Fuck," Rick said. He held up his hands. "I'm shaking, I'm shaking so fucking bad."

Carl took his fingers in his, kissed them. "What will be will be," he said. "We keep trying if not, no big deal." He looked at me. "No big deal, Katie, if it's not... if you're not..."

I nodded. "I know."

I put my hand on my belly, hoping, just hoping my instincts were right. The sickness, the tiredness, the weird flutters.

"Let's do this," I said, and set off for the bathroom.

Carl stood so still as I pissed on the stick, but Rick was pacing, twitchy.

I took a deep breath, and my fingers were shaking as I held that test, waiting for the result to show up.

My God, the tension was palpable. I had to laugh just to break the atmosphere.

"Shit," I said. "I can hardly stand it. My heart!"

"Mine, too," Carl said.

"And mine," Rick added.

I closed my eyes, and I couldn't look, couldn't look as the time came. I had to force myself, heart pounding as I looked at the result.

A gasp, and a sharp breath, and the strangest feeling, the strangest shock.

"What?" Carl said. "Is it? Are you? Are we?"

"We are, aren't we?" Rick asked. "Oh my God, we are."

I nodded, and I couldn't stop smiling, couldn't stop the tears pricking my eyes.

I turned the test result to face them, two solid blue lines.

"Congratulations, guys," I said. "You're going to be daddies."

EPILOGUE

Katie

I waved to Jack as we passed him in the Range, but Rick and Carl hardly noticed him, they were too busy looking at the yard beyond. *Happy birthday*, he mouthed, and I gave him a thumbs-up.

"Fuck," Rick said. "This is really coming on."

"Last few days really," I said, and I was proud and excited. I couldn't take the grin off my face.

We parked up on the new flash paving and I let out a groan as I dropped from the Range, waving away the guys as they tried to fuss me. After all I was pregnant, not an invalid, and I'd had worse, so much worse.

A stint in a wheelchair had made pregnancy feel a doddle in comparison, even if I was waddling like a big fat penguin.

The new stable block was almost constructed, a gleaming brick and steel structure directly opposite the old stalls. "They're bigger," I said. "A lot bigger than the early plans."

"Only the best for our furry boy," Carl said. "He'll love that." He peered inside, and so did Rick, and I knew it looked good, I knew it all looked good here.

I'd been dreaming about it long enough.

"Talking about our furry boy." Rick grinned, and held up some mints.

I led the way, slowly, not just because my swollen belly took the breath from me, but because there was so much for them to see. A refurbished school, piled high with new woodchip and bordered with decent solid fencing. A new jumping paddock, with really swish poles and fences — not that I'd be the one using them, not for the foreseeable, if ever.

These days Samson didn't come running when we arrived at his gate. His limp was less pronounced than it used to be, but he was still lame. It didn't seem to bother him all that much, not with a couple of new little field buddies to keep his interest.

He took his time to join us, letting out a snort as he presented his snout for his mint treat, and the ponies came trotting up, wanting in on the action.

"I'll miss you," I said to him, scratching his ears. I pointed at my belly, as though he might understand. "I'll be back soon, just as soon as I can. You'll have to put up with Auntie Verity in the meantime."

Carl and Rick mock groaned.

"Auntie Verity!" Rick laughed. "Bloody hell, Sammy, she'll have you doing all that poncey footwork again. What a bummer, eh?"

It turned out Verity was as tenacious in all aspects of life as she had been in the office. She was still adamant Samson would recover enough to hack out again. I hoped she was right.

One of the ponies nipped at Carl's leg through the bars, just playing, but it was enough to make him groan. "Vicious, these little bastards," he said. "They hate me."

I laughed. "They don't hate you."

"I don't know how those kids aren't scared of them, I really don't."

But the village kids weren't scared of them at all. Not even close. The village kids loved them, just like I'd always hoped.

And I hoped our little girl would, too. Just as soon as she was old enough to meet them.

After all, I'd chosen them for her, just in case. Just in case she shared my insatiable love of all things equine.

"We'd better get going," Carl said. "Table's booked for half-one, we'll be cutting it fine."

"They can entertain themselves if we're late." I let out laugh. "Just as long as Olivia doesn't laser Mum to death with her evil eyes."

"I'm sure they'll draw a truce for one day," Carl said.

"You're the birthday girl." Rick kissed my cheek. "We're on your timetable."

"Yes," I said. "Quite rightly so. *And* I'm expecting birthday favours." I grinned. "Butlers in the buff when we get home tonight, I expect to be hand fed chocolates and showered with rose petals."

But fate it seemed had other plans.

I'd only managed a couple of steps across the school, three at most, when I felt the gush of fluid down my legs.

"Oh shit," I said. "Oh God, oh my God." I looked at Carl and Rick and they were looking at me, eyes wide. "It's happening, it's really happening."

They smiled, they really smiled, and I did, too.

My heart pounded, and I couldn't hold back the giggles, laughing to myself as Rick and Carl dithered with phones and car keys.

They cancelled lunch before I was in even back in the Range, changed our destination in the Sat Nav, like we needed it. Like we didn't know exactly where we were headed. We'd driven it a hundred times, just to make sure, just to practice.

I put my hand on Carl's wrist before he turned the key in the ignition, took one last breath before our final journey as a family of three.

"This is it," I said. "This is really it, I hope you're ready."

"We're ready," Carl said. "We've been ready since the moment we met."

"Are we ever fucking ready?" Rick added. "We couldn't be more ready."

And so was I, I was ready, too.

Ready to meet our little girl.

THE END

ACKNOWLEDGEMENTS

As always, there are so many people to thank for the contribution to this novel!

Johnny, my tireless editor, here's to another completed novel! You've done me proud, taught me so much, and never fail to make me smile in the process. Thanks for all the sparrow farts and the eagle eyes. Couldn't do this without you.

Letitia, thanks so much for the incredible cover and graphics. I think this one if my favourite of all. You amaze me, and I'm so grateful.

Tracy, my PA and sounding board. What can I say? Love your face, and I love it hard. I appreciate all your hard work so much.

Michelle and Lesley, it was a pleasure to see you both in Birmingham. You are incredible, thank you for all your support and help with the street team. I'm grateful for everything you do.

Leigh, for the formatting, thank you for making this look beautiful. I know I'm writing this before you've actually made it look beautiful, but I absolutely know you will. I've seen the magic you work, and I've also seen the dedication you put into the projects you're involved with (Liverpool – thank you so much!) You're awesome. Keep on doing that awesome shit. ☺

Lisa, you've been an incredible sounding board and an incredible friend, as always. Thank you so much. Your beautiful family mean the world to me.

Clarissa, thank you for the chat. Your input and honesty were so valuable and appreciated. <3

My street team – ladies, thank you so much! Thank you, thank you, thank you! I'm always honoured that you enjoy my work so much you take the time to promote it. Super-duper appreciation from me. <3

My Dirty Girls (and now boys, too!) – seriously, I love our group so much. It's fun, it's honest, it's non-judgemental, supportive, and a million different flavours of awesome. Your feedback is invaluable and your support humbles me. I'm so proud of our little haven, I really am. Thank you all!

To my beta team, your guidance and enthusiasm on this novel were massively valued. Thank you!

Bloggers and reviewers – thank you so much for everything you do for me. You've made it possible for me to get word out about my novels, and I've been overwhelmed by the support I've received from this community from the very beginning. You tireless enthusiasm inspires me. Thank you!

I have so many friends to thank! So many! My author buddies Siobhan, James, Jo, Paula, Mia, Azalea, thank you! My friends who get to put up with my crap in person – Maria, Nicola, Kate, Boo, Dom, Kirsteen, Lauren and Andy (who does the hot businessman thing so inspiringly well ☺)

Jon, thanks for the love and support. I don't know how you put up with my shit. With the incessant book chatter, and the mood swings, and my insane waking hours, but I'm glad you do. Love you. <3

And of course, my wonderful family, Mum, Dad, Brad and Nan. There aren't enough words to say how important you are. Love you all. x

About JADE

Jade has increasingly little to say about herself as time goes on, other than the fact she is an author, but she's plenty happy with this. Living in imaginary realities and having a legitimate excuse for it is really all she's ever wanted.

Jade is as dirty as you'd expect from her novels, and talking smut makes her smile.

She lives in the Herefordshire countryside with a couple of hounds and a guy who's able to cope with her inherent weirdness.

She has a red living room, decorated with far more zebra print than most people could bear, and fights a constant battle with her addiction to Coca-Cola.

Find Jade (or stalk her – she loves it) at:
www.facebook.com/jadewestauthor
www.twitter.com/jadewestauthor
www.jadewestauthor.com

Sign up to her newsletter via the website, she won't spam you and you may win some goodies. ☺

Made in United States
Troutdale, OR
11/18/2024

25030202R00246